EMBERCLAW

Also by L.R. Lam

Goldilocks

The Dragon Scales Series:
Dragonfall
Emberclaw

Seven Devils Duology (with Elizabeth May):
Seven Devils
Seven Mercies

Micah Grey Trilogy:
Pantomime
Shadowplay
Masquerade

The Pacifica Novels:
False Hearts
Shattered Minds

EMBERCLAW

L. R. LAM

HODDERSCAPE

First published in Great Britain in 2025 by Hodderscape
An imprint of Hodder & Stoughton Limited
An Hachette UK company

The authorised representative in the EEA is Hachette Ireland, 8 Castlecourt Centre,
Dublin 15, D15 XTP3, Ireland (email: info@hbgi.ie)

1

Jacket design and illustration by Micaela Alcaino
Interior design by Fine Design
Map by Deven Rue

A CIP catalogue record for this title is available from the British Library

Hardback ISBN 978 1 399 71553 9
Trade Paperback ISBN 978 1 399 71556 0
ebook ISBN 978 1 399 71554 6

Typeset in Cochin LT Std

Printed and bound in Great Britain by Clays Ltd, Elcograf S.p.A.

Hodder & Stoughton policy is to use papers that are natural, renewable
and recyclable products and made from wood grown in sustainable forests.
The logging and manufacturing processes are expected to conform
to the environmental regulations of the country of origin.

Hodder & Stoughton Limited
Carmelite House
50 Victoria Embankment
London EC4Y 0DZ

www.hodderscape.co.uk

To the readers who told me *Dragonfall* and the Lumet did feel like home.
It meant and means the world to me.

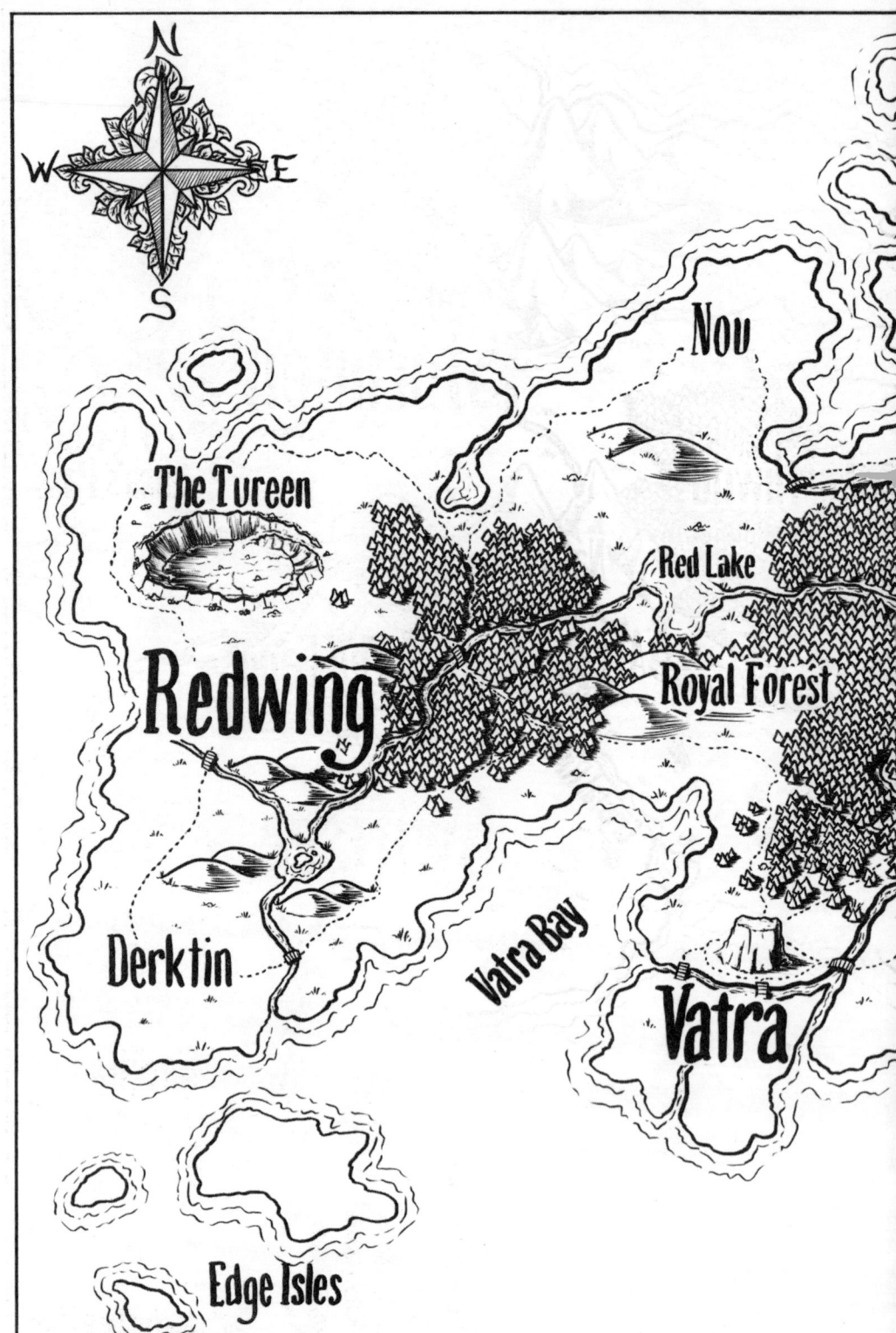

The Spine

Stormfell

Northwild

Zama's Pass

Nalore Monastery

Atrel

The Fangs

Vatra River

Crystal River

Swiftsea

Cardia

Loc

Cartographer Deven Rue

Dear reader and scholar: contained within, please find a brief summary of the previous events of the Dragon Scales Prophecies, should the reminder prove useful to you. A glossary of terms remains at the end.

—THE TWELFTH ARCHIVIST OF VERE CELENE

On the Night of Locked Tombs, Arcady Eremia, a desperate thief, broke into their grandsire's tomb beneath the Citadel of Loc and recited a secret spell. On the other side of the Veil, Everen Emberclaw, the last male dragon, stole a prophecy and fell through the storm between worlds.

Though Arcady's spell altered the carvings on their grandsire's drag-onstone seal to give themselves a new name and identity, they had one last barrier: money. If Arcady stole a rare dragon relic and sold it on the black market, they could afford university tuition and take the next steps to clear their grandsire's name as Plaguebringer. Arcady also had an-other secret to hide: they were a survivor of the plague themselves, one of the Struck, meaning, according to Lochian society, they should be banned from using magic at all.

To his horror, Everen discovered he was trapped in his human-like pret-erit form, and that he had partially bonded with a human. When he scried his sister Cassia, she suggested he convince this human to trust him enough to finish the bond by the night of the Feast of Flowers, when he could drain the human's magic and kill them to open a rip in the Veil. Then, and only then, could he hope to save his kind. But first: he had to find this human.

Sorin, a priest of the Order of the Dragons, had trained to be an assassin under the guidance of Magnes, the Head Priest, since she was a child. On the night of her first kill, she learned the act brought her no pleasure, but Sorin knew dragon relics must be kept within Loc's borders. Magnes claimed that a false god had slipped through the Veil and must be destroyed to protect the world from chaos.

On the night Everen and Arcady's paths finally collided, they discovered that, due to their half-bond, a wound on one of them would be echoed on the other, and they could not touch without Arcady stealing some of Everen's magic and causing him pain. While Arcady initially wanted nothing to do with the stranger who claimed to be a prince from a land beyond the borders of the Lumet map, Arcady later decided they might as well make use of him.

Arcady trained Everen as a thief and recruited Kelwyn, their fence and the owner of the Last Golden antique shop, as well as two members of the criminal gang called the Marricks. Their leader, Larkin, was still furious with Arcady for stealing from the gang in the past, but the pile of wraithwright coins from selling the relic meant Larkin might be persuaded to forgive and forget.

As the human and the dragon worked together, Arcady gradually lowered their defenses, and Everen began to doubt fate's path. Since arriving in the Lumet, Everen had been plagued by dreams of a set of dragon scales, with the human and dragon worlds hanging in the balance.

After Sorin's assassination of a Jaskian captain who smuggled dragon relics drew too much attention, Magnes was furious with her. Later, he took her to the forest and they fought a wolf-like wraith that emerged from the Veil. Her injuries from its claws drove home the dangers if the Order failed its protection of the boundary between worlds—and if she disappointed Magnes.

In Vere Celene, the volcano known as the Reek rumbled. If it erupted, all dragonkind would fall.

On the night of the auction at Widow Girazin's manor, Arcady disguised themselves as a noble merchant, Sar Ikari Dwell, and Everen pretended to be their guard. The auction grew heated, with a mysterious stranger competing for the dragon claw relic, but Arcady emerged the victor. Afterward, however, their disguise failed. To escape, Everen discarded his human disguise, spread his preterit wings, and jumped from the tower window with Arcady in his arms.

Sorin, concealed as one of the guards, threw a knife after him, but couldn't bring herself to make it a killing blow.

Arcady, reeling from the revelation that Everen was more than human, demanded answers. Everen gave some, but not all. Arcady eventually treated his wound and Everen revealed that Arcady had taught him well: he had pickpocketed the claw Arcady thought they'd left behind, so the night hadn't been a failure. Upon their return to Vatra, Arcady instructed Kelwyn to set up the deal.

Arcady and Everen finally admitted their attraction to each other, and though neither fully intended it, their bond completed. Everen, knowing he could no longer kill Arcady, hoped to avert fate as the Feast of Flowers grew closer.

After Everen and Arcady awoke from a shared nightmare, Everen found a stash of notebooks and realized Arcady had been stealing his visions of the future for years. Everen, convinced it was deliberate, lost his temper and burned most of the drawings. Through the bond, Arcady discovered Everen's secrets. Furious, Arcady banished him and pulled away from their connection.

Arcady, Larkin, and Kelwyn headed outside the city to a barrow hill to sell the relic to the real Sar Ikari Dwell, but Sorin arrived, killing the drakine and their guards.

Everen, in full dragon form, landed at the barrow hill and took Arcady to the rip in the Veil. Larkin escaped into the forest with the claw, but Sorin found her. Sorin took the relic, but let Larkin live if she promised to leave Loc behind.

As the Feast of Flowers arrived, Queen Naccara and her dragon warriors flew through the storm and fought to emerge in the human world, but both the Veil and the wraiths within drew them back.

Arcady and Everen's shared magic was drained by the rip in the Veil, and Arcady lost control and turned Starveling. Arcady remembered nearly dying of the Strike and realized they and Everen had unintentionally first connected through the Veil as children.

Sorin arrived in the clearing and a Starveling Arcady attacked her. Magnes saved Sorin, and she gave him the claw.

As Everen fought dragons and wraiths, fate opened its eye. In all paths, one of the worlds fell. In most, both worlds were aflame. To save humans and dragons, Everen urged Arcady to speak the same spell they'd uttered on the Night of Locked Tombs, and as they did, Everen dived into the storm.

The severing of their bond was the greatest pain either of them had ever known.

Back in Vatra, a broken Arcady discovered Larkin had stolen both Ikari Dwell's money and Arcady's original seal. Though Arcady had lost nearly everything, they still had the money they'd started with. They decided to enroll in the university, even if they might not be able to stay longer than a year.

Sorin, though her faith had fractured, chose to become one of Magnes's Eyes and guard the Veil away from the Citadel.

Magnes had worn many names over the years, but his first was Ammil: the previous last male dragon. With the return of his claw, he regained full access to his power and could enact the next step of a plan three centuries in the making.

Everen, imprisoned in Vere Celene, wrote to Arcady, lamenting all that had gone wrong. Yet, deep in the dark, he heard the golden chime of the bond, leaving him with a sliver of hope.

PART I:
DIVISIONS

As above, so below.
As what was, so shall become.
Whatever you do, remember this:
you must not wake the Dreamer.

    —Unsigned, undated half-burned fragment from the Vere Celene
        Archives, recovered from the fire begun by Ammil Aldwing

One volume has closed and the next opened.

I wish I could promise that fate arced its way straight and true toward *fairness* and justice. If there is one thing I have *learned, it is that life, especially when touched by magic, is never tidy.*

Herein lie more accounts of the Dragon Scales Prophecies, gathered from written records, interviews, or by scrying directly into the past. I will not pretend it was comfortable to hear some of the innermost thoughts of people I know or once knew.

I cannot shy away from writing it all down, tempting as it is to burn certain pages. I made a promise that I would show it all. For better or worse, I must let it stand. Try not to judge us too harshly, dear reader.

There is a duality within these pages: hope and despair. Triumph and loss. Intimacy and betrayal. Life and death. Hatred, but also so much love.

This is the story of the dragon scales and whether humans and dragons found their balance.

—*THE TWELFTH ARCHIVIST OF VERE CELENE*

I.

EVEREN:

WITHOUT BREATH

It is difficult, even now, to think back to my time imprisoned down in the dark. When my sister could no longer risk sending me parchment and ink, I wrote to you in my head, Arcady. Again and again, I apologized, but I heard only silence.

Three hundred years before I was hatched, Ammil, the last male dragon, went mad. At some point, in that black cave, I am sure I broke with reality myself. Those dreams I had of you early on felt so real. I clung to them because it was easier to step out of my empty life and into yours, even if it hurt. You thought me dead or gone for good. I knew I deserved every bit of your hatred and more, but I craved these tiny glimpses.

The sound of your boots hitting the cobblestones as you walked through the streets of Vatra at night, hands in your pockets and shoulders hunched. Going to a bookseller's and purchasing blank journals, quills, pen nibs, and ink. And books. So many books. It was hard not to remember half-burned pages dancing in a room, the smell of soot in the air, and the fear on your face.

I would awaken ashamed.

Sometimes, everything that happened in the human world seemed a dream. Had I truly been that desperate to prove I was everything dragons had foretold? In those months together, you were dragon-like in your own way, hoarding your secrets, scaled defenses hiding the softness beneath.

You eventually trusted me, and it nearly killed you. *I* nearly killed you, and I would never forgive myself for it. All I could do was cling to the hope that what I had done was worth it. That the human world of the Lumet and the dragon world of Vere Celene were spared, at least for a time. The wounds in the Veil had stitched over, and I hoped the barrier would hold until I could find out how to save them properly.

When I was first imprisoned, I told Cassia of my dreams of a dragon perched on a set of scales and my visions of the end of all things. My sister searched the archives for any references or hints that might show us a way forward. Though I have trusted her with everything, my sister would be Queen one day. An Emberclaw's duty must always be, first and foremost, to dragonkind over kin.

I stayed there, in the gloom, and I missed you as much as flight, as much as breath, as much as magic.

2.

MAGNES:

THE CHANCELLOR

D eath lurked on dark wings.

The scent of sickness was thick in the air: astringent bandages, old blood, and wounds long gone sour. The curtains of the Chancellor's room were kept closed against the fire of sunset. The mage lights were dimmed, the atmosphere hushed, almost holy.

Magnes had grown almost fond of Yrsa of Swiftsea over the years. He might hate her for what she and the others had done during the Schism, to him and to Monarch Laen, but Yrsa had largely done right by Loc as Chancellor these past twenty-eight years.

"Magnes," Yrsa rasped. "I'm sorry." Despite the heat of late summer, Yrsa was swaddled in thick robes and blankets that did nothing to hide how much flesh she had lost the last few moons. Her face was little more than thin skin sagging over a skull. The hazel eyes were still bright and unblinking, whether from fever or the drugs the Master Healer had decanted down her neck. She heaved a wracking cough.

"For what, Yrsa?" Magnes asked when the worst subsided.

"For being . . . weak enough to die."

With his sharp hearing, Magnes caught each stuttering heartbeat in that frail chest, counting down the time she had left. The tumors dotted throughout her brain and organs had grown too large for surgeons to remove and too stubborn for healers to shrink with magic.

It was a shame that humans lived for such a short amount of time. Only Monarch Laen, the human Magnes had once bonded with, had lived nearly three centuries due to their shared magic. He'd watched so many pass on to whatever came after death—on the battlefield, by his hand, through illness, or simply old age and a body wearing out. He supposed time was relative. To a human, a sparrow living but three years seems short. A sparrow, in turn, lives so much longer than a moth. A dragon lived a long time, but not forever.

"You're not weak. You've never been that," he reassured her. Yrsa of Swiftsea had shifted the trajectory of the world nearly as much as a prophecy.

"Still. I wish . . . I wish I could have held on longer. The Consul has . . . successfully extended the mandate twice—would they do it a third time in . . . two years?" She breathed hard from the effort of speaking.

Magnes had always admired Yrsa's intelligence. Even through her illness, her mind had stayed as sharp as a dragon's. It was Yrsa who dreamed up the ten-year term for the Consul and worked in a legal loophole to extend the mandate in times of crisis. It was Yrsa who liaised with the Stewards of the Court on many of the day-to-day runnings of the country. She had never shied away from the heavy work. The ugly work.

She coughed wetly, blood staining her teeth.

Yrsa's skin was so translucent the veins were stark as a plague survivor's Struck marks. Her eyes were brighter and sharper than he'd seen in months. He straightened. He hadn't thought it would be so soon. He knew that telltale shine. Dying animals often had a last burst of strength at the end.

"Yrsa," he said, softly.

"I'm not afraid."

"Do you want me to send for Carym and Ketrel?"

She shook her head. "Ketrel barely remembers me these days, and Carym will be too deep in his cups at this hour. It's better, like this." She smiled through cracked lips. "We had a good partnership, didn't we? You, and I. And once, the others." Another pause to cough. Blood splattered the blankets. Her breaths came short and fast, and he heard the hummingbird flutter of her heart.

"We were fearsome," he said.

The last few months had been a delicate balance. Magnes had ensured the Citadel Court wouldn't realize how weak the other Chancellors were. His faithful Eyes monitored the Veil. Jask remained a challenge: despite the Order's best efforts, too many relics were finding their way south. His spies had helped plant seeds so the sightings of dragons on the night of the Feast of Flowers worked in his favor. Rumors were thick that the gods were foretelling the return of good fortune to Loc.

Yrsa's wavering hand reached for his cheek, a fingertip resting against his skin. It was not the first time they'd touched, but this time, Yrsa's seal surged, glowing purple. Her eyes widened as the magic flowed through her.

Once, her weather magic had been strong enough to call down tempests. The other side of the power of those blessed by the violet "god" was the latent ability to read the mind. Magnes had appeared as no less than three consorts at Monarch Laen's side, working hard for generations to ensure that type of magic of the mind was well-feared and forbidden. Yrsa had never nourished it, but even if she had, Magnes should have been plenty strong enough to push her away, especially now that he had his long-missing claw and the power that came with it.

Yet there on the cusp of death, Yrsa saw flashes of countless thumb brushes against her wrist over the years. A well-timed whisper nudging her or the other members of the Consul in the direction of his choosing. She saw right to the truth of him.

Who he'd been. What he'd done. What he was. Not a god. Something far more real than that.

Magnes jerked back, but it was too late.

"No," she breathed. "You couldn't—you aren't—" She struggled to sit up, remaining half in his mind despite breaking the physical connection. "Guards!" she cried out, voice surprisingly clear.

Magnes had long ago discovered each of the Chancellor's greatest fears. Yrsa hated, more than anything, being played for a fool. And here, at the last, she had discovered that Magnes had used her for decades. Pulling the strings, shaping Loc in the way he thought was best. He had always been the one in control. This country was *his*. She opened her mouth—

Magnes pressed Yrsa into the bed, and her breath wheezed from scarred lungs. It would take no effort at all to break her ribs like kindling. He let himself unfurl, his human features fading to reveal orange eyes with slit pupils. Yrsa struggled, the whites of her eyes showing.

Magnes held a fingertip to the hollow of her throat, the nail darkening to a pointed talon. She dug into his mind, but there was no need to hide his secrets from her any longer. He felt every bit of her terror and pain as she tried to fight back. She'd resigned herself to dying, but not like this.

In his other hand, Magnes held a pillow, and he placed it, gently, over her face. He could use magic, but it might leave a trace. Simpler was often better. Her hands grasped his forearms, her brittle nails raking across his thicker preterit skin, legs kicking weakly beneath fur covers. He pressed harder.

It didn't take long. All too soon, the feeble motions stilled.

Magnes raised the cushion. Yrsa's face was awful: the tongue lolling, eyes half-open, blood vessels burst around her blank eyes. Carefully, he closed her mouth and slid the eyelids shut.

"Thank you, Yrsa," he whispered to her corpse, bending over and brushing his lips against her forehead. "You did your job well."

Gathering himself, he exhaled, drawing up his human illusion before folding his features into an expression of heartbreak. "Guards! Healers!" he called, tinting his voice with urgency and grief. "Come quickly!"

"I looked away but a moment, and They were gone." He let his throat catch on the words as the humans streamed into the room. The Chancellors always referred to each other in the honorific pronoun in front of others. Only in private had formalities fallen.

He rose, backing away as the healers tried, fruitlessly, to bring the Chancellor back from the dead. He stayed until they covered her face with a sheet, and he led a prayer as the healers bowed their heads.

"Their body remains, but soon we will send Yrsa of Swiftsea's soul to the gods," Magnes finished.

"May They fly on swift wings," the Master Healer said, spreading their fingers wide in a benediction to the five gods. "Chancellor Yrsa died in the presence of Your All-Holy Eminence, and I am sure it was a great comfort."

"I leave the Chancellor in your capable hands, Healer Lordon."

Magnes strode through the Citadel until he reached his tower, taking the steps two at a time. Once the door was shut behind him, he let his human form fall away once more. He bowed his head, his longer, darker, feathered hair falling into his face. He clenched his hands into fists. There was the barest white scar at the base of his pinkie finger, the sole sign that the digit had been missing for centuries. He opened the window, the cooler air swirling through the tower room, and forced his breathing to slow, his heartbeat to calm. Magic crackled along his skin.

He was meant to have more time, but already his mind spun. With luck, he could convince Loc to wait until the next election to select a new Chancellor, especially if he could find a distraction or delay.

After years of planning, everything was finally falling into place. A few more steps, and another delicate rebalance of the scales, and no one and nothing would be able to stop him.

Change was on the wind.

3.
ARCADY:

DAWN

I no longer dreamed of dragons—I only dreamed about one.

I spent so much effort *not* thinking about him while I was awake that my sleeping self couldn't lock the bastard out. Asleep, I didn't always hate him. His arms would come around me from behind, with his fingers at my waist, dancing up my ribs. He'd press his palm flat against the metal of the seal setting in my chest, the tip of the index finger hooked over my collarbone, and he'd hug me tight, like he couldn't bear to let me go. I'd feel his breath on my neck as he whispered into my ear.

"I will find my way back to you."

Even asleep, I knew it wasn't real, but there, in dreams, I let myself arch against him as his hands continued to drift. I let myself pretend we hadn't broken, that he wasn't dead and everything between us shattered to bits. I let myself be greedy.

But it was always the same. I'd blink, he was gone, and I was awake and tangled up in my bedsheets, skin damp with sweat. There, in the darkness, I was free to hate him once more. At least until I conjured him up the next night.

When dawn broke on my last morning at the Last Golden, I'd already been awake for two candlemarks.

After I'd dreamed of Everen, I'd fallen back asleep to nightmares of wraiths screeching against a night sky. By the time Kelwyn—erstwhile proprietor, illegal fence, and friend—was lured from his room by the scent of coffee percolating on the stove, I'd already poured him a cup. I added milk and stirred five times, first in one direction and then widdershins, just as he liked. Kelwyn took it, his eyes snagging on my fine clothes, the subtle paint around my eyes, the rings on my fingers, and the bag packed neatly by the door.

"You've certainly left it late enough," he said, sipping carefully.

I lifted a shoulder, then poured my cup of coffee. "Saved a bit of coin by delaying taking up my dormitory as long as I could."

Kelwyn blinked his way toward wakefulness as I made him breakfast, for once. A dollop of butter sizzled on the pan on the stovetop. I added sliced onions and garlic. The sliced sausages went in next, then mushrooms. I cracked the eggs last, one-handed. Kelwyn toasted slices of bread above the open flames of the grate. We layered our plates and sat at the table by the window and ate in silence. The cobbled street below was quiet, in that lull between when the bakers had gone to work and when the shopkeepers had yet to unlock their doors. I took another sip of my coffee, already feeling a wistful nostalgia. Our morning routine had been perfected, and who knew when we'd next perform it?

Kelwyn leaned closer to the windowpane, the morning light catching his face as he tilted it toward the Citadel.

"Still can't believe you'll actually be up there," he said. "Looking down on the rest of us like a proper member of the nobility like a little drakine."

"Don't fret, I'll never be proper." I aimed for lightness. "You'll be glad to have the place to yourself again."

I knew I hadn't been an easy person to live with the last few moons.

The first time Kelwyn had taken me in after everything went to shit, over a year and a half ago, I'd just left the Marricks. Three months ago, my plan to steal and sell a dragon relic to cover all four years of university costs had imploded rather spectacularly. People had died because of my actions. There was no way to pretend otherwise. I'd lost myself on the night of the Feast of Flowers, and parts of me were missing.

No matter how much I polished myself up, I was sure the cracks still showed.

"Dunno," he said, taking another sip of coffee. "I've almost grown used to tripping over you. It's like having my own grumpy, hissing cat."

Kelwyn and I hadn't spoken about Everen. Kelwyn had run at the first sign of trouble, and I didn't blame him for saving his own skin. He must have all sorts of suspicions—had he seen a dragon take me up into the sky? So far, though, he'd kept them to himself, and I was pathetically grateful.

A fortnight after I'd moved back in with Kelwyn, my shirt had gaped open one evening. By the way his gaze caught on the hollow of my throat, he'd noticed that my black Struck marks had crawled a little further up my skin. He'd known exactly what that meant: at some point in the months since he'd fitted my new seal setting, I had turned Starveling. We didn't speak of that, either.

Neither did we discuss Larkin, aside from acknowledging that she'd fucked us both by taking all that wraithwright and only leaving a couple of coins and a note to rub salt in the wound. Kelwyn had done some digging, but none of his contacts knew where she had gone. The other gangs had closed over the Marricks' territory like a scab on a wound.

But Larkin was out there, somewhere, and she had something of mine: the old seal that said my true name, Arcady Eremia. That would come back to haunt me, one way or another.

Kelwyn tapped his fingers on the wooden table, bringing me back to that cozy, cramped room in the Last Golden.

"So what's the plan?" Kelwyn crossed his arms. "Every time I ask you about money, you've fobbed me off, but I know you don't have enough."

Over the last few months, I had been clouded over with anger and grief. At night, I walked the city streets for hours. I'd spoiled for fights a time or two, just to feel something. Kelwyn never commented on the scraped knuckles, or that one black eye. Arnica salve would appear on my bedside table, and that was that.

In between drunken fights and fractured sleep, I'd done as many jobs as I could. Sneaking into homes to crack safes. Stealing at marketplaces, in taverns, in churches—anywhere someone might have heavy pockets.

"I'll figure it out," I said, but in truth, I had no clue what I'd do. My best hope was to study my arse off, scour the library, and steal as much as I could on the side to buy more time. If I was lucky, I'd be able to limp along to the end of the academic year, and in that time, I'd find something of the truth. I had to.

"It's not easy to keep up a ruse day-in, day-out for so long."

"Are you . . . seriously trying to explain how con jobs work to me, Kel?" I chewed my food, even as my stomach tightened. For this job, I would wear my true face. Arcady Dalca wasn't a temporary identity I'd pick up briefly and set down. Unless I cleared my family name, I would never be Arcady Eremia again.

He waved a hand. "Yes, yes, you're the expert. I forgot. I'm just . . . I expect it's not worth warning you to stay out of trouble?"

"I seem to have a way of sticking my nose in it, no matter what I do."

I made my way to the door, picking up my leather satchel. I'd already sent the rest of my things ahead to the Citadel via courier like a good drakine would.

"You'll still visit?"

"If you make your lavender biscuits."

His mouth opened, and for a moment, I worried he'd say something too real, too honest for the both of us. I shook my head once, in warning. Kelwyn's mouth closed. "Not good-bye," he finally said.

"Not good-bye," I agreed.

Yet the door clicked shut behind me with a horrible finality.

Out on the street, it was too bright, and I squinted against the sun. I could feel Kelwyn watching me from the window, but I didn't glance back. Squaring my shoulders, I made my way through the city.

I didn't keep my fingers idle.

With a film of magic across my skin and a burst of salt on my tongue, I drew on one of my many false faces. My grandsire's stolen seal glowed blue beneath my shirt. Since the night before the Feast of Flowers, my power was stronger than it'd ever been, but it wasn't all mine—it was hot and smoky, like I had a cinder in my throat. A dragon's magic. Everen's magic.

Don't think about him.

A careful bump into a guilder on Ruby Street, and I had a bracelet for my trouble. Squeezing my way past a merchant in the close quarters of the Blackwell Market netted me a few coppers and a silver sul.

I shrugged off the shapeshift and slipped the silver and shell brace-let on my wrist. Might pay for an extra night or two of accommodation at the dorms. Maybe a sennight, if Kelwyn got a good enough price.

At the bottom of the hill, I nibbled a handful of nuts to refuel my magic. I passed one of my stolen copper suls to the driver and climbed into the horse-drawn cart filled with other students, craning my neck toward the series of ramps leading up to the spires on top of the hill.

As the cart began the ascent, some students stared at me curiously. Most of those I'd be studying with were old money, with bloodlines that could be traced back to the founding of Locmyria under Mon-arch Erisyn the First. I swallowed down my nerves. My seal would match the Citadel Records. Arcady Dalca had once existed, though they had died in the first Strike along with the rest of their family. My maire had selected the name and woven it into my grandsire's spell, but I didn't know how well the false identity would hold if someone went digging.

I held my head high, even as my stomach fluttered. I couldn't show weakness.

Finally, I was going to learn more of magic's rules. I'd learned simpler spells not associated with the gods, like wards and cantrips. I'd demonstrated shape-shifting well enough to gain admission to the university, but barely touched my magic's other side of waterweav-ing. I could light a flame, thanks to Everen, and I could just about move stone a little with my mind, thanks to the tutoring of my paire, who had been blessed by Piater. What else would I be able to learn with access to some of the brightest minds in Loc?

At the outer wall of the Citadel, I showed my seal to a stoic-faced guard, who ushered me through the gate into the courtyard.

The sunlight made the Citadel's yellow stone shine pale as new butter. The spires rose toward the sky, the Lochian flag waving from the tips. Columns carved with dragons kept watch with jade eyes, and mosaic panels on the lower walls depicted saints or scenes from myths. The morning light glinted off leaded panes of glass. I'd laughed the last time I was here when I'd realized the windows and doors weren't that large simply to show off wealth. It had once been practical: so dragons could fit.

I was just about to find my dormitory when a gong echoed across the Citadel.

For a heart-stopping moment, I thought it was a different, impossible chime, but others winced at the sound. Another klaxon, and a third. My throat tightened. Whatever it was, this wasn't planned. I'd only just arrived, and something was about to change.

The mutterings around me rose, and people streamed onto the cobbles of the courtyard. Windows opened and others leaned out.

What would be important enough to bring the Citadel to a halt?

I chewed on my lip as I scanned the horizon and the sea, my mind racing with possibilities. The water was its usual slate gray. No red of a crimson tide, at least. The last of the toxic algae had been chased away by Kalsh, Zama, and Jari mages by mid-summer, but it'd still devastated the harvests. Food prices were eye-watering.

Reports of Starvelings were more common than they had been this time last year. What if war had broken out with Jask, or worse, the Strike was back? Maybe the Veil had frayed and wraiths had returned? Or dragons?

A stab of almost-hope, quickly dashed.

Finally, the double doors of the balcony opened. Robed figures in wraithwright masks emerged. An emerald-clad Citadel Herald came to the front, resting their hands on the stone railing. All waited, the wind whistling through the gaps in the buildings. The chill brought gooseflesh to my skin, the hair on my arms standing straight.

At first glance, someone might think the figures were the three Chancellors of Loc, but one wore the robes and the horned mask of the Head Priest of the Order of the Dragons. A Chancellor was missing. My fingertips went colder.

"Subjects of Loc," the Herald began, their magic-amplified voice reaching the corners of the crowd. "We have sad tidings. Even now, wyverns are being sent with missives, and heralds are gathering in the stables to help spread the news." A pause, and the crowd held its collective breath. Somewhere, a babe wailed and was hushed by a parent.

"After a brief illness, we regret to share that Chancellor Yrsa of Swiftsea's soul has been borne upon the wings of the dragon gods."

Gasps and whispers whipped through the crush.

"Chancellor Yrsa of Swiftsea," the Herald continued, "was a loyal servant of Loc for the past near-thirty years, forging this country to utmost strength after the Schism and navigating us through the two Strikes of plague. Their untiring love and devotion for this land was clear, and we owe a debt of gratitude that we can never hope to repay."

I swayed on my feet, dressed in mostly stolen finery. Though the Herald kept speaking, the ringing in my ears drowned out the words.

The Chancellors' wraithwright masks, polished so bright they reflected like mirrors, swiveled back and forth as they took in the crowd. Around me, a few people began to weep. Some seemed performative, but I also spied genuine grief. Even if the Chancellors largely stayed hidden in their wing of the Citadel these last few years—the excuse trotted out was that they needed to remain free of influence and distraction as they listened to the gods' will—many were loyal. I supposed it was easier to love whoever kept you rich.

I edged my way back through the crowd of strangers, my breathing quick and shallow. Despite the autumn chill, I was too hot. I shuffled toward the red sandstone university building, where I found a servant who led me to my room. When the door closed behind me, I dimly took in a bed, a desk, a fire, and a wardrobe. A tapestry on the wall had the University of Vatra coat of arms—a wyvern in flight, its claws curled in front of a full moon. I leaned out of the open window, gulping in cool air. Below me lay a courtyard, clusters of students muttering among themselves as they took in the news. Ivy climbed up the stone walls, already turning a vibrant red as if trying to match the stone.

When I could finally breathe again, I leaned back, closed the window, and collapsed on the bed.

I'd been working toward this day for so many years. Since I'd found my maire's notebook in the ashes of my old life up in the mountain hamlet of Atrel over a year ago, it had consumed nearly every waking moment. Yrsa of Swiftsea, along with the other Chancellors and the Head Priest, had dubbed Barrow Eremia the Plaguebringer. Somewhere far below my feet were the tombs of all the pariahs of Loc. My grandsire, my taie, had been buried more than half-dead but still breathing. I shivered every time I remembered that pile of bones and his grinning skull.

Yrsa of Swiftsea had never answered for their crimes. Now, they never would.

I'd dreamed of taking the whole Consul down in one fell swoop. Of being able to see the faces behind all the masks: the three Chancellors, the Head Priest, and as many of the other Stewards and advisors in power at the time as I could manage.

I knew the Chancellors were older, but I hadn't even heard a whisper that Yrsa was ill. They'd kept that quiet. I hoped, with a fierce burst of fury, that the Herald had lied about it being brief. I hoped it'd been painful. I hoped they had suffered. I dug my fingernails into my palms.

I'd given up so much to be here. I'd had so much taken from me.

"Lal seu al-lei lutra," I said. Even though our bond had broken, I still understood the dragons' language in a way some Old Tongue linguists could only begin to dream about. I dragged my nails through my hair and along my scalp as the silencing charm took hold.

And I screamed.

4.

EVEREN:

AS ABOVE, SO BELOW

On the third full moon after I had been imprisoned, fate cracked open its eye and gave me a sliver of insight.

It began with a nightmare: a rip of darkness and an unspooling of shadow. All was as pitch dark as the deepest caves of Vere Celene or the one beneath the Citadel where I had first fallen to the human world.

The dragon scales rose before me, as they had so many times before. The fulcrum changed, twisting from heavy metal into a tree of white light, the branches reaching to the heavens and the roots to the depths of the worlds. The scales hung from its branches—the human world on one side, the dragon on the other, still askew and out of balance. A snake twined around its trunk, its scales the hue of the humans' wraithwright coins: a dark gray shining with different colors.

—*As above, so below. As what was, so shall become,* fate whispered to me. I would listen to anything it had to say.

It was Vatra as I had never seen it before. The city was smaller, the stone less weathered. As I watched, dragons banked, flying over the buildings and landing gracefully, one by one, in the grand amphitheater of the Citadel, surrounded by a crowd of people. All felt festive: music drifted on the air, the humans smiled, and the dragons' feather crests lay flat in satisfaction.

In the center of the amphitheater, a young human in strangely cut clothing gazed up at a blue dragon, little more than a hatchling herself. No, I corrected myself—it was a young drake. The dragons present were an equal mix of sexes. Other humans and dragons clustered at the sides, watching as the youth stepped forward, closed their eyes, and let their magic unfurl in an invitation. After an aching pause, the dragon accepted. Gold sang between them. The human wore no seal. This was the furthest into the past I had ever seen: the Great Betrayal was over seven centuries ago.

The dragon hummed, the magic swirling around them. The human opened their eyes and placed a hand on the tip of the dragon's nose, their expression so full of love that it pained me. The crowd, human and dragon alike, called out in celebration. Without hesitation, the human climbed onto the dragon's back, settling into a saddle at the base of the neck, just above the shoulder blades. Magic shimmered between them, and the dragon took off into the sky for their first flight to help cement the bond.

—How did it all go so wrong from here? I asked the ether.

The tree returned, without the snake and scale. I suspected it was made of something I had seen in small cylinders: dragonstone. The white of it shimmered with the colors of magic—a red shadow, then purple. Blue, green, and gray.

Five humans stepped into the reflected glow of the tree. They raised their hands, and I recognized one of them as the youth I had watched bond with a dragon, now middle aged, their expression twisted with fear and jealousy. The five worked their magic, chanting spells, but I could not catch the words.

A shimmer, and ancient Vatra spread beneath me once more.

Instead of peaceful flight, dragons writhed in the sky. A rip appeared above them. Lightning flashed, and I caught the familiar silhouette of Vere Celene on the horizon. As I watched, the storm lowered, swallowing the dragons and the island whole. A flash of lightning blinded me.

The long-dead humans finished their spell. The tree was so bright it was as though it had been poured from starlight. Dragons had long suspected that the humans had stored our stolen magic in a repository of some sort. Here was our confirmation.

Some of the mages wept, clutching their chests as if part of them had been ripped out. I recognized that pain, for I had felt it myself: they had severed the bonds with their dragons.

"What have we done?" the one I had seen gaze up at a dragon with love whispered.

—*As above, so below*, came the voice of fate once more. *As what was, so shall become.*

The dragon scales and the snake returned. There was a wound in the serpent's side, pulsing red and painful. One eye opened just enough to show a splinter of starlight.

—*Whatever you do, remember this*, came the voice of fate. *You must not wake the Dreamer.*

The serpent's head bucked to the side, and the ground shook. Its mouth opened, baring its fangs. Wisps of smoke emerged from the snake's mouth, and the air filled with hissing, clicking, and a long, high scream.

My awareness whipped across years and back to the present. A dragon slept in one of the remote fields of Vere Celene. When her head rose, I recognized Sidar, one of the hunters. The green dragon's wings opened in alarm as a rip in the fabric of the world appeared above her, showing a slice of a storm the color of a bruise. Smoke poured from the tear, nearly invisible in the night, twisting into shapes of smoke with purple eyes, black teeth, and wings of wisp. The creature opened its mouth and screamed.

Roaring back, Sidar launched herself into the sky to face them.

I awoke back in my cell, but the scream echoed.

—*Cassia*, I bellowed, sending the thought as far and as wide as I could. *My Queen! Miligrist! Anyone!*

I clawed at the sides of my prison, desperate to escape. In preterit form, I could stretch my wings, but there was no hope of escape. The magic barrier over the twin openings of my prison would stop me. I felt the rip in the Veil tugging at my awareness.

Another shriek echoed, shivering down my spine.

For the first time in my living memory, there were wraiths in Vere Celene.

5.

CASSIA:

WRAITHS

Cassia gasped, disoriented, her hands clutching the edges of the scrying pool. When she scried, she usually saw the present, yet that night she had been dragged along into Everen's vision as he slept. Already, the details were fading around the edges, like a dream. She knew she should stop and write it down so it would not be lost, but there was no time.

She raced through the corridors, nearly tripping on her robe. Her lungs ached. As soon as she made it above ground, she stripped her robe and ran faster, finding her gait and growing into her full form. Other dragon warriors, wakened by the unearthly sounds, joined her. Would they be enough? Mace, Thist, and Pan, Sidar's mate. A gray, a green, and a blue. They'd lost Glisten in the human world and Feith in the storm on the night of the Feast of Flowers. Plenty were trained to hunt, but not as many to fight.

Cassia stretched her awareness toward her mother.

—Go! the Queen commanded, and Cassia felt her struggling to her feet, grunting in pain.

Cassia stretched her neck, wings working hard. She knew exactly where the rip in the Veil was—something deep within her was drawn to it. The other dragons followed.

—*Why are the monsters here?* Mace asked. *Why now?*

—*All I know is Sidar needs us*, Cassia thought back. *And we must come to her aid.*

Pan's fear was palpable in every wing beat. Cassia banked, following the coastline. They raced to the west side of the island. She hovered, claws closing on air, dread pooling through her like scrysilver.

The rip floated above the horizon, edged in purple lightning. The emerging monsters were winged, distorted echoes of dragons. Necks too long, jaws too large, and purple eyes too bright. The one nearest to her opened its mouth, hissing and clicking, before it swerved and attacked Sidar, black teeth biting deep into the hunter's neck.

Sidar roared in pain, shaking her head and trying to loosen its grip. Cassia dove, scraping her claws through the wraith. Beneath the smoke was something denser but somehow still insubstantial. From Everen, Cassia knew a dragon's touch weakened the wraiths, and here was the evidence: the beast let go of Sidar, giving a last screech before disappearing.

Pan dove and raked her talons along another creature. It shrieked and twisted into itself, losing its form. Remnants of smoke scattered to the wind. Cassia plucked a monster by a wing, hurling it into another wraith. Mace flew through them both with a snap of her teeth.

The dragons were ferocious in their fury. Cassia opened her jaws and bellowed, heart pumping with the thrill of the hunt.

It did not take long. The dragons' teeth and claws tore the wraiths to nothing. Scant minutes later, no new creatures swooped through the Veil, and the edges of the gap between worlds began to close.

Cassia's wings pulsed as she hovered in mid-air, lured by the hypnotic glimmers of the storm. What would it be like within the gaps between worlds? Part of Cassia yearned to fly through and fall to the Lumet herself. To live among the creatures she had seen in her scrying. She wanted to walk the streets of Vatra and the Citadel where dragons and humans had once lived in harmony. Everen had failed—but what if *she* could succeed?

Cassia shook her head. She knew better than to repeat her brother's folly.

Mace destroyed the last wraith, and the Veil closed over once more.

As the thrill of the fight left, long stripes of pain flared along Cassia's back—the claws hadn't pierced her flesh, but her scales were bruised. Sidar moaned in pain, and Cassia's head whipped toward her. Sidar bled from her neck and half a dozen other wounds, the red stark against the green. She struggled to keep herself aloft. She groaned, magic rippling over her scales as she shrank in mid-air, too exhausted to keep her full form. Pan flew above her and, as gently as she could, caught her mate in her claws. Sidar howled in pain before going limp.

Cassia led the others back to the weyr in weary triumph and fluttering fear. Pan had a deep scratch at her side but flew with utmost care. One of Mace's eyes was closed, blood staining her snout. The attack had narrowly missed the eye itself.

The Lady of Vere Celene appeared, her folded wings catching the moonlight. In silence, the dragons flew between them, landing on the banks of the bathing pool.

Every dragon in Vere Celene had emerged from the caves, waiting for the warriors' return. Once, there had been thousands, but they had been whittled down to a scant few hundred. The Queen crouched in dragon form, her red jewel glittering at her forehead, her shoulder bound in bandages: even months later, the wound from a crossbolt still pained her and she could not fly. Cassia knew her mother would be ripping herself to shreds that she hadn't been able to fight.

Pan landed on one claw, carefully placing Sidar's small, unmoving form in the sand, her pebbled skin stained scarlet. Pan nudged her mate with her snout, magic questing for any spark of life. A few of the dragons skilled with healing came closer, but all knew it was too late.

Pan raised her head to the sky and keened her loss.

Throughout the weyr, every dragon echoed her call, the collective note shifting and layering until it became the song for the dead, guiding Sidar's soul back to starfire. It reverberated across the island of Vere Celene.

Even from here, Cassia sensed Everen's grief. Without those shared visions, the dragons wouldn't have had the scant warning they did. What would have happened, if wraiths had descended upon the weyr itself? How many more dragons might have been lost?

Cassia hoped fate never told them.

6.

ARCADY:

ECHOES

I dreamed I was in Widow Girazin's manor, but it was empty. No guards, no glittering elite. Red light streamed through the windows, stained by the eerie crimson tide. My footsteps echoed as I chased Everen through the maze of wood-paneled corridors hung with priceless art. White marble statues watched me as I passed.

Everen was too quick. He'd pause at the end of a landing, taunting, but he'd be gone by the time I arrived. The more I chased him, the more easily he evaded me.

"Wait!" I kept calling. "Wait!"

I caught the echoes of his self-important laughter. I was again only a cast-off thief rooting for scraps, when we humans had worshiped his kind as gods. He'd known the truth all along.

In my waking hours, I told myself I was glad I spoke the spell that banished or killed him. I did my best not to think of him at all.

But asleep? Asleep I was full to the brim with regret.

I gave up in yet another posh bedroom, leaning against one of the sturdy wooden posts of the bed. The dream felt real enough. The wood was almost solid along my spine. Almost.

I blinked, and Everen was in the doorway. Between the sadness that surrounded him and the dark clothing he'd worn the night of the auction, he seemed in mourning.

I knew why I dreamed of this location, this night—because this was the last time I'd thought him human. As soon as we'd jumped from the tower, I'd learned some of his lies.

He focused on me with all the intensity of a dragon. He lowered his head and stepped forward, his lips meeting mine like a punch. I hissed in a breath, and his tongue flickered into my mouth. He pulled back with a hard exhale, as if my touch hurt. Pain and the memory of his magic ripped into me, tingling along my skin. He threw me onto the bed, balancing on his elbows as he gazed down at me. I felt the weight of him against my legs, my groin, my stomach. So close to real.

"Do you still hate me?" His breath whispered against my cheek.

"Yes," I said, even as my body fought not to arch.

He pinned my wrists above my head with one hand, the leather of his gloves between us. "Good," he said, his human illusion rippling away. His ears pointed, his teeth sharpened. His voice was so low I felt more than heard it, and his green eyes glowed. "You should."

He trailed a gloved finger along my neck. His hand came around my throat hard enough to make my breath catch. Sensations were blurred and muted, but my body tingled with magic and desire. In my new life at the Citadel, I had to keep myself under tight control. Here, curled up in the corner of my sleeping mind, I let myself go. I lifted my chin, exposing my throat while staring him down. I was not afraid, but the threat of danger made me feel alive. His hand tightened on my neck until I felt my heartbeat in my ears, and then let me go. I gasped in another breath.

He didn't kiss me again, even as I lifted my head toward his. One-handed, he ripped open my imagined finery and shrugged off his coat. I felt the tips of his fangs on my neck at the pulse point. My hands scraped along his back over the thin fabric of his shirt, feeling the two long, fine lines on either side of his spine that started at the top of his shoulder blades and ended at the bottom of his ribs. His wings were hidden by magic, but I'd never forget the first time I'd seen them.

His lips brushed the skin of my neck, and he hissed in pain. I wanted more, even if it hurt him. Especially if it hurt him.

I pushed up against him, and his free hand pressed my upper stomach, forcing me to still. He freed my hands, and I tangled them in his hair as he took his time working his way down my body, lips pressed against the fabric of my undershirt, gloved fingers finding ways to make me gasp. With one sharp movement, he ripped open the fastening of my trousers. His palms slid beneath me to cup my arse before he pulled off the offending bit of clothing. I was exposed and vulnerable. My Struck marks were dark and jagged. I fought the urge to hide from even this false version of him.

"Do you wish this were real?" he asked. His breath played on my lower stomach, then across my hip and down to my inner thigh.

He paused, not giving me what I wanted, what I needed. He took off the gloves, hands hovering. Dimly, I felt the heat of them.

I wanted his fingers, his tongue. I wanted to revel in the sight of a dragon prince kneeling before me. I wanted to break apart and gasp out his name, and then make this echo of Everen do the same.

"I wish you weren't dead," I whispered.

He raised his head and met my gaze in a challenge, one leather-clad hand snaking to rest on my hipbone, his touch hot as a brand.

"Maybe you need only find me, Arcady."

Another blink, and he was gone.

I woke up on the other side of the room, my shin throbbing where I'd bumped into the trunk at the foot of my bed. It'd bruise, and it wouldn't be pretty.

I was breathing hard. My hand rested on the doorknob, as if I were going to search through the corridors of the dormitories for Everen.

I forced my heartbeat to slow, rubbing my shin. Sleepwalking was a new and distressing development. If I hadn't hurt myself enough to wake up, would I have left my room? Coldness spread through me. The last thing I needed was other students thinking me odd enough to look closer. My fingers went to my open collar, drawing it closed protectively. The wardrobe mirror showed me my wild hair and flushed cheeks. I crossed the room and splashed cold water on my face.

I'd hidden a thin box in the gap between my wardrobe and the wall. I dragged it out and opened it on my bed. Nestled inside were two dream journals that had survived Everen's angry flames, as well as my maire's notebook I'd found in our cottage in Atrel. I flipped through the notebook carefully, the soot staining my fingertips. Most of the spells inside were hedge magic or healing balms. My maire had built on my grandsire's research but only given me one new spell: the one that had given me my new seal and identity.

I'd started my first dream journal when I was ten, and it had survived the fire. Most of the drawings were vague and abstract, but I paused on an image of a group of dragons in mid-flight. The next showed a tree and a snake. Fruit hung from the tree's branches, and

I'd written symbols I didn't recognize around the edges of the page. In the corner, I had scrawled 'I didn't like this dream,' my handwriting rounded and childish. I shivered and closed the cover.

Today was the first day of classes. I had agonized over my choices half the summer before Kelwyn had snapped at me to piss or get off the pot. I'd picked a history class that focused on the Schism and the Strikes to give me an excuse to access sources in the library relating to my grandsire. My most advanced magic class was intermediate Kalsh with a focus on waterweaving. While I was dead good at shapeshifting, I had less practice with the blue dragon god's elemental power.

For the other magic class, I'd gone with alchemy, which fell under fire's remit. This should have been hardest for someone blessed with Kalsh's power, but I had an ember of a dragon's fire magic.

I hunched my shoulders and popped the stone seal out of the metal setting at my chest, rolling it between my fingertips. For years, this little piece of stone had been down in the dark in a tomb next to a pile of sodden bones. Before that, it'd nestled right over my grandsire's heart. Now, it rested over mine.

Soon enough, I'd walk through the same corridors as my maire and my taie. I'd made it to the place my paire had never been allowed to study, much as he'd wished for it.

Despite a poor background, Barrow Eremia had worked his way to a position as an advisor to first the crown and then the Consul, discovering new innovations in magic along the way. Most people were drawn to the magic of one of the five "gods," but with enough grit, education, and energy, those with magic could learn at least the basics of other types, and some even went on to master them. My taie had been water-touched, like me, but had mastered all five branches of magic, which was unheard of. He must have made his share of enemies along the way. When they needed someone to blame for the

Strike, the drakines had been all too quick to turn on him. I needed to know why.

Carefully, I packed up my notebooks and put them back in their hiding place.

"I miss you," I whispered. "I miss you all."

Dawn was breaking, the light inching across the courtyard. I was too late for morning training, which was a shame, as hitting things and sweating might have helped chase away both the dream and my nerves. During orientation, I'd learned the basic layout of the university and introduced myself to some of the students, but today was the first day of proper classes.

I was, of course, bricking it.

I took my time dressing, trying on one set of clothing only to immediately rip it off and don another, leaving the discarded items scattered across the unmade bed. Finally, I settled on a russet brocade vest with brass buttons, dark brown trousers, and a green silk shirt. I attached a gold oval brooch to the high collar—plated, of course—painted with an enamel rose. I combed my curls into something resembling order and tied them back with a ribbon. I didn't bother with paint aside from a daub to hide the circles beneath my eyes. I'd noticed many other students didn't wear much day-to-day. With a last anxious glance at my reflection, I shrugged on my school robes, leaving them unfastened, and made my way to the courtyard.

Time to become Arcady Dalca.

7.

EVEREN:

THE QUEEN'S DECREE

Three days later, I foresaw another wraith attack. I sent my warning to Cassia, and the warriors took off and once more destroyed the creatures. This time, the dragons sustained only minor injuries. Yet I was sure it would happen again. And again. The Veil was weakening.

The following morning, the boundary at the top of my prison released, like a bubble bursting. The sun darkened with a familiar silhouette — I would know the rise of that feather crest and the curl of those horns anywhere.

A rope lowered and I clung to it, using my feet to help as my sister pulled me up by the strength of her jaws.

I fell to my knees as soon as I was out of my prison, overwhelmed by the scent of dried grass and dirt and the sight of the unending, gray-smeared sky above me. I unfurled myself to my full form for the first time in three months. I was not in a good state — my muscles were wasted, and my first few flights would be short and pathetic. I craned my neck toward the sky, spreading my wings, desperate to leave the ground behind.

—Not yet, brother mine, my sister said. *The Queen has summoned you.* Her draconic expression gave nothing away.

I lowered my wings, resisting the urge to whine like a hatchling. *—But the sky. I need the sky.*

—After, my sister reassured me. *We will fly together. I promise.*

Going back down into the dark so soon after being released was one of the hardest things I have ever done.

Cassia led me through to the largest cavern in Vere Celene. A human might call it a throne room, though there was no throne. Here was where my mother did much of the business of ruling. Dragons came to her here with grievances, or measures to put to a vote. Five thousand dragons could have fit inside it, cheek to jowl, if five thousand had been left.

Each step I took on my four limbs echoed throughout the cavern. I kept my wings tight across my back, my feather crest lowered in respect. It felt too much like groveling. Mace, her right eye closed and crusted with a nasty scab against her silver scales, stood at the Queen's side. My mother's scales were dull, and her bones showed through her hide. Fresh lacewing bandages peeked out from the edges of the leather wrapping at her shoulder. She stood stiffly, favoring her injured shoulder. Cassia, ever the Heir-in-Waiting, came forward to crouch at my mother's other side, while Miligrist arrived last, cataract-clouded eyes revealing nothing. Here were the dragons who ruled Vere Celene through crown and fate.

—Everen. The Queen's greeting burned like ice fire. Who would she be to me today? The Queen? My jailer? Or was she simply a mother faced once more with an errant, unruly son?

—Mother, I hazarded. *Are you . . . well?* I ventured.

—Do not concern yourself with it. Her green eyes took me in from crest to tail. *I have been trying to decide what to do with you.*

— You threw me into the dark and planned to leave me there unless I proved myself useful. Now I have, so you are considering letting me out. I should

have been more deferential, but the anger at being confined for three moons built in my chest.

—*Whatever you might be thinking, I will not go back into that prison,* I warned her. *I would sooner fly off to the horizon and die.*

My mother's crest puffed up. —*That could be arranged.*

I lifted my chin. —*If you were going to kill me, you would have done it by now. So why am I still breathing?*

Smoke curled from my mother's nostrils. —*For one meant to see everything, you have always been so oblivious. I put you down there for punishment, but also for your safety.* She tossed her head, eyes flashing. *I was not the only one furious at you. Dragons were queued up to challenge you. I wonder if I should have let them.*

—*There has not been a challenge since before I was hatched. They would not have dared if you forbade it.* My jaw clenched, my wings half-rising from my back. *If they yet listen to you, that is.*

—*Fly carefully, Everen.* The Queen's green eyes were hard. *You had your path, and you defied it. Our plans are nothing but ash. I could not let that go unpunished. Miligrist and Cassia tell me the prophecies say your story is not yet finished, and so you live.*

She opened her mouth, showing me the ember of her throat. —*Whether you remain alive depends on your behavior.*

My mother had often thought me petulant over the years. You, Arcady, had called me a spoiled prince enough times. I grew up pampered, fed by promises of my eventual saviorhood. Many dragons had fawned over me, even if my mother never coddled me. Miligrist told me myths that hinted at the legacy I would grow into, while Mace taught me to hunt and to be strong and unflinching in the face of danger. I was so desperate to be what the dragons wanted of me and then railed against the cost.

—*I warned you of the wraiths' attacks,* I pressed. *I take it you told our mother and Miligrist of our shared vision, Cassia?*

—I did, my sister said.

—Surely Miligrist has seen them too. I would not show my belly first. Miligrist looked away, her feather crest wilting.

—Miligrist? I asked

She silently conferred with my mother. Finally, the old Seer raised her head.

—Since the Feast of Flowers, the scrysilver has shown me nothing. I thought the Veil was too thick, but your vision weaves a different tale. Her feather crest drooped even further. *Perhaps my time is past.*

Part of me was filled with sympathy for Miligrist, but the rest was caught between triumph and horror.

—I saw the snake and the tree in visions before, but so very long ago. I thought we avoided this branch . . . Miligrist paused, expression soulful. *Come. The scrysilver might show you the truth. Will you seek it?*

I swallowed past the fire in my throat. *—I will.*

My mother left the cavern, limping but keeping her head high. Miligrist followed, then Cassia, then Mace, and I was last: the lowest in the hierarchy.

My fear grew with each step. What if I did not see anything?

What if I did?

It had been so long since I'd been down to the pools. The molten metal gleamed, and the air smelled of sulfur. I transformed to preterit, as did the others, and we donned the simple lacebark robes kept in the cavern. I leaned over the pool, seeing my silvered reflection. The scrysilver swirled with formless colors. How many times had I bent over this surface, desperately hoping fate would show me the way forward? I had less magic since the Feast of Flowers, for some of mine remained with you. Perhaps severing the bond had given me back my powers of prophecy.

—Show us the way, Everen, my heart, Miligrist sent. *For I no longer can.* Grief rose from her. She had spent so long in the scrying pools that Cassia and I used to jest she was never fully present. Who was a Seer without her visions?

I closed my eyes, reaching for the magic within myself and the scrysilver. I bent down, barely kissing the surface, and tasted sulfur and sunlight.

I called fate and waited for its answer.

My sister placed her hand over mine, fingers tightening as she took her own kiss of silver so she might join me. Together, we let Vere Celene fall away and the storm between worlds rise around us.

We were not truly there. I did not feel the frozen rain or the unearthly wind, but it frightened me just the same.

When I had first entered the storm, a being had nearly caught me in its current, but our golden bond had dragged me back.

This time, I saw it more clearly: an enormous serpent twined through the gaps between worlds. The sheer scale of it was difficult to imagine.

—The Dreamer. My sister's thoughts were tinged with awe. *The Dreamer between worlds. There have been scant mentions of it in one of the oldest of prophecies that survived the fire from the time of the third Archivist.*

Its sheer size and power filled me with numinous wonder. Red pulsed brightly from a wound in the snake's side.

—What did the prophecy say? I asked.

—"As above, so below. As what was, so shall become. Whatever you do, remember this: you must not wake the Dreamer."

If I had been in human form, I would have shivered.

—We have seen enough, my sister said. *The longer we linger, the more dangerous it becomes, even in visions. Come away. Come back.*

I slammed into awareness, the acrid taste of scrysilver on my tongue. My legs had collapsed, but Mace had caught me. Across the pool, my mother gazed at us. A new emotion rose off her, one I was not sure I'd ever seen: fear. Miligrist wrapped her arms around herself, shivering.

I staggered to my feet.

— *We dared not speak of the great serpent between worlds,* Miligrist said. *Only trusted Seers knew of its existence.*

I, the failed Seer, had not been worthy, then. I pulled my lips from my teeth, resisting the urge to spit out the remnants of scrysilver.

—*All we know is that if it wakes from its slumber, it will be the end of all things.* Miligrist's white eyes glowed like twin moons.

— *Why haven't I seen any of this before?* I asked.

— *You have already learned fate is not a straight path. It turns and winds like the coils of the serpent.* She blinked. *Perhaps you changed it.*

—*I told the truth the night of the Feast of Flowers,* I said slowly, working through it. *And now you realize it, too. The other dragons trying to come through risked waking the Dreamer.*

— *You went through the storm without issue on the Night of Locked Tombs,* Mace said. *We had no reason to think it would be any different for us.*

—*Maybe it would have been, but the serpent is injured,* I said.

— *So it sleeps more lightly. Yes. At this point, you now know as much as we do,* Miligrist said. *Fate has us flying near-blind.*

—*I want you to admit it,* I said to my mother. *Admit I was right, that my choice saved dragons and humans. That fate chose to show* me *the truth. Not Miligrist. Not Cassia. Me.*

My mother's expression hardened, the jewel on her forehead glimmering.

— *You suspected it then,* I pressed. *But you know it now.*

She was silent for so long that I thought she would never give me the satisfaction. She shifted, and her grimace showed sharpened fangs. — *You were not wrong,* she said, each word seeming to pain her as much as her wound. *Fate, it seems, showed you true.*

The words were so sweet I wanted to savor them.

—And so now, Mother, what will you do with me?

Mace's uninjured eye was sharp. *Careful*, she probably wanted to say. *Mind your mother's temper.* Mace had hovered around the edges of my world since I was a child. If Miligrist was like my grandmother, Mace was the stern aunt. Over the past few months, she had been my other jailer, bringing me food and water if Cassia was detained. Mace's loyalty to my mother was unshakable.

— We are short of warriors, Mace said. *You will fight the wraiths and warn us of any rips in the Veils.*

I nodded. *—Of course.*

—You will also scry for any more visions, my mother added. *But you will tell no one else what you are doing.*

That gave me pause. *—The other dragons do not know about Miligrist, do they?*

Miligrist's clouded eyes closed in pain.

—No, my mother admitted. *And it will stay that way. Dragons are angry. They are scared. They need stability.*

—More than they need the truth?

She ignored that. *—You may move through the weyr freely, but you will be closely watched by Mace, Cassia, or Miligrist. You will not scry alone, and anything you see will be recorded in detail. Is that agreed?*

—Agreed, I said without hesitation. That was more than I had hoped for, but still, I dared push her. *I saw a future of peace. Not dragons ruling humans with fear and fire. This is what I will always work toward.*

The dragon queen stared at me, unblinking. *—Perhaps there need not be such death, but I swear to you this, here and now: I will never bow to a human. I think you overestimate them. They will fear us, and humans always attack what they fear.*

I believed she was wrong, but part of me feared she was right.

—Lastly, my mother continued, and my hopes sank. *I hereby strip you of the name Emberclaw and of your titles. No one will refer to you*

as a prince of the realm. To do otherwise would give you the illusion of too much power, or that you have not been punished enough. You, Everen once-Emberclaw, must learn your place.

It should not have come as a surprise, but it hit me like a blow. The breath left my lungs. The muscles in Cassia's jaw worked — she had not warned me. Would it have hurt less if she had?

Queen Naccara stared through me. Her dragon features were so similar to mine. The slope of the snout, and the way the eyes tilted up at the corners. Our scales were the exact same shade of red. I had no father, for the rising temperatures of Vere Celene meant dragons lay eggs borne solely of themselves. Only females had hatched for centuries. All save me.

She had always been far more concerned with being a ruler than being a mother. And I knew, in many ways, she was a good Queen, especially after seeing how much the humans let some of their own kind suffer. She had always kept herself apart from me because of what the last male dragon before me had done. She had been strong. But now the Queen was injured. Her reign was weaker than it had ever been in no small part because of me. Would anyone dare try to take that power for themselves?

— Do you understand? she asked.

If I misbehaved, or if the Queen felt me a threat to Vere Celene or her rule, I would be thrown back into prison or outright killed. Visions or no visions. Chosen one or not. This was the sole chance she could give me.

— As you wish, my Queen, I managed, keeping my voice steady as I stared at the dragon who no longer claimed herself my mother. There was nothing more to say.

8.

ARCADY:

QUICKGOLD

The laboratory was in the basement of a remote corner of the university grounds. I chose a seat near the front so I'd be able to hear the professor. The long tables and the walls were lined in the same black stone. I'd bet good coin that the chairs, though wooden, were regularly spelled to be fire-resistant. On the tables were basic laboratory equipment: between every other seat was an unlit oil lamp with a melting tray above it. Each table had a selection of round-bottomed beakers. There were also glass trays and a long, tiny glass spoon. An eye dropper. A plain black box. It was locked with a simple enough charm, but I figured I shouldn't start my academic journey with a bit of magical lockpicking, so I left it alone.

The other students filed in. I was still learning everyone's names and genders. The majority of students were from drakine or guilder families. A few were acolytes from the Citadel Order. They wore normal robes like the rest of us, but their shaved heads stood out, and they stayed in the monastery wing instead of the dorms. There were a handful of scholarship students from merchant backgrounds.

Everyone knew who they were, and they stuck out like sore thumbs. There were no students from villein or lower tradespeople or merchant stock, for all that the Citadel pretended the university was open to all.

As a relatively poor, orphaned drakine, I wasn't much higher in social standing than a scholarship student. A few days earlier, two drakines, Delin Sanron and Kala Jonrir, had spoken to me long enough to learn my background and then promptly up and left, practically mid-sentence. They had skin so perfect that I suspected they both spent small fortunes on potions from healers. Kala had jet-black hair that fell, perfectly straight, to his shoulders. Delin's chestnut hair was elaborately braided. I recognized their type: they'd both likely been proper terrors at the academy when they were younger. They'd worked the worst of the outright bullying from their system and were now content to stand in the corner and talk shite and cast the occasional dirty look instead. Easy enough to ignore.

I nodded at Rahela Easel, one of the students I was most hoping to befriend. She was from a well-connected family, knew everyone, and was friendly with all. She had a round face and black hair that she wore nearly as short as a priest's, and she had a generous smile with a dimple on one cheek.

Just as I was about to motion for her to come to the seat next to me, one of the acolyte students slid into it, folding their forearms on the table, hands gripping opposite elbows. My shoulders lowered as Rahela sat near the back.

Professor Hayden arrived last. They were tall, with cropped brown hair and light skin, and Their lips were painted a dark purple. Instead of voluminous robes, They were dressed in a treated leather jerkin and trousers and good, sturdy boots. The ties at the side of the jerkin were loose, and I caught the subtle swell of the belly. I suspected the professor was pregnant.

"Well, this won't do at all," They said, taking us in, but a smile played at Their mouth. At our visible confusion, the smile widened. They went to a corner of the lecture hall and opened a door so seamless I hadn't noticed it.

"Put your robes in here and for today, roll up your sleeves and return to your seats. For future lessons, I recommend wearing formfitting clothing — nothing trailing. While I'll charm you once we begin using fire more often, the spell wears off quickly, and my goal is to have no student light up like a candle this term. Understood?"

As we hung up our robes, I wondered if that meant a student *had* caught fire before. I rolled back the green silk of my shirt to show half of my forearms. The acolyte next to me was better prepared — beneath their robes they wore a shirt with tight sleeves to their wrists. I stifled a sigh. I'd have to go buy something similar with more of the coin I didn't have to spare.

"Wonderful," Professor Hayden said when all the students were ready. The professor pushed up Their sleeves, revealing the red dragon tattoo around Their left forearm, which signaled the mastery of Their chosen god. A second dragon outlined in gray showed They could use Piater's magic almost as well. The outstretched wings reached Their elbow. With everyone in the Citadel often wearing long robes, this was the first time I'd seen one of the tattoos in the flesh, so to speak. I wondered if I'd ever have the chance to wear one myself.

Professor Hayden narrowed Their eyes at us. "Now, firstly, why do you think alchemy falls under Aura's purview instead of Piater's? Metal and elements come from the earth just as much as stone, after all. Yet those with the silver god's power tend to move objects with the mind or manipulate non-living matter directly, without fiddling about with beakers and the like. Any guesses?"

Another hesitation before Rahela raised her hand. "Because a lot of alchemical processes have to do with heat and energy. So transmutation is the other side of fire magic beyond simply control of the element."

"Very good. If someone is very strong in red magic, it's often easier to pick up silver, and vice versa. All five magics have blurred boundaries rather than hard delineations. Someone strong in either purple Zama or blue Kalsh magic could make it rain—it's merely a matter of whether they affect air pressure or force the water itself to fall from the clouds. Fire needs both air and wood from the earth to burn. Different approaches for the same end result. Yes, yes, I know none of this will be particularly groundbreaking to you, but it bears repeating."

They gestured to the equipment on the tables. "Today, we'll start with a simple alchemy experiment. There's nothing inherently magical in this one beyond the general charm of the world and its intricate workings. There is plenty of theory for you to get through before you'll set things aflame or attempt to transmute anything, I'm afraid."

They spoke with such enthusiasm that it was contagious. I think I had an intellectual crush. I could listen to this professor talk about how magic worked all day. This was what I'd been working for: a chance to sit in a lecture and soak up as much of the knowledge about how the world worked as I could. The professor leaned against Their desk at the front, reaching into a pocket to take out a lump of something dark.

"Alchemy is about transformation. It is the most beautiful, elegant blend of magic and science. Though of course, I might be a little biased." Professor Hayden laughed. "Many innovations in magic come down to this practice. For, of course, magic is not permanent. If you try to build a tower with magic holding it together, it will crumble eventually unless you constantly re-spell it, which is expensive, wasteful, and dangerous. But if you transmute something via alchemy, it might last longer, for it's the actual science and understanding of the natural world, sans magic, that helps keep the mortar strong. However: what's the risk we have to keep in mind for, say, transmuting metals?"

They held the dark lump on Their open palm and, as we watched, it brightened to gold. A gasp went through the room at the display.

I took a deep breath and raised my hand, and Professor Hayden nodded at me. The students' heads turned in my direction, and I tried not to wilt under their stares. I was Sar Arcady Dalca. Drakine, privately educated up in the mountains. Poor compared to a lot of drakines, but confident in my place in the world.

"It doesn't last. So people might change lead to gold, but then someone might open their coffers one day to find out they've nothing but lumps of lead. It happened to my uncle," I lied. "Though only for a few coins, luckily enough."

"Very good," Professor Hayden said, and I felt a glow of triumph. As we watched, the gold in Professor Hayden's hand darkened. They tossed the lead and caught it before setting it back down on the desk.

"Chrysopoeia is the main branch of alchemy, but only the absolute strongest masters can shift a base metal to a noble one in a way that is essentially permanent. For most, it will start to degrade—the weaker the alchemist's power and command, the sooner it reverts. Why would we want more noble metals at our disposal?"

Several hands went up this time. "It's valuable," said Oran Winward, a dark-haired student at the front. Their parents were guilders.

"Yes, of course, noble metal is currency. But noble or precious metals are also more resistant to corrosion, which can be useful for a variety of reasons, both magical and non-magical. And metals are associated with certain elements, and therefore different gods or constellations in the sky."

Professor Hayden tested us, calling on students one by one until we'd laid out the basics: gold was associated most with Aura's fire and alchemy. Copper for the living elements of earth and Jari and healing. Platinum for stone, metal, and Piater's ability of telekinesis. Silver for water, shapeshifting, and Kalsh, and wraithwright for weather and Zama. Of the other half of Zama's magic—mind-reading—nothing was said. It'd been forbidden for years, and if anyone was caught using it, it was a death sentence. I'd had no small amount of panic when I'd realized part of the bond with Everen involved speaking mind-to-mind. Though, really, it would just be one more entry in a long list of why I'd be killed if anyone found out who and what I was.

Oran raised their hand.

"Yes?" Professor Hayden raised Their eyebrows with a half-smile.

"What about the Elixir of Life?"

Something flickered in Professor Hayden's expression before Their smile widened. "Ah, there's always one who asks about it. It's quite the fairy tale, isn't it? A potion that can increase your power and decrease the cost of using magic. This is, of course, especially covetable after the Strike. A panacea that could help you live forever and solve all our earthly woes." Their tone was teasing. "Alchemists are at their heart scholars and scientists. There is no concrete proof that the Elixir of Life has ever been successfully created. It's an unreachable goal, but that doesn't mean we shouldn't keep striving to find it. Who knows what else we might learn along the way?"

Professor Hayden clapped Their hands. "Now. Today is just a bit of fun. In addition to transmutation, amalgamation is important in alchemy." They held up a block of grayish metal with a small, shallow divot bored in the center. "Any guesses as to what this is?"

The students shook their heads. "Great, that means I can surprise you later." They placed it on Their desk. "We'll come back to this."

Professor Hayden raised Their hands. *"Luetakya,"* They said, and the laboratory echoed with *snicks* as the boxes on the desks unlocked. "You'll be sharing materials with the person next to you."

The acolyte beside me opened it before I could. Inside were three glass trays. In the center was a dollop of quicksilver, and on the right, thin sheets of gold leaf. The acolyte took out the three trays carefully and set them between us.

The professor passed around gloves and goggles. "Who can tell me what we have here?"

My new partner raised their hand. "Quicksilver and sheets of gold." They were faintly familiar, though I hadn't spoken to them before. Shorn hair, brown skin, serious expression. Acolytes weren't high on my befriending priority list, as mercenary as that sounded. I was more focused on the offspring of those who might have killed my grandsire.

"Good," the professor said. "Now, though the harmful toxins absorb slowly, please avoid touching the quicksilver anyway. If you do, wash your hands. Do not heat it for any reason, for the vapor is also dangerous. And for the love of the gods, do not drink it. Don't ask me why I have to give *that* obvious instruction."

A laugh rippled through the class. "Now," They continued. "Are these elements base or noble?"

"Gold is noble, obviously," another student with black braided hair said. "Dunno about quicksilver."

The dollop on the tray had coalesced into a silver pebble. I had dreamed of huge pools of something like it, hidden far underground in a world that wasn't this one. I didn't know if the dragons' scrysilver had quicksilver in it. Whatever it was, according to Everen, it could became a portal to the past, the present, and the future. I leaned closer, squinting at the distorted reflection on the surface of the liquid metal. If I looked hard enough, what might I see?

My lab partner picked up the tray, shattering my concentration. I leaned back, aiming for nonchalance. Around me, students moved the trays gently, watching the quicksilver move as if with a mind of its own. Others carefully poked at it with the eyedropper, letting the drops fall and the liquid metal come back together as if magnetized. The professor had us separate the quicksilver into two droplets, using extra glass trays, and then we fed one of them a sheet of gold. Exclamations rose as the gold crumpled and gradually drew into the quicksilver until they melded together. I picked up another leaf and did it again, fascinated. The acolyte draped the next gilded leaf over the quicksilver, as rapt as me, a smile playing around the corner of their mouth. Soon enough, we'd fed it all the gold.

"Give it a poke with the spoon," Professor Hayden urged. "See how it's changed in texture and color, so it's almost buttery? Some call this quickgold. They use this technique in mining to draw out the gold when the pieces are too small to easily pass through a sieve. Eventually, you can melt away the quicksilver—carefully, so you don't breathe in the fumes—and only the gold remains. This is how they gild bronze statues, for example. The two elements of gold and quicksilver are bonded briefly, but not for good."

I fought down a grimace, passing the spoon to the acolyte. It was hard not to follow the obvious metaphor. A human and a dragon had amalgamated a bond before we'd forcibly separated ourselves. I was just all that was left, and I wasn't anything as precious as gold. The grief threatened to choke me, and I forced it back down.

"Now. Have you all forgotten about my earlier little experiment?" Professor Hayden gestured at the metal on the desk. Sure enough, I hadn't given it a second thought once we'd started playing with quicksilver and gold. The metal block had changed, with something white emerging from the center.

"It can be a little slow naturally, so I'll hurry it along," They said, and Their seal flashed silver and red. We watched as white filaments pushed up into a tower-like shape. It seemed organic, almost alive, closer to a plant or fungus. Eventually, unbalanced by its weight, the white tower toppled over, the tendrils still growing.

"Anyone figured out what it is?" the professor asked.

Rahela's hand once more. "Aluminum reacting with quicksilver?"

"Very good. Quicksilver will form amalgams with many substances, with different results. Amalgams have their uses, and many elements bond with others in nature, like sulfide, where it instead burns. Throughout this year, you'll be learning how to break apart elements of the earth and combine, heat, and make something stronger or new as a result. A grasp of alchemy will help you harness the power of fire itself."

The class had gone quiet and rapt. The professor grinned at us. "Now that you've finished, let's have a bit of a clear-up."

"*Kéavén piutusam*," They said, and Their seal flashed bright enough the red played against their collarbones. The professor had said "combine quicksilver," but quicksilver translated closer to "blood-metal," as if the metal were a living thing.

The quicksilver detached itself from the gold, leaving behind a small, irregular nugget. The classroom watched as the drops of quicksilver rose, coming together until an orb about the size of a fist floated above our heads. With another burst of magic, the professor coaxed it all into a beaker and corked it neatly. The sheer amount of power and control in that display, even though They made it look like less effort than flicking a finger, made my mouth fall open.

"Before next week, please read the first two chapters of *The Fundamental Principles of Alchemy*. And for our next lab, please sit in the same seats. The person you worked with today is your partner for the rest of the year, so better say a brief hello if you haven't already made their acquaintance. Have a good first sennight of classes," They said with a last smile. Students burst into conversation, a few trailing to the front of the laboratory to ask the professor questions.

I met my new partner's eyes. They had freckles across their nose and cheeks, and the mage lights made their light brown hair shine nearly blonde. They were also glaring at me with something bordering on hostility, which took me aback.

"Arcady Dalca," I said, sticking out my right hand and signing "any" with my left. Turn on the charm, and the acolyte would warm to me soon enough, I was sure. "Pleased to meet you."

After a hesitation, they signed "she," and reached out and took my forearm as I took hers—the polite way to handshake if you weren't wearing gloves. The acolyte winced and pulled back. "I am Sorin of the Order of the Dragons."

9.

SORIN:

PRACTICE GROUNDS

After the Feast of Flowers, when Magnes had asked her what she wanted for her life, Sorin had taken the quiet option of being His Eye.

Sorin's summer in the forest hadn't been easy. She'd cursed when her horse threw a shoe in the middle of a torrential summer storm. She'd burned her porridge on the campfire more times than she could count, and though the Veil was quieter since the Feast of Storms, she'd fought the odd wraith with her dragonbone blade before they could linger long enough to cause harm.

She'd spent the warmer season following the leyline along the Red River through a swathe of Royal Forest she'd eventually thought of as hers. The forest, with all its greenery and beams of golden light, became her new cathedral. She didn't know if she still believed dragons were gods. How could she, after all she'd seen? She no longer prayed. Not to Jari and Saint Wyndyn, not to Piater and Saint Dolard. Not to Zama and Saint Etter. She had lost her faith and clarity, but she was perhaps still lost and wandering. She'd watched blooms open in the morning and close at night. Picked berries off the vine, sun-warmed sweetness bursting along her tongue. Listened to birdsong and the steady clop of her horse's hooves. Out there in the forest, she had found something like peace.

The time in the forest had had another effect on her: the longer she spent away from Magnes, the more she felt as if she were waking from a dream.

During the last new moon, Sorin had climbed the steep mountains of the Fangs to the gray, imposing keep of Nalore Monastery, where the Eyes rested between treks protecting the Veil. Built directly into the stone, the royal family had fled to the fortress whenever Vatra was attacked. In its depths was a grand library, a mirror to the one in the university, to ensure no knowledge was lost in another dark age. The books were copied magically, but the monks painstakingly traced the words so the ink wouldn't fade.

Sorin had arrived at the monastery with Jaculus perched on her shoulder, out of breath from the thin air. She wanted nothing more than a hot meal and a warm bath. Instead, she'd opened the door to her room to find Magnes sitting by the fireplace, waiting for her. Her stomach had dropped, and she'd fought the urge to turn and flee.

Her wyvern squeaked in alarm and fluttered to his perch in the corner, watching Magnes warily.

"Tell me honestly, my child," He'd said, toying with His glass of wine. "Are you bored yet?"

She'd stared at Him, dumbstruck once more. That summer, she had often wondered if she should have made a different call. While Sorin loved the forest, she realized she'd spent years with her Vow of Silence and broken it only to speak once more to no one but her wyvern or horse. She couldn't imagine wandering that leyline for months on end, cut off from life more thoroughly than when she'd hidden in the background of the Citadel.

Sometimes, Sorin dreamed of learning her healing magic well enough to find work in a small hamlet somewhere along the coast or in one of the small mountain towns. She imagined living in a small cottage, far enough from the town that she woke up and fell asleep to the sounds of the sea or the forest. People would come to her, and she could help rather than hurt them. Until she'd had the time and quiet in the forest, she'd never dared to properly picture a future outside of Magnes's sphere. She'd always known she'd serve Him until she was nothing but ash on the wind.

Hadn't she?

"Come back to the Citadel," He'd said. "I have need of an Eye in the university."

In her years as an acolyte, she had toyed with the idea of going to the university to strengthen her command of magic. Priests all received basic training for the magic of their chosen blessed god. Magnes had taught her other spells, and she'd picked up more from study or when she occasionally helped professors at the university. With her Vow of Silence and work as an assassin, it hadn't seemed possible to do anything more.

"I know I promised you a respite from it all," He said. "I have honored that. In this role, you need not kill. There's no one else I trust with this. It's too important, my child. So. Will you come?"

Sorin swallowed against her growing foreboding, but curiosity plucked at her like a harp string. "What would I be doing?"

"I will not pretend it will be easy," Magnes warned her. He reached over, peeling back her sleeve, revealing her red scar, still fresh and angry. He brushed His bare fingertips over the skin and she flinched. She had not dared go to the Citadel Healers for the wound. Some of her misgivings melted away, her desire to please Him returning.

"You must watch the one who gave you this."

She felt her face slacken. The interloper from the auction. The one who could command a dragon. The Starveling who had tried to kill her. Her scar burned. She pulled her arm back. Jaculus spread his wings in agitation before settling back down.

"They are at the university?" she asked.

"I want you to stay close to them," Magnes said. "Report everything you notice about how they wield their magic, no matter how strange it might seem. And above all: never let them suspect. Tread carefully, and trust nothing they tell you. They are working for an agent of chaos, a pretender who could destroy everything we have worked for."

Sorin swallowed.

"The Veil is thicker, but it and the world's magic remain sick, Sorin," Magnes said. "I know a way to heal it for good, to make sure The Lumet is safe once and for all. The false god and the human are at the nexus of it. They always have been. But I cannot do it alone."

She knew there was no option to refuse. Not truly.

"I will be your Eye," she said.

Magnes leaned forward and kissed the top of her head. "I knew I could count on you, my child."

Even as she leaned into his touch and wanted to bask under His praise, the smallest corner of her mind still hated Him for it.

The morning after Sorin's first alchemy class was bitterly cold; autumn had well and truly arrived.

Sorin had been back at the Citadel for nearly a sennight, and it was both like and unlike the many years she'd spent here. She visited Jaculus in the Rookery first thing before heading down to arms practice. She flexed her hands, willing warmth into her fingertips.

Around her, students lined up in the armory, plucking their chosen weapons.

Three months ago, she would have used the honorific pronoun in her head for any student. Now, she reluctantly had to admit that they were on equal social footing, at least while they all studied together.

Sorin chose a battered trident. She fancied a challenge that morning. Plenty of the other students went for polearms—glaives, halberds, scythes, and lances. Some picked shorter axes. Edin Vayne, a dark-haired fourth year, always chose a sword. She was a good fighter, that one. A handful of students snatched pre-strung bows from hooks, planning to head to the far side of the grounds for target practice. Gemiean, another acolyte, chose a mace, the brave soul. The last time she remembered him using it, he'd given himself a bump the size of the moon on his forehead.

He shot her a smile, and she returned it. She remembered what Gemiean had been like as a child. They'd nudged each other's shoulders to try and make the other laugh first when they should have been praying at altars. He'd often flicked a bread crumb at her at mealtimes to get her attention from across the table. When Magnes had chosen her to be His, she'd pulled away. All these years later, he was taller, broader, but just as prone to his snaggle-toothed smile.

Sorin hefted the trident. It was heavier than the thin-tipped spear she usually trained with. Tridents were often for ceremonial fights or used as staves during parades, yet it was still basically a pitchfork. She strapped herself into her practice armor and pulled the helmet over her freshly shorn skull.

The amphitheater was a carved-out ledge two-thirds of the way up the volcanic plug of the Citadel. The stone walls lifted at the edges like the slope of a shallow bowl.

The armorer, Colla Hulm, paired off Their charges with sharp shouts and gestures. Hulm stood ramrod straight, military history apparent in every line, sharp eyes missing nothing. Hard as petrified wood, and—as some students joked, well out of earshot—just as old. Without the shelter of the outer walls, the wind found its way through any gap in clothing. Above them, the spires of the Citadel were just visible over the crenelated guard towers.

Sorin shuffled her feet along the hard-packed earth of the training ground. Her partner was Willem Ansel, an auburn-haired drakine from a particularly well-connected family. He stared her down, adjusting his glaive. Willem was a head taller and had more muscle. Armsmaster Hulm tended to alternate partnering people who were close physical matches versus those who weren't.

"It's not like they give you a choice on the battlefield," They'd say each time a student complained about a mismatch. Never mind that, if war were ever to break out, Sorin knew none of these drakines would fight. Even military family drakines like Damon Aldburn would be senior officers or generals, safely away from the fray on the back of a horse.

Sorin rested lightly on the balls of her feet and raised her trident. One could learn a lot about someone by how they fought. Willem held his glaive in a loose two-handed hold. His grip was good, but his stance was sloppy. The students' collective breath misted in the air, but the fog was thin enough to barely gray the grounds.

Armsmaster Hulm made the rounds and touched each weapon with a fingertip and a muttered spell to activate the protections for the next half a candlemark. Hulm's magic was Zama's. The spell created a tight barrier of air around the dull edges, so a hit meant a bruise instead of a cut. Sorin was always in awe at the strength needed to be able to enchant twenty weapons at once. The Armsmaster fell upon a pre-packed breakfast as soon as They were finished, chewing as They watched the fights.

Willem kept his position, focusing on Sorin. His brown eyes were bloodshot, and Sorin suspected he was hungover.

"On my count!" Hulm called. "One, two, three . . . fight!"

Sorin breathed out slowly through her mouth. Willem came in fast, bringing the blade down hard. Sorin caught the polearm in the tines of her trident, the clang muffled by the force field of air. She could twist and tug the weapon from Willem's grip with ease, but she shouldn't win a fight so soon. She was meant to be an acolyte who had spent her life lost in study and prayer, not one who knew the quickest way to kill someone.

Sorin freed her trident and circled. Willem feinted, but the cant of his hips gave him away, and Sorin blocked it, though she felt the reverberations of the impact in the bones of her arms. She let out a muffled grunt.

Sorin thrust forward with the trident at Willem's unprotected side, giving him what would become a decent bruise on the ribs.

He swore and retreated a couple of steps, adjusting his grip on the glaive.

Another few furious attacks, another equally furious blocks. Sloppy. Very sloppy.

Don't be proud. She could almost hear Magnes's voice in her head.

She chanced glancing at Arcady Dalca, though she doubted that was their true name. Arcady and Damon were both using staves, and it was obvious this Arcady, whoever they truly were, had not been properly trained. Damon would win any second.

When Sorin had stepped into the alchemy lab on the first day of class and met Arcady's eyes, it had taken everything within her to keep her face blank. To not remember those same features twisted with hunger, black lines spreading over their skin as they turned Starveling. Their breath, hot on her cheek, and the feeling of teeth digging into her flesh.

A quick movement out of the corner of her eye: Sorin grunted, using the staff of the trident to block Willem's glaive. The long blade had come closer to her ear than she would have liked.

Sorin threw off the glaive and swung hard with the trident, tripping Willem, though he recovered before he fell. Willem was a decent enough fighter when he was fresh, but that morning his reactions were slow. She blocked, barely catching his blade with the tines of the trident, but he held on grimly.

Sorin no longer felt the cold. Sweat dampened her brows as she freed her tines and struck. Her joints ached from the impact. She swung out a leg, but Willem dodged it. His left side was consistently open. All she needed to do was tangle his glaive again and flip it from his grip. Before he could recover, she could move in close enough to punch him in the stomach, following up with a right hook to the jaw, and then kick his ankle to pin him and make him yield. It would be easy.

But not only would it break Hulm's rules for good sportsmanship, she would have given her target a bruised jaw, a sore stomach to go with his already-bruised ribs, and possibly an injured ankle or knee. And others, including Arcady Dalca, might wonder how a priest could win so many bouts in a row.

Don't be proud.

Sorin sighed and shifted her weight, intentionally making a clumsy feint. Willem latched onto it without hesitation. And it was Sorin's trident flying to the ground, and Sorin who tripped. Willem held his forearm to her neck, his other hand pressing her firmly enough into the ground she couldn't move, but not hard enough to hurt. The sun had just risen over the Citadel, and pink chased the morning mist away.

"Yield," Willem panted. At least she'd tired him out.

Part of Sorin still wanted to fight.

Don't be proud.

Sorin let her head fall back, hitting her fist against the ground three times.

Willem stepped back and offered his hand to help her up. She took his forearm, grudgingly. Once upright, she shook out her limbs. She'd fallen well, with no pain. She'd have the usual soreness after working her muscles, and a slight twinge at the joining of her sternum and ribs. She picked up her trident, the humming quieting as the spell faded.

Hulm made Their way through the students. "Sar Edin, good work as always. Nicely done, Sar Willem, despite you not being at your best, eh? Acolyte Sorin, make sure to watch your right side."

Sorin grunted.

"Well fought," Willem said, just as winded as she was. "Thought you had me there for a moment."

The interloper trotted over to them, trailed by Damon. "Bravo, Willem. Afraid Damon absolutely thrashed me," Arcady said.

"Turns out even this bastard hangover couldn't keep me down," Willem said with affable politeness. Damon gave Willem an inscrutable look.

"Bad luck, Sorin." Arcady flashed her a grin. To outside eyes, they seemed just like any other student on the grounds, though they hailed from a poorer drakine family of little standing. Sorin, however, had caught the exhaustion lurking behind the easy smiles and the dark circles beneath the face paint. *What are your secrets?* Sorin wondered.

"Alchemy's next. I'm surprised you didn't sign up for that one, Willem," Arcady said. "Rahela and Sorin here did."

"Oh, there's a very simple reason for that," he said, grimacing. "Professor Hayden is my maire. Practically taught me alchemy since I was in diapers, anyway, whether I wanted the instruction or not. Come to me if you get stuck, though. I know the tricks and shortcuts."

Sorin spotted the resemblance in the shape of the nose and the high cheekbones. Willem and the professor had different surnames, but that wasn't unusual. Often, it depended more on which noble name the family wanted to carry on, and the Ansel line was older than Hayden's.

"My sympathies," Arcady said. "But I'll almost certainly take you up on the offer." Willem gave them a sardonic salute before ambling away.

Arcady smirked and stuck their hands in their pockets, feigning nonchalance.

Sorin narrowed her eyes. Here she was, doing Magnes's bidding as soon as He'd crooked His finger. By working with Him, though, Sorin could satisfy her curiosity about someone who had nearly outsmarted the Head Priest of the Order of the Dragons. A person who had called down a god, and then banished Them and the other celestials back beyond the Veil.

This stranger was pretending to be normal and beneath notice. Sorin knew all about that. One thing was certain: once Magnes had learned whatever He needed to know about this person, Arcady Dalca would disappear and never be seen again.

10.
ARCADY:

ELEMENTAL

I took to university life like a fish to water, if the fish was a salmon battling currents upstream. Yes, I was well aware that salmons died once they spawned. I had to hope my luck would be better.

Over the first few days of classes, the Citadel was a flurry of activity in preparation for Chancellor Yrsa of Swiftsea's funeral. Bouquets of purple-black roses were on every landing, and black ribbons twisted around columns or were tied around the upper arm of anyone wanting to publicly signal their grief. Despite being at the university for over two sennights, I kept getting lost in the corridors that all looked the same, and it took me too long to find my lecture halls or labs. I diligently scribbled my notes in Kalsh and history class, but it was obvious that no matter how much I'd studied on my own, I had giant gaps in my knowledge. My education had been erratic and self-led. Many of the textbooks I'd been able to access had been older editions I'd found on Binder Street, with notes and doodles from past students in the margins.

Drakines had grown up living and breathing magic, whereas for years I'd rarely done more than shapeshift and cast the odd charm or ward. I stayed quiet, knowing I had no choice but to keep swimming. Grades at the university were pass or fail, but if you did not pass, you did not progress. There were far fewer fourth years than first years. More than that, I didn't *want* to simply scrape by. I'd worked so hard to get here. I wanted to be brilliant—to follow in the footsteps of my grandsire's early career before it all went wrong.

While I'd always been busy, my schedule had been largely within my control. I liked routine but always built in flexibility for when I took to one of my obsessions or tangents. Now, my time was rigidly accounted for. I'd wake up before dawn, still exhausted, and drag my arse down to the practice grounds a few times a sennight. I'd always been more of a night owl than a morning lark, so this was, frankly, torture. I could scrappily win some brawls, and I knew how to use a knife, but I'd never properly learned how to fight with other weapons or to follow the rules of combat with others of higher status. It was like another one of Kelwyn's courses in etiquette, but with pointy metal bits. Afterward, I'd slink off to the private baths, sweaty and bruised, before heading to the Great Hall for breakfast.

I wasn't sure I'd ever grow used to the mountains of food laid out on those tables at mealtimes. The cost was factored into the eye-watering amount I'd paid for my room. I was determined to get my coin's worth, and so I stuffed myself silly.

I needed the energy, though, as I was doing more magic than ever before. I had Kalsh on secondday.

Professor Plink was flighty and dreamy. They'd clearly walked hundreds if not thousands through these basic opening waterweaving exercises and I suspected They could do it in Their sleep.

We all had bowls of water on our tables. I angled my way to join Rahela Easel, Damon Aldburn, and Willem Ansel. They were all in second year, and I was determined to weasel into their group. The problem was they'd been friends since academy, and while they'd been polite enough, they had no real reason to give a fig about me.

Rahela was short and soft, with dark hair and eyes and warm brown skin. Willem, tall with auburn-ish hair and light brown skin, oozed a confidence that the world would lay itself out for him just the way he liked, whether he tried hard or not. Damon was average height but well-muscled, and rather devastatingly handsome, with similar coloring to Rahela. They were quiet but would occasionally come out with a joke so off-color it'd have impressed the Marricks.

Rahela was taking no less than three magic classes, which was impressive. Damon's paire had been high up in the military, and they would likely leave university after this academic year, as their family had already bought their commission. They were related to Chancellor Ketrel of Stormfell, who had overseen the military coup of the Schism. I'd learned Willem Ansel was Professor Hayden's child, but his other parent, Sar Kesia Ansel, was likewise very well-connected in government and related to Carym of Redwing. The Ansel family was one of the oldest, richest drakine dynasties around.

"Water is everywhere," Professor Plink said, eyes half-lidded. "The clouds above, the air we breathe, in our very bodies and in the ground beneath our feet. Look at your bowl. All you have to do is tap into the blue god Kalsh's desire, and the water will bend to your will. It starts with a drop, but one day you might command a river, a lake, an ocean. See what you can do. What shapes you can make. You know what to say."

I leaned over my bowl of water, and the others did the same. My reflection was a very unflattering angle—I could see right up my nose.

"*Kjetim-lei ak-kaš*," Rahela said, and neatly raised a globule of water. I heard the phrase echo around the classroom. It simply meant

"I call upon Kalsh" and was meant to help focus and access the blue god's magic.

Willem created a few ripples. Damon took longer, but managed a small stream, like a fountain.

My bowl's surface remained smooth. My anxiety heightened.

Focus on your own journey, my maire had always said. *Doesn't matter what anyone else is doing.*

I let my eyes unfocus, tapping into my seal's magic and trying to connect with the water. Colors played across the surface in a flash of red and green until they settled into an image.

When I'd seen dragons previously, they'd been fighting or flying. This one was calm. Two horns rose from either side of a feather crest. The way the head perched on the long neck reminded me of a swan. The dragon's head moved, green eyes staring right at me, the slit pupils widening. I felt the force of that gaze like a crossbolt to the chest. Everen. I'd know him anywhere, in any form. This is what he'd look like if he were alive and well.

I leaned back with a gasp, my heart hammering.

"Are you all right?" Rahela asked.

I fought to control my expression as I felt the power of that dragon's gaze, right down to my fingertips. "Fine," I said, my voice too high. "Just studied too late." I'd slept four candlemarks, and it'd been light and broken. Was that enough to make me see things that weren't there?

"In the first sennight?" Willem scoffed, with all his seniority as a second year. "This is when it's all sweet as pie. Just wait until exams. Then none of us sleep."

Across the room, Sorin glanced at me before turning back to her bowl of water. She had only managed ripples, from what I could tell, which pleased the petty part of me. My alchemy partner was so far immune to Arcady Dalca's charm. Considering how much work I'd put into crafting an imminently likable persona, this annoyed me. I'd wear her down, I'd decided. It was simply a matter of time.

"Again," Professor Plink waved an arm lazily from the sidelines.

I turned back to the water, pinching the skin at my wrist to bring me back to my body.

"*Kiév vojra*," I whispered, and magic rushed into my seal, strong and sure. This spell was more of a direct command, meaning "shape water." Either approach could work. I tasted sea salt on my tongue as I lifted a sphere of water and arced it over to Willem's bowl before bringing it back.

"Not bad," Damon said. I noticed they sat further away from Willem than strictly required, and glanced at the drakine with a strange mixture of forlornness and resentment when they thought he wasn't looking. Something had gone wrong there.

Willem raised another stream of water from his bowl and let it splash, but he was obviously bored. If there was one thing I'd learned about Willem, it was that he had no patience at all. He'd a well-earned reputation for being the student who dragged everyone out to taverns. He'd always drink the most and come home the latest. He was constantly on the hunt for new experiences to interest him. All I'd have to do is make myself amusing enough to be worth keeping around.

I raised my dollop of water and, with a twist, shaped it into something resembling an arse. Willem laughed, loud enough that it caught the professor's attention, and I let the water drop back into the bowl with a splash.

"Childish," Rahela said, but she dimpled and, when the professor glanced away again, made a peachy bum.

Willem raised his water and lengthened it out to a penis with lopsided bollocks.

"Wil!" Damon hissed.

Professor Plink cut Their eyes in our direction, and we erupted into stifled giggles as our water splashed back into our bowls. Juvenile? Yes. Extremely. But it'd been just silly enough to crack deeper through their defenses. Sometimes the simplest option worked best.

When I emerged from the class, I felt a glow of triumph. It was a start. I put my glimpse of a dragon in the water down to nothing more than fractured sleep and lingering grief that I just couldn't shake.

My Schism & Strike history class was on triday mornings. I was obviously impatient to get through the first and focus on the latter.

Professor Fullin had been lecturing for at least forty years. "I'm well aware I'm living history by this point," They said in that first class. "I remember what it was like before, during, and after the Schism. Something about history you must always remember: nothing about the past can ever be captured in its entirety. So many people's stories are never recorded, especially those who never learned to write. We pick apart the facts and try to reassemble the tale as best we can."

According to Everen, the past could be found, if only you knew how to scry for it. Humans didn't have that luxury. I leaned forward, curious. Surely the professor had known my grandsire. Maybe even taught him?

My grandsire had proven himself at university when Monarch Laen ruled Locmyria. It was Laen who had given Barrow Eremia his own laboratory after he'd won the old University Trials and stayed on through to graduate studies. It was Laen who had appointed him magical advisor to the court, despite his low birth and lack of title. The Consul had overthrown Laen as thoroughly as my grandsire. I'd heard all the old reasoning for the coup—that the Monarch killed people to bathe in their blood to stay eternally youthful, and loved creative punishments for real or imagined crimes. When they were executed, though Laen was over two hundred years old, supposedly their beauty had not waned. They'd outlived three consorts, trading each out for a younger one at their side.

Part of me was curious to learn more about the Last Monarch of Locmyria and how they'd been overthrown. No portraits of the Monarch hung within the Citadel, of course, but the textbook had a recreation. Monarch Laen was as beautiful as the stories said, but there was a hard glint to their eyes and a cruel twist to their painted mouth.

Laen's bones were sealed away in a stone casket not far from my grandsire's. But while Laen deserved their punishment, as far as I could tell, I didn't believe my grandsire did.

I'd skipped ahead in the textbook, but so far it hadn't said anything new about Barrow Eremia, the supposed Plaguebringer. My taie was always painted in the worst light possible—a villain with nothing but evil in his heart. Yet I'd seen his love and kindness firsthand. There'd be answers, somewhere on this hill, either in a book or someone's head. I only had to find them.

My excitement punctured once Fullin began Their lectures. The professor had a melodious voice that enchanted others, but to me, it was a lullaby. I dug my fingernails into my thighs to stay awake, barely taking anything in, and when the lecture finished, I tried not to sigh in obvious relief.

When I wasn't in classes or arms training, I pretty much lived at the library.

The first time I saw it, I nearly cried. I'd made my ragged collection in the Loc & Key, but they'd mostly been battered copies with the pages loosening from the spines, piled high wherever there was space. Now and then, I'd splurged on a new book or stolen one if the opportunity arose. I'd seen some fine libraries in those grand homes I'd broken into to crack safes with Lightfinger a lifetime ago.

The University Library put all of them to shame.

It was larger than the Citadel Cathedral. The grand, towering stacks were filled to the brim with books. Everything was lit by mage lights that cast an amber glow. Spiral staircases made of solid oak, with carved and gilded handrails led to the balconies on the upper levels and more seemingly endless stacks. The arched ceiling was painted with the constellations of the sky, dragons roaring along the edges, snouts pointed toward the golden sun at its center.

There were study rooms tucked among the stacks, armchairs well broken-in with warm mage light fires to chase away the chill. Willem had been right. The first sennight, most of the students were out in the courtyard, soaking up the autumn sunlight rather than studying. Meanwhile, I checked out as many books as I could find on the Strikes and began reading. I pored over autopsy reports, transcripts of political speeches, census data. I focused on where the first Strike outbreaks occurred (the Fang mountain hamlets), how it spread (quickly), and how the Council responded (far too slowly).

Any articles or books by my taie had long since been culled from the library. I couldn't find anything written in his own words. Why had he been so consistently blamed? Why had *no one* doubted it or come to his defense?

"It'll be here," I kept muttering to myself, as if wishing hard enough could make it come true. "It'll be here somewhere."

I worked nonstop from sunrise to well after sunset. I'd study at the library until the evening meal and then come back to my dormitory and study some more. Sometimes I'd take out my maire's notebook, reading through it as if it would magically reveal something the other hundred passes hadn't.

The benefit of working so hard was it meant I couldn't dwell on the recent past. I buried all my guilt, grief, hatred, and frustration. If I was studying, I couldn't worry that I might have sacrificed so much to get here simply to discover maybe I wasn't as good at any of this as I'd hoped. Perhaps, after all the heartache, I'd still fail. What if there wasn't anything about my taie to find, or, worse, I might regret what I did discover?

When I couldn't keep my eyes open any longer, I'd tie my wrist to the bedpost to stop my body from wandering off, and I'd take what solace I could in my dreams of a dragon who I shouldn't have missed, but I did.

II.

ARCADY:

THE WAKE

Chancellor Yrsa of Swiftsea's funeral was as lavish as I'd expected. The Grand Cathedral of the Citadel dwarfed Lacewing Cathedral in the city below—more marble, more stained glass, more incense, and an even larger gilded dragon's skull shimmering with jewels. I wondered what that dragon had been like. Had they bonded to a human, and had that human betrayed them, too?

The ceremony went on for more than two candlemarks, the church crammed to the brim with some of the most important people in Loc. The rest of the Consul sat at the front like wraithwright-dripped statues. I stared at the backs of their heads with such hatred it's a wonder they didn't feel it.

The two Chancellors of Stormfell and Redwing always wore their masks in public. For the last few years, they'd mostly kept to their private wing of the Citadel. Supposedly, it was so they could better focus on the business of ruling and remain closer to the will of the gods.

I smelled bullshit.

The Head Priest might eat in the Great Hall, but even that was rare. I'd never been close enough to grab more than an impression: tall, hawkish features. Dark hair shorn short as any other priest's. From their age, they'd probably been a youth during the Schism. While sometimes I'd think of the clergy in the honorific pronoun despite myself, thanks to my paire's devotion, the Head Priest who had sentenced my grandsire to death got none of it.

After the funeral ceremony, Yrsa of Swiftsea's corpse was gently placed on the pyre of kindling, dried lavender, and roses. Their face was hidden by a plain wooden mask instead of wraithwright. Not even the Citadel was that wasteful. The Head Priest lit the pyre with a spell, and the Citadel smelled of smoke and burning flowers for the rest of the day. Yrsa of Swiftsea was no more.

The feast afterward made the meals I'd had in the Great Hall so far look like plain fare. Meat, fowl, and fish from all corners of Loc. Strange mousses or sticky sauces with unfamiliar spices. Fruits from the Myrian cloud forests I'd seen at the fanciest markets. I devoured a prickly pear from the Blackstone desert. I had pinched one from a market a few years ago, but I hadn't known how to prepare it and it'd been sour and astringent. In the Citadel cooks' hands, it melted on my tongue and was sour-sweet. I ate five, mentally tallying how many coins my feast likely cost. I tried a little of everything. By the time dessert rolled around, I couldn't move, as much as I wanted to devour all the tarts and cakes topped with elaborate meringues and marzipan.

The food was whisked away by servants, and the revelers prepared to go upstairs to the ballroom. There would be drinking, dancing, and a wake until dawn, but the long sennight and the food had made me sleepy. I wanted nothing more than to go back to my room and pray my three glasses of wine would be enough to give me a solid night's sleep without dreams or nightmares.

"No, no, no," Willem said when I made my excuses. "You're being dreadfully dull. Up you come. I want to see you dance. I bet it'll be as amusing as your fighting."

I bristled, but there was no true malice in his tone. If he decided to adopt me as an amusing backwater pet, I'd have to lean into that, even if it rankled.

He linked my arm with his, and I let myself be dragged upstairs. The ballroom had chandeliers of glittering mage lights, and candles around the edges of the room burned with blue and purple flames. Musicians waited at the ready. Willem pushed another glass of wine into my hand, and I held it dutifully but only pretended to drink.

When the last of the stragglers had arrived upstairs in their finery, the Herald stepped onto the stage at the far end of the grand marble floor. The Chancellors had retired to their rooms, of course, but the Head Priest was to the side, masked and expectant. I had that same tingling sensation I'd had along my skin when I'd first arrived at the university.

"Esteemed citizens of Loc," the Herald began, shepherding away any remnants of conversation. "We thank you for celebrating the life of Chancellor Yrsa of Swiftsea today. The Consul has something very exciting to commemorate and celebrate Their legacy." They cleared their throat, letting the pause build anticipation.

"For centuries, there was a grand tradition here at the Citadel. It celebrated the talents of the next generation, highlighting those who would become the best and the brightest magic users of our times. However, in the upheaval of the Schism and the Strikes, it was suspended."

Whispers whipped around the ballroom, and I tightened the grip on my wine glass.

"Surely not . . ." Rahela whispered, eyes wide.

"It is with great honor and excitement that we proclaim the recommencement of the University Trials," the Herald said, puffing up with importance. "For those who choose to enter, there will be three tasks over the next four moons. Three chances to prove your mastery over magic. The winner will receive a full scholarship for their remaining time at the university for as long as they wish to continue studying. Two others will receive a partial scholarship. Their successes will be a testament to Chancellor Yrsa of Swiftsea's legacy."

The ballroom erupted into an excited uproar. Willem bumped me on the shoulder, nearly knocking over my wine in his excitement.

"Oh this," he said. "This will be a bloody good show."

"We urge all interested students to put their name forward so we can begin to make arrangements," the Herald continued. "Be aware that if you enter, you must sign for it with your seal, and it is magically binding. The first trial will happen in a moon's time. We look forward to it, and we are sure the whole Citadel will enjoy seeing the potential of our youth and the future generation of leadership. Now, let us return to the wake, and give Chancellor Yrsa of Swiftsea the farewell of a lifetime."

The ballroom erupted into shocked murmurs. I'd read about the University Trials. My grandsire, after all, had won them back when he was at university before the Schism while wearing the very seal now pressed against my skin.

I'd begged him to tell me about the Trials so many times when I was young. He'd made it all sound so exciting. Since he was from villein stock, the scholarship had given him the security to stay and push his experiments and the borders of magic and become one of the most celebrated people in Loc before he'd become the most hated.

I'd finished my wine without noticing. Willem pushed another glass into my hand, and I took a deep gulp, letting myself be pulled into the revelry. I danced first with Willem, then Rahela, and even Damon and I took a spin across the marble floor.

I watched a cluster of fourth years chatting to each other. Edin Vayne had dark hair, a nose with a bump in the ridge, and always wore jewelry so fine it made my thief's fingers itch. Lowe Balcil, who I knew used any pronouns like me and I'd settled on 'he', was very good at both Kalsh and Jari magic, according to Professor Plink — who was always singing Balcil's praises. The other two I hadn't learned the names of yet. One had hair in long braids and spectacles they kept pushing up their nose, and another had red hair a brighter orange than Everen's.

Don't think about him.

My excitement punctured. How could I hope to come close to students who had nearly finished their studies, having trained with all the resources at their disposal since they were children? It didn't matter. I had to try. I had been drowning, and here was a lifeline. I had no illusions this wouldn't be difficult, and that if anything, I'd be even more out of my depth. A partial scholarship was the best I could hope for, but without worrying about tuition, it'd be enough for me to cling to this new life that much longer. If this had been in the cards last year, I wouldn't have had to get myself nearly killed thrice over stealing that damned dragon relic. Still. It was a chance.

The dancing continued, and the wine flowed. I stayed out until dawn, and I enjoyed every moment. Yrsa of Swiftsea was gone, and while I hadn't been able to make them pay for their crimes, their death had given me a gift.

I wouldn't waste it.

12.

SORIN:

DRAGON BONES

How many times in her life had Sorin woken to the red glow of a candle's flame, hurriedly changing into robes before pressing the catch at the corner of her room? Once more, she made her familiar way through this hidden passageway. She could have done it with her eyes closed.

She entered the hidden room in the back of the library, knelt, and waited. Magnes entered moments later. His presence, as ever, sizzled like lightning and ozone. He was blessed by Zama and had control over weather and storms, but His true power was the ability to read someone's thoughts, memories, and dreams.

He placed His gloved hand on the back of Sorin's head, offering a wordless blessing, and she leaned into it before she rose to face Him.

She kept her mind blank, trying not to think of her doubts or her fractured faith.

"Your All-Holy Eminence," Sorin said. It was still strange to speak to Him aloud instead of signing in Trade.

"My child. Show me," Magnes ordered. He took off His glove, His bare hand hovering over her cheek.

Sorin tried not to quake. She had sent him detailed written reports, hidden every three days in a puzzle box on top of the chest of drawers in her room. Whenever she returned, it was always empty. Either another Eye came to claim it, or the box itself was somehow spelled.

During her three moons in the forest, she had meditated, struggling to control what thoughts she brought to the front of her mind versus burying deep down. At first, it'd been impossible. As soon as she tried not to think of something, there it would be, crowding out everything else. After countless candlemarks of practice, she had improved. But was she good enough?

He made her kneel again before taking her chin in His bare hand.

Memories of her first alchemy class swirled around them, ghostly and transparent. The morning on the practice grounds. Watching Arcady in the library, and later following them to sit in the corner of the tavern that students favored. She'd nursed her drink, hood up, and eavesdropped. Her memories were deliberately jumbled. Would He notice she was holding back, and if He did, would He push harder?

His rummaging didn't hurt, but it made her feel utterly exposed. Finally, Magnes's hand drew back. If He suspected what she'd done, He gave no sign. She fought the urge to rub her aching neck, willing her heartbeat to slow.

Magnes's smile widened. "Good. Good. Continue your observations."

"Your All-Holy Eminence," she said. "Why . . . why haven't you . . ."

"Simply touched them and read all their secrets for myself?" He finished.

"Yes."

"Because I can't. Their mind is closed to me."

She blinked. "How?" Was it possible to hide oneself completely from someone with mind magic? She curled her toes but kept her face blank.

He hesitated, then relented. "Their shared magic with the pretender shields them."

"The dragon," Sorin breathed.

"The false idol," Magnes corrected, expression hardening. He gave her a long, searching look. "Come. There's something you must see."

She fought down a wave of trepidation. Whenever He showed her something in the depths of the night, it often ended in blood.

"Fear not, Sorin," He said, as if guessing her thoughts. Had He?

Magnes pressed the hidden panel and opened the door to the passageways. He entered and she followed, taking up the crimson candle once more. They moved from the library to the main university building. Finally, He brought her through a set of wards she had never been able to pass. He pressed a panel and entered another room, and the mage lights threw it into sharp relief. She nearly gagged at the smell of new leather, smoke, and decay.

The next thing Sorin noticed was the dragon's skull.

It was as large as the one in the Citadel Cathedral. But where that one was ancient and yellowed, this was fresh and white. The empty eye sockets seemed to stare at her, pinning her in place.

Sorin tore her eyes away and took in the rest of her surroundings. It was an old laboratory, with black stone walls similar to her alchemy classroom. The tables were topped with dust-coated beakers and other long-abandoned equipment. Careful columns of vertebrae were stacked next to the skull by size. Ribs rested upright against the walls. Femurs and shin bones lined up on another table. The small pieces of bone from the feet. Or were they called paws?

Sorin shivered. There were twenty claws, wicked sharp and black. The slope of the hips and pelvis on one table. Wing bones on another, impossibly delicate for how much weight they must have once borne. Leather from the wings stretched across racks. Shelves with glass bottles full of blue scales glittering in the low light. She picked one up, tilting the glass bottle back and forth, scales clacking like beetle shells. Most relic scales were dulled at the edges by time, but these, she suspected, would be sharp as knives.

At the back of the room were barrels that must be filled with pre-served meat or organs. Dried ligaments and tendons coiled like rope and hung on hooks. Fat melted down to tallow candles without a wick.

It was a god, disassembled.

"Is this the one that died in the clearing?" she whispered.

"Yes."

Magnes had called them false idols. While she didn't know exactly what she believed anymore, she fought her rising gorge. Relics were supposed to be from the past. Not from a creature she had seen liv-ing and breathing before it had fallen, overwhelmed by wraiths and hitting the forest floor with a horrible, sickening crack.

It couldn't have been easy to move this here undetected. Sorin imagined Magnes's chosen monks swarming the body, stripping meat from bone, ensuring no part was wasted.

The teeth of the skull looked like polished alabaster. She took a few steps closer. Magic hung in the air. In the hush, the room felt sac-rilegious and holy all at once. She knew she should feel grateful that He trusted her enough to see this. Instead, she wanted to be sick.

"There are thousands of relics here," she said. *This is wrong*, every part of her body screamed. *This is all wrong.*

"Yes," He said, eyes glittering in the dim light. "Even if some of the older relics find their way south, this helps ensure we can defend ourselves."

From what threat? In her time in the forest, the wraiths she'd fought had been barely more than smoke. Magnes had given her the calculations of where along the leylines the Veil was likely to be thinnest on the new moon. Even if she hadn't been there with her dragonbone blade, those paltry creatures may not have done more than wither a few trees before slipping back through the gaps between worlds. Was Magnes afraid of the Veil breaking once more? If she asked, she doubted He would tell her.

Her gaze was drawn back to the skull, reminding her of the Cathedral, the funeral, and the announcement at the wake.

"I would . . ." Sorin paused. "I would ask about the Trials. If I might."

"You may." He was clearly amused by her boldness.

"Why did you bring them back?" she asked.

His smile widened. "Why do *you* think I did, my child?"

Everything with him was always a test, but something had shifted. He was treating her like an Eye instead of a knife. Part of her was honored by His trust; the rest was terrified.

She gathered herself. "The Trials distract from Chancellor Yrsa of Swiftsea's death. The court will find it entertaining — more so than something like a snap election. It will help buy you more time while you figure out who is best placed to be the next Chancellor of Swift-sea. Someone who wishes to serve the country rather than Their own agenda. Otherwise . . . you might risk the Court wanting a clean slate and an entirely new Consul, either by election or by blood."

"You see much," He said, and was that a faint hint of surprise? "Transitions of power are always dangerous times. Drakines have forged Their own alliances and enemies for centuries. A Chancellor chosen from one family would upset five more. I cannot rush it. Loc wouldn't shy away from a coup any more than Locmyria had, especially if the drakines thought they could get away with it. Some are pushing for the Ansel diplomat, but . . ." He grimaced and trailed off. "I don't trust Sar Ansel as far as I can throw Them. Why else?"

She considered. "The Trials are also a chance to test what those from the university have learned. As you said, they are the next generation, the future of the country. Perhaps there's a likely Chancellor in the making there, though not for a few years yet."

He chuckled. "It doesn't hurt to think decades ahead. I've plenty of life in me yet."

Not for the first time, she wondered how old He truly was.

"And?" He pressed.

Sorin sucked on her bottom lip. She had seen how the interloper's eyes had lit up as soon as the Trials were announced.

"This is a way to test Arcady Dalca's magic somehow, isn't it?" she asked. "To see how being bonded with a false god has changed or altered it." Her eyes raked over the lab equipment. "You're laying a trap."

His laugh was warm. "You're taking well to this, Sorin. I should have made you an Eye years ago."

She flushed with warmth at the praise, despite herself. It was strange to hear her name on His lips. "I still don't understand why you'd need to."

"You mean why not simply arrest this Arcady Dalca, lock them in the dungeons, and be done with it, even if I can't read their mind?" He asked, and she flinched, remembering Widow Girazin.

"Yes."

"Because it's not yet time. There's so much more to be done."

"To what end?"

"The Veil has been patched, but another threat hides. An old problem I have not yet been able to solve. There is a way, I believe, to use this person's magic to hold back the tide of chaos and heal something that was hurt long ago. If that happens, no one will be able to challenge me or my authority again. Not anyone else on this hill, not Myria and its Monarch. Not Jask and its Boy King. Loc will be strong, and we will be free of all that lurks within the Veil and beyond."

Beyond? Sorin's skin prickled as a finger of ice traced her spine. "What must be healed?"

The edges of his lips curled. "Tell me, my child: how do you think *you* fit into the Trials?"

She frowned, picking up one of the black claws. "Oh. I—I wasn't planning on entering."

"Oh? Why ever not?" His sly delight made her stomach clench.

Her fingertips tingled. "I've no delusions about the level of my magical ability." She wouldn't ever pretend she could compete with drakines who had been raised with the best schools and tutors. In magic, she was thoroughly average. She'd barely been able to demonstrate enough of it to be allowed entrance, and she knew she'd scrape passes at best in alchemy and waterweaving.

"What if you were wrong?" Magnes rose and drifted over to a table that had been hidden from Sorin's view by the skull. This table was filled with new equipment, free of dust. Something bubbled in an ampule, curls of white smoke rising toward the ceiling. There was a closed book near it, leather-bound with no title on the cover or spine.

"Y—Your All-Holy Eminence?" Her mouth was dry.

Magnes carefully took the ampule off the low heat and poured it into the vial, stoppering it and handing it to her. The glass was strangely cool against her palm.

"This can focus and enhance your magic for brief periods."

Her stomach twisted. The liquid was thick and opalescent. She stared uneasily at the dragon remains, and considered her alchemy professor's lecture. "Is this . . . the Elixir of Life?"

He chuckled. "No, not quite, but it's an elixir sure enough. You won't live for centuries by drinking it, I'm sorry to say. But it is still something rather extraordinary. You must make sure to fuel yourself properly and rest afterward. Combined with my training on what the tasks entail, it will enable you to do well. Very well."

If she asked what was in it, she would get no answers.

"This is cheating," she managed.

"Hah. This is winning a game that is a matter of life and death. You don't understand now, but you will, child. I have been setting these pieces on the board long before you drew your first breath."

Sorin had always known that she was nothing more than a minor piece in His grand scheme. But she also knew she was holding something powerful.

He clasped her hand with the vial in both His gloved palms. "This, of course, is a secret you must and will keep." He angled His body and touched His forehead to hers. She fought the urge to flinch back, desperately attempting to think of nothing. "Remember. You need only believe that the gods work through me."

She leaned back. "I trust in you," she whispered. "Always."

"Good," He said. "Then let us get to work."

She was grateful He didn't seem to realize that she had lied to Him.

13.

ARCADY:

NEW FRIENDS & OLD ENEMIES

When the Trials were announced, I thought nearly all five hundred students enrolled in the university would throw their hat in the ring.

To my surprise, it turned out plenty were either too cowardly, realistically guessed that they wouldn't make it past the first trial, or so rich they knew they didn't need the scholarship and therefore had no need to stick their head over the parapet.

Fifty students put themselves forward, in the end. Less than five were other first years. Willem and Rahela were among the eight second years. Damon hadn't entered. I pressed my seal into the parchment, the flare of the seal's magic promising that I would enter the Trials. I was more than half-convinced I'd made a mistake, but I wasn't about to turn back.

Willem dragged Rahela and me to a popular student tavern at the base of the hill called the Wyvern's Kiss to celebrate. It was all warm woods and stained glass, and the wooden tables were sticky with spilled drink.

I buried my face in a tankard of overpriced ale as Willem grew more gregarious with every empty cup. Even drunk, he had a knack for charming everyone he met. He wouldn't make a half-bad diplomat like his other maire if he managed to rein himself in enough.

Willem slung his arm around my shoulders, pulling me tight to his side. I slid my hand in his pocket and freed him from a few coins. It was foolhardy to steal from someone I was trying to befriend, but I still needed all the coin I could get, and Willem's head would be all the better tomorrow if he bought fewer drinks tonight.

"How do you think you'll do, Arc?" he said too loudly into my ear. "What type of magic are you gonna use for the first task?"

We'd had to demonstrate our proficiency with our main magic to enter the university. For the first task, we had to show what we could do with a magic type that wasn't as innate.

"Fire, I think," I said. "You?"

"Water's my only hope, of course." His eyes flashed with a hint of competitiveness. "We'll see who's stronger, eh?"

"I know how I'll do," Rahela said, taking a long sip from her glass before flashing her teeth. "Brilliantly."

"Hear, hear," I said, raising my tankard.

"Pity Damon couldn't come out tonight," Rahela said to Willem with an air of false innocence. "Haven't seen them as much of late."

Willem hunched. "They've turned into a right stick in the mud, haven't they? I swear, everything I say seems to annoy them these days."

"That's because you can be very annoying," Rahela teased. "But we love you for it."

He stared into the depths of his empty glass glumly.

"Oh, stop being stubborn and just apologize, Wil," Rahela urged.

"Willem!" Edin Vayne waved at him from across the pub. "Come settle a bet!" Willem perked right up, and swayed over to her.

Rahela watched him go. "Oops. I think I upset him."

"What's up with him and Damon, then?" I asked.

She shook her head. "Don't know, exactly. They had a falling out over the summer. Willem wanted to pull a prank, and they got caught. Damon's parents gave them a right bollocking and almost took away their military commission. It hasn't been the same between them since. I've felt a bit caught in the middle."

I'd learned more about Rahela in the last few sennights. She had a lot of family living in Myria that were staunch monarchists. I'd learned in history class that some in Loc were still loyal to the old crown, too, and believed in reunification, with Monarch Laen's second cousin, Monarch Gena of Myria, overseeing both countries. Since childhood, Rahela had spent summer and winter breaks on the Myrian side of the border. She'd probably spent more time than she'd liked caught in the middle in other ways.

"They'll work it out, I'm sure." I didn't particularly care about Willem and Damon's tiff. I glanced at her. "Hey, you've seen people in Myria using their wands, yeah?" I asked, both because I was curious and because I'd already learned the best way to distract Rahela was to let her educate you about her latest interest. Rahela would be a professor one day—I'd bet a fortune on it.

She nodded. "Of course. All my Myrian family use them, now."

"Does it work the same?" Myrian wands were a relatively recent development since the Schism. While there was some dragonstone in Myria, there wasn't as much as in Loc. Seals had been confiscated from many of the poor in Myria, and the dragonstone broken into smaller pieces to be put into wands for the rich. In some ways, Myria was even more obsessed with class than Loc, which said something. But what would happen to magic there if they ran out, and what lengths would they go to for more? Monarch Gena of Myria was cunning, from what I'd heard, and knew that those who were loyal to

Laen lurked in Loc. Would they try for reunification, especially now that Loc was a Chancellor down?

Rahela grew animated. "That's the thing. Plenty are just as magical as someone who uses a seal, despite it being less dragonstone per person. This is what I want to investigate. Maybe study abroad for a year at the university in Nika. It's something to do with the material they use for the wand, I think—just like in alchemy where different types of metal are associated with the gods, it's the same with wood. Elm for Jari, and so forth. Or maybe it's something else entirely." Her eyes shone. "Do you ever get overwhelmed by just how much more information there is to know, or mourn the fact you'll never be able to learn it all?"

I had a rush of tipsy fondness at her enthusiasm. "More than you can ever know." I raised my glass. "To knowledge and magic's secrets."

She clinked her glass with mine, and I drained my drink, fighting down a yawn.

"I think I'm going to head back up the hill," I said. "You coming?"

She lifted her glass. "I'll go after this, and I'll make sure to drag Willem along with me."

"Good call. See you in class tomorrow, Rahela."

"Night!" she said, cheerily. And, right there in the middle of the pub, she took a book out of her satchel and started reading.

Once I was outside, I breathed deeply, savoring the crisp air after the stuffiness of the tavern. I was in a good mood, and the couple of drinks I'd had warmed me from the inside. I was surviving my classes. I'd befriended some students. I hadn't made much headway in finding information yet, but it was still early in the year. And if I somehow managed to do well in the Trials, I wouldn't have to rush.

A Struck beggar outside the tavern rattled their cup for my attention.

"Can you spare a coin or two, good sar?" they signed in Trade.

I sighed and dug around in my pocket for the money I'd just pinched off Willem. As I bent down to place the coins in the cup, I caught sight of the beggar's face, and froze.

It was Wren. I hadn't seen the art forger for the Marricks since just before the Feast of Flowers.

I tried to back away. His hands came up, eyes flashing in warning. "No point running. I'll find you again."

My eyes darted to the tavern, not wanting any student to walk out and wonder why I was speaking with a Struck beggar.

"Nearest Marrick hideout," he signed. "Ten minutes. You knew Larkin would come calling at some point. It's time to pay the piper." He put his hood up and took off into the night, blending into the shadows.

I shoved my hands in my pockets and walked through the streets. I knew Larkin had stolen my old seal, but I had foolishly hoped it would take her longer to figure out how best to threaten me with it. The nearest Marrick hideout was an abandoned brewery on the edge of the merchant district. Wren waited for me there, the door propped open.

"How bad is this going to be, Wren?" I asked. "What's waiting for me in there?"

"It's just me," he signed. "I promise. We're simply having a chat."

"Ah. Blackmail then, is it?"

He gave me a sad smile and slipped inside. I hesitated, calculating whether I could take what little money I had left and make a run for the docks, stow away on a ship, and leave it all behind.

Of course, I followed him in. Too curious for my own good, really.

The brewery smelled of old hops beneath the damp and mold. The copper tubs had long been sold or stolen, but a few barrels remained.

I perched on one, my eyes scanning the corners. As far as I could tell, Wren was telling the truth. We were alone.

He lit a candle so it was bright enough to sign.

"Larkin's not in Loc," he began.

"So that rumor's true, then," I signed back. "Why'd she leave?"

"My guess is someone threatened her."

"And why did you stay?"

"Because . . ." a careful shrug. "I didn't agree with some of her methods."

"Like fucking over Kelwyn and me?" My signs were sharp and jerky.

He nodded. "It wasn't right."

I cleared my throat. "She's Larkin. I shouldn't have expected her to change her stripes. Lesson truly learned this time. Yet here you are, ready to deliver her message. Out with it, then, Wren." I tapped my foot against the barrel with a hollow thump.

He took out an envelope from his inner pocket and handed it over. I broke the wax seal and unfolded the letter. There was the doodle of a lark and her familiar scrawl.

Darling, I know you're rather angry with me, and I don't blame you. I thought you'd like to know that wraithwright has already funded half a dozen Struck communes in both Loc and Myria. We've also started a travel corridor for any Struck who wish to go to the Trader side of the Glass Isles. None of this would have been possible without that coin. Even if you didn't give it out of the goodness of your heart, this might give you some comfort.

I snorted. I wouldn't pretend my reasons for needing that money were selfless, but they weren't as selfish as she thought, either. Better the money went to the Struck than staying in some rich merchant's coffers. I sighed and kept reading.

I'll leave you to your new false life, but first I just need one teeny thing. Wren will take it from here. Do this for me, and you'll get what's yours back. Maybe I'll even throw in a few wraithwright coins as a sweetener.

Be a darling and burn this, now, will you please?

The beginnings of a headache thrummed at my temples, but I dutifully let the corner of the note catch in the candle flame.

"We need access to your alchemy teacher's research," Wren signed.

"Professor Hayden?" I said it aloud, but he read my lips and nodded. Whatever I'd been expecting, it wasn't this. Once it'd burned enough, I dropped the flaming letter into a barrel of stagnant water.

"Do you know what sort of projects the professor worked on when They were younger?" Wren asked.

"Something to do with alchemy, I'd imagine." My lips twisted wryly.

He gave me a long-suffering look. "Larkin says They were researching the Elixir of Life. A panacea so powerful it could heal anyone of anything. Even the Struck."

I snorted. "Professor Hayden obviously hasn't actually cracked it, or They wouldn't be teaching alchemy labs for first years, would They?"

"The unofficial word is that They helped make it, or something like it, once. But Their research was destroyed."

That caught my curiosity.

"Larkin has heard that Hayden has been trying to recreate it in secret. Might even have cracked it again, or nearly."

"And Larkin knows this . . . how, exactly?"

Wren shrugged. "She says her source is good. Another alchemist in Myria is my guess."

"You have to admit this sounds like a fairy story, Wren. Someone trying to get Larkin to part with some coin in exchange for some false hope." There were plenty of charlatan alchemists wandering the Lumet, offering tonics and tinctures that were little more than flavored water at best or something that could actually poison you at worst.

Wren gave me another look. "Larkin also figured, given who Hayden worked for, you might be particularly interested."

My stomach twisted. "Oh? Why's that?"

"Professor Hayden was the Plaguebringer's assistant when They were younger. They worked on this Elixir together."

I froze, the headache deepening and my heart rate speeding up.

Wren nodded at my carefully blank expression. "Yes. She showed me what she stole from you."

I said nothing, barely even breathing.

"She didn't ask me if it was real. She knew it was."

I swallowed. Not for the first time, I wished I'd buried my old seal out in the middle of the forest or thrown it out to sea. Somewhere where no one would ever find it, much less use it against me.

"How did you do it?" he whispered, his gaze lingering on my chest.

"Do what?" I asked. Larkin herself had taught me to always deflect rather than risk revealing more than you wanted.

Wren came closer and placed one fingertip on the stone seal hidden beneath my shirt.

Every muscle in my body tensed. Wren was good at reading body language. I'd given myself away already.

"Everyone knows you can't cast off your own seal," he signed. "Yet you have. And if that seal was your old one, I can see why."

My tongue was stuck to the roof of my mouth.

I said nothing. His fingertips went to his face, tracing the lines from the Strike. Wren's eyes darkened with anger as his fingers danced. "Loc is full of ghosts because of him. Both the dead and those still half-living. And here you were, an Eremia right under our noses all along. Larkin, as you might imagine, was impressed but mostly furious."

"He didn't release the Strike," I whispered, finally. No point in denying it, even if every word I spoke was a potential weapon. "Everything I'm doing, all I'm working toward, is to prove that."

He came closer, peering at me like he was trying to determine if I was real or a forgery.

He took his marble seal from the chain around his neck, glancing at the black-veined stone before slipping it back beneath his shirt. "Could someone else do it? Take a seal from a dead person to change their name and regain their magic?" His expression was so hungry that I swallowed down my unease.

"I don't know." I didn't want to give him false hope. "I don't think so. It'd be too dangerous to try."

His face rippled with disappointment. "I suppose it wouldn't matter anyway, would it?" He gestured to the markings on his face. "I'd never be able to hide. Not like you."

I sucked in a careful breath.

"Oh, Arcady." Wren tutted. He reached up, gently, and pulled my shirt down enough to bare the marks. "I knew it the first time you set foot in the Cote. Struck recognizes Struck." He spoke those words aloud with the voice he could no longer hear. He traced the ones on my collarbone so lightly I shivered, then he pulled my shirt back up and patted my shoulders. "I never told Larkin, you know. Not in all those years."

I forced my tongue from the roof of my mouth, finding my voice. "That's very kind and I'm grateful and all, but you're still here blackmailing me on her behalf."

He returned to signing. "I thought you'd rather hear it from me. And I wanted to see if my suspicions were true. What will you do? Larkin won't hesitate to blow up your new life if you don't do what she wants."

"It's a bit more than that, Wren. Exposing me won't just get me kicked out of the university. It'll get me killed."

His eyes softened in sympathy, but he didn't bend.

"When does she need this information?"

His signs were crisp, business-like. "Larkin realizes it might take some time, and that you'll be busy with the Trials. She wants it as soon as you can manage. After all, you might not even last the year."

I exhaled, shakily.

"It's a funny old twist of fate, isn't it?" he said, and I tried not to scowl. *Fate* had become my most-hated word in any language. "If we came to you with this, you would have gone searching anyway, wouldn't you? No blackmail required."

I sighed. "This is what we do, don't we? Hold things over each other's heads and betray each other time and again. Will it be you next, Wren?" I didn't know what Larkin would do if she found out I was Struck.

He held my gaze. "I consider you family, Arcady."

I gave him a small half-smile. "You only have to look at my toppled family tree to know that doesn't mean much." Part of me hoped he was telling the truth. Wren had always been the honest sort, as far as a thief and an art forger went. "How do I next get in touch with you?"

"Give me an update at the next Night Market. I'll be there."

I grabbed Wren's upper arms. "Wait," I said aloud. "Kel doesn't know about any of this, does he?" My voice was low and urgent, my face almost too close for him to lip-read.

"Your real last name, you mean?" he signed with difficulty. I dropped my hands. He shook his head. "Not as far as I know."

"You can't tell him. Please," I signed. "*Please.*" Wren had allowed me the space for secrets. Kelwyn had, too, but with the expectation that I'd eventually come clean. He'd collected most of them. Kelwyn would probably take me being bonded to a dragon god relatively in stride, but if I told him he'd been helping the grandchild of the Plaguebringer for years? He'd never forgive me for that.

Wren patted my cheek. "See you soon enough, Arcady. Good luck."

Once he left, I dropped to the dusty ground of the brewery and let myself fall apart. My muscles shook with tension, and I sucked in breath after breath but still felt like I was choking. I don't know how long I stayed there. Time stopped meaning anything—all was the endless panic of the present.

Eventually, the fear ran its course, and the cold seeped down into my bones. I rubbed my face, stood, and brushed off the worst of the dirt from my clothes. It took me a long time to walk back up the hill. I kept having to pause to fight down the fear. Finally, I made it to my room. My aching body went through the steps of getting ready for bed—stripping off my clothes, shrugging on a nightshirt, brushing my teeth—but my mind was far away.

In bed, I stared at the ceiling of my dormitory. The wyvern on the tapestry stared back at me, its open mouth a cruel grin in the dim moonlight. A few hours ago, it'd seemed I'd found my footing, and here was something else to stumble on. On some level, though, I knew this was another potential way to find out the truth, especially after I'd realized how thoroughly they'd censored any information about my grandsire.

After lying there for candlemarks, mind spinning, I rummaged around in my trunk and found a half-full flask of rum. I'd worked hard to break the habit of hiding at the bottom of a bottle like I had over the summer, but that night I wanted nothing more than to drown out the sorrow. The rum was cheap, and harsh, but I drank it down like medicine. Soon enough, it worked its way through my veins. My limbs went heavy, and the bed was so soft. I just remembered to tie my wrist to the bedpost.

But my dreams brought the opposite of relief.

14.

EVEREN:

GLIMMERHAIL

I was no longer a prisoner, but I was a pariah.

Word spread fast that I was no longer a prince of the realm. If I arrived at the bathing pools, most would leave, and the rest would turn their heads. Some would hiss as I passed. Even Hyacinth, or Adile, both of whom I had playfought and later learned to hunt alongside when I was older, snubbed me. Pan, Sidar's mate, made no attempts to hide her hatred. She bumped into me or snapped her jaws when no one was looking.

So I did as I was told. I kept my head down. During the day, I hunted, Mace or Cassia at my side. As I flew searching for fish, dolphin, or whale, I realized that while I might be out of the cave, the dragons' collective prison was our island in the middle of an endless sea, slowly boiling us alive.

The dragons had pooled their magic to erect a protective barrier around Vere Celene. It might not keep the wraiths from the weyr if they came in high enough numbers, but it would at least give us a warning. Whenever a rip in the Veil occurred, I'd feel a sharp pull in my belly, my magic tingling with awareness. I sensed it first, but all dragons eventually caught the dread of an impending fight. There was no pattern. Morning, dusk, the deep of night. An attack each day, then silence for three. We could never relax.

I took out my frustrations on the wraiths, ripping them to shreds of smoke, unnerved by how they felt both real and unreal between my teeth. The bitter taste of them lingered for hours on my tongue. Their echoing shrieks and the strange hisses and clicking sent shivers down my spine and into my bones. They were nightmare creatures without a hint of feeling other than hunger. Did the Dreamer send them, or were they something else?

In the last moments of each fight, I would hear the whispers of the storm between worlds. I was as drawn to it as the night I had fallen through to the human world. Mace or Cassia hovered nearby, ready to stop me if I made any sudden moves, but the rips, so far, were always too small. If they ever were not, though . . . then I did not know what I would do.

Thankfully, while several dragons were injured in the fights, no one had come close to dying since Sidar. Not yet, at least.

As the days passed, I bowed my head and I did what was expected of me, even if I was no longer an Emberclaw.

At night, I often slept outside, desperate for an open sky above me rather than stone. Mace or my sister were never far. The only time I went below was to scry, but there had been no more visions since I had learned of the Dreamer. My sister dipped into other humans' lives in the present, and sometimes I joined her, hungry for any glimpse of the Lumet. Together, we would watch groups of humans in taverns, or a guard patrolling a wall of a city I didn't recognize. A sailor at sea desperate for a glimpse of land on the horizon. A wandering priest riding a horse through the forest. Each time I hoped to see you, or even the Citadel, yet the humans were always strangers, and many were in Myria or even Jask instead of Loc.

My sister had to write down the visions as soon as she emerged, or the details would fade. A few times before I returned, she had been so ill after scrying that Miligrist had to carry her back to her rooms and she fell into a deep sleep, awakening to remember next to nothing. She'd grown stronger with practice, but I helped, at least, taking notes and giving context to what I had learned in the human world.

A few weeks after I was freed, the autumn equinox brought the dragon holiday of Glimmerhail. It was a time when day and night, light and dark, were balanced, and so we believed that fate was easier to read.

During the day, dragons drifted in and out of the nursery, singing to the clutch of eggs buried in the hot sand. The eggs had been there for nearly a year, laid by several dragons, and yet there was no sign of quickening.

When the light began to fade, the dragons feasted, though it of course paled in comparison to anything from the human world. Many dragons transformed down to preterit, both because it would take less food to be satisfied and because the tongue could taste more flavors.

There was charred meat from the plains deer whose herds grew smaller each year. We cracked open the bones for marrow. Fish from the ponds to the north or the salt-water shallows to the east. Oily whale and dolphin flesh. The organs and blood were saved to consume in dragon form, when our stomachs could handle them better. Nothing could be wasted. Beyond meat, there were roots and wild greens, and slabs of mushrooms from deep in the caves.

I watched my kind with new eyes after my time away. More dragons stayed in their smaller form since I had fallen to the Lumet. Plenty hacked painful coughs, the ever-present smog of the Reek taking its toll on lungs. I wondered if I would ever see another hatchling, or if this was it: that even if we survived the wraiths and the Reek didn't erupt, it would still be a slow decline as we were picked off one by one by starvation, or sickness, or simply time. We were long-lived, but no dragon was truly immortal. We were weakening. We were dying.

Humans and preterits were not as different as dragons would like to believe. There were low rumbles of laughter or the hum of pleasure from a dragon as they spoke mind to mind. Still, it was a comfort to see them relaxing rather than solely surviving. Pan hung back, simmering with a grief I could feel even from the other side of the gathering.

I kept my distance, too. Mace, my guard, lurked nearby and watched me with careful eyes.

After we ate, most who could turned back into their dragon forms and settled around the bathing pond between the shoulder blades of the Lady of Vere Celene. I perched on a ledge above. While I did not feel welcome enough to join, I wanted to watch.

The dragons began to hum. On the night of Glimmerhail, the dragons cast enough magic to chase away the smoke and clouds. Soon, the stars shone above us, bright and glorious and full of the fire we worshipped most.

Cassia held a chalice of scrysilver in her hands as she stepped to the edge of the pool.

—*On this night of Glimmerhail, we ask starfire to show us true*, she intoned. *May their light lead the way to a brighter future.*

She held up the cup to the Queen's lips.

Once, I would have taken the next sip. Instead, Miligrist stepped forward.

One by one, my sister went around the pool, holding the chalice up to each dragon's lips in order of rank. Hyacinth closed her eyes as she drank. Thist's tail curled. Garder's eyes rolled back in pleasure. This was the sole time any aside from Cassia, Miligrist, or I sampled scrysilver.

Cassia took the last taste before pouring the leftover liquid into the pool. It eddied out, the water gradually glowing the same white-blue as the stars above. The humming grew louder.

Together, each dragon placed a talon or hand into the water. Wordlessly, they sent through a wish, a hope, and a desire for a future in a world where dragons thrived.

Pan broke out of formation, stumbling back from the pool and roaring up at the sky.

—*No wish can bring her back*, she cried, the pain so intense all dragons bowed beneath it. *She's gone.*

Coral, one of the healers with scales such a light red they were closer to pink, came to comfort her. Pan's head drooped, horns nearly grazing the rock, her whole body shivering. On the night of Glimmerhail, with scrysilver in their systems, dragons all felt each other's emotions more intensely. Even though I hadn't tasted it, I reeled from her grief, too.

—*Come*, Coral urged. *Come away and rest now.*

The other dragons watched Pan leave, leaning heavily on Coral's larger bulk, wings tight across her back. Pan paused, staring up at me, and the hatred in those slitted blue eyes almost drove me to my knees.

—*It's your fault she's dead*, the dragon hissed, letting everyone else hear the thought. *These wraiths are your doing. You have doomed us all and yet you walk and fly free.*

The fire in my throat burned. On some level, wasn't it true? Coral nudged Pan to the cave entrance, but the dragons' collective gaze fell heavily upon me. How many others wondered why the Queen let me be among them, even if I was no longer their prince?

—*Find your peace*, the Queen said. *We all have our pain and our fear for the future. Pour that into the scrysilver, and Miligrist, our great Seer, will help us find the way through fate. We have had a setback, but we are not defeated. Dragons will prevail.*

She sounded so regal, so imperious, that the dragons settled back into their places around the pool. After a muffled start, the humming rose again, chasing away the last of the unease and making the stars shine all the brighter.

Cassia's preterit voice came through, high and strong, as she sang the song of Glimmerhail, the yearning condensed into rising and falling tones. The song faded. Cassia held out her arms and with a burst of magic, became a dragon once more.

Miligrist rose to her four feet. Her milky eyes stared at the waters of the pool. She was the sole dragon left who had lived in the human world, though she had been but a hatchling at the time. She waded into the water, standing shoulder-deep. As one, the dragons stretched their necks up toward the stars, letting loose plumes of fire from their throats. I could feel the heat of it even from my perch. They bowed toward the water, long necks stretched toward the glow. Miligrist slipped beneath the surface, pausing until her eyes and feather crest were above the water, before disappearing.

The dragons rose, making their way back to the caves in silence. They had faith in their Seer and the scrysilver warmed them from within. It was said if a dragon fell asleep thinking of their deepest desire after drinking the liquid on Glimmerhail, it would come true. Soon, only Mace and the Queen remained.

—*Sleep*, Cassia said, allowing me to overhear. *You must rest. I'll watch over him. I'll record all.*

The Queen pressed her jeweled forehead to Cassia's snout, communicating silently. I wondered what they said. Eventually, the Queen and Mace left the edge of the pool. Miligrist remained under the water, but I knew she would find no truth in its depths.

My sister stood alone on the banks.

—*Everen*, my sister said. *Come.*

15.

EVEREN:

THE DREAMER

I approached the edge of the banks. We were alone.

Miligrist's head emerged from the water, and she made her way back to land. Her body language was dejected. Even with the power of Glimmerhail, she had seen nothing.

Cassia gestured to the chalice with her snout. The bottom was coated in scrysilver.

—*Drink*, she instructed.

I dipped my head into the chalice, lapping up the last of the molten fluid. It both burned and froze as I swallowed, pooling in my belly. The world grew sharper about the edges, and the stars above brightened further.

The water lapped at my feet. Cassia and I moved forward until we were wing-deep. I turned my head back toward the Archivist Seer.

Miligrist settled on her haunches to keep watch. —*May starfire show you true*.

Cassia and I exhaled, clearing our minds. I tried to banish my fear, my doubt, my self-hatred.

The reflection of the pool darkened to black, the stars' echoes glimmering on the surface until they, too, snuffed out. Cassia and I gathered our strength and submerged ourselves.

Coolness slid over my scales. Everything around me grew dark, sound muffling as I sank to the deepest part of the pool. I sensed more than saw Cassia floating at my side.

—*Fate, open your eye*, my sister said.

A glimpse of that future we wanted so desperately floated in my mind's eye: dragons flying over present-day Vatra on warm winds. The vision faded to show the tree with the snake around its tail, the scales hanging in balance from its branches.

My lungs burned, already desperate for air.

—*Show me*, I said. *What am I meant to do next?*

The scales tilted, and I saw myself back within the storm, flying with purpose.

—*On the Night of Locked Tombs, when the last male dragon has come of age*, the voice of fate echoed the prophecy I had once stolen. *The Lady of Vere Celene points the way.*

The vision of myself flew harder, my wings working.

—*A Veiled storm and a golden chime . . .*

I watched myself fall to earth in a snow-covered forest.

—*. . . will guide him to the fading light of home.*

That version of me was tired, in pain, but all of that faded when I saw . . . you. You, Arcady, snow swirling around you as you stared up at me in wonder, not hatred, one hand reaching up toward me. I tried to reach back, but the vision faded.

I hovered once more in the deep, dark of the pool. My sister shifted, her wings propelling her through the water as smoothly as air.

Cassia drifted closer. —*Don't you see, Everen? It's the bond that guided you through and kept you hidden from the Dreamer.*

White bloomed into the dragonstone tree of magic. The injured serpent was twined around its trunk once more. The snake's head thrashed, its tail flicking restlessly.

The scales tipped, the human world rising and the dragon world falling. The serpent's wound at its side pulsed red. The snake's eyes opened, showing a whirling gyre; the darkness at its center luring me closer. The serpent uncoiled from the trunk. Its body shortened, wings rising from its back, legs emerging before forearms. Once it was a full dragon with scales the color of wraithwright, a burning claw swiped towards me, its jaws opening wide.

I inhaled water, choking, drifting down to the bottom of the pool. I could almost feel that talon slicing across my neck.

My lungs burned as I resisted the effort to gasp and choke down more water. I had turned myself around. Which way was the surface? I was lost.

Just as my vision began to fade, a body came beneath me, and my sister pushed me up from the deep.

Bubbles emerged from between my fangs. My head broke the surface, and I sucked in smoke-scented air beneath the still-shining stars.

Cassia dragged me unceremoniously from the pond and dumped me on the bank. I hacked up more liquid. My crest was sodden and heavy against my skull, my wings waterlogged.

My sister was frantic with concern, and it battered at my awareness. I felt as exposed as the wound of the serpent. I pushed her and Miligrist away as I came back to myself and the present.

When I could breathe more normally, I dragged myself upright, widening my wings and shaking off the worst of the water.

I had never, not once, seen Cassia this frightened. Miligrist, meanwhile, seemed . . . not surprised, but resigned. My stomach tightened in foreboding.

My body ached from my near-drowning, and my head pounded. I shook my head, shaking a few more droplets from my crest.

—*Parts of the vision seem clear,* I said, *but other aspects are opaque.* The past, the future, and the symbolism of the dragon scales all blurred together. I was dizzy with it. *What does it mean?*

—*Divination is always more art than science,* Miligrist said. *Sometimes it's only obvious in retrospect. But care not what I believe as an old dragon who now sees nothing. What do you think fate is trying to tell you?*

I sought that sense of peace and certainty. —*The serpent must be healed so it may sleep deeply once more.*

The old Seer bowed her head. —*I would agree.*

—*Whatever way the scales fall, I return to the Lumet.*

Miligrist silently urged me on.

—*The vision claimed the bond would guide me through,* I said. *But even if the Veil were to open for me, the bond is broken.*

Miligrist cocked her head. —*You have felt nothing of it since you returned?*

—*I thought I did, at first. Recently, there's been nothing, no matter how I might wish otherwise.* The fire in my throat seared.

—*Sleep,* Miligrist said. *All will be clearer in the morning.* She took a few ponderous steps before pausing to look back at us. *Come with me, Cassia. The vision must be preserved. What you both saw tonight might be some of the most important ever recorded. But after, you must watch him. The Queen doesn't want him on his own too long.*

—*Can I trust you to stay out of trouble for a moment?* my sister asked.

I swayed. —*I want nothing but sleep.*

—*Go, then,* my sister said. *I'll be quick.*

I took off into the sky. The warm night air dried the last of the water from my feathers. I flew to the far side of the island, landing at the edge of the cliffs where Cassia and I usually slept since I'd been let free. Waves crashed far below, and the orange and red of the

Reek glowed through its mantle of smoke. I pressed my wings tight along my back. When I had returned to Vere Celene, I had thought I would remain on this rock until my last breath. It was a strange luxury to be alone.

Cassia had not lied. Before I even began to drift to sleep, she landed at my side.

— *What is Miligrist not telling me?* I asked my sister as she curled herself into a circle and tucked her wings away.

— *I do not know. But if she is holding something back, she will have good reason for it.*

I exhaled hard through my nostrils, my gut twisting. In the Lumet, after you and I had stolen the claw from Girazin's tower and you had discovered what I was, I'd had a dream with Miligrist in it. *Stop*, she had said, as the dragon's claw reached toward me. *We're not here yet.* Were we, now?

— *What if I cannot return to the human world?* I asked.

— *You did it once. You can do it again. And this time, I don't believe any will try to stop you.*

— *Not even the Queen?*

— *Not even her.*

We drifted into silence, the stars above us slowly fading as the smoke returned.

— *Go to sleep, featherheart,* my sister sent. *Miligrist is right. You'll feel better in the morning. I'll be here, at your side.*

— *Of course you are. You are my guard, after all.* My thoughts were bitter.

She made a disgruntled noise in her throat. Her gaze rose to the hidden stars. Sleep would not find her easily.

I brought my wing over my head. I did not think sleep would find me, either, but exhaustion tugged me toward dreaming. As I did every night, Glimmerhail or not, I fell asleep wishing for you.

16.

ARCADY:

WAKE UP

I knew I'd dream about him.

Red played against the back of my eyelids. Tonight, we were in my dormitory—we hadn't met here before. His glowing wings lit the room red and orange. My hand was still tied to the bedpost.

He lay beside me and I sighed. His lips rested on the skin of my neck, and his fingertips traced the outline of my shoulder over my nightshirt.

I arched back toward him. His fingers found the hem of my nightshirt and pulled it up. Everything was real and unreal. I hadn't just been blackmailed. I didn't have to think. I merely had to feel. The alcohol had transferred into the dream judging by how everything tilted pleasantly around me.

I turned onto my back, and he hovered over me.

I realized, with a jolt, that he was entirely naked.

I drank him in. I didn't think I could conjure up anyone more beautiful to me if I'd tried. The green fire of his eyes burned. The glowing red wings covered us like a canopy.

I reached out with my free hand, needing to touch him—the bulge and dip of his arm muscles, his shoulder, the planes of his chest. He was completely unselfconscious of his body in a way I had never been. I reached lower, feeling him grow harder in my palm. There was something so satisfying, so powerful, about knowing it was because of me.

"Arcady." He said my name like a prayer. "I had hoped I would dream of you."

My body was singing. He pinned my free wrist and leaned down, pressing his body against mine. I arched my neck and brought my lips to his throat and heard his answering groan. I loved the weight of him on my wrists, the feel of him across my stomach.

His lips went lower, and he kissed the hollow of my throat and the sensitive skin at the outline of my seal setting.

"Free me," I panted, and with a flick of magic, the scarf at my wrist burned away.

I was bolder in my dreams than when we'd been together in the flesh. I made a noise of pure want, deep in my throat, and met his lips in a searing kiss.

Yes, *yes*. I wanted this. His hand came between us and touched me. I deepened the kiss, hungry for more, *more*. My dreams were where I tortured and indulged myself. In another life, maybe we could have had this whenever we wanted.

"I wish you were here. I wish this were real." I gasped as he did something clever with his hand.

"Arcady—" he said again, pulling away, a line appearing between his eyes. The sound of my name made me want to cry.

"Is this—?" he began, but I put my fingers to his lips.

His hands went to my wrist with that preternatural quickness.

"Arcady, I think—"

"Shh," I said. "Too much talking. We won't have long. We never do." Soon enough I'd wake up, aching and alone, with a splitting headache and an absolute belter of a hangover.

He peered at me. "Arcady, are you . . . drunk?"

"Mhmm." I leaned forward to kiss him.

"Arcady, stop."

I peered up at him, squinting. "Why would we *stop*?" I asked, plaintive.

"Because . . . I don't think this is simply a dream."

His words took a moment to register through the fog of desire and alcohol, and when they did, I snorted. "Of course it's a dream, silly. You're dead." My voice caught on the last word.

He pushed me back by the shoulders, his gaze intense. "I am not dead, Arcady. I made it back through the Veil. I am asleep in Vere Celene. Right now."

"No, you're not," I said. "The bond broke. I felt it." My eyes pricked. There was that ache in my chest and throat, the twist of my gut every time I thought of him. "This is supposed to be a *nice* dream, and I've had a shite day. Help me forget, my dream dragon ghost." I leaned back and hit my head against the headboard. "Ow," I said, faintly surprised. "That hurt?"

He grimaced and climbed off me, wrapping the sheet around his waist. He took in the details of my room. "You made it to the university, didn't you? I dreamed you had, but I did not know if it was true. I had hoped it was."

I sat up, pulling my nightshirt down. The back of my skull thudded. Dread punctured my confusion.

This felt truer than any dream.

I rose, stumbling back, needing distance between us. At the sight of the window, I froze.

Outside, an endless storm raged. All at once, I was entirely too sober.

"You must feel it, Arcady." Everen's voice was hushed.

At first, I didn't know what he meant. Then I caught it. A corner of my mind had been nothing but absence, like a socket of a pulled tooth. It was so faint it would be easy to miss: a tiny, golden hum.

"It is me," Everen whispered, his eyes as wide as mine. "I do not know how, but I think I found you. Or you found me. We are meeting somewhere in the middle, in the storm, in dreaming."

His words after I'd chased him through the corridors of the mansion in that earlier dream came back to me. *Maybe you only have to find me, Arcady.*

"No." Panic fluttered in my throat. "Because if we're both here, that means that you—that we—" Heat worked its way up my cheeks.

His gaze raked over my bare legs and the open neckline of my nightshirt.

"How long have you been a part of these dreams?" My voice went too high on the last word, tinged with panic.

Surprise, then sly amusement. "Are you saying this is not the first time you have dreamed of me like . . . this?"

It was a mortification so pure, so all-consuming, that I thought I would combust on the spot. My breath came faster. If he was right, then he was not dead and he was here in my hungry, lonely dreams.

"Do you still hate me?" he whispered. "For what I did?"

"Wake up," I said. I put my hands to my temples, squeezing.

"Arcady, please, I—"

"Wake up, wake up, *wake up!*"

I screamed the last two words into the darkness of my dormitory.

I was standing by the window. Across the room, the singed scarf dangled from my headboard, and the room smelled faintly of smoke. Outside, the university courtyard was silent and empty. It was a candlemark or so before dawn. My head was killing me.

Gathering my courage, I focused on that corner of my mind I'd been avoiding. And, sure enough, there was a stitch of gold across the worst of the darkness.

"Shit," I said to my empty room.

PART 2:
DIVINATIONS

To balance the scales, you must find the tree.
Branches stretch high and roots run deep,
only the magic within holds the key.
The first unlocking cut the world in twain,
to leave such a deep and festering cut.
The second attempt to heal was in vain:
illness struck and the future nearly shut.
Though the third unlocking will not fix all,
dragons may rise and yet others may fall.
While a coil unkinks and worlds collide,
the wound still aches and another threat hides.
To banish the rot, trust not what you see,
branches stretch high and roots run deep.
Dig deeper: beyond golden must you be.

17.

EVEREN:

REEK & RUIN

I awoke on the cliffs of Vere Celene, blinking the remnants of the dream-that-was-not-a-dream from my double-lidded eyes. My sister slumbered. I should wake her, but I wanted—I needed—to think without anyone else hovering. Everything was always clearer from the sky.

I was still regaining my strength, but the wind rustled through my feathers and along my scales, and my heart soared along with my wings as dawn fought to break through the gray sky. My jailers would come collect me, soon enough, and I would be told off like an errant hatchling.

I did not care.

Despite the dangers of what I had learned, I was elated. Once, not so long ago, I had despised the thought of being tied to you. Now that I knew we were connected once more, I never wished to let go.

All will be clearer in the morning, Miligrist had said. Had she known?

I shivered as I flew through the protective ward the dragons had made to keep out the wraiths. I made my way toward the Reek and flew until I could feel the heat of the magma on my scales, and my lungs and throat burned from the smoke. As a dragon, I was not afraid of fire. Orange-red lava oozed from the volcano like a pustule, and steam hissed where the molten rock hit the sea. The Reek had been slumbering since before I was born, but one day it, too, would wake. Over the last few months, I had sensed the occasional faint tremors from the depths of my prison.

Whatever you do, remember this: you must not wake the Dreamer.

The Reek, too, risked awakening.

In the dream, you had been embarrassed and angry, but there had been relief there, too. I would take that. All those details that would have blurred in normal dreams had been clearer than I could even imagine. The little dots above your eyebrow, the way one side of your mouth tilted up more than the other. The taste of your lips and the way your waist had felt beneath my hands. Undeniably you. It had been so difficult to draw away to tell you the truth when all I wanted was to pull you closer.

Somehow, despite the odds against us, we had found our way back to each other.

Out of the corner of my eye, I caught the flutter of wings. I expected Cassia or Mace, but it was Pan.

—*Pan*, I greeted her, warily. She looked terrible—her feathers were ratty from a lack of preening. The pupils of her red-rimmed eyes were slits, and she bared her teeth, aggression in every line from the tip of her crest to the end of her tail. I was acutely aware that we were far from the pryde of other dragons and the protection of the weyr.

— *Why did you come back?* Pan threw her thoughts at me so sharply, I flinched. *Why did you stop it all? We could have been in the human world, even now, ruling all of it. And Sidar would be at my side.*

—*She would not*, I forced myself to say. *We would all be dead and gone. It is the truth, Pan, I swear it.*

—*Liar!* She let out a high, piercing cry. *You have been corrupted, Everen once-Emberclaw. You brought the wraiths back with you. Why else would they be here when they never have been before? The Queen is weak for continuing to let you live.*

My claws curled. —*You dare question your Queen?*

Far off, I sensed Cassia and Mace coming to my aid.

—*Each day you walk among us as if you're a part of this weyr,* Pan spat, her thoughts venomous. *As if you will still be the one to save us when you have killed us all. I cannot stand it. The dragons that remain live, breathe, and eat, for now, but we'll all be corpses soon enough.*

—*Pan, stand down,* Mace commanded. *Now.*

My wings flapped furiously as Pan crowded me in mid-air. My talons curled in on themselves reflexively. Her eyes were wild and desperate, the pupils narrowed to slits.

—*Pan,* my sister called. *You overstep. In the name of Queen Naccara, and as future Queen of Vere Celene, I order you to stop. I understand you're hurting. But I promise you, this is not the way.*

—*You will be queen of nothing, Cassia, and we all know it.*

Cassia reeled in mid-air, her neck stiff in anger.

—*It is too late for me,* Pan thought. *I can't face all those sunrises and sunsets without her. I won't. We were mated for over a century. Do you even understand what that means? You have been alive but a handspan of years compared to us. And you, you were low enough to throw your kind away for a creature you knew but a few moons.* She bared pointed teeth, hissing. *A human.*

—*Pan,* I said, my heartbeat hammering. *I am sorry, I am, with all my soul, and I will mourn Sidar*—

—*Do not keep her name in your skull. Do not dare.* Pan raised her chin, claws extended. *By starfire as my witness,* Pan said, drawing forth her magic to underscore her words. *I challenge you, Everen once-Emberclaw. Tomorrow at sunset, we will see this through.*

A flare of magic played over her blue scales, and I felt the echoing call across mine as the spell took hold.

Cassia let out a roar, and Mace snarled, but Pan's eyes blazed in triumph.

The queen had warned someone might challenge me, but in my arrogance, I thought no one would dare. This was old magic, and none had dared use it in years. Even if dragons had their disagreements, we were too small in number to ever risk this. Pan had sealed her promise with magic. It was not dissimilar to a human breaking a contract signed with their seal. Every moment after sunset would grow more painful for us. We would have to fight.

And there would be only one survivor.

18.

SORIN:

THE WYVERN RACE

The morning before the first trial, Sorin turned the vial of Elixir in her hands. She unstopped the cork and smelled it, catching something sickly sweet and floral with an undernote of metal. She capped the bottle before doing it all again.

She'd taken a couple of mini doses as Magnes had trained her for the first trial, but for this one, she was meant to drink half the vial.

For all she knew, it could be lethal at that dose. Perhaps Magnes had sensed her doubts and thought an assassin ending herself by her own hand a fitting end.

The morning bells rang across the Citadel.

Finally, she knocked the Elixir back. It burned, tasting like it smelled — floral, metallic, and earthy. She grimaced even if, strangely, she wished to drain the bottle.

The euphoria crept up on her. It started subtly, with a buzzing deep in her bones. A tingling in her fingertips, her toes, even her eyelids. Her brain was sharp and clear, yet strangely calm. She was filled with a deep certainty that all would be well.

Her magic waited just below her skin, ready for her call.

She ate her belated breakfast and prepared for the wyvern race, the entertainment before the first trial of the tournament. Sorin had dithered for days before finally entering Jaculus's name.

There was a merry atmosphere throughout the Citadel, and Sorin was caught up in it. Music drifted on the wind, and bright bunting was a colorful counterpoint to the black and deep violet that had draped the Citadel for Chancellor Yrsa of Swiftsea's recent funeral. Some of the other students fidgeted with nerves, but Sorin's had melted away. The corners of her mouth curled up as she fought the urge to hum along with the reverberations in her body.

The shallow crater of the amphitheater in the hillside had been transformed from its daily use as the practice grounds. Raised seating curled in a crescent, and the autumn sun turned the sandstone of the citadel walls the color of lemon rinds. The amphitheater was full of the sound of flapping wings. Dozens of wyverns hovered above, and others perched and preened on the shoulders of their owners, their feather crests and wings brighter pops of color compared to their darker bodies. The air was bright and cold, but Sorin didn't feel it.

Sorin whistled and Jaculus peeled himself from his feathered brethren and fluttered down to her.

"Are you ready, little protector?" Sorin asked Jaculus. He chittered in response, rubbing his head against her cheek. She'd entered him into the race partly as an apology. Between her training, her classes, watching over Arcady, and training with Magnes at least thrice a sennight, there had been no time to slip away into the Royal Forest with a wyvern on her arm. He didn't deserve her neglect.

The people of the Citadel streamed through to take their seats, many clutching mugs of warm apple cider or mulled wine from the stalls in the courtyard. As the stands filled, wyverns dived overhead.

"Bet gold on Ambrosia," Sorin heard a passing drakine say to Their friend. "Good odds, but not as popular."

"I was considering Lindwyrm," said the other.

The drakine snorted. "That one has come dead last in the past four races. I've heard rumors of croup."

To the nobility, this was nothing more than a diversion and a chance to win some coin. Gemiean had told Sorin he'd bet three coppers on Jaculus that morning. Since the start of term, he'd made a few friendly overtures, and they'd studied together in the library a few times. He'd spent most of his teenage years at a monastery and was back briefly but would soon transfer to another. He had confided in her he'd rather study on his own than with all the stuck-up drakines. She understood, though she was sad to be losing an ally.

Sorin knew people were betting on students, too. "What are the odds on me for the first trial?" she had asked.

His grimace had been all the answer she needed.

Sorin took Jaculus down to the starting lines, the warm honey of the drug dripping through her veins. She nodded at the other students who had wyverns as she set Jaculus on his assigned perch and tied a bright green ribbon around his neck. Jaculus made a nervous noise and Sorin scratched under his chin.

Willem Ansel had boasted often enough that his family had a whole crop of wyverns at his hunting lodge in Redwing Valley. He'd sent for his swiftest, a blue named Livet. Rahela's wyvern was a silver named Elspeth.

"Beautiful creature," Sorin complimented Rahela, and she basked in the reflected praise. She wore a tunic made of fine Myrian silk beneath her student robes.

"Yours seems a little . . . small, I have to say," Willem said, casting a critical eye over Sorin's green wyvern. Jaculus had either been the runt of the litter, or his growth had been stunted by starvation before

Sorin had found him in the forest as a hatchling. He puffed up, as if offended. Sorin ran a soothing hand along his back.

"He's fast," Sorin said, but Willem's interest had already waned.

"Is Livet ready to lose to my Elspeth then, Wil?" Rahela teased.

"She'll thrash your molting lizard, yes," Willem drawled, and Rahela laughed.

"Care to put some coin on it?" Rahela asked, rubbing her fingers together.

Willem's eyes sparked. "Always."

They enthusiastically haggled, finally settling on four gold coins to the winner and drinks the next time they were out at the tavern. Sorin shook her head at the sum.

The head Wyvernmaster, wearing formal hunting leathers stitched with gold thread, gave the wyverns a last check, searching for signs of doping, sickness, or spells. Magnes had assured her that the Elixer wouldn't be detected by any of the professors. In her haze, she couldn't find it in herself to worry about being caught.

The call of a horn echoed across the grounds. It was time.

Sorin stepped forward, the drug lending her a confidence she'd never known. Jaculus's head bobbed, feeding off the energy of the crowd and his owner. His neck strained toward the starting line. Sorin had put him through his paces as soon as she'd entered him in the race. He knew exactly where to go, and he was just as eager as Sorin to prove himself.

She scratched Jaculus right between his wings in the place he loved most, pressing her lips to the soft spot on his forehead above his crest. Jaculus had defended her from wraiths, had given her comfort after she'd stared down at a corpse she'd created.

"You can do this, my little shadow," she whispered against his feathers. She adored everything in that moment. Her wyvern. The other students. The crisp wind, the sky, and the cold, winter sun.

A klaxon called, and the Wyvernmaster walked to the center of the amphitheater. Sorin gave Jaculus a last kiss on the forehead before stepping back to join the other racers.

"May their wings fly true," They said, voice spelled louder. "And may the gods bless us all this day."

The Wyvernmaster's hands raised, ribbons fluttering from Their gloved hands. They brought them down in one fast, hard motion and the wyverns launched themselves from their perches.

Sorin clasped her hands to her chest as more than one hundred wyverns took wing, jostling each other as they looped once around the arena before speeding off to the cote on the other side of Vatra. It was the first of the long line of roosts along the watchtowers of the coast.

"Come on, Elspeth!" Rahela called, hands cupping her mouth as the wyverns became tiny dots punctuating the blue of the sky.

Sorin thought she caught Jaculus's joyful cry among the others, and her face broke out in a grin.

"Jaculus!" Sorin cried, reveling that she could raise her voice after so many years of silence. Was this what it was to be happy?

One of the other students clapped her on the back, but Sorin's eyes were on the sky. Anxiety punctured the warmth of the drug. There was always a chance a wyvern could be clipped by another racer's wing and injured or attacked by a bird of prey.

The students about to compete were tense and distracted, but the rest simply enjoyed the display.

Finally, finally, the roar of the crowd announced the return of the wyverns, instincts, training, and the thrill of the chase guiding them home. They were little more than blurs, and Sorin's eyes strained for a glimpse of green ribbon and familiar iridescent feathers. She jumped up and down, screaming as loudly as everyone else.

The wyverns arrived back in the amphitheater with the sound of flapping and screeching calls. They circled the outer edges of the arena, flying over the cheering crowd below. They began the final three laps along the ribbon-marked route, jostling each other. Sorin winced as two wyverns collided, spinning away with cries of pain. Another few caught themselves and glided down to the ground. A last wyvern fell, hard, their owner rushing forward in concern. Sorin's throat closed as she searched for Jaculus among the jumble of feathers and wings.

There.

Her breath caught when she spotted how close he was to the front. His small size made him nimble, and he wove between the other wyverns, gaining precious distance as the creatures veered into the final lap. A few more crashed, and another simply gave up, fluttering away to perch on an outcrop and tuck its scaled head under its wing. The remaining creatures gave their last bursts of blurring speed — and then —

Another klaxon as the wyverns passed the finish line.

A few moments passed as the experts confirmed the results, the crowd cheering or arguing who they thought had won or placed.

The Wyvernmaster came back onto the field.

"A fine race, a fine race," the Wyvernmaster called. Sorin rose on her tiptoes, hands clasped over her heart. She was surrounded by a press of whispering students.

"In bronze, we have Jaculus, in silver, Lindwyrm, in gold, Verdell, and the wraithwright goes to . . . Curtall!"

Fourth. Her little wyvern had come fourth out of over a hundred. She thought she'd burst with pride. Students clapped her on the back.

Verdell was Edin Vayne's violet wyvern and Curtall and Lindwyrm were both owned by one of the richest drakines in the Citadel who raced wyverns professionally. The fact that Sorin's little runt of a wyvern had come anywhere near the front was incredible.

Jaculus circled over Sorin's head, keening his pleasure as if he knew he'd done well. She raised her arm, but he was too keyed up from the race. She gave a sharper whistle, and he settled, his head nudging along her cheekbone.

"Well done, you marvelous little thing," she said.

"That was brilliant," Willem said, a tad grudgingly.

"How did your Livet do?"

"Thoroughly middle of the pack." He smiled, but annoyance sparked in his gaze. "But still did better than Rahela's Elspeth."

Rahela glowered, dug in her pockets, and passed over the gold coins.

Jaculus perched on Sorin's shoulder. She could feel his little heartbeat racing when he leaned against her cheek. Sorin made her way forward through the crowd toward the podiums. The Wyvern-master hung the ribbon and medal around her neck, the eyes of the Citadel on her.

There was Magnes, right at the front. His eyes met hers behind His priest mask, the gilded horns curling over his ears. A stab of fear punctured her glow. She held her breath. She was no longer invisible, and He had urged her to join the tournament, after all. Surely, He would not be angry at her for wanting to be seen?

Magnes raised His gloved hands and gave her a sardonic little clap. Her knees shook with relief.

The race had helped distract her from what was next. She clutched her ribbon in damp hands, the bronze metal digging into her palm. The opening entertainment was over, and now it was time for the true test.

Her magic thrummed in response.

19.

ARCADY:

THE FIRST TRIAL

The morning of the trial, I was yet again half-tempted to run away from the university, from Larkin and Wren, from everything. Yet I had signed my false name with my stolen seal, and I couldn't break my promise. No matter how far I ran, I also wouldn't be able to escape the dragon in my head.

I'd not slept a wink, equally afraid of dreaming or not dreaming about Everen. My magic seemed the same, despite that barest golden thread, but I was still terrified it would somehow affect the trial.

When the sun rose, I went down the hill and called on Kelwyn. I'd not had the time to visit the Last Golden since I'd left for the Citadel. He offered me a loaded plate of eggs, black pudding, mushrooms, and potato scones. I'd been eating and training so much that even with the constant magic use, I'd managed to put on a little fat and muscle since term had begun. My stomach was all tangled with foreboding.

Kelwyn asked me light questions about the university as I doggedly chewed and swallowed, barely tasting the food. I told him about the students, the classes, my professors. He was curious about the meals in the Great Hall, of course. I answered listlessly.

"Are you all right?" He broke our unspoken rule and peered at me. "I expected some nerves, sure, but there's something else."

I opened my mouth, imagining for once telling him the whole truth. *You see, the dragon I thought I killed has instead been linked to me in dreams where I consistently undressed him, and I managed to wake myself up from the sheer mortification of it all once I realized. Now I'm afraid to sleep.*

"Larkin's blackmailing me," I managed. That part I figured I should share.

"What?" he exclaimed, and it didn't seem forced. He hadn't known.

"Aye. I have to spy on my alchemy professor and try to steal Their research. It's some treatment that might help the Struck."

He put down his fork. "Fuck. Should have seen this coming, I suppose."

"I suppose I should be glad she's not asking for anything else."

"Unless she changes the rules of the game partway." I grunted. I'd decided I'd make her give me that seal back one way or another, even if I had to hunt her down in Myria.

"What's she got on you?" he asked.

"My identity won't hold up under any sort of scrutiny," I said. "All it'd take is a note urging the university to take a closer look, and I'll be back out on my arse." I couldn't tell him about my seal or my true name. Wren knowing so much was already bad enough. If I was caught being a Struck, too, I'd be arrested, my seal confiscated, the works.

Kelwyn frowned, sensing my evasiveness. He'd always been under the impression I was actually a drakine who had lost my family in the Strike. It wasn't a thousand leagues from the truth: my grand-sire had been given privileges and we'd lived in a house as grand as any noble's before my parents and I had fled Vatra. The rumor was he'd been on the cusp of gaining an official title before his death.

"Oh, before I forget," I said, rummaging in my pocket and passing him the silver and shell bracelet I'd stolen the first day of term. "Can you sell this for me?"

He appraised it critically. "Aye, maybe three silvers and a few coppers."

"Better than nothing. Ta." Distraction achieved.

"Come on," Kelwyn said, tucking the bracelet away and grabbing his coat. "We don't want to be late. I've already missed the wyvern race because of you needing a feed."

I stared at him. "You're coming up to the Citadel?"

"What, you didn't think I'd heard the rumors about the Trials down here and not realize you'd have put your name in immediately? I bought my ticket as soon as they were announced. Figured you could use a friendly face in the crowd."

My eyes started stinging. "Kel. I don't know if I can do it," I whispered. "What if I just make a fool of myself? What if I'm not good enough?"

"The only way to find out is to put yourself in the arena. You went to all this trouble—you're not about to tap out at the first sign this won't be easy, will you? That's not the imperious imp I know." He reached out and tweaked my nose. "You've faced much worse than this."

I laughed and wiped at my eyes. He had no idea.

We took the cart up the hill together, acting like strangers, but he sat close enough that his arm pressed alongside mine in wordless reassurance.

Soon enough, I stood in the amphitheater with the forty-nine other students who had signed up for the Trials. I wore the clothes I'd purchased for alchemy after my first class, the dark material spelled to be less flammable. I heard from the others that Sorin's wyvern had placed bronze in the race, but that was about all that made its way through my anxious fog.

Even with Kelwyn's face in the crowd, every passing moment made me more convinced I was about to embarrass myself in front of him and the whole damn Citadel.

"How are you holding up?" Rahela had a flower tucked behind one ear, and another attached to a vine curled around her wrist. Students were allowed to bring small materials like this into the trial, as long as the professors checked them for tampering beforehand.

"Oh, grand," I said. "Definitely not nervous at all. Luck be with you."

"Saint Ini bless you, too," she replied by rote. "I'm scared too," she admitted, her lips thinning. Her chosen god was indigo Zama, but for the trial she'd be demonstrating her ability with green Jari. Even though we were in competition, I found myself wanting her to do well.

"You'll smash it." I nudged her shoulder and smiled, and she returned it.

A Herald came forward to announce the trial. On the raised dais, the Head Priest in his horned dragon mask and the two remaining Chancellors in their wraithwright masks sat beneath a canopy. Something about their bearing was subtly different from the funeral. Not for the first time, I wondered if they were body doubles trotted out for events like this and the parades down in the city. Maybe that was just the paranoid thief in me, but it's what I'd do. Let someone else handle the boring pomp and ceremony and assassination risk. I'd hole myself up in my palace and scheme. Or take a nap. I bloody loved a good nap.

Gods, I was tired.

"Five gods keep you all," the Herald intoned, spelled voice carrying to the back of the amphitheater. I swallowed, eyes raking over the seats filled with drakines, guilders, Citadel officials, merchants, knights—anyone who could afford a seat. All the eyes on me made my skin itch.

The professors and healers were in the front row, close enough They'd be able to intervene if a student lost control. We'd been informed of the dangers, time and time again, before we'd pressed our seals into the ink.

Professor Plink leaned forward, more animated than I'd seen Them in Kalsh class. Professor Hayden's hands rested lightly on Their pregnant belly. I tried not to stare at Them too obviously. I still couldn't quite believe that, if Larkin's source was reliable, my favorite teacher had once worked with my grandsire, and now I'd have to find a way to steal from Them. That was tomorrow's problem.

"We are delighted to open the University Trials here at the Citadel for the first time in generations," the Herald began. "Our luminous students of the University of Vatra are the stars of the future. Through Their talent, diligence, and hard work, They will shine as They demonstrate Their magic for us today.

"For this first task of the Trials, our students must show They can access a different type of magic than that of Their chosen god. Those who show this mastery over self will progress to the next task.

"May you be lifted up upon the dragon gods' wings and prove your might." The Herald lowered their upraised arm, the crowd cheered, and the Trials began.

The Herald called out names, and the first lot of ten students stepped into the amphitheater to their well-spaced designated spots. I didn't know many students in this initial group, but more than a few seemed green around the gills.

A third of them stated their spells and managed no magic at all. Nerves gained the upper hand. A few others conjured the minimum — wisps of clouds around their hands, or a couple of drops of water, or the tiniest spark of fire. Not enough. Iona Lyn, a studious-looking student with glasses I knew from alchemy class, created a bright enough flame hovering over their palm to be impressive. Kala Jonrir, one of the

students who had been so snooty to me at the start of term, gathered a
rain cloud overhead and a wind whipped through the amphitheater, his
dark hair dancing around his face. The professors made Their notes,
but I suspected only two in that group would progress to the second
trial, if that. Some of those students were in their third or fourth year
of study and had failed. My stomach wound itself tighter.

This was folly, and yet I burned to do well. While I was exhausted
and stressed, the last few sennights had, in some respects, been exhil-
arating. I wanted to prove that I could be more than I was: a Struck
with no money, no standing, and a soiled name.

The crowd grew restless. They wanted a real show.

Willem was in the second group, and he gave Rahela and me a
sardonic salute as he sauntered forward. He succeeded with a decent
demonstration of Kalsh magic, the water twisting into a large infinity
symbol folding in on itself. He smirked, and I knew he was tempted
to turn it into something rude and offend the entire Citadel in one
go. He lost his focus, and the water splashed to the ground, but it
was possibly enough for him to scrape through. Professor Hayden
clapped as hard as They could. I glanced away.

Delin Sanron planted a seed and a small rose bush bloomed before
our eyes, which drew a round of applause. He beamed, pleased, a
blush rising to his cheeks.

A third year, Olwyn Biela, who was so short and young-looking
he could pass for still being in academy, had brought a small pile of
scrap metal with him. He muttered a spell as he raised the metal mid-
air. The seal at his chest glowed with silver light.

The metal melted, the gray warming to red-orange as it twisted
into undulating shapes. It was hypnotic enough to distract another
student, and their spell folded. Olwyn grunted, a line appearing
between his brows as a shape began to emerge. Before I could guess
what it would be, Olwyn lost control.

Liquid metal splashed his skin, and he screamed, the sound echoing across the amphitheater.

Even from where I stood two dozen paces away, I caught the hiss of metal on skin and the smell of burning flesh.

The crowd gasped as Olwyn fell to the ground. Some covered their faces, but others watched in horrified fascination.

Healers rushed forward, muttering spells, seals flashing green beneath Their robes. The metal cooled on Olwyn's flesh into a splash of gray droplets. It was a mercy when the healers sent Olwyn unconscious.

There was a delay as officials settled the crowd and Olwyn's limp form was carried away toward the infirmary.

"Gods above," Rahela breathed.

Through my horror, a bitter part of me wondered if the audience was now entertained.

The Chancellors had not moved. The Herald came up and spoke to the Head Priest in lowered tones. Would the Trials be canceled before they'd truly begin? After a whispered exchange, the Head Priest leaned back.

The Herald returned to the amphitheater, shaken. "We have word that the student's wounds are severe, but not life-threatening. As we have warned, injuries during the Trials are a risk, but the professors and healers on hand are ensuring they are as safe as they can be. However, we offer you the choice here and now: any students who wish to rescind their name may do so. The university will break the seal-promise spell without repercussions or judgment."

A lengthy pause as the students eyed each other.

Harlowe cracked. "Sard this," they said as they left their spot. A few others followed, shoulders hunched under the scrutiny. Yes, we'd been told of the dangers, but it was something else to be confronted with them. I hoped Olwyn would be all right. At least he'd have the best healers in Loc.

Pride alone wouldn't let me follow them, but inside, I quailed. I studied the others. Twenty had already been tested. Five had quit. That left only twenty-five, including me, and I wasn't sure how many would progress to the second trial. Sorin stared blankly at the spot where Olwyn had fallen.

Another ten students came forward. Lowe Balcil, a fourth year, showed a sharp aptitude with Kalsh. It was like Willem's display, but with far better command. Lowe was of average height, with round cheeks that were always flushed. He kept control and wove rings that circled his body.

Edin Vayne raised a pile of small rocks and had them orbit around her head, and her control was impeccable. She wore a brass circlet, as if she already knew herself a victor. Usually, when a student tapped a magic that wasn't innate, they grimaced with the effort, but she was peaceful, a faint smile playing around her mouth.

"Edin is one to watch, isn't she?" I said to Rahela as Edin let the stones fall gently to the ground.

"Definitely."

Rahela and Sorin were in the fourth group, meaning I'd be in the last, in the smaller group of five. I was on the edge of pure panic. Few first years had entered the first trial, and none so far had done well. The crowd had already seemingly forgotten what had happened to Olwyn. The atmosphere was jovial again. People sipped mulled wine or leaned closer to chatter among themselves. To them, this was all a lark.

Everyone in the fourth group managed at least a measure of magic, making them the strongest showing so far. Flames or lightning hovered over a few palms. Teasel Miti, a tall student I barely knew, with a shock of orange-red hair, manipulated metal without injuring himself.

I'd expected Sorin to use Aura's magic, as she was in alchemy with me, but to my surprise, she held her hands apart and created a sphere of a mini storm. She focused on the largest of the rocks that

Edin had used earlier, still clustered at the outer edge of the amphi-theater overlooking the city. Sorin muttered her spell, and a small bolt of lightning emerged from the storm and hit the stone, cracking it right down the middle. The crowd went wild for it.

Sorin grinned, swaying as though drunk on success.

Rahela went next and held out her arm. Her mouth moved, her seal flaring. As we watched, the vine grew, twisting its way up her arm. Soon, it covered most of her body in green tendrils, and with a last muttered word, the vines erupted into fresh pink peony blos-soms. The crowd applauded, impressed by the display.

Rahela, embraced by flowers, walked to the other side of the amphi-theater, hands shaking as she ate a few sweetspheres. Both she and Sorin had done advanced magic. I was both impressed and intimidated.

It was my turn. My self-assurance shriveled further. Someone gave me a gentle shove from behind, and I stepped forward and took my place along with the other students. The audience's collective gaze crawled over me, and I felt exposed. I found Kelwyn again, and he slyly gave me a rude hand gesture, knowing I'd prefer it to something encouraging. I smiled, despite myself. Waiting for the signal, I took a deep, steadying breath.

The klaxon called, and we began.

I reached for my magic, my seal flickering. My Kalsh magic was no good here. I let the crowd and my fellow students fade to a dull roar, focusing inward. I reached into my seal for the magic I'd stolen from a dragon.

Drawing myself tall, I raised my hands, tasting soot on my tongue.

"*Reukas vé.*" My voice cracked. *Ignite more*, I'd said, but I only caught a hint of smoke.

"*Reukas vé,*" I said, louder. This time, Everen's stolen magic caught like a match, but the flame above my palm was pathetically small. The flame sputtered.

Shit.

I was just about to close my palms and give up when I caught a golden chime echoing through my mind from across the Veil. I had thought of a dragon, and far away in another world, a dragon thought of me. My emotions were heightened, and with our hampered, rekindled connection, it seemed we could subtly sense each other even when we were awake.

I glanced in panic at the professors in the first row. No one had noticed our bond when we'd both been in the same world, even if we spoke mind to mind, but I also hadn't been around some of the strongest magic users in the country, had I? Yet none of them glanced at me more than anyone else.

My dragon sent a formless question. The pathetic flame still burned above my palm, sputtering as it fought the wind. I was running out of time. Every second I delayed, my chance to impress the professors decreased.

Sard it.

—*Help me*, I thought back through the bond, as hard as I could, and the gold in my mind hummed.

"*Reukas vé*," I tried once more, my voice stronger.

Everen's magic answered.

The flames above my palms sparked to life, burning bright enough they'd be seen from the back row of the audience. I could let the spell go and end it there, and that might be enough.

I chewed my lip. So far, my magic and my hunger were under control. It was like the professor said in waterweaving class: the element wants to do your bidding—you simply have to be strong enough to convince it.

The gold hum grew louder. It was instinctual, as if Everen were there, crouching in my mind, behind my ribs, whispering in my ear. I used a hand gesture Everen had shown me once before. The fire rose above my head.

My fingertips danced. My seal burned bright red, and brimstone was acrid on my tongue. I closed my eyes tight and told the fire what I wanted it to become, picturing it in my mind's eye. Everen's magic was around me, strong and sure, like a caress.

"*Kiév kio tiɾ viuɾkar*," I said, telling the fire to burn in a particular shape.

The roar of the crowd and the heat against my face told me I'd done it. I opened my eyes.

I'd chosen a dragon, of course. The flame's shape was little bigger than a wyvern. It flapped its wings, once, before collapsing into smoke.

Dimly, I staggered to the edge of the amphitheater and fell upon the food I'd spirited away in my pockets, my hunger roaring to life. The crowd was on their feet, applauding. Kelwyn had his hands around his mouth, whooping with glee.

Looked like the students had provided sufficient entertainment, in the end.

The professors conferred. The Herald congratulated us before announcing that twelve students would progress to the next phase. The Herald read out their names. The fourth years were Lowe Balcil, Edin Vayne, Delin Sanron, Kala Jonrir, and Teasel Miti. The third years: Jordin Miti, a tall student with brown skin and corkscrew curls, who had been borderline in the first group with fire magic, Cind Melody, a half-Myrian student with blonde hair who had been in my group and used green magic, and Iona Lyn, a student with brown hair and green eyes who had used Aura's magic. Of the second years, Rahela and Willem made it through.

Mine and Sorin's names, the only two first-years, were called last.

—*Thank you*, I thought out into the ether. *Thank you.*

Gold flared in response.

20.

ARCADY:

CELEBRATIONS

Three hours later, as the sun began to set, the common room was full of drunken students.

The ground floor of the dormitories was where students congregated if they weren't studying in the library. It was full of comfortable, well-used armchairs and sofas, the tables stained with decades' worth of mug rings, and thick rugs softening the floor. The eleven students who made it through were celebrating, and others drowned their sorrows. Someone had draped a garland of flowers around me at one point, but half of the blooms were squashed. It'd been over forty candlemarks since I'd last slept, but I'd passed through exhaustion to something else.

The anxiety hadn't magically disappeared once the trial finished. I kept gulping down more drink against the dread clawing its way up my throat. Winning the first trial had felt too good to be true. How long before it all went to shite this time?

Willem stood on one of the tables, a tin crown askew on his head as he conversed earnestly with Damon. There was far too much background noise for my weaker hearing to pick anything up, and the angle wasn't right for proper lip reading. Damon's expression rippled and they shook their head. Willem's face went pleading, and he placed his hand on Damon's shoulder, who shrugged it off. Jumping down from the table, Damon pushed their way through the throng of drunken students before disappearing.

Rahela was surrounded by a gaggle of students. She still had a pink flower from the trial tucked behind her ear, and she'd spelled it so the bloom opened and closed in time with her breathing.

Sorin sat in the corner clutching a cup. She listed slightly in her seat, eyes distant. Another student said something to her, and Sorin blinked slowly, gave a lax smile, and laughed. About time she loosened up. Sorin was possibly the most serious person I had ever met, and that included Everen at his most pompous.

"I'm just so impressed," Vilm, from my alchemy class, kept saying to any of us who had gotten through to the second trial. He was a tall, reedy slip of a thing, with wide, pale blue eyes.

"Thank you, Vilm," I said when he'd gone around the room to congratulate each of us a third time. His enthusiasm was strangely wearying. Iona Lyn and I exchanged a glance. We'd spoken long enough earlier that we'd finally made our proper introductions, including gender. She pushed her spectacles up her nose, hiding a smile as Vilm went in search of more mead. I rubbed the skin above my seal, trying to chase away the tightness in my chest. Iona had done well with fire, but her innate magic was water, I believed.

Edin Vayne came over with a jug. She raised her eyebrows, and I held out my near-empty glass for her to top up.

"Thanks," I said, taking a long sip. The cider was spiced with cinnamon and clove and had a pleasant, dry bite. It felt like drinking autumn.

Edin said something to me, but I couldn't catch it in the din.

"Can you repeat that?" I asked.

"So you're through to the second trial," Edin said, louder, eyeing me up and down. "As a first year. I didn't think any would get through, much less two, I have to say."

Her tone was chilly, so I pitched mine extra toasty. "I know, I'm shocked, myself. Got lucky. You did brilliantly." I raised my glass, and she clinked it with the cider jug. "They say you're the one to beat."

She laughed, her frost melting, but there was an easy smugness about it that made me suspect she well knew it, too. "Thank you. The second one will be harder, though, I suspect."

Was that a warning?

Jordin and Teasel drifted over. Despite their different coloring, between their same last name and similar features, they must be siblings or cousins. The Miti family was quite influential in Loc—lots of judges and solicitors, in particular. A Miti judge had presided over my grandsire's trial and sentenced him to death, after all. My stomach twisted, but I forced a smile.

"We were just gossiping about the second trial," I said. "Any guesses?"

"The professors said they'll explain what it is next sennight," Teasel said. "I don't have a clue what it'll be. Do you?"

"It's an offensive of some sort, I suspect," Edin said, still speaking louder for my benefit, but other students were clearly eavesdropping. "That's how the old Trials went. The first was magic against self, the second magic against others, and the third magic against nature."

I'd suspected the same. I'd spent an afternoon rifling through the library and reading up on the old Trials. Death was rare, at least— the university had some duty of care, after all—but an alarming number of students had been injured in them. After what happened to Olwyn, it was hard not to be spooked.

"Mm, you're probably right. A duel then," Jordin said, expression hard to read. Both Jordin and Teasel did well on the practice grounds.

"That'd be my guess," Edin said cheerfully.

"Well then we'll meet once more on the battlefield of the amphitheater," I said, my words slurred. The lack of sleep meant the drink was going to my head, and I'd used a lot of magic. My body was deeply unhappy with the abuse.

"Spell well," Edin said, lifting the cider. "Now I must continue my sacred duty of ensuring no one has an empty cup." She drifted away.

My eyes were gritty and dry. My nerves were in tatters, and the too-crowded, too-loud, too-warm common room was abruptly far too much. I congratulated Cind and Lowe on my way out before slipping out into the courtyard, sucking in deep breaths of cold air. The sky was yellow-orange. I'd learned the university was at its prettiest during the golden hour.

The peace was marred by the sounds of someone throwing up onto the ivy. I smirked when I realized it was none other than my surly alchemy partner. Sorin was doubled over, her whole body shaking.

"Take it you're not much of a drinker?" I asked, and she startled.

"N—no," she said. She was a little gray, a little wary, and thoroughly miserable.

"Here," I said, holding out the last of my cider. "Don't drink any more, but you could swish your mouth out, at least."

She stared at it warily, like she thought it poisoned. Eventually, she took my advice, spitting out the liquid and wiping her mouth with her sleeve. "My thanks." It was amazing how grudging those two words sounded.

"So. We're the two first years who got through," I said, conversationally. "That bit with the lightning was dead wicked."

"Mm," she said. She'd barely said a word to me unless it was something to do with alchemy. She rarely spoke to anyone, in fact. I'd maybe have put it down to shyness, except for the way she kept glowering at me when she thought I wasn't looking.

Sorin closed her eyes, breathing through her nose. She held onto the wall to keep upright.

She took a couple of steps, then stumbled.

"Come on," I said. "I'll help you back to your room."

"I don't need your help," she spat.

I sighed. "All right. Out with it. Have I pissed in your teacup or something?"

"Wh—what?" she blinked at me, her eyes having trouble focusing. She had long eyelashes, and her irises were a light brown, almost tawny, the pupils blown. Her full lips were parted. If she wasn't so damned hostile, I'd probably have found her attractive.

"You've taken against me since day one. Have I done something to offend you?"

She scrunched her nose, the constellation of her freckles shifting. She rubbed her forearm, swaying on her feet. "I'm here to learn. I don't need friends."

"Well, you definitely won't make any if you keep up this frankly impressive level of grumpiness. Though I seem to be getting the brunt of it, I've noticed."

"Sard off," she said, and I couldn't help it, I laughed. I received another dirty look for my trouble.

"What? It's strange to hear a priest swear. Like seeing a cat wearing trousers."

Sorin took three whole steps before falling back to her knees. "Oh," she said, as if surprised the ground was so close.

I sighed and hauled her up, throwing one of her arms around my shoulders. She made a complaining noise but leaned heavily on me all the same. She smelled of sour sick and cloves.

"Don't you . . . want to stay?" she asked, gesturing loosely at the sounds from the common room. "Willem will be annoyed with those who leave early."

"I've had my fill of celebration. Wil's so drunk already that I highly doubt he'll take a final attendance," I said. I desperately needed to sleep, no matter what I might find in my dreams.

Sorin didn't say anything else as I led her back to the priests' rooms near the Cathedral. The sun was low enough that it dazzled me, and Sorin groaned, her head lolling forward.

She fumbled with the door. I only caught a glimpse of her room—it was completely bare and much smaller than the student dormitories, without even a rug or a tapestry. There was an empty wyvern perch in the corner. I wondered why she'd entered the Trials. As an acolyte, her tuition and board were already covered by the Citadel. A similar desire to prove herself, I guessed.

"Thanks," she muttered.

"You're welcome." I leaned forward, whispering theatrically, "See, I'm not that bad."

She blinked at me owlishly and closed the door in my face.

I scoffed and made my way back to my room. My feet dragged, and I paused in the courtyard, admiring the last of the sunset. Fingers of red spread out across the sky, and the clouds were brilliant orange.

"What a day," I said to no one. My mouth was so dry, and the anxiety returned, hitting me like a wave. Something hooked in my torso and *pulled*, making me gasp. The golden chime clanged discordantly in my mind.

This was wrong. With a lurch, I realized this fear I'd been fighting all day . . . not all of it was mine.

I staggered back to my room, stumbling near as badly as Sorin. My vision darkened around the edges. I caught scattered impressions — flapping wings and the sound of snapping teeth. I felt something sharp and painful bite into my shoulder, and I just swallowed down the scream.

I slammed the door to my room shut, and promptly collapsed.

21.

EVEREN:

THE CHALLENGE

I had no heart for this fight.

I had spent the day away from the others, gathering my strength. At one point, I dozed and found my way to you. You had a challenge of your own to face, even if I only caught disjointed flashes. Once, I would never have stooped to help a human. Now, I had not hesitated. Perhaps Pan was right — I had changed.

When it was time, I walked out to the flat area by the bathing pool. I was in my full form. The dragons around us were utterly silent, so still they could be made of stone. With so few of us left, a challenge was not only a tragedy, it was a waste. Soon enough, the pryde would sing another dragon's soul to eternal sleep. How many in Vere Celene hoped they would sing for me instead of Pan?

The queen's preterit face was stony. Despite the heat, she was wrapped in deer pelts. She was outwardly implacable, but I sensed her unhappiness at the display. Even she had no power to stop what Pan had begun.

Pan and I faced each other as the sun slipped below the horizon. My opponent's tail lashed as she bared her teeth. She was nothing but coiled anger and wounded grief.

She snarled. I lowered my head, bunching my shoulder muscles and whipping my tail. My sister's concern washed against my scales.

I knew I would not die that day. This was not my ending. Even if fate had not whispered to me, I was larger, younger, and stronger than Pan. Yet she was a fully trained warrior of Vere Celene, and, blinded by her sorrow, she had little left to lose. She could hurt me.

With a roar and a plume of fire, Pan leaped into the air, using magic to help propel her upward. She twisted, her flight graceful and her lines long. With a heaviness in my chest, I rose to meet her.

We circled each other, our feather crests raised in challenge. I had never seriously fought a dragon before—the closest was play fights with the other hatchlings that resulted in little more than scraped scales. Wraiths could be vicious, but they were not armored. Dragons had a weak point at the throat and another high up on the stomach, just below the rib cage.

Pan attacked first, rising higher before diving at me. I banked, angling my wings, but she managed to rake her claws down my back. I roared.

The wind rose off the ocean, and I caught a thermal to swing around to Pan. The fading sunlight illuminated the veins in her wings. Once more, she struck first, trying to come in below me to swipe at my stomach, but a kick with my talons sent her back.

I breathed hard, my muscles still weaker than they should be. I was also missing the chunk of my magic that now belonged to a human another world away.

Pan opened her jaws wide enough that I saw the ember of her throat before she let loose another blast of flame. The fire played along my haunch, but it took more than that to burn a dragon.

I feinted a few times, driving her back with a few short bursts of flame. Below us, a circle of dragons craned their necks to watch. No one would interfere. This was between me, Pan, and starfire's fate.

—*Fight me!* Pan yelled. *Fight me, you coward.*

My wings worked harder as I gained altitude. Was I merely delaying the inevitable?

I dived, tucking my wings tight, landing on Pan's back. She roared, her head twisting back, jaws snapping. She rolled and I lost my purchase.

I grabbed one of her claws with mine, and our wings worked as we twisted like two leaves in the wind. She opened her mouth wide before reaching out to bite down on my shoulder with enough force to puncture my scales. I roared in pain but held on as we tumbled, the ground growing ever closer. She tried to shake her head from side to side to shred the meat of my shoulder but lost her grip. I did not. With effort, I dragged her back down to earth with a loud crash.

Dirt and dust rose in a cloud around us, the dried grass crunching beneath me as I came to all fours. Pan was disoriented, and I pounced.

Pinned beneath my claws, Pan gave a higher cry. She worked her head, but I had her by the throat, my body weight across her chest, her legs unable to kick and disembowel me.

I clenched my jaw and held her harder, wrangling her into submission. I saw the exact moment she knew she was defeated. Like a snuffed flame, the fight went out of her. Her muscles went slack, but I did not loosen my grip.

She was down. I had won.

She lifted her chin, exposing her throat. I had to finish it. Already, the magic of her spell plucked at me, tightening like a vice around my bones. The longer I delayed, the worse the pain would become.

I had heard tales, long ago, of drakes who had fought so long and so fiercely without giving up that both of them died.

I chanced glancing at the other dragons. Some seemed impressed that I had won the fight so quickly. Yet by hesitating to go in for the kill, I was losing face. Their disapproval at my reluctance tinged the air around me. It was a grim business to kill for anything but meat.

The Queen met my gaze.

—*Finish it*, she commanded.

Every moment I let Pan live clarified what I had already known, deep down, as soon as I had returned: there was no place left for me here in Vere Celene. My mother was right. I was no longer an Emberclaw, not in any way that mattered.

Or maybe Pan was right. Maybe my time in the human world had made me weak.

The magic tightened. I grunted with the pain of both the power and the wound at my shoulder.

—*I wish there were another way*, I said to Pan. *I wish it had not come to this.*

If only she had not called upon an ancient magic. If only I had not flown off on my own, giving her the opening to challenge me in the first place. Pan's nostrils flared, her mouth open as she panted, pointed teeth glistening. She turned her head enough to meet my stare. There was still so much grief. Most of her had died the same night as Sidar.

—*Send me to her*, Pan said. *Send me to her.*

I could not tell if she regretted what she had done, or if she realized hating me would not bring her mate back. But this, at least, I could give her.

I reared my head, the muscles in my neck tightening.

I struck true.

22.

ARCADY:

A RECKONING

I came to awareness gradually, but I wasn't awake.

I was in the Loc & Key, or a dreamy echo of it. I hadn't been back to the shop in the real world since the night of the Feast of Flowers, when I'd found Larkin had already been there before me and stolen her ammunition for my blackmail.

Still. Something in me ached as I took in the locks along the wall of my old home. How many of those had I taught Everen to crack? There was the pillar where I'd tied him up that first night we met, when we both realized, with dawning horror, that we were connected in both body and magic.

Everen emerged slowly, like a ghost coming to haunt me. He moved stiffly, favoring his preterit shoulder. His wings were hidden away. It was difficult not to flinch. I hadn't caught all of what had just happened to him in Vere Celene, but I had understood enough.

He'd just killed a dragon.

And it'd broken him.

Everen leaned against one of the bare walls. Painfully, he slid down until he was sitting, wrapping his arms around his knees while favoring his shoulder. His red feathered hair fell into his face.

"I suppose we have much to discuss," he said.

"Yes." I was trying to hide my fear of him, but I was sure I'd failed. When I'd first seen him in this not-quite human form, everything about him had screamed 'predator.' When trying to sell the relic at the barrow hill went terribly wrong, he'd arrived as a proper dragon, plucked me in his claws, and carried me to the rip in the Veil. I'd seen him destroy monsters from the storm between worlds. I'd seen him fight his own kind. There had been an efficient savageness to him, both then and in the challenge he'd just finished. I had to remember: even if he could appear human, he was anything but.

"Speak," he said, voice wooden. "Please. I do not know what to say."

The specter of so *much* hung between us. I'd cycled through every possible emotion when it came to him. I'd cried for him, raged at him, longed for him. How would I have felt, if I'd known he was alive this entire time? Where did we even begin to go from here?

Part of me didn't want to believe, but most of me knew, deep down, that this was real. Or as real as dreams could be.

"You're not dead," I said.

"No."

"We broke our bond, though. I broke it."

He nodded, expression wounded. "Yes. You did."

"Then how is this possible?"

He made a helpless movement with his hands. "That is the crux of it, no? The rules of this are unwritten. As far as we know, no other human and dragon ever connected across the Veil like we did as child and hatchling. When I was searching for visions and you were . . ." he trailed off.

"Dying of the Strike. Yes," I said, shortly.

"We stayed bonded without knowing it for years. It seems even our severing could not kill the connection for good. I think the bond has . . . regrown. We cut the plant but did not rip out the root."

I met Everen's green, draconic eyes. He was changed by the last few moons, and by what he'd done that evening. I glanced away first.

"I thought I had lost you," he whispered. "But every night as I fell asleep, I reached for you. I believe you reached back."

I swallowed, hard. The silence between us grew oppressive. I stared at a spot of peeling wallpaper.

"We're both asleep now?"

"Yes."

"Then why—earlier—"

"Strong emotions break through. We are flying in the dark, but that is my best guess." He grimaced. "I cannot . . . I cannot talk about what just happened. Not yet. Anything but that."

I searched his face again. His devastation made it difficult to be as furious at him as I wanted to be. I didn't want to pity him, or to have the urge to kneel and take him in my arms.

"Fine. As long as we don't discuss the last dream." I wasn't above bargaining.

His gaze skimmed along my body and embarrassment curled through me. The barest hint of a smirk at the corner of his mouth was better than that awful blankness, at least.

"As you wish," he said. "What . . . what did I sense this afternoon? Why did you need my help shaping a fire spell?"

"The university has announced a return of the Trials," I said, my voice tight. "A tournament where the students show off their magical skills. I think it's a distraction because one of the Chancellors died, so we're the entertainment while the Citadel figures out what to do next. But if I win, or even nearly win, I'll have my tuition paid."

I plucked one of the locks from the wall. My picks were in their usual place, too. I hopped up on the bar. It was so strange — I knew I was asleep and none of this was real, but the wooden bar was solid beneath my arse, the lock heavy in my hands, and the pick's shapes familiar and reassuring. I placed the lock upside down between my knees and got to work.

I swallowed. "I won't be able to stay long unless I do well at the Trials. If the bond keeps growing back, will it affect my magic?" The lock clicked open with a satisfying sound. "I can't risk that."

"When we were younger it did not, and you still have my stolen power. All I did was help guide you in how to use it."

That was one relief. Everen grew motionless, and I braced myself for whatever he'd say next.

"I am sorry, for what it's worth," he whispered. "For all of it, and how it ended that night."

I snapped the lock shut again too viciously.

"Ask me anything, and I promise to tell the truth," he said.

I scoffed. "Yes. Because you've been an absolute pinnacle of honesty in the past."

I set the lock aside and jumped off the bar. I walked across the room and pulled back the curtains of the shop. Instead of a cobbled street in Vatra, lightning flashed purple, illuminating black storm clouds and the few stars bright enough to shine through. I shivered.

"Are we actually in the Veil?" I whispered.

"I do not know."

I let the curtain drop. "I was doing fine on my own before you fell into it," I leaned against one of the shop pillars. I was still standing while he sat, his face tilted toward me. It helped me feel that bit more powerful to stare down at him.

"Were you?"

"I was fine enough." My breath left my lungs. "I would have found a way to get that claw, somehow. Then you crashed into my life, changing my whole world, and you lied to me. For close two moons, I thought you were on my side, and you tried to take everything from me." I laughed, mirthless. "Now I can't even sleep in peace."

If I opened the trap door in this dream version of the Loc & Key, the back room would be full of soot and all my burned drawings. Everen bowed his head, the shame rising off him in waves, but I wasn't done. I'd bottled this up for too long, and it turned out I had plenty more to say.

"You stole my dreams. Then you stole my magic, and you opened the *sky* with it. I saw dragons and monsters. If they'd broken through, then it would have been my fault, and I'd have been as evil as the whole world thinks the Plaguebringer was." My voice shook and I knocked the back of my head on the pillar in frustration.

"And now you're here, back in my head, and you're looking at me like that, and I don't know what to do or how to feel. I don't." I crossed my arms.

He was silent for a time, choosing his words. "I did not want to take your magic that night. It happened despite my will. And I gave it back, in the end, along with some of mine."

My turn for silence.

"I do not know where we go from here," he said, finally. "I have spent months expecting never to see you again. Tearing myself up for all I had done. All the choices I wish I had made differently. All I want is to make it up to you. All I want is for you not to hate me."

There was that open, wounded expression. *Did* I hate him? If I had, would my sleeping mind miss him so much that it reached through worlds to find him?

When I'd faltered in the trial, he'd offered me help, and I hadn't been too proud to take it. The anger was still there—it'd take more than a dragon staring at me all tortured and sad to chase that away.

But he must have seen something soften in my face, despite myself.

"Truce?" he whispered.

I worried my lip between my teeth. I hooked my arm around the pillar and half hid behind it. "Tell me everything. From the beginning." I kept my voice brisk, walling out any vulnerability. "Leave nothing out. If I catch you lying, I'll swear I'll find a way to throw you out of my dreams."

Everen launched in without hesitation. His lightly accented voice told me about dragons and Vere Celene. The stolen prophecy. His first few days in Vatra, learning what he could of the human world before he found me. He spoke until his voice went hoarse. He told me what his mother the Queen, Miligrist the Seer, and his sister, Cassia, had asked of him. He claimed they had let him find the prophecy, knowing he was so desperate to prove himself that he'd do anything to make it come true.

"Like kill a human," I said.

He looked away, the muscles of his jaw working.

"The night I burned your drawings—I thought you were the one playing me from the beginning. That you knew you had stolen my visions and my destiny and used it to trap me. I thought you would be just as ruthless as the humans who had stolen dragons' magic in the first place."

I leaned back, letting the pillar hide whatever my face might give away.

"By the time I realized I had been wrong, it was too late. I know I frightened you, and I will be ashamed of that as long as I live. After, even."

I slid down the pillar until we were at the same level, reluctantly raising my head to meet his gaze.

"When it came down to it," I said, "you didn't kill me, did you? You couldn't."

"No."

I glanced up at the ceiling of the shop. "What I did was worse, in a way. I said the spell, expecting it'd kill you."

"I asked you to."

"I still did it."

We stared at each other in an impasse.

"I do not know how long we will have. Do you wish to spend it arguing over who is more at fault?" he asked.

That startled me into a laugh, breaking some of the tension.

"What now, then?" I asked. Things weren't all right between us, not even close, but at least I felt I finally knew most of the missing pieces.

"Fate, it seems, has arced forward and tangled us up again." He hesitated. "I have had a few visions in dreams of my own."

"Oh, gods. What now?" I said with a very different inflection. Maybe those dreams I'd had had always been his and I had unknowingly stolen them. I still resented their loss.

"The worlds remain out of balance," he said. "You and I must put it to rights."

I shook my head. "Oh, no. No. I can't be dragged back into dragon nonsense. It came close enough to getting me killed already, and I have my own share of problems. Fuck your fate, Everen."

His expression was rueful. "If you help me, I might be able to help you with the trial. I did already, after all." He cocked his head. "Have you not realized what the Trials truly were?"

"What do you mean?" I asked, dread slithering through me like a snake.

"The Trials are old," he pressed. "Very old. We have records of them here in the library. What do you think the university was for, before the humans betrayed us?"

A tingling ran across my skin. It was so obvious, it was a wonder I hadn't put it together earlier. "To train dragons and riders."

His eyes gleamed in the darkness. "Yes. To prove their magic worked in tandem and they would be able to fight together. The tasks will have changed over the centuries, but having a dragon at your call might prove a distinct advantage, no?"

I swallowed, my throat dry.

"We have to work together once more, but this time we have to trust each other from the beginning."

"I don't know if I can," I whispered.

He stood slowly, as if afraid of startling me, and drifted closer. From his stiffness, I wondered how much the bite at his shoulder pained him. Despite everything, I wanted to step into his arms. I wanted to raise my lips to his and make him earn his forgiveness.

He caught my waver. He always saw too bloody much.

The edges of the lock shop blurred.

"The dream is ending," he said. "Listen: this is important. There is something hiding between the worlds, and it is injured. The wound is infected, and it is restless. If it wakes up, nothing either of us want will matter, for humans and dragons and every living thing will all be dead."

I sucked in a breath.

"Tell me," he said, eyes unblinking. "Did any of your dreams ever involve a dragonstone tree with a serpent twined around its trunk? Or a serpent that sleeps in the gaps of the worlds?"

The ringing in my ears returned. The lock shop was fading, growing transparent. Stars surrounded us, and another bolt of lightning flashed, throwing his features into sharp relief.

"I knew it," Everen said, growing animated. "We cannot ignore this. We tried, and even so, we found our way back to each other. Is it worth fighting the inevitable again, Arcady? There is a way, to mend the dragon and human worlds." His voice grew rougher. "There is a way to mend us, too."

He reached out with his uninjured arm, but the lock shop dissolved around me, taking Everen with it.

I awoke on the floor of my room. My head had narrowly missed the fireplace grate when I'd fallen. I sat up, my muscles protesting. I pulled down my shirt, remembering teeth piercing my—his—scales during the dragon fight, but the skin of my shoulder was unbroken. We weren't bonded enough for that.

Fear still pulsed through me. I crawled across the room and took the thin box from its hiding place behind the wardrobe. Tossing the notebooks on the bed, I grabbed my first dream journal.

I flipped to the sketch of the tree and the symbols that I now recognized as alchemical. Those smudges at the bottom of the tree could be silhouettes of several people, arms upraised as if speaking a spell. The serpent had a dark slash along its side.

Like a wound.

"Fucking fate," I said into the darkness.

23.

EVEREN:

LICKED WOUNDS

I hissed, my claws twitching as Cassia, in preterit form, daubed a poultice on the bite wound at my shoulder.

—*Stop moving*, my sister admonished.

I settled, resting my dragon head on my side and ensuring my wings were pushed out of the way.

—*Were there any wraith attacks last night?* I asked. I had slept deeply and then spent the day hiding from the others, licking my wounds.

—*No, all was quiet.* There had been a lull since Glimmerhail. Perhaps the Veil was healing. I hoped so, but I doubted it. Cassia daubed more medicine onto my scales, her feathered hair covering her face.

—*How are you?* my sister asked. *Truly.*

—*How else could I be other than heartsick? We both knew who would win, but she still forced me to be her executioner.* I had had my fill of people forcing me to do things without my say. My mother had done it. Miligrist. You. Fate. Even Cassia.

She was silent for several heartbeats. —*From another angle, you put her out of her misery. It was a mercy.*

I shifted, wincing as my wounds pulled. —*I killed a dragon, one of my own, in front of all of Vere Celene.*

And you, Arcady, I added privately. You might not have seen it clearly, but you had sensed more than enough. It had been written on your face in the dream of the lock shop. I will have to live with that for the rest of my days.

—*Brother mine,* Cassia breathed. What else could she say?

I hissed at another stab of pain. The bite at my shoulder was in the same place where my mother's wound festered. —*How bad is the Queen's injury?* I asked. *Truly?*

Cassia hesitated. —*She has been giving me more responsibilities. The healers tell me nothing. She sleeps much of the time.* She drew her lips back from her teeth in worry.

—*Is she dying?* I asked.

Cassia toyed with the hem of her lacebark robe. —*I don't know,* she admitted, as if doing so shamed her.

I sat with that, trying to imagine a world without my mother in it.

—*How does she feel about the challenge?* I chanced. The mother who had disowned me had not called me for an audience. I had not expected her to.

—*She was not pleased.* Cassia wiped her hands clean on a scrap of lacebark cloth. *But not for the reason you think. You proved yourself with that fight, in some ways.*

—*It was largely a one-sided fight. And I hesitated, at the end. That made me look weak.* I felt sick. *Killing one of your own does not feel like a triumph. It never will.*

—*No,* Cassia agreed. *But you showed that, even if it hurts you, you do not shy away from what you believe must be done.*

I shifted uneasily. —*What are you saying?*

—*You should be careful,* she said. *Some dragons might follow you, in the right circumstances, especially if they learn you are now the one sifting through fate. Some will hate you more after what happened. Maybe others would challenge you. You, my brother, are divisive. Loved or hated, and nothing in between. In the eyes of our Queen, that makes you dangerous. Mace and Miligrist see it, too. They would put you back down in the dark if they could.*

Her words unsettled me. I stretched, feeling the medicine and the magic in my bones doing their work. The wounds were superficial. By the next morning, my body would feel better, even if the mind would take far longer to heal.

I followed my sister's reasoning. The Queen was physically weakened. The future showed itself to me, not Miligrist, not Cassia.

My mother had ruled for centuries, always promising dragons a return to their true home, and yet she had tried to lead her warriors through and failed. I had gone where she had not, and if the vision from Glimmerhail was to be believed, I would do it once more. If I brought the dragons through properly this time, their hatred of me would vanish in smoke. I would be their chosen one again. Their loyalty would be unshakable.

My sister's expression was somber when she watched me put it together: if I wanted to, I could do more than reclaim my name. I could be the king of dragons.

—*Then you have realized I am dangerous to you, too,* I said. *Even once our mother's time is past, you are her heir.*

—*Indeed,* she said, evenly.

We stared at each other. Even if she had lied to me in service of the Queen and Miligrist, I had always felt that, deep down, we were united.

I wanted to tell her I did not want her crown jewel, but something stopped me. The tiniest corner of my mind wondered if it would be a lie.

I rested my head on my forearms, half-lidding my eyes, unable to read her expression. —*Sometimes, I think our mother regrets not killing me as soon as I broke from my shell. It would have been easier.*

Cassia shook her head. —*No. She fears you, yes, and what you risk. But you are still of her, Everen.* My sister's thoughts were soft. *Even if you emerged male and the subject of so many prophecies. Even if you're at the nexus of all of this. She does love you, despite all of it.*

I tilted my head at her. —*Is love with chains truly love at all?*

She had nothing to say to that.

—*I do not even know if I will be able to return on the Night of Locked Tombs.*

—*You will.* Her thoughts rang with certainty. *Your human will draw you through. And once you are away, our mother's rule will strengthen again. Until you leave, keep your head bowed and stay away from the others. We need risk no more challenges. Scry, hunt, eat, fight wraiths, and sleep. Nothing more. Nothing less. Then go to the human world and do what fate asks of you.*

—*What do . . . what do you think of humans?* I sent my thoughts through to her hesitantly. *Do you hate them, as she does?*

Cassia put away the medicines, settling back on her haunches. She stared off into the distance. It was strange, to see her so small while I was in my larger form. Usually, we were both dragons or both preterit at the same time.

—*No.*

—*Why not?*

She cocked her head. —*I may not see what's to come when I scry, or even what happened in the past, but I see how things* are. *When I'm deep in my visions, it is like I become human. I have spent so much time experiencing their hopes, their dreams, their fears. Their flaws, but also their strength.* She blinked, once. *The more there is understanding, the harder it is to hate.*

She paused. —*I have asked our mother to watch the reflections of the scry silver. She refuses. She clings to the hatred, believing it gives her strength.*

—*Yes,* I agreed. *Yes.* I opened my eyes. *The second dragons are back in the human world, she will turn on me. No matter what she promises, she would*

raze humans to the ground without more than a pause to breathe more fire.
You would not. If you were Queen. You, I think, would try for peace.

—*Stop, Everen. Stop. This is all treason.* She stood, gathering her supplies, her movements jerky.

At the threshold, she hesitated. —*There is still time for her to unlearn her hate*, she said.

—*I would rather you be right than I.*

My sister turned and fled, but I knew my words followed her.

24.
SORIN:

WARD & SWORD

S orin spent the day after the first trial in bed, her stomach roiling with nausea. She struggled to sleep, and when she did, she woke drenched in sweat. She was unable to keep anything but liquids down, so she drank ambrosia, a concoction of ground almonds, milk, honey, and fruit. Her head felt as though needles had been stuck through her temples and in the space between her eyebrows.

When the worst of it passed, it was as if she'd risen after a fever. Though Sorin was weak as a newborn foal, the next morning she shrugged on her robes and tottered to her history class. She focused on the back of Arcady's head throughout the lecture, wondering what they had done the night before and how they'd managed to show such control in the first trial. Magnes had observed Arcady closely in the task. Sorin had felt the power of that stare even from behind His wraithwright mask. Sorin had put her latest written missive in the puzzle box on her chest of drawers but received no summons. Had He learned what He wanted?

"You see," Professor Fullin said, and Sorin tried to drag her attention back to the professor's words, "the trade tensions between Jask
and then-Locmyria were always delicate. Jask would often accuse
Locmyrians of allowing the pirates from the outer edges of the Glass
Isles through their defenses deliberately, letting them attack Jaskian
ships as long as the Locmyrian ones sailed free." They drew lines
along the map of the Lumet pinned to the wall with a long pointer.
"Locmyria, in turn, accused the Jaskians of forcing their ships into
dangerous currents and whirlpools in Jaskian waters. Many Locmyrian ships set sail from Vatra, never to be seen again."

Rahela raised her hand. "Was Jask responsible, or were the currents simply dangerous?"

Professor Fullin shrugged. "Only the sailors at the bottom of the
sea can say for certain. Still, it was an insult, and Locmyria responded
by imposing trade sanctions on certain Jaskian goods like whale-
bone and ambergris. It was a very pointed message: we will raise the
cost of you coming anywhere near our waters. This deliberately led
to the War of 742—the last big war before the Schism. 742 was a
particularly bloody one, and we will focus on it in more detail when
we next meet. Over the next sennight, please read the fifth chapter
in your textbook and continue considering topics for your essay due
before the Spirit Moon break. It'll come upon you faster than you
expect, I promise you this. Dismissed."

Sorin blinked her way back toward wakefulness. Arcady darted
up to the front of the classroom as the other students packed their
things and headed to the Great Hall for the midday meal.

Arcady asked the professor a question Sorin didn't catch, but
the professor shook Their head. "Even I would struggle to obtain
access to those documents, young Dalca," They said. "They're in the
restricted section of government records."

Muscles worked in Arcady's cheek as they clenched their jaw. "Perhaps I could conduct interviews from someone who was there, or testified against Barrow Eremia?"

Sorin's interest sharpened.

The professor sighed. "There's one of you every other year, I'm afraid. The Plaguebringer is a macabre subject, so I understand. Many a student has wanted to dig into that trial. But I ask you to remember that this is very recent history. The Strikes are a sensitive subject for many. Focus on an aspect of the plague, by all means, but I would suggest a topic where you can use established sources. We don't require original research for a first-year paper, even if I appreciate the enthusiasm." They gave Arcady a smile that didn't reach Their eyes.

"Ah. I understand. Thank you, Professor. I'll keep that in mind." Beneath Arcady's easy smile, Sorin sensed gritted teeth.

"Something the matter?" Sorin asked out in the hallway.

"Oh, nothing," Arcady said, striving for lightness. "I'm back to a blank sheet of paper, but I'll find something."

"What was your idea?" Sorin's curiosity was burning.

"Doesn't matter. Professor Fullin was right—way too much work for a first-year paper, and I've enough to be getting on with. My back up choice was Monarch Laen and the final years before the Schism. There are more biographies available in the library on that subject, at least. What will you write about?"

Sorin swallowed. "I haven't given it a second's thought yet." She was idly considering looking into the history of the Order of the Dragons. "May I copy your notes from alchemy? I'm sorry I missed the lab on firstday. I was unwell."

Arcady took her in. "No offense, but you still look pretty unwell. Too much drink again?" Their tone was teasing.

"No."

Arcady raised an eyebrow at Sorin's shortness. They reached into their bag and passed them over. "Here. What are partners for, eh?"

The following triday, the twelve students who would be in the second trial shivered on the grounds of the amphitheater, their breath misting in the air. While they hadn't gathered as early as they did for morning practices, the sun was low in the sky and winter was well on its way.

Armskeeper Hulm was dressed in Their usual battered leathers, Their face as inscrutable as ever. On the benches next to Them, twelve practice swords were neatly lined up, and there was a platter of sweetspheres for whoever needed them. Joining Hulm was Professor Ultred, who taught classes on the "lesser" magic of wards, charms, and spells that weren't generally associated with a specific god. Their willowy tallness and long black hair contrasted against Hulm's sinewy muscle and shorn gray cut.

"Today, I am *honored* to introduce you to the basics of the *second* trial," the professor said. "The date of the second trial will be *just* before the break for the Spirit Moon."

Excited and nervous murmurs broke out among the twelve. It wasn't long to prepare—less than two sennights.

"Now," Professor Ultred continued. "This challenge is *significantly* different from the other two in that it's a *duel*: a blend of magic and fighting prowess, hence why Armskeeper Hulm and I are both here today. Unlike the other two tasks, as you might have suspected, it is not a *solo* challenge. You will fight *in pairs*."

While the students had already suspected it was a duel, this part was a surprise. Sorin's muscles stiffened as the students spoke over each other.

"I know, I *know*," Professor Ultred said, raising Their hands. The professor was certainly fond of speaking with an emphasis on certain words. "This is exactly why it's such an *important* challenge. A mage rarely works *alone*. To banish the red tide this summer, for example, required no less than *ten* mages blessed by different gods. Jari to wither the algae and treat the soil, Kalsh to shift the currents to help flush out the tainted areas, Zama to coax rain but keep away the worst of the storms. Their combined spells were a *careful choreography*."

"Do we get to choose our partners?" Rahela asked, eyeing the others.

"They have been *randomly* assigned," Professor Ultred said, and the students exploded.

"What if one of us does perfectly but the other is absolute dogshite?" Willem demanded. Arcady was equally indignant.

"Then neither of you actually did well enough to progress, did you?" Armskeeper Hulm said, stone-faced. "Because you didn't work as a balanced pair."

"That's not fair," Kala exclaimed.

"And what would I say to that?" Armskeeper Hulm asked.

"That there's no fairness on the battlefield," Kala said, glumly, and Sorin swore Hulm hid a smile at all the students' combined outrage.

Armskeeper Hulm let them carry on before raising Their hands. "You can complain about it all you like, or you can get on with it. You passed the first trial. I thought you'd all be made of sterner stuff than that."

That quieted everyone.

"*That's* more like it," Professor Ultred said. They took a small scroll of paper from Their pocket and read out the names.

Willem was partnered with Lowe Balcil, who had done well in the first trial, so he seemed pleased enough. Rahela was paired up with Edin Vayne, which delighted her. Delin Sanron and Kala Jonrir were paired together. Jordin and Teasel were disappointed to be split up. Teasel was paired with Iona, and Jordin with Cind. Which left . . .

"Sar Arcady Dalca," the professor called out. "And Sorin of the Order of the Dragons."

"What are the odds, eh?" Arcady asked. "First alchemy partners, and now duel partners."

"What are the odds," Sorin echoed, her fingertips tingling. Magnes's influence, rearing its head once again. "Maybe they paired the first years together, even if it's supposed to be random."

Arcady made a contemplative noise. Sorin fought the urge to bite her lip. This was sloppy of Magnes. Too many coincidences and Arcady might begin to suspect.

Armskeeper Hulm clapped. "Settle. We've much to get through before afternoon lectures begin. Now. Some say that wards and charms are little more than hedge magic. They're more generic and don't call upon a magic user's gods-touched ability in the same way."

A few students shifted uncomfortably, as they'd probably thought exactly that.

"I know, I *know*," Professor Ultred said. "Wards are considered rather *basic* spells. But remember: flexible does *not* mean lesser or unimportant. Here at the university, you're already learning how to *best* harness your *innate* magic. The Trials have *always* meant to stretch students' powers in *different* directions and show how you adapt under *pressure*."

The students looked daunted.

"Casting a ward on a building or object is a damn sight easier than casting it over *a person*," They continued. "Much less *two people*. Much less two people where *one* of them is using magic of their own to try and *destroy* their opponent's *ward*."

Sorin's interest sharpened.

"Ooh," Rahela said. "This is battle magic."

Professor Ultred smiled. "*Very* good. Legend has it that ancient mages were strong enough to cast wards over *whole armies*, meaning protected soldiers could sweep through a battle and cut down everyone in their path without the other side having a *chance*. If the other side had a similarly skilled mage, then it was all rather more . . . *dramatic*. Only the stronger magic users survived."

Professor Ultred clapped Their hands. "*One* of you will keep up the boundary and *the other* will penetrate their opponent's. Armskeeper Hulm and I will demonstrate, but we'll need a *volunteer*. Edin Vayne, will you do the honors?"

"Certainly," Edin said, stepping forward smugly. The Armskeeper passed Edin one of the practice swords, and the professor reached out and took Edin's free hand.

"*Vanoté leu ek kasutul leu-al*," the professor said. "It means 'protect myself and my friend.'" Sorin felt the burst of magic. Their seal glowed white, rather than a specific color of a god. The barrier that rose around the two of them was almost invisible, shining iridescent as oil mixed in water where it caught the sunlight. The ward was large enough that both people fit inside comfortably. Professor Ultred dropped Edin's hand.

"*There*, the ward is in place. Armskeeper Hulm, if you please?"

The Armskeeper picked up one of the practice swords.

"*Tis-té tusamkue*," Hulm said. "This translates roughly as 'breathe life to the sword.'" Immediately, Their sword flared purple.

"The sword will simply have some of your *innate power* within it, making it easier to pierce the other side's boundary," Professor Ultred said. "Edin, let's see if you can manage."

"*Tis-té tusamkue*," Edin said, her voice ringing out across the amphitheater. Sure enough, her sword glowed green. They grinned.

"Bravo, you took to it quickly," Armskeeper Hulm said. "Swords up, Edin."

She raised her weapon.

"And we *begin*," Professor Ultred said, Their ward growing stronger.

Armskeeper Hulm struck immediately. Edin reacted just in time, their sword clanging together. Ultred's ward followed Edin's movement, keeping her protected.

The fight was brief and furious. Armskeeper Hulm didn't hold back, and Sorin appreciated the chance to see a master at Their work. Within three moves, Hulm had unarmed Edin, and Professor Ultred kept the ward. While Edin staggered to her feet, Ultred's power flared and the ward thickened.

Hulm stabbed, slashed, and swung. Again. Again. The ward grew weaker each time. Hulm planted Their feet and gave one more stab, and the ward popped like a bubble.

Professor Ultred and Armskeeper Hulm faced each other, breathing hard, before bowing. The students applauded.

"Whichever pair drops the ward *first* loses," Professor Ultred said. "That can happen because either the warder becomes too *weakened* to keep up the spell, or because the attacker's magic *punctures* it. So it's a blend of both the *skill* of the attacker and the *strength* of the defender. It can be elegant and symbiotic when it works *well*, but it can also immediately expose a pair's *weaknesses*. Today, we're only *introducing* you to the spells. Start *weaker*—do not pour too much into it. You need to learn the *foundation*. Too *much* power, and the ward will be unbalanced—and dangerous. Likewise, when you are fighting with swords, though they are dulled, the magic will make them more *hazardous* too. If a ward drops unexpectedly, you can be injured. Take care: we are aiming for no more . . . *mishaps*."

Along with probably every other student, the image of Olwyn's face studded with cooling molten metal flashed in Sorin's mind.

Sorin and Arcady paired off in front of each other.

Sorin had limited experience with wards—most of what she'd learned had been through Magnes's hidden corridors. Luckily, most drakines had never bothered much with protective magic, either—noble families often employed warders rather than casting the spells themselves.

While several performed both spells decently, no one covered themselves in glory.

A few times, the wards dropped without warning and the power of it knocked down the students. Sorin watched Willem land hard on his backside, gasping. Lowe apologized and helped him up.

"Too *much*," Professor Ultred admonished. "Remember: less is *more*."

Sorin found it easier to imbue the metal with magic, and Arcady was better at warding.

"Well, that decides who does what in the trial, doesn't it?" Arcady said, and Sorin nodded. She'd take offensive, and Arcady defensive.

Arcady re-cast their ward, this time pouring magic into it slowly and carefully. "*Vanoté leu ek kasutul al-lei,*" Arcady said. The white transparent boundary surrounded both of them, muffling the sounds and sights of the other students.

Arcady's eyes closed as they concentrated on the spell. Sorin heard a strange buzzing in her ears, and for a moment, her surroundings blinked out.

She's in the forest. It's late in the afternoon, and the heat of summer makes the air close. She feels like she's choking on it as she leans lower over her horse, urging it faster. She's running. Running as fast as she can, like a monster chases her.

Sorin staggered as Arcady dropped their ward. The sounds and sights of the practice grounds rushed back in.

"You all right?" Arcady asked.

"Fine," Sorin said, clearing her throat. "Fine." She shook her head, disturbed by the flash of memory. When had that been? That summer . . . ?

When lunchtime finally arrived, the professor and the Arms-keeper drew the practice to a close. Despite the sweetspheres she'd had between spells, Sorin was starving and couldn't wait to fall upon the food in the Great Hall. One thing was certain: this challenge was even harder than the first trial, and no students, not even the fourth years, would be able to coast easily.

"In a few days' time, we'll have one last practice where we'll put this together and you will try dueling properly, but before and after that time, I highly suggest you come to arms practice every morning for the next two sennights. Do not train your wards with your competition—you'll all have your idiosyncrasies or your weaknesses, and you won't want to expose them."

"The better prepared you are, the better your chances," Professor Ultred said. "You can come to me with questions, but no professor can tutor you privately for fairness. I look forward to seeing how you perform for the second trial, and we both wish you the best of luck."

Professor Ultred paused, and every student heard the unspoken words beneath: *you'll need it.*

25.

EVEREN:

THE DRAGON ARCHIVES

We did not see each other every time we closed our eyes. One night you gawped open-mouthed when you appeared in my world instead of yours. I had spent so much time in the archives that it must have bled into my dreams. The rough-hewn walls rose around us until they were lost in a darkness that turned into the storm-filled sky of the Veil. Gentle mage lamps cast a warm glow. Scrolls were tucked neatly into alcoves carved right into the stone, lined in leather to keep out the damp. Other shelves contained older tomes of tooled leather books and vellum, lacewing bark paper, or parchment pages, many faintly stained with soot from that long-ago fire.

I fought down a smile at your wide-eyed wonder. You were, in a way, the first human to see these archives, even if it was in a dream. You tried to take a scroll off a shelf, but that is where the limits of the dream made themselves known. In the Loc & Key, you knew every lock on the wall and so could pick them up with ease. If I showed you a book I had read, you could touch and open it, but since I did not have a perfect memory, many of the written words were blurred, scribbled nonsense, as they often were in dreams.

"Strange," you muttered, putting it back.

The deeper caves that held the written prophecies remained locked to me. I had only been in them the time I had stolen my sister's key, and only, in the end, because she had let me.

"Tell me what Larkin is asking you to do," I said. "I am missing pieces of it all."

You were running your fingertips along spines, testing which books moved and which did not. You shot me a sideways look, and there was that usual internal battle: whether to share or whether to hoard secrets.

You slid into a chair, backward, tilting it forward so the back rested against the table and the two legs hovered in the air. Miligrist or Cassia would have been appalled. I sat next to you as you told me about Professor Hayden.

"Where do you think the professor's research might be?" I asked.

A shrug, which threatened to unbalance you. "For all I know, They were smart and destroyed it all, and there's nothing for me to find. I'll have to hope Larkin decides not to punish me for that, but she's not exactly known for being merciful where I'm concerned."

I nodded. "Have you found anything regarding my visions?"

You grimaced. "You were right, it seems." You reached into the pocket of your nightgown and took out a notebook. You blinked in surprise. "Huh. That worked. I fell asleep with it, and it came with me." You slid it over. "There. I marked it with the ribbon. This is from when I was ten."

As soon as I saw the soot stains, I recognized it as one of your dream journals. I clenched my jaw, cursing my past self for losing control. Who knows what other answers I might have destroyed in my anger?

I opened the page to a drawing of a tree and a serpent.

I sucked in a breath. "Strange. None of my visions had anything hanging from the branches." My fingertip hovered over the silhouettes at the bottom, and your younger self proclaiming you had not enjoyed the dream. I could not say I'd particularly liked having the vision, either.

Meeting like this and focusing on a task was almost—almost—like slipping back to our earlier dynamic, when we had been focused on stealing the dragon claw. Your body language was closed off, arms wrapped tight around your torso. Since that first dream, you had not touched me, and I had not touched you, much as I wanted to. You reached into your pocket, took out a second book, and pushed it over to me.

"The library didn't show much, but I decided to get creative and look to myths and stories," you said. "I might have found something."

I opened the book to the page with another ribbon.

"The Mage of the World Tree," I read.

You leaned forward. "This mentions a tree with 'roots so deep they connect worlds.'" You pointed to a particular phrase on the page. "The story said you can find the tree where 'veins meet the sharpened teeth at the heart of the truth,' which sounds . . . both vague and gruesome. It's supposedly where wishes can be granted and prayers answered, because the magic is directly bestowed by the gods. You have the usual story of a foolish young person trying to journey to it because they're desperate to live forever. But they phrase their wish without considering the loopholes and end up paying the price—they join the tree and become another piece of fruit on its branch. Forever living but not alive."

You tapped your lips. "I have no idea if it ties into anything, but I thought that was interesting." You flipped to another page near the end of the book. "The Jaskians also have a myth about a serpent so large it could swallow the world. They believe the King is the one who keeps the serpent from their shores, along with other evils like dragon demons and magic. They're both old stories, but I'm not sure how old."

"It sounds like it could be connected, but it does not give us anything specific enough to go on, does it? Anything else?"

Your eyes shifted to the side. "I haven't exactly had much time, what with everything else on my plate." You rubbed your temples. "It's a lot to balance, you know. I have to study longer than everyone else because I'm playing catch up. There's the second trial to prepare for, and it turns out you can't even help me with that one."

I shook my head. "I know." We had discovered that when you warded yourself and your partner, I could barely feel the bond at all. I could help stabilize the spell from afar, perhaps, but little more.

"On top of all that, I'm sneaking about trying to find anything I can about Professor Hayden. I have to break into Their office sooner rather than later. Now *this*. I can't even rest in my dreams because I meet with you. I'm so fucking *tired*." You sounded petulant, but I could not blame you.

"I know. I know it is not easy." I paused, certain I was about to make things harder. "I had a vision when I scried in the silver earlier today. One I have had before, the night of Glimmerhail. The more you have a vision, Miligrist says, the more certain it will come to pass."

"You're looking entirely too serious for my liking," your shoulders hunched.

"Both times, I saw myself flying through the storm, following a golden thread. I heard the same prophecy I stole, the one that references the Night of Locked Tombs. Then I heard you, calling out your grandsire's spell." I hesitated as your eyes grew wider, as you suspected what I would say next.

"If the vision is true, I am meant to come back to the Lumet. On the anniversary of the first time I fell. Once again, you call me through."

You went still. I knew this would raise your hackles. But we were running out of time, and the longer I delayed, the more it felt like the lie of omission it was.

"We have to find a way to heal the serpent together. I was able to pass through because of the bond—because of it, my presence did not disturb the Dreamer." I gestured around to the dragon archives. "Even this—when we dream, we are somehow puncturing the Veil like a vision in scrysilver, but the Dreamer does not seek us."

You were shaking your head slowly. I resisted the urge to grab your shoulders.

"There is a link and a pattern here, Arcady," I said, my voice growing more desperate. "My return. The tree. The serpent. Your grandsire. This Professor Hayden. Your dreams, my visions. More threads we have not even unpicked. It's all interwoven. It's all connected."

You wrapped your arms around yourself and rocked, shaking your head. "Back and forth, and now back again?"

"Like stitching a thread. Fate did say deep sutures make the strongest scars," I whispered.

Your breath caught.

"The longer I stay here in Vere Celene, the more dangerous it is for me." My throat closed. "My mother and sister both see me as a potential threat to their rule. Other dragons could easily challenge me, and if enough of them try, who is to say they can't nudge fate off the path? There is no place for me here. Not any longer. But perhaps there is with you."

You stared at the shelves of scrolls and dusty tomes. I was at risk of losing you. Whenever things became too real, you slithered away, forcing yourself awake.

"Will you help me?" I pleaded. "Would you call me through once more? I cannot do it alone."

Your face closed. "If I brought you through, wouldn't it risk us half-bonding once more?"

"Perhaps," I said. "Probably. If the trust were not there."

"We *know* the trust isn't there, Everen," you said, panic curling around the edges of your words. "It can't be. Not after what we did to each other. We're talking, like this, and we have our truce, but we can't pretend things are fixed."

"I have seen to the truth of you," I said. "I will not make the mistake of doubting you again."

You closed your eyes. "Wake up," you whispered. "Wake up."

"Arcady." My hand went to yours, and I felt another spark of gold magic. Your eyes opened wide. I shifted closer, until we were barely a breath apart. You searched my face.

I brushed the backs of the fingers of my other hand along your cheek. "Does even part of you want me back?" I whispered.

"No," you said, drawing your palm away from mine, but we both heard the obvious lie. I let my hand fall.

"I can't," you said. "If my magic is affected, I'll never have even a hope of winning the Trials. Any training you could offer me is useless if I don't have the raw power. Maybe after they're finished, but before . . . ?"

"If we managed to fully bond, then by contrast you would have *more* access to my magic. The dragon riders and dragons of old were symbiotic. You would be more powerful than any of the other students, you would even live longer than any human. You could very well be unstoppable."

You bowed your head, but I caught the flash of greed and longing.

"See?" I asked. "You are tempted." My fingertips traced the line of your jaw. You swallowed.

You blinked, and the dream snapped back into focus. "Wait. Wait. Did you . . . did you just say I'd live longer than any human?"

I paused. "I thought you had read enough of the old tales? The dragon-partnered mages lived for centuries."

"I thought that only a story." There was the stiffness in your muscles, the wide-eyed disbelief. "You . . . you're saying I'd be immortal?"

I opened my mouth, my throat making a clicking sound. "No," I managed. "Not immortal. But yes, you might live a long time. It might already have started, I do not know. We were bonded, briefly, after all, and you still have some of my magic within you. If we re-bonded properly, you certainly would live a very long time. A dragon sacrifices some of their own life to give the human more time."

You opened your mouth, your lips shaking. "Then why did those mages betray dragons, then, if your kind was oh so generous?"

I shook my head. "Because the humans wanted more than symbiosis, I suspect. They wanted dominance."

You licked your lips.

"What if I'm too hungry, Everen? You trust me, but do I trust myself?" You swallowed. "Every time we touched, I took your magic. And I *wanted* it."

"This time, it would be freely given," I said.

"Why would I believe this is anything other than more manipulation? I don't know what to think. I never do when it comes to you." You exhaled. "I have to think. Wake up." You raised your voice on the last two words.

"Please," I said as the dream began to fade around us once more. "Please simply consider it. The Night of Locked Tombs is after the second trial."

"Wake up. *Wake up.*" Your eyes squeezed shut as you chanted the two words over and over. The archive dissolved into sparkling dust, leaving us suspended in the Veil.

"Please let me find my way back to you, Arcady," were my last words to you before I woke up alone in the dark.

26.

ARCADY:

THE NIGHT MARKET

As the second trial grew closer, I tried to balance my new life. Sweaty practice in the mornings, meals at the Citadel, lectures, and alchemy lab. Long afternoons in the library, surrounded by the smell of old paper. I'd often study with Rahela, Willem, and Damon. Or, rather, Rahela, Damon, and I studied, sometimes speaking to each other in Trade so we didn't disrupt the other students, and Willem napped on one of the sofas with a book over his face to block out the light.

A few evenings a sennight, Sorin and I would meet in an abandoned classroom in an out-of-the-way corner of the university building, pushing the desks and chairs out of the way to give us enough room. I doubted another student had stepped foot in it in decades.

I could keep the ward up decently but dropped it at the slightest distraction. Sorin would also act strange the longer I held the spell, sometimes staring off into space so blankly, I'd have to clap to bring her back.

"Where did you go?" I'd ask.

She shook her head. "Nowhere." She'd refocus but remained contemplative. She glowered at me less, though, over the past few sennights. While I wouldn't call us friends, I'd maybe say we'd graduated to acquaintances. I was glad, in the end, she'd be my partner for the second task over any of the other students. She was disturbingly good with a sword. All I'd have to do was keep the ward up long enough for Sorin to break her way through our opponent's defenses, and we had a chance at winning.

But on the night of the new moon, a few days before the second trial, I snuck out of my new life and back into my old one.

I'd found a note in my pocket—I don't know when Wren had put it there or how I hadn't noticed. A three-word reminder: *The Night Market.*

I'd balled up the note and thrown it into my dormitory fire.

The Night Market always took place in one of the seedier parts of town, often not far from the docks. At first glance, it seemed like a regular market. But look a little closer, and some of the wares would make anyone blanch.

I hadn't been to the Night Market since I'd bought the illustration of Girazin's dragon claw that had set everything in motion. Even a thief didn't want to spend more time there than necessary.

Night was thick on the streets of Vatra, and it felt like coming home. I drew my cloak tighter around myself, but my lips curled up in a smile. I knew these smells. I knew every twisted wynd of this city. It was comforting to have tall tenements rising on either side of me, half of the windows a warm, candlelit yellow. Cats trotted along the tops of walls to patrol their territory. Dogs rustled through alleyways searching for food, and rats scuttled along gutters.

This new moon, the Night Market was tucked into a courtyard in a tenement that had been largely abandoned both due to the Strike and damage to the foundations. The boarded-up doors and windows still had the remnants of the red crosses on them. Even years later, they made me shiver. Sharp-eyed people in large cloaks looked me up and down at the entrance, but they let me through.

The stalls were squashed together like drinkers in a too-crowded tavern, and the air was thick with the smell of incense. I spotted a stall run by a petite keeper with graying red hair in a long braid dotted with crystals. A bead dangled from the tip of their goatee. Rocks and crystals of all colors, shapes, and sizes glimmered beneath mage lights. Labradorite seemed like gold, green, or gray auroras trapped in cracked stone. Black tourmaline. Jade, carnelian, and citrine. Others were for protection: glassy obsidian, ruby. The stall keeper's seal glowed with silver magic, protecting their wares from theft and probably making the stones themselves glimmer brighter.

There were plenty of stalls with weapons. Some were in the Jaskian style, and others Myrian. For any weapon bought officially, you had to seal-sign for it, and the Citadel might have a record. But not here.

While the Struck were rare in the city, there were enough at the Night Market that even someone as marked as Wren wouldn't attract too much attention. So many of the Struck scraped together their coins and bought the various tinctures and potions that claimed to heal their marks. They always came away disappointed.

I grimaced at a stall that sold vials of animal or human blood. Some drank blood in the belief it'd keep them safe from the effects of too much magic and save them from turning Starveling. A few months ago, I might have said that was poppycock, too, but Everen and I accidentally swapping blood had cemented the bond. Even though these shopkeepers were charlatans, maybe there was some truth in it.

A pinch at my shoulder, and Wren was at my side.

"Thought you might have your own stall if you asked to meet here," I signed at him in greeting, but he shook his head.

"I met a buyer, but I still sell things in the shadows. I'd never be so obvious as to have a stall." He took a false dragon eye out of his pocket, made of glass, and passed it to me. It fit in the center of my palm, just bigger than a marble. The iris was orange, the pupil a black cat's eye. It even had an upper and lower lid of gray skin made out of some sort of clay and eyelashes of black feathers. It was so realistic I half-expected it to blink.

"It's gorgeous, Wren. Unnerving, but gorgeous."

"Keep it," Wren signed, making a shooing motion with his hands when I tried to pass it back. "It's a gift."

"That's kind of my blackmailer to give me a present, I suppose," I said, tucking the glass eye into my pocket.

We paused in an out-of-the-way corner of the market. "What have you found?" he asked, keeping his hand movements small and low.

I sighed. "I did manage to break into the professor's university laboratory a few days ago," I said. I'd gone during dinner when I knew Professor Hayden was in the Great Hall, but I'd been shaking as I broke the wards and manually picked the lock. If I had been caught, that would have been that.

I'd gone through everything quickly but methodically. There were experiments in various stages on the table in the corner. I'd read the spines of Their books on the shelf, flipping through most of them in search of hidden papers. I'd spent longest on Their files in an old cabinet of curiosities. It'd taken ages, but Larkin hadn't given me much to go on.

"I didn't find anything," I said. "Is Larkin even sure her source is good? The professor's current research is on alchemical symbolism and such. Nothing on the Strike, the Struck, or any Elixir. Are you sure they're not just filling her head with fairy stories?"

"She says the source is sound and that it's real."

I glanced at the people milling between the stalls. I caught the scent of Pollen even before I saw a middle-aged merchant couple buy a bottle of the pungent drug preserved in oil. I'd smelled it at places like Cinders. Pollen had ruined the fortunes of many a drakine or well-to-do merchant. It gave euphoria, but the effects faded faster after each dose, meaning you were always chasing that first high. Larkin had always told the Marricks if she ever caught us with the flower from Myria, she'd kick us out on our arse quicker than we could blink.

I shook my head. "What if there's nothing for me to find?"

Wren rubbed his lips. "There will be," he signed, insistent. "And it's still early enough in the year. You're friends with Their child, aren't you?"

"I've tried," I signed back. "All Willem has said about his maire's research is that 'it's very dull.'" I breathed out, hard. "Look, I'll keep searching, but I need you to work on staying Larkin's hand."

He nodded. "I'll do what I can." He hesitated. "If things do sour, I want you to know that Driscoll has stayed behind with me. I've got a fair amount saved up for passage. We're thinking of heading to the Trader side of the Glass Isles one of these days. It's a warmer climate. After this is all finished, one way or another, you could join us. If you wanted."

I smiled sadly at him. "I'm not sure Driscoll would love me tagging along." The youngest member of the Marricks had had . . . choice words for me after I'd stolen from Larkin and fucked off, I'd heard. "You're always trying to invite me back where I'm not truly wanted, Wren. I think I'm stuck in Loc for a while yet. Focus on your own plans. When should I next check in?"

Wren shrugged. "Whenever you find something. Leave a note with a drawing of a wren in it at the brewery. There's a loose brick on the left-hand side of the door when you come in, near the bottom. If you don't leave a message within a moon, I'll come find you."

"Fine. I'd better go. Take care of yourself, all right?"

"I will." He tapped me on the shoulder. "I haven't told you I'm proud of you yet, have I? Heard you did well in the first trial. You've always wanted this. Try to enjoy it."

"It'd be a damn sight easier with no blackmail."

"I know. I'm sorry for it, for what it's worth."

We clasped hands, and then I made my way back through the Night Market and all its dangerous wares, making my way back up the hill, where I shrugged off that old life and put my new one back on, wondering how long I'd be able to wear it.

27.

SORIN:

PAST MIDNIGHT

W hen the candle at her bedside burst into red flames, fear spiked Sorin wide awake.

She had dutifully written her detailed missives every other day and hidden them in the puzzle box in her room. A few nights ago, Willem had invited his friends out to drink at the tavern, but something about the way Arcady declined had snagged at Sorin's instincts. Her gut had proven correct when, later that evening, she had caught Arcady slipping out of the Citadel.

Sorin had followed Arcady to the Night Market and watched from the shadows as they met with someone Struck. She'd kept her hood up and lingered near a crystal stall, following most of their hidden conversation in Trade.

Sorin had learned that Larkin Nash was blackmailing Arcady into spying on Professor Hayden's early research.

She'd left it out of her update. It wasn't the first time she'd lied by omission, but this was the largest so far. She hadn't mentioned leaving the Citadel at all. She could have sworn no one trailed her that night to the market, but what if He knew anyway?

Even as the fear pulsed through her, her heart leaped for another reason. Part of her waited desperately for his call.

For she had nearly run out of Elixir.

Sorin had taken a dose before Professor Ultred and Armskeeper Hulm introduced the second task, and more sips before she'd practiced wards and swords with Arcady.

She tilted the near-empty vial above her tongue, shaking out the dregs of the potion. A sigh shuddered through her as the warmth hit her veins. Even knowing how much her mood would ebb afterward, she wanted the focus, the power, the confidence to believe she could do whatever she wanted.

Including hide things from Magnes.

Every time she practiced warding with Arcady, she had more flashes from the forest.

She was always running in them, always terrified someone or something was chasing her. Jaculus would cry above her, encouraging her to go faster. The images were disjointed. She couldn't remember what happened before, or after, but she knew they were real.

And that Magnes had made her forget them.

She didn't know why, or how many times. She had seen Him use forbidden mind magic before. When He had interrogated the siren at the brothel, He'd asked Mirel about a winged god, then made her forget what she had seen. He'd needed to touch her with his bare skin to work His magic, so Sorin suspected she was safe from His influence only as long as He didn't lay His hands on her.

She couldn't ignore his summons, so she pulled on her robe, took up her candle, and entered the corridor. She didn't meet him in the library any longer.

When she entered the hidden laboratory, she noticed immediately what was missing. The great dragon's skull and the rest of its carefully harvested body parts were gone.

Magnes watched her closely. The ampule on the table next to him bubbled on its burner, sending out that metallic, sickly-sweet scent that made Sorin's head spin. Another few vials lay next to it, filled to the brim with Elixir, and her eyes fixed on them.

"Sorin, my child," Magnes greeted her.

"Your All-Holy Eminence," she said, inclining her head. She felt her heartbeat even in her palms. Her eyes kept returning to the vial.

"I am sorry I have not been able to call you as often as I should," He said, and her head rose in surprise at the apology. "It has been . . . a busy time. This is the tensest relations have been with Jask since the last days of Monarch Laen."

He had lost weight, and the faint lines around His mouth were deeper.

Of course, with Yrsa gone, most of the running of Loc fell to Him. He was the head of the country in all but name. Of the Chancellors left behind, one had lost most of Their memory and the other was addled by drug and drink. Plenty of Loc suspected it, though none spoke of it openly. Magnes was holding the country together in His palms, and the weight must be heavy.

"Sometimes I miss her power," he said. "How very formidable she was. How at one point, it seemed no one would ever question it."

Sorin's brows drew down as she stepped forward and picked up one of the vials, resisting the urge to clutch it to her chest. "You were at court before the Schism? You knew Monarch Laen?"

His head rose, His eyes clearing. "I speak of Chancellor Yrsa of Swiftsea," He said, but Sorin was not sure she believed Him.

"The Elixir has worked well for you so far, has it not?" His tone was brisk.

She nodded, knowing better than to press Him.

"Use your words, Sorin, since you were so determined to give up your Vow to get them back."

She coughed. "Yes, it has worked well. But I've run out." Her latest dose was taking stronger hold, and she welcomed that beautiful, slow surge of happiness and peace. This. This is what she had once thought faith would bring her.

"Go slow with it, Sorin," He warned.

"I will." Sorin also now knew why He'd warned her. She'd caught the same sickly smell at one of the stalls in the Night Market: Pollen.

"You see, though, why it's something we must keep secret."

"Yes." She would also keep to herself that she'd realized that Elixir was almost certainly what Arcady had broken into Professor Hayden's office to find for Larkin Nash.

"It's a boon I choose to share with those worthy of it."

Once, those words would have made her heart sing. She clutched the vial tighter. "Thank you for your faith in me," she forced herself to whisper.

He smiled, though His eyes stayed tired, and adjusted the heat below the ampule.

"Have you decided who might become Yrsa's successor?" she asked, the drug making her bolder. His body language was open, and she didn't sense any anger. The fear in her uncoiled, just barely. "If you had another to help, perhaps the burden would be less."

He heaved a sigh. "It's more I know who I don't want it to be. I learned too well how dangerous it can be to align yourself with someone who drinks down power only to become addicted to the bottle. Someone who hurts for the joy of causing pain." His gaze went distant, and Sorin shivered. Yet again, she suspected He was not speaking of Yrsa of Swiftsea. Who, then?

He shook himself. "The Balcil family is proving particularly power-hungry, and while there are a few strong magic users in other families, I wouldn't trust them as far as I could throw them. Same with the Easel or the Sanron families. Perhaps someone from the Rhium line?" He paused, tapping His lip. "Never mind. We have some time yet, and much to do before I decide." He turned His full gaze upon her, and she did her best to meet His orange-brown eyes without quaking.

He took off His glove, holding up His bare hand. "Come, Sorin."

Sorin had hoped the reports were detailed enough that He would not actually check within her mind. Instead of praying in the mornings, she now meditated, sorting through her memories, burying what she didn't want Him to see. She had managed once, but would her luck hold a second time? And if it didn't. . . what would He do to her?

He sensed her hesitation and crooked His finger. "I'll be gentle." One corner of His mouth quirked.

She pressed her fingernails hard into the soft palm of her hand and stepped up to Him. If she did this, He would not touch her until after the second trial, and she would walk out of here tonight with more Elixir.

She closed her eyes, feeling the light touch of His fingertips on her cheek before He took her chin in His grasp. In the next blink, there He was, dripping through her mind like oil. Everything He touched, He might stain.

Memories rose around them like ghosts. *Arcady with a line between their brows as they added a few drops of sulfur to a beaker in alchemy class. The same look of concentration when they practiced holding the wards in an old, abandoned classroom.* The threading together of memories wasn't so different from keeping up a ward, Sorin had discovered, and practicing for the second trial might have also helped her here. Sorin felt like she was being peeled open like an orange, trying to keep the seeds of so many secrets hidden from Him deep within her flesh.

Arcady bent over a bowl of water in Kalsh's class. Their seal glowed a subtle blue, but Sorin thought she caught a flash of another color—gold? Red?

Magnes paused here. Sorin's neck was still craned upward, chest open, hands balled into fists at her sides. She shook from head to toe with the effort of keeping herself together. Magnes smiled in triumph, letting go of her chin.

She fell to her knees, gasping, as the stitched memories around her collapsed into dust.

"It's as I thought," He said, more to Himself than to her. "Just as I thought."

She stared up at Him, one hand on her chest, the purple glow of her seal slowly fading. The Elixir protected her from magic's hunger, but she felt hollow.

The vial was nestled in her palm, and the sight of the silver liquid gave her comfort.

"Keep taking your medicine," He said. "Especially whenever you're doing magic around the interloper."

How much Pollen is in this? she wanted to ask. *How long until I can't turn back from the need for it, and what happens when you stop giving it to me?*

"You've done well," He said, and His thoughts were clearly somewhere else. "No need for further practice this night. Head back to bed, my child."

"You should rest, too," she risked.

"I should." He turned from her, fiddling with one of the flames beneath the burners. "But not just yet."

She was dismissed.

She scurried back through the corridors, the three vials of Elixir burning a hole in her pocket. It was only once she was back in the privacy of her room that she let herself go boneless with relief.

She had one more tool in her arsenal. Perhaps the person whose mind Magnes couldn't read might know how to keep hers safe.

28.

ARCADY:

THE GOLDEN TREE

The next few nights slipped past in a blur of study, practice, classes, and more study. At night, Everen and I met in that strange in-between. I still tied my wrist to the bedpost to stop my sleepwalking.

It was strange to feel like I was racing, even though most of the time I was furiously hunched over a desk, my fingertips stained with ink. When I could spare the time, I searched the library for anything about the crystal tree, or Professor Hayden, or any of my various problems.

For history class, I had indeed decided to write about Monarch Laen, since there was much more information about them available. I narrowed my focus to the last few years before the Schism and what factors led to the violent coup. It did turn up an unexpected reference to my grandsire that had slipped through the censorship cracks: Monarch Laen's last consort, Consort Genat Lant, had evidently thought highly of Barrow Eremia and said "the advisor's approach to magic and developing new spells was revolutionary." I couldn't find out what had happened to that consort after the Schism. They had simply disappeared.

Alchemy remained my most difficult course, but I enjoyed it the most, despite the challenge of the material and my increasingly complicated emotions about my instructor. Professor Hayden was encouraging and explained things well, but gently called us out if They suspected us of cutting corners. This made it hard to hate Them enough to even drop the honorific for Them in my mind.

There was something about the blend of magic and science of alchemy that deeply appealed to me. How, if any one step was out of balance, the whole experiment would be ruined. It was like baking rather than cooking, which was amusing, considering the few times I'd tried to bake something for Kelwyn, I'd always burned it. I hadn't found time to visit him since the morning of the first trial, and I found I missed him. I'd have to sneak away to see him—and his pastries—sometime soon. He'd probably have sold that silver bracelet by now, and I wouldn't say no to the coins.

The lesson of our last alchemy class before the second trial was tricky. Granted, they were never easy. Our first attempt to transmute lead into gold a few sennights earlier had, of course, roundly failed. No one in the class had managed the barest shift in color from dark gray to gold. This was a class designed for non-Aura mages, after all, so we were all at a disadvantage.

"I won't lie to you," the professor said, one hand resting absent-mindedly on Their stomach. "Most of you will never manage it, even if you were to focus on it with single-minded determination. It is an exceedingly difficult magic, even for those chosen by Aura."

"So why bother?" Vilm asked.

"Because it wouldn't mean it was wasted effort. Of course, you could see it as always failing, or a complete waste of time, or impossible. But you could also see it as always striving. Someone once said to me: if it weren't impossible, how might it be done? And I still attempt to live by that."

I clutched the edge of the black stone table with slick palms.

Part of me had wondered if Wren and Larkin's belief that Hayden and Barrow Eremia had worked together was nothing more than a rumor. When I'd been a frustrated brat as a child, crying that something was too difficult, how many times had my grandsire said those very words to me? *And if it weren't impossible, how might it be done?* The professor had even used the exact same inflection.

Any last doubts evaporated like steam.

"That's the way of the alchemist," Professor Hayden continued. "To be undeterred when the experiment fails and see what needs shifting or tweaking and test it once more. To always wonder if what's broken can be fixed. That's how you make advances, both in magic and in life."

Why did you testify against him, Professor Hayden? I wanted to ask. *What did you both work on, and why did only he take the fall?*

Professor Hayden had laid out our next experiment. I forced myself to focus on the task at hand, even as my stomach twisted.

Sorin and I both frowned in confusion as we opened the box to reveal a pile of dried seaweed, a beaker of distilled water, and a lump of lead. There was a beaker of some type of vinegar and another that smelled like bleach. We had a written list of instructions in the professor's tidy hand, duplicated with magic.

Sorin and I set up the equipment and began cooking down the seaweed to a fine ash. Some of the students struggled to light fire with Aura's magic. If neither of the pair could, Professor Hayden did the honors, but it didn't bode well for their success in the class.

The air of the lab soon filled with the scent of salted smoke. When the seaweed was completely charred, Sorin carefully mixed it with distilled water, swirling it to dissolve the compounds. I shaved small strips of the lead and combined them with each solution before setting the seaweed and the solutions on the burners to cook.

Doing the steps with the aid of magical fire meant it all went quicker than it would otherwise. The liquids turned murky, one shifting a lighter gray than the other.

"What do you think this'll actually do?" I asked Sorin, who shrugged. She stuck the tip of her tongue between her teeth as she concentrated. Quite a few students were sweet on Sorin, with her muscles and stoic silence, but the acolyte remained woefully oblivious, which I found amusing.

Across the room, a cry of dismay and a plume of acrid black smoke announced someone had taken a wrong turn.

I peered at our liquid. So far, so good. The seaweed ash came off the heat first. The lead compound had turned muddy.

"Hmm. Did I cook it too long?" I fretted.

"Contaminants in the vinegar, maybe," Sorin said. "Dissolve it in the water and see."

I did as she bade, filtered it again, and it looked more like the instructions said it should.

The moment of truth: I mixed more of the bleach and vinegar and put it in the concentrated solution. When the water turned a deep yellow-orange, I held it up in triumph.

"Good, yes, like that!" Professor Hayden said as They passed, patting me on the shoulder, and I hated how I still wanted to bask in Their praise.

"It's iodine," Sorin said, quietly smug. "We made iodine from seaweed."

"You know, I heard a rumor about you," I said to Sorin as we waited for the lead solution to precipitate, my tone carefully conversational.

"Did you now?" Sorin said, guarded, eyes on the gently bubbling liquid.

"Is it true you took a Vow of Silence for years?"

Sorin's brown eyes cut to mine. "Who told you that?"

"Gemiean," I said. "Said you never faltered, not even when you broke your collarbone at practice. Not a peep." I shook my head in amazement. "I'm not sure I could go even one day without saying a word."

Sorin shrugged. "It wasn't that difficult. I was allowed to use Trade to communicate something essential, and I could whisper the words for spells since that was in service to the gods. It was basically that I didn't communicate anything personal. Soon enough, though, I learned no one had much to say to me at all, and I had little to say back."

I thought that sounded lonely. "How long was your Vow?"

She chewed her lip. "Six years, eight moons, and five days." But her eyes went down and to the side. She was lying about something. I tucked that away.

"Almost there," I said, nodding to the solution. "Just mix together, heat, and see if it's worked." I squinted. "The instructions simply say, 'you'll know if it has.' That sounds ominous."

Sorin did the honors, and when the iodine hit the lead, it turned a brilliant, impossible yellow. I used my magic to gently heat the beaker.

"What made you decide to break the Vow?" I asked, carefully watching the color of the bubbling liquid.

Sorin was quiet for so long, I wasn't sure if she'd answer.

She squinted at the solution as it began to clear. "I decided the gods likely did not want or need my silence. And that maybe I had something to say, after all."

There was something fragile underneath her shielded expression. Wren had said Struck recognized Struck, but I'd learned that broken also recognizes broken.

We took the liquid off the heat. The solution gradually cleared, golden flecks falling through it like snow. The glitter was mesmerizing.

"It's beautiful," I whispered.

"Hey! After your speech, we didn't transmute lead to gold, did we?" a student asked.

"I'm afraid not," Professor Hayden said with a small smile. "This is simply the laws of nature being nearly as magical."

Several other students around had made the same solution, but it'd gone wrong for about half of the class along the way. Sorin and I leaned closer, our heads nearly touching as we watched the golden flecks fall.

"Now, keep watching," Professor Hayden said.

Gradually, the gold flecks coalesced into a shape.

"No one knows exactly why this happens," Professor Hayden said. They leaned forward, the seal hanging from the chain around Their neck swinging forward. "But it's a common phenomenon with alchemical experiments made with magical fire. Maybe it's simply a bit of beauty to be enjoyed. My suspicion is that it's because magic always comes back to nature. Nature loves to be in balance. It always yearns to grow."

The flecks had become a golden tree with a solid trunk of twisted threads. As we watched, it sprouted branches of filaments. In a corner of my mind, a dragon caught hold of my emotion, wondering what it was. My fingertips tingled. It wasn't difficult to imagine a hidden tree just like this, made of crystal and full of magic.

—*Everything is connected.* I didn't realize I'd sent the thought out into the ether.

—*Yes*, Everen breathed back from across the Veil.

29.

ARCADY:

THE SECOND TRIAL

At first, the second trial seemed ages away, and then, in a blink, the morning of it dawned. Sorin and I had practiced every evening the last sennight, and each night, my dreams with Everen left me with more questions than answers.

The students competing in the trial clustered together in the Great Hall, loading up on as much food as we could. I managed a good ten slices of bacon, chewing them with the single-minded determination of an athlete about to race a long distance. Iona, Jordin, and Teasel were quiet and grim. Rahela and Willem appeared far more relaxed than I was, and Edin was quietly confident. Cind's constantly bouncing leg beneath the table fed my own anxiety.

We headed out to the amphitheater. In an echo of the first trial, the stands were once more full of drakines, merchants, and the tradespeople or servants who had scrimped and saved to buy a ticket in the cheaper seats at the back. People spoke animatedly to each other, and I wondered what the odds were on me this time.

The sky was clear, without even a cloud in the sky, but it was cold enough our breath was visible, as if we were dragons. I crossed my arms over my chest, shifting my weight from foot to foot to help keep warm. Sorin's lips were pressed into a thin line, and she played with the leather-wrapped hilt of her sword. She was different since breakfast—full of energy, but calmer. In control.

"We can do this," I said. "We've practiced, we have the skills and the power."

"All we must do is not fail," Sorin said.

"Is that all?" My lips twisted.

Her eyes roved over the crowd as if she were searching for someone. Did Sorin even have friends outside the Citadel? Kelwyn was sitting in nearly the same seat, and something in me loosened at the sight of him. I was less comforted when I spied Driscoll further up in the stands. All set to report back to Larkin, I supposed. Wren wouldn't have been allowed in with his marble seal. I swallowed at that, resisting the urge to rub my collarbone, as if I could erase the Struck marks beneath my shirt.

This time, I was here early enough to see the pre-trial entertainment. Instead of a wyvern race, it was a dance troupe from Myria. Their movements were hypnotizing as they rolled hips and shoulders in time to the flute and cymbal music, scarves fluttering in the breeze. I let myself fall under their spell as they danced, trying to drive away all my nerves about what I was about to face. Across the Veil, a dragon was there, ready, waiting. He'd given me some advice, but this time, I had to rely on myself and Sorin.

When the last note of the music faded, I was forced back to reality.

The same Herald came out into the amphitheater, holding out their arms as silence fell. The eleven other students and I fidgeted, aware of the eyes of the crowd on us.

"We are delighted to begin the second task here at the Citadel for the revival of the illustrious Trials," the Herald said. "Our luminous students of the University of Vatra are the stars of the future. Through Their talent, diligence, and hard work, They will demonstrate Their magic for us today.

"For this second trial, our students must work in pairs. One will defend their team with a ward, and the other will attack the opposing team with a magic-imbued sword. Those who show this mastery over others will progress.

"We will have three pairs against three pairs, and all will begin at the same time." The announcer took a sheaf of paper from their pocket. "Rahela Easel and Edin Vayne will fight Willem Ansel and Lowe Balcil."

I bit my lip as I watched the four students reach out and shake hands with each other before stepping onto their spots, which were marked with chalk. Professor Ultred and Armskeeper Hulm gave us our last bit of advice the day before, which pretty much boiled down to what Sorin had said: *don't fail.*

Edin and Willem wore the swords, and Rahela and Lowe would be the warders.

"Arcady Dalca and Sorin of the Order of Dragons will pair against Delin Sanron and Kala Jonrir."

"Here we go," I muttered as Sorin and I stepped forward. My nerves must have traveled through the bond, because I felt a rush of reassurance from Everen that I tried to ignore.

I shook Delin's hand, then Kala's. They were both clearly delighted that they were battling the poorly bred drakine and the penniless priest. My resolve strengthened. Sorin gave me a small nod before tightening her grip on the sword hilt, staring down Kala. Denlin had done well enough on the wards in practice that I knew I'd have my work cut out for me.

"Lastly, we have Iona Lyn and Teasel Miti against Jordin Miti and Cind Melody."

The last group shook hands and stood on their marks. Jordin and Teasel had the swords—it would be sibling fighting sibling.

We were spread out enough to have space and to give the crowd the best view. I felt their eyes on me and the skin on the back of my neck prickled.

"May you be lifted upon the dragon gods' wings and prove your might," the Herald lowered their upraised arms, and with a roar of the crowd, we began.

"*Vanoté leu ek kasutul leu-al*," I said, and the spell leaped to my call.

"*Tis-té tusamkue*," Sorin said, and her sword glowed green.

I kept the ward close to Sorin as it required less energy. I was relying on Sorin's skills with a blade to help break the other team's spell faster.

With the ward up at full strength, I could barely feel Everen and his bond. If I was going to progress, it was down to me and Sorin. A different sort of partnership.

Sorin darted forward, her green sword meeting Kala's glowing silver one with a loud clang. Delin's and my wards grew brighter, white sparks flying off their weapons. Delin and I hung back out of harm's way. Already, I grimaced with effort. My seal flared, magic pouring into the spell. I had to keep it flexible enough to move with Sorin, but strong enough not to break.

The sounds of metal on magic filled the air. I couldn't spare a glance at the other pairs, but I was sure all the students clashed just as viciously.

Sorin and Kala circled each other, searching for weaknesses, the boundaries bulging and retreating, twisting and untwisting. If the wards tangled, it made them weaker.

Sorin made a parry, and Kala blocked it. Out of the corner of my eye and through the swirling colors of the spell, I barely caught Edin and Willem battling. Willem's movements were almost lazy as his red sword blocked every swing of Edin's red sword. I couldn't spot the last pair. Were they still fighting, or had one duel already ended?

Focus. Focus.

I fed my ward a steady stream of power. While Everen couldn't help me as directly as in the last trial, the extra store of magic I'd stolen on the Feast of Flowers was a boon. It mixed with my Kalsh magic, though the ward remained the opalescent colors of oil mixed with water.

I felt sweat at my temples and the small of my back, as if I were swinging the sword right alongside Sorin. This task felt, in a way, like a bond. With the ward around us, I could anticipate what she'd do next. Her magic burned brighter than when we'd practiced on our own. I fed my ward more magic as we worked in tandem.

Come on, I urged silently. *Find an opening.*

As if Sorin could hear me, she renewed her efforts. Her sword moved so quickly it blurred. My wards trailed her like the Myrian dancers' scarves.

There. Kala staggered back, nearly losing his footing, leaving Delin's ward undefended.

"Now!" I said aloud. I could barely hear the roar of the crowd. Everything was muffled within the barrier. I heard the rasping of our breath and the scrape of our boots against stone. I smelled our magic, a mixture of sea salt and the green of plants, with the barest hint of smoke and fire.

But Sorin, instead of rushing forward, stiffened and fell to her knees.

"Sorin!" I cried, but she didn't seem to hear me. Kala charged forward, and the ward thickened as I pured in more magic. It held, barely, but I was almost drained. If Sorin didn't pick up her sword — we were lost.

And somewhere beyond the boundary of our spell, someone was screaming.

30.
SORIN:

THE GREEN SWORD

When Sorin had stepped onto the amphitheater, she had been confident. She knew how to fight, and the Elixir she'd taken that morning flowed through her veins. Her magic was well-tuned, and she was ready to let it sing.

Magnes sat on the raised dais, and she felt His eyes on her through His mask.

When the clash began, Kala attacked with a ferocity Sorin hadn't anticipated. Each blow had so much force behind it, she feared that if the ward dropped and Kala managed to land a strike, blood would flow.

Arcady's magic was thick as a blanket around Sorin, tasting like sea salt and a hint of smoke, and it held through Kala's barrage.

Sorin's ears rang, her muscles shaking despite the Elixir. Kala came, again, again, like waves crashing to shore. Sorin desperately kept the other student at bay, blinking away the sting as sweat dripped into one eye. Her breathing was too fast, too shallow. Even the Elixir couldn't keep her calm and controlled.

Kala sensed Sorin's weakness, fighting like someone possessed. Sorin blocked everything Kala threw at her, but some of her footwork was poor.

The ringing in her ears rose to a shriek, and the amphitheater winked out.

Sorin sees herself from above, as if through her wyvern's eyes. She's racing through the dawn-dyed forest, urging her horse to go faster, faster, leaning low over the saddle. She glances over her shoulder.

Sorin blinked back in the area in time to catch another swing of Kala's sword, the wards brightening between them.

Blink. She could barely see the other student and his shining silver blade through the swirl of the ward. *Clang. Clang.* Each meeting sent a reverberation through Sorin's arm down to the bone. She could still smell the loam of the forest over the scent of Arcady's magic. The fear crawled up her throat, choking her.

Out in the crowd, she felt Magnes's eyes on her, making the hair rise on the back of her neck. Blink.

Her horse is running too fast across a forest path that might have hidden roots. If her beast trips, it'd be a broken leg, or worse. But if she can make it in time—if she can get just a little further—

Blink. Sorin forced herself to focus on the amphitheater, to keep her footwork tight, to coil enough power in her shoulders to hit back hard. Her magic bled into the sword, the metal glowing green. All she had to do was cut the smallest hole in the opposite team's ward. To have her sword kiss the metal of Kala's blade rather than being cushioned by Delin and Arcady's wards.

The terror galloped through Sorin like the echoed sound of her horse's hooves. Why couldn't she *remember*?

The Elixir gave her energy. When Kala began to flag, Sorin twisted, catching his blade and disarming him. The sword clattered to the ground, the silver glow spluttering as Kala scrambled for his weapon.

Delin's muscles shook with the effort of keeping up the ward. It wouldn't take much.

"Now!" Arcady called behind Sorin.

But the ward had chased away a mental fog, revealing a knot, hidden deep within her skull, like the tangled root of a tree. For all her meditations, all her trainings, Sorin had never known it was there. Now the spell was so obvious, it was a wonder she'd ever missed it.

And there was only one person who could have put it there.

Faster—faster—if she can make it to the sea by morning, if she can find a ship that will take her—she just has to get far enough, fast enough before He realizes she's gone—

Blink. Kala rose slowly to his feet, picking up the sword, but Sorin barely registered it.

Magnes was watching her, even now. Did He realize what she'd seen, or had Arcady's magic protected her, like it had kept Magnes out of their mind?

Kala adjusted his grip on the hilt of his sword. The crowd's noise rose to a dull roar.

"Sorin!" Arcady yelled behind her, their voice strained with the effort of holding their magic. "Fight!"

Sorin forced herself to her feet and raised her sword in the nick of time.

Clang. White sparks rose in an arc, and Arcady cried out. The ward wobbled, but held. Far off, she heard more shouting from the crowds. Sorin's body moved through habit and years of training even as part of her mind remained far away.

Arcady breathed hard behind her, the sound of it catching at the back of their throat. It reminded Sorin uncomfortably of that cave in the forest clearing. The ward shuddered as Arcady struggled to keep the spell intact. Were they strong enough, or would Arcady turn Starveling like they had on the night of the Feast of Flowers?

Sorin steadied her stance.

Kala hesitated as he calculated his next plan of attack.

Sorin's palms were slippery with sweat. There was another way: all it would take was lowering the blade here and now. Let Kala take one more swing. No ward, no sword. No task, no trial.

They would both lose, and Sorin's seal promise to the university would be broken.

She could run, run toward the sea like her heart wanted. The green of her sword was as brilliant as the leaves in the summer forest, lit from behind with the last of the sun like stained glass. Arcady could run, too. If they stayed, after all, what would Magnes do to them?

Kala readied his blade for another swing.

Blink.

> *The branches of the trees reach for her, twigs breaking and falling to the dirt. The wyvern calls out, wings beating hard, keeping pace. Does he, too, dream of the horizon?*
>
> *A shadow falls over them both. The wyvern gives a mournful sound. He knows what is coming. He drops lower, flying toward his human.*
>
> *"Hush," she says. "We had to try, didn't we?" She always remembers, right at the end.*

Far off, she heard Jaculus shriek from the Rookery tower far above them. He circled above as if he could come to her defense. The Elixir focused and refracted her magic, and her sword glowed brighter.

Sorin finally stopped dancing away or defending herself—she ran to meet Kala. Were those screams? She couldn't let herself look.

Sorin hit the ward with everything she had and the felt the exact moment it sliced through Delin's spell. The ward fell in tatters. A scant second later, Arcady dropped theirs, and the sounds of the Citadel roared back to life.

They'd won.

Sorin was on hands and knees, gasping, drawing another, smaller ward over her body and mind, trying to draw the scattered parts of her together.

She raised her head, sight blurred with tears. The screaming hadn't stopped. Chaos surrounded them. Arcady was slack in horror, hands raised over their mouth. Sorin blinked, taking in scattered details. Blood splatters stained the stone of the amphitheater. A cluster of Healers in green robes on the other side of the arena bundled away two figures on stretchers.

Sorin caught growling and a scuffle as several people held back a hissing Starveling. Dread struck her in the gut as she saw the too-wide mouth, the black eyes, the dark marks crawling up skin. They fought with unnatural strength, head jerking side to side, mouth snapping, desperate to eat anything or anyone.

Sorin recognized the Starveling as Lowe Balcil. Her gaze snapped back to Arcady, who met her eyes. Sorin realized she was clutching her forearm, and she forced herself to release her grasp on her hidden scars. She stretched her fingers wide before clenching her hand into a fist. A professor hit Lowe with a spell, and she crumpled, unconscious. More professors swarmed until Lowe was hidden from sight.

"Willem," Arcady whispered. "Where is Willem? And Edin?"

Rahela was sobbing into Iona's shoulder. The older student wrapped her arms around Rahela's side, her own face stoic with shock.

Kala had let his sword fall from numb hands, his loss of the trial forgotten as he, too, took in the carnage around them. Very few in the Citadel would have seen a Starveling turn, much less one of their own. Everyone up here was too rich and too well-fed. How could Lowe have let herself risk growing so hungry?

Teasel and Jordin were hand in hand as they fled the amphitheater. Cind rocked back and forth. Rahela and Iona were led away by a professor. Iona's face was tear-streaked. Oran Winward had frozen, staring blankly, until Vilm gently tugged at their sleeve.

No Edin. No Willem. Had they been hurt?

Her eyes flicked to the empty dais. No Magnes.

Sorin felt too exposed, too raw. She turned and fought her way from the crush.

In the quiet of her room, she tried not to think about blood splashed on stone or tangled roots unearthed in her mind. She thought of the sea, the shush of waves, the straight line of a horizon. She imagined herself on the deck of the *Iris*, the Jaskian ship she had sunk in the harbor of Vatra with its dead captain aboard. In this vision, They were still alive, steering the ship toward open waters.

Since she was a child, she had always thought of Magnes with the honorific pronoun, no matter what. She had honored the Head Priest above all else. But now? She knew, at least within her own mind, she would let it fall.

If she was brave enough, the next step was untangling that knot and facing whatever else Magnes had hidden within her skull. And she suspected she would need Arcady's help to free her from him.

PART 3:
DECISIONS

Back when the world was newer, a youth wept over their parents' bodies and promised to one day cheat death and live forever. They spent their life in pursuit of this and studied with the great mages who could raise mountains or level them in turn. The youth used magic to heal any injury, but even though they had not yet lived many years, they knew each day was another day closer to eventual death.

One of the mages told the youth of a tree of magic with roots so deep they reached the heart of the world and branches so tall they tangled with the land of the gods. It alone had the power to defeat death. The mage warned that though many had gone searching for eternal life, no one had ever found it.

Death is what makes life worth living, the mage said, but the youth, of course, did not wish to listen. Finally, the mage relented and said the tree could be found where veins meet the heart of the sharpened teeth of truth. It took more precious years before the youth learned what that meant.

The journey was long and dangerous. The no-longer-as-young mage was tested along the way—vanquishing beasts and enduring both cold and hunger. Each task brought them face to face with death, and each time, they defeated it. Surely, they thought, this meant that one day, they would be able to defeat death for good.

Eventually, they found the tree, luminous as a star. The youth knelt at its base, eagerly making their wish.

But youth, as we know, is wasted on the young. Without fully considering their words, the mage wished to be more powerful than any magic user, so powerful death itself could never find them. A voice told the youth to climb the branches to receive their wish, and they did it without hesitation, sealing their fate.

The tree took them into itself, turning the youth into fruit upon its branch.

The fruit hangs there still to this day. It does not wither, but neither does it bloom. The only way to truly beat death is to become a god, and no mere mortal can. None of us know how much time we are given. Far better to spend however much time you have well.

Death is for the living.

31.

ARCADY:

AN INVITATION

There was no celebration after the second trial. No drunken students in the common room, no students standing on tables and raising overflowing cups in triumph.

The university grounds were silent during the last week before the Spirit Moon break. I worked in a daze, finishing my history paper on Monarch Laen, which was due on the last day of classes. History texts and papers had no clear consensus on the role of the consorts. Some believed they distracted Monarch Laen from the business of ruling. The Monarch's lavish parties and the increasing glee they took from killing and violence was well-documented, and the consorts were always present. Others believed they functioned like secret advisors during pillow talk, whispering poison in the Monarch's ear and driving them to deeper cruelty. Still others believed the final consort, in particular, was fully in on the coup against Laen and helped bring about the Schism. I concluded, rather weakly, that whatever the consorts' role, they had certainly been underestimated.

And, of course, at night, every time I closed my eyes, there was Everen. We met in dream versions of the lock shop, the dragon archives, or even once, the Cote where we'd schemed with the Marricks. With each dream, that gold between us grew stronger.

We had found nothing more on the location of the tree. What he needed from me hung over our every interaction like thick smoke. Everen had said he meant to return to the human world.

And I was meant to help him do it.

"If it's going to happen, it'll happen, then, won't it?" I'd said once, bitterly. "I don't even have any say in the matter."

Everen had only stared at me with those expressive green eyes and I woke up, alone.

A few days after the second trial, the students who had progressed met in the Citadel infirmary. Willem and Edin were awake, and the Master Healer had confirmed they'd both be discharged the following day. Edin's arm was in a brace. Willem had been badly scratched, with a few broken ribs, but overall, he'd been lucky. It could have been so much worse.

Rahela, Cind, Jordin, Sorin, and I had pitched in and brought a ridiculously large bouquet of roses and a packet of the finest marzipan sweets from Daisy's Confectioners on Silver Street. Edin ate a couple, but Willem gobbled half the box in one go.

I'd pieced together more of the details from the trial. Lowe Balcil had used too much magic, and the impact of the ward imploding had knocked Willem down. Lowe, his eyes black and mouth open, had rushed Willem, almost ripping out his throat, by all accounts. I was glad I hadn't seen that part.

Edin had swiped at Lowe's back with her sword, distracting him. He'd attacked her instead, breaking her arm, but she'd managed to hold him off long enough for the professors to step in. I was still haunted by the memory of Lowe's twisted face. I'd seen a Starveling down in the city with Everen, but never someone I *knew*. During the Feast of Flowers, I'd also turned Starveling myself, but I thankfully remembered nothing except how deeply I'd hungered and how desperate I'd been to escape it.

"What do you think will happen next?" Cind asked. "Will the Trials continue, or will they be canceled?"

I'd been wondering the same thing. To do well enough to progress and then yet not have the chance for the scholarship would be a blow, but at the same time . . .

Lowe remained in the intensive care ward. The healers had brought him back from the brink, but the damage was already done. Because he'd turned Starveling, especially so publicly, his dragonstone seal would be replaced with marble. He'd leave the university and never work with magic again. The shame of it would follow him and his family for years. It was a stark reminder that this was what I faced, at least, if Larkin turned me in.

"I expect the university and the Consul are discussing it now," Edin said. "It doesn't reflect well on the university that a student turned Starveling so publicly. The Citadel is shaken, by all accounts."

I understood why. Drakines rarely turned Starveling, after all. The nobility had so much more access to food, training, and education. They also had a staunch, misplaced belief that it was the poor or the Struck, especially, who were weak enough to turn. But anyone, no matter their station, must pay magic's cost.

"No one died, though," Jordin pointed out. "There was an injury in the first task, and the Trials continued. This one might, too."

Rahela nodded. "I don't think they'll cancel. That would make Loc and the university look weak. They'll want to see it through, but I suspect the university will probably give us another chance to tap out now if we don't wish to continue."

We all exchanged glances. Edin's face was set with determination. Rahela, Cind, and Jordin were also competitive enough to stay. We all burned to prove ourselves—it's what had gotten us this far.

Sorin chewed her lip. She'd been keeping to herself since the second trial, and I echoed her unease. Part of me knew that if the opportunity came to free myself of the seal promise, I should probably take it. If Everen came through, and our magic was compromised, what hope did I even have in the third trial? But to give it all up after I'd come so close . . .

"I expect we'll find out after the Spirit Moon break, in any case," Edin said.

"Not a decision I have to make, at least. I lost quite dramatically," Willem said, chewing another marzipan.

"Bad luck, chum," Jordin said. "On multiple fronts."

Willem waved his hand, then winced in pain. "I never truly thought I'd make it through anyway. No skin off my nose. I do feel awful for Lowe, though. Just awful."

Everyone went quiet. What else was there to say?

We had two sennights of freedom stretching before us for the Spirit Moon break.

Everyone chattered about their plans at breakfast. Rahela was traveling to Myria. A few other students might visit their kin who had settled on the other side of the boundary, but most would be staying with their families in their larger houses along the Citadel hill or their manors out in the Lochian countryside.

I'd planned on hunkering down at the Citadel over the break, studying like mad and deciding whether to let a dragon back into the human world. As an acolyte, Sorin would be staying behind, too.

"Oh no, you can't *stay here*," Willem said when he heard our plans. "You simply must come with me to my hunting lodge in the country."

"Oh, I'm sure we couldn't impose," I said, tamping down my excitement. "After all, you'll be there with your family for the holiday, right?"

Willem's easy grin faltered. "Well. No."

"Why not?" Sorin asked, cocking her head.

Willem poked at his breakfast glumly. "Something came up with my mam's work. An incident off the coast with some sunken boat. Jask is blaming Loc, Loc is blaming Jask. You know, that old chestnut."

"Ah," Sorin said. "Do you know anything about how it's going?"

Willem blew into his hands. "I'm not even supposed to know that much. But my mam is still out there, and my maire is going to meet her now that classes are finished. I wouldn't be allowed to go, and even if I did, it wouldn't exactly be festive. Sounds like it's a sarding mess." He set aside his napkin, his expression tightening. "But anyway, I . . . I'd rather not be alone for the Spirit Moon. I'd . . . I could use the company. I've asked Edin, too. She saved my life, after all, and she doesn't get on particularly well with her family, I know that much. So. Will you come?"

His faltering smile was hopeful. He was out of the hospital and physically healed, but the mental marks of what had happened would take longer to fade.

"We'd be honored to join you, then," I said. "Right, Sorin?"

The priest nodded.

Willem smiled so widely I could see his back molars. "Excellent!" he said, his haunted expression leaving him. "It'll be brilliant. Good food, better wine, and we can even go for a hunt!"

He chattered on and I smiled patiently, but inside, I was resisting the urge to raise my fists in triumph.

One: if I were a professor hiding potentially forbidden research I didn't want anyone to find, I'd put it in the grand family home in a remote swathe of the forest.

Two: if I were to draw a dragon back through to the human world, the middle of nowhere was not the worst place to do it.

32.

SORIN:

THE HUNTING LODGE

Sar Kesia Ansel came to see Their family off as the carriage was readied. Everyone's breath misted in the air—winter had set its claws in, and Sorin could barely feel the tips of her fingers.

Sorin's eyes widened when she realized they'd be taking a horse-less carriage. Those were reserved for the very rich. The carriage had to be re-spelled with Piater magic by a master mage after every journey, and often the driver was someone strong enough in gray magic to help move it along if needed, which wasn't cheap considering most servants didn't use much magic at all. Even Edin seemed impressed.

While Sar Ansel was returning to the coast to sort out the Jaskian snarl, Professor Hayden had decided to come out to the lodge after all, which delighted Willem.

"Are you sure you can't come, too, mam?" he asked.

"I wish I could, sweet, you know I do," Sar Ansel said, kissing his cheek. They were statuesque and more than a little intimidating, with hair in a long braid and brown eyes that missed nothing.

There was a tightness around Their mouth. Whatever had happened regarding Jask, Sorin suspected it had Them worried.

Magnes would have gone Himself to lend the delegation more importance, which made her weak at the knees in relief. Jask and Lochian relations were tense at the best of times, but since Loc and the Order of the Dragons knew Jask was trying to steal its dragon relics, it was even tenser. She had spent hours meditating and searching for that knot in her mind. Without a ward, she couldn't find it on her own, but she knew it was there.

"I know it might be odd to spend time with your professor outside of the classroom," Professor Hayden said with a half-smile, "but never fear, I'll be locked away trying to finish some projects before the babe arrives, so I won't lurk too much. Promise."

Arcady seemed particularly displeased at the change in plans, though they were trying not to show it. Surely Arcady had been planning on looking for the professor's research at the lodge. It's what Sorin would have done. How would they manage now?

Sar Ansel patted Willem's cheek. "I'm glad you will be among friends, Willem. But don't go too wild out there, if you please. I'd appreciate not receiving a missive from your maire telling me you got drunk and fell in the pond. Again."

Professor Hayden chuckled as Willem made a face. "I maintain the mud was extremely slippery and my state of inebriation made no difference."

Professor Hayden and Sar Ansel embraced, pressing their foreheads together, before hugging their offspring and rocking back and forth. There was such genuine fondness and love between them that Sorin had to glance away.

"Thank you for letting us stay at your estate," Edin said, bowing her head toward Willem's parents.

"Yes, Sar Ansel. Your generosity is most appreciated," Arcady added hastily and Sorin inclined her head in gratitude.

"It's our pleasure," Sar Ansel said. "Enjoy yourselves."

Willem, Arcady, Edin, Sorin, and the professor climbed into the carriage, and the driver hopped up to the cab. Three wyverns circled overhead: Willem's blue Livet, Edin's violet Verdell, and Jaculus. They'd follow the carriage or perch on it when they wanted a rest.

With a muttered spell from the driver, they were on their way.

Sorin enjoyed watching the streets of Vatra from the window and then, once outside of the city, the sprawl of woods to either side of the Royal Road. She'd missed the forest.

Conversation stayed light. Sorin sat back, watching and listening. Arcady was determinedly upbeat in contrast to the darkness of Sorin's thoughts. The Elixir comedown from the second trial had not been as difficult as the first one, but it had still been unpleasant. Sorin hadn't interacted much with Edin beyond the Trials or occasional sparring on the practice grounds. All Sorin knew was that professors loved Edin and between her smarts and family connections, she'd probably rise to the top of society. She might even become a Chancellor one day.

Professor Hayden soon closed Their eyes, hands resting on Their stomach, and Sorin followed Their lead.

The carriage was swift and the road clear, so by the time they arrived at Willem's estate, it was only mid-afternoon. Sorin blinked awake, groggy.

"*This* is what you call a hunting lodge?" Arcady asked when they passed a bend in the road. Sorin was equally incredulous.

Professor Hayden chuckled. "I reacted the same way when I first saw it."

The lodge was at the top of a steep cliff with a good view of the surrounding landscape. It was made of stone browner than the buildings of Vatra. Maybe a few centuries ago, it had been a simple dwelling, but over the years the Ansel family had added more wings, towers, and turrets. More . . . everything.

Professor Hayden yawned as They dismounted from the carriage. "Please excuse me, but I'll leave Willem to settle you in. The drive quite took it out of me, I'm afraid, and I'm going to rest until dinner." They inclined Their head before They made Their ponderous way up the sweeping stairs to the main door.

Sorin tried not to ogle when they entered the entrance hall.

"Come on," Willem said. "I'll show you around and then to your rooms. I don't know about you, but I'm absolutely gasping for a mulled wine."

Everything was spotless. Dried flower bouquets were arranged in vases at every landing. Everything was deep blues and greens with gold or silver accents, the furniture maroon and mahogany. Chandeliers made of intertwined antlers hung from crown-molded ceilings and deer and boar heads on the walls served as a grim reminder of past hunting trips. Willem waved at the portrait gallery, which showed a parade of severe-looking drakines with echoes of Willem's features trapped in gilded frames.

Sorin had known Willem was from one of the richest drakine families, of course, yet she was startled to be confronted with the sheer scope of Ansel wealth on display. This wasn't even his family's main residence.

They ascended the sweeping staircase to the upper rooms and passed a closed door with faint banging sounds behind it. "Of course she's already in her laboratory instead of actually resting," he said with a roll of his eyes. Arcady's expression sharpened, and Sorin pretended not to notice.

Their bags were already in their rooms, which were as lavish as expected. Sorin cleaned herself up and changed into her spare priest robes. Night fell, so much darker out in the forest compared to the city with all its lights.

This was the night before the longest, darkest night of the year. The time when people contemplated the year that had passed and looked to the one ahead. A time to remember those lost and cherish those still living.

Over the next few days, Sorin was determined to learn more of Arcady Dalca's secrets.

33.
ARCADY:

THE SPIRIT MOON

I t's far too stuffy and echoing in that grand dining room, isn't it?" Professor Hayden said with an airy wave of Their hand. "I don't think we need to stand on ceremony tonight, do you?"

"Stuff ceremony," Willem agreed.

We'd all dressed for dinner. I'd decked myself out in a doublet of blue silk and trousers so loose they were like skirts, with a few painted silver stars on my cheeks in honor of the festive season. Edin: a deceptively simple blue houppelande. Professor Hayden: velvet robes of deep green with ornate, trailing sleeves. Willem was clad in clothing similar to mine, but wine-dark. The paint on his eyelids reminded me of orange monarch wings. Sorin had opted for her usual priest clothes but allowed Willem to paint her face, too. The orange brought out the reddish-blonde tinge to her short hair and made her darker freckles look like fairy dust scattered across her cheeks. She kept glancing at herself in the ornate mirror on the wall, as if she'd shapeshifted and didn't recognize herself.

"It's nice," I said, honestly, and I swore she almost blushed.

The drawing room was all tartan and oil paintings of hunting scenes I found a bit distasteful, but the fire warmed the room. There was a harpsichord in the corner, and the servants had set up a spread of food. Fancy cheeses and meats surrounded by plump grapes imported from Myria. Roasted chestnuts, caramelized pecans, and meat pies with a glistening glaze on the pastry. We ate our fill by candlelight and the mulled wine flowed. After dinner, Willem fetched a good brandy from the cellars.

Edin was obviously at home in the sumptuous surroundings, but I'd only gone into houses as fancy as these long enough to crack a safe and then crawl out a window. Sorin was used to gilded cathedrals and the beauty of the Citadel, but I'd seen how plain her monk's cell was. She, too, seemed anxious about spilling crumbs on the velvet settee.

A few candlemarks later, Willem was, of course, absolutely sozzled. Sorin and Edin were tipsy, and I was stone-cold sober but pretending not to be. Willem attempted a few carols on the harpsichord, but he was, in a word, terrible. Every time Edin and I started singing, he'd lose the thread of the melody, and we'd devolve into giggles. One of the servants who came bearing dried apricot tarts with double cream winced as they set them down.

"I know, terrible isn't it, Arine?" Willem called over his shoulder.

"Yes, quite, young sar," Arine said, and Professor Hayden laughed. Arine was of medium height, with brown hair just beginning to gray down to their shoulders and ice-blue eyes. They had a kind face. It was easy to imagine a young Willem running through the corridors or sliding down the banisters of the spiral staircases, and either Arine or Professor Hayden telling him off for it. I couldn't imagine Willem had been particularly dedicated to practicing the harpsichord.

"Willem, please, leave the poor instrument alone, I beg you," Edin said. "What has it ever done to you?"

"Please do us all a favor and save us from my playing then, maire," Willem wheedled. "Please?"

His maire smiled at him indulgently. "If you insist."

Professor Hayden settled on the bench, placing Their hands on the keys. They played far more skillfully than Willem had. Edin led the singing, and, of course, she did that as well as everything else. Sorin hummed more than sang, and I realized that because of her Vow of Silence, she'd likely never sung them. Her voice was untrained, but not half-bad.

After a few more songs, Edin took over the playing. I took a bit of satisfaction when she stumbled over a few notes.

Professor Hayden came and sat next to me on the sofa, and I clutched my wine glass tighter. Their hand rose and They flashed "she" at me. "We're in my home," she said. "I think we can leave some formalities behind by now, no?"

"I suppose so," I said, responding with the sign for "any," though she already knew it. She inclined her head.

"It's nice to see Wil smiling," Hayden said. "It's been hard since the second trial."

"I can imagine," I said. It was strange to listen to Hayden speak of things other than alchemy and the elements. She was, of course, more than simply a professor. She was a person with a son, another babe on the way, a wife. Even beyond the blackmail, I wanted to pry for so many details. What jokes my grandsire had made, or what he'd looked like bent over a beaker on the cusp of some breakthrough. Everything. Anything.

"You did well during the ward and sword challenge," Hayden said with a raise of her glass.

"Thank you," I said, raising mine back before we both took a sip. "I'm enjoying alchemy class, and I'm not kissing up. It's a fascinating subject."

Her eyes crinkled. "I'm glad. You're doing well there, too. You and Sorin seem to be good partners."

"We work well enough together." I paused, biting my lip, trying to figure out how to play this next bit. She wasn't drinking alcohol because of the babe, but Hayden's guard was down. Time to chance Saint Ini and see how my luck held.

"Are you working on any interesting research outside of teaching?" I asked, nonchalantly.

She swirled her grape juice in her glass. "I'm finishing up a few bits and bobs before I give birth in late spring."

"On transmutation?" I pressed.

"No, I drifted away from that in the last few years. My current research isn't terribly interesting, I'm afraid."

"Oh I doubt that very much," I said. "I keep thinking about what you said in class a few sennights ago. That if you approach an impossible problem by asking yourself how it might be done, it might not be so impossible after all? It's helped me when I've been tearing my hair out during my studies."

She chuckled. "I'm glad. I've found it a good reminder myself over the years."

"Who did you say shared that with you?" I asked.

"I didn't." She shot me a glance out of the corner of her eye, and I tried to look innocent.

"An old friend I lost years ago," she allowed. "I still think of him often."

I ground my teeth together, barely stopping myself from asking why she'd helped kill him, then, if he'd meant so much to her.

"Ach, it's late." Her eyes flicked to the clock. "Far past my bedtime. I'll leave you all to carry on the party without your professor hovering."

"Good night, Professor Hayden," I said.

She smiled. "Good night, Arcady."

She paused on her way out to kiss the top of Willem's head and whisper something in his ear before bidding the rest of us farewell.

After Hayden left, the talk soon turned to classes or gossiping about other students. Edin made the mistake of making an offhand mention of the trial, and Willem's jolliness wilted.

He swayed in his seat and leaned toward her, gesturing with his cup. "My parents haven't told me they're disappointed I'm out of the Trials, but . . ." He hiccoughed. "To be honest, I think they were fairly surprised I made it past the first."

"You're a talented mage," Edin protested.

"That's a lie, but it's an especially kind one coming from you, Edin," Willem said with a raise of his glass. He took a long sip. "I don't know . . . my parents are so godsdamned *brilliant*. And it's not like I can even be mad at them for going off and saving us from war with Jask or discovering the mysteries of the alchemical world. It's just . . . hard, sometimes, I guess, to stand in the shadow of it and know I'll never do anything very dazzling myself." He drained his glass.

"You don't know how the second trial would have gone if that ward had held," Edin said.

Willem gave her a pointed look. "Spare the platitudes. I knew I was out the moment Lowe and I were up against you and Rahela. Nearly dying in front of everyone, though? Embarrassing, that. I'll probably never stop thanking you, my bold rescuer."

"Anyone would have done what I did," Edin demurred.

"No, they wouldn't," he said.

Edin was distinctly uncomfortable with Willem's drunken out-pour of emotion.

"Don't have a sarding clue what I'm gonna do with my life," he continued, waving his hand. "Suppose my parents are about to have a chance to try again. Maybe this next one will be a bit smarter than me."

"Oh Gods, Wil. Enough of this." The annoyed words were out of my mouth before I could bite them back.

Willem squinted at me, blearily.

I cocked my head at him, dropping Arcady Dalca's affable persona entirely. "Wil. Are you . . . expecting sympathy?" I gestured to the sumptuous room around us. "You're so rich you could never lift a finger and be more than fine. Your parents are often busy, but . . . you know. At least you still have them, and they love you. Count your blessings."

Sorin was wide-eyed. I was being too blunt, but it was too late to take the words back.

Edin nodded, though, as if I'd echoed everything she'd wanted to say.

Willem's face crumpled and he buried his head in his hands. He laughed, but it was watery, and he hiccoughed. "I'm sorry. You're right. I'm the *worst*."

He looked so pathetic that all three of us burst into laughter. I went over and hauled him to his feet.

Willem clung to me, holding me tight. "I'm sorry," he wailed.

"It's all right, Wil, we forgive you for being a rich toff." I gave him an awkward pat on the back. "Though your family is probably even richer than the Ansels, Sar Vayne," I said to Edin over Willem's shoulder.

"We're about the same," Edin surprised me by answering. "But Willem's parents are a good sight nicer than mine, is all I'll say." She cleared her throat, eyes shuttering. I'd heard rumors Edin hadn't spoken to her parents in years, but no one knew why. "Right. Self-pity is definitely my sign to end the night."

"Good idea. Come on, Willem. Off you get to bed in your fancy mansion so we can go hunting on your extensive grounds tomorrow. All right?" My words were teasing, but I kept my voice soft.

Edin and Sorin both started helping him up the stairs before Arine and another servant arrived to take over.

"Is he . . . all right?" Sorin asked.

"He'll be fine in the morning," Arine said. This wasn't the first time they'd tipped a very drunken Willem into bed, I suspected, and it wouldn't be the last. "Willem . . . feels things very intensely."

"Hey. Stop talking about me," Willem slurred.

"I didn't say it was a bad thing, did I? Come on, young sar," Arine said, gently.

On the way to my room, I spied the sliver of light at the bottom of the door to Professor Hayden's laboratory. I shut the door to my room and changed into my alchemy clothes, which turned out to be excellent for both university trials and sneaking about. At least I was getting my coin's worth.

I waited for two candlemarks.

I thought of Willem and Edin, wondering what my life might have been like if my grandsire hadn't been put to death by the state.

Would I have felt pressured to follow in my grandsire's greatness, just as I now felt the same pressure to clear our family name? Would I have been as oblivious as Willem to what life was truly like for most people in Loc? I knew full well how lucky even I was compared to most. Because I'd found Kelwyn and then the Marricks, I'd never gone truly hungry or slept on the streets with only the rats for company.

I finally caught the sound of the door opening and closing and Professor Hayden's footsteps as she passed my room. There was no point torturing myself with what-ifs. I felt Everen with me. He couldn't see through my eyes beyond an occasional flash, but as we grew closer to the Night of Locked Tombs, it was becoming easier to speak across the Veil.

I took my lockpicks from the hidden pocket of my satchel, tucked some blank paper in my pocket, and snuck through the corridor of the hunting lodge.

—*What are you hoping to find?* he asked.

—*Answers.*

The lock was dead easy. I was inside Professor Hayden's laboratory in less than five minutes. The wards were on the perimeter of the grounds, and Willem had brought us right through them, never suspecting one of his new friends might betray his hospitality.

None of the tables showed any active experiments; the beakers were all neatly packed away. Alchemical tomes lined the bookshelves. I peered at the spines before taking out a couple and flipping through the pages. I paused, my Struck-blunted ears straining at every sound, hoping that Professor Hayden didn't decide to come back to burn another mage lamp at midnight.

In their university office, Hayden had had volumes on chrysopoeia, transmutation, and alchemical symbolism. Here, though, I noticed quite a few on the intersections of health and alchemy. My breath caught.

One was called *Elixirs and Panaceas of the Ancient and Modern Ages*. I sucked in a breath, wondering if Larkin's source was actually not entirely full of shite. I opened it to find dense alchemical equations I could barely read, much less puzzle through. I put the book back and focused on the grand cabinet in the corner. It was the double of the one in Hayden's office—a matching set.

—*If there's anything, it'll be in here somewhere,* I sent to Everen. *If there's not, then I'm stumped, and Larkin won't be happy.*

—Happy hunting. Despite everything hovering between us, Everen's presence in my mind helped me feel that bit braver.

The lock on the cabinet proved trickier. Once it clicked open, I hesitated, the fear rising again. I sensed no wards, but what if Professor Hayden realized someone had snooped? There was also the constant push and pull in my head and my heart since I'd arrived at the university. I was desperate for answers, but I feared what I might find.

When I'd broken into Hayden's other office, I'd rushed, afraid of being caught. Part of me had worried I'd missed something.

Here, I took my time. Many files were similar to what I'd seen in the other office. Papers on transmuting lead. Write-ups of various experiments, both successful and unsuccessful. Nothing related to what Larkin wanted.

I put back the last file, breathing out slowly in frustration. I crouched, running my fingers along the seams of the cabinet.

When I heard the *snick*, I gave a muffled hiss of triumph. I drew out an unmarked folder, and my hands shook as I flipped it open. There were a few sheaves of rough sketches—earlier drafts of research that Hayden must have hidden when everything else was taken. The first paper showed alchemical symbols in my grandsire's hand. My fingertips tingled.

My eyes roved hungrily over the document. It was an equation, with lines drawn across symbols, arranged in a crosshatch pattern. A few parts were circled, with additions in Hayden's handwriting. I recognized the sign for quicksilver. Here, then, was more incontestable proof that my grandsire and Professor Hayden had worked together.

The next page was a log of dates. But below each one, in Locmyrian: *Experiment: failed.*

Experiment: failed.

The dates ranged from a few years after the second Strike ended to only a few months ago.

Experiment: successful, but with side effects. More testing required.

I exhaled.

Everen caught whatever my emotion was.

—Is this what you wanted to find?

—I don't know yet.

I took the blank paper from my pocket. *"Džav lasevan ful-as,"* I said, and the words and diagrams appeared on the blank pages, every angle and pen stroke just the same. I'd have to trace over them with ink before the magic faded. "Thank you, Rahela," I muttered, carefully putting the originals back where I found them. She'd taught the copying spell to me one afternoon in the library when I'd asked to borrow some of her Kalsh notes.

I re-locked the cabinet, slipped out of the laboratory, and tiptoed back to my room, hiding my papers in the same pocket as my lockpicks. My heartbeat was hammering. I hadn't sensed any wards, but what if Hayden suspected someone had gone into her laboratory?

I changed into my night clothes and tied my wrist to the bedpost, but sleep was slow to find me. Was she testing Elixir? If so, what—or who—was she testing it on? What were the side-effects? I shivered, dread pooling at my stomach.

When I finally drifted off, it was as though I blinked and Everen was with me in the room of the lodge. He wore a robe of strange material, and his feathered hair was tousled, his dragon-green eyes half-lidded as he leaned back against my pillows.

—I don't know if I should give what I found to Larkin, I said. *Not before I know what it means, anyway.*

—It is more than you have discovered so far, yes? He stretched his arms over his head, the robe gaping and giving me a tantalizing glimpse of his chest.

—Yes. I stared at the fire burning low in the grate. *My grandsire always seemed so careful around magic. He knew how dangerous it could be, but he always said magic would tell you its limits if you listened. There must be more to it.*

—Do you think he figured out this experiment years ago? Everen blinked at me slowly in the half-darkness.

My mind spun with the possibilities. *—If he cracked it, the Citadel stole his research, and that's why Hayden has been trying to re-create it. If it was something that could heal the Struck, what else could it heal? If it made it easier for the poor to learn magic, for example . . .* I trailed off. *I could see the Chancellors killing for that. But then . . . how did it go wrong? Was the Strike the result?*

Everen shook his head. *—Maybe. It could be something that came through the Veil, or a consequence of magic being out of balance and both worlds sickened. I don't think there is much more we can glean for now, but this gets us closer.*

He turned on his side, looking at me. I was all too aware we were in a bed together. Despite everything, part of me wanted to drag him to me, but I kept my hands to myself. This was already complicated enough.

—Tomorrow is the Night of Locked Tombs, he said. *Your grandsire wrote the spell that drew me through and sent me back. This is all connected, Arcady. You know that as well as I do.*

—I'm afraid, I whispered.

—I am not, strangely enough, he said. *Since the vision, I have felt almost at peace.*

I considered this. *—You didn't know what stealing that prophecy would do any more than I knew what else speaking that spell would do. I didn't exactly have the full information to consent to completing the bond the first time, either. Have we been able to choose any of it?*

He grimaced. *—I do not know what will happen tomorrow night. But I do know you are so stubborn I am not sure even fate can make you do something if you do not wish it.*

No other human was bonded to a dragon. I could have more magic, more life, more time than anyone in the Lumet. Why *wouldn't* I take it?

The dream started to fade as deeper sleep took hold. I felt the ghost of his lips on my forehead.

—If you call me, I will return, he said. *Whatever we face together seems impossible. But if it weren't . . . ?*

—But if it weren't, I sighed, echoing my grandsire's words, *how might it be done?*

I felt his lips smile against my skin, and then he was gone.

34.

SORIN:

THE HUNT

Sorin had drunk enough the night before that her head should have been pounding something fierce, but Professor Hayden had given them a wonder tonic with breakfast. It tasted like death, but within half a candlemark, her headache had fled. Perhaps that explained why, even though Willem drank like a fish, he made it to arms practice or an early class relatively bright-eyed.

Willem, despite a vat of the tonic, yawned and winced at the sunlight. Sorin supposed it couldn't work miracles, after all.

Willem was still enthusiastic about the hunt. In addition to bows and quivers of arrows, he loaned Sorin and Arcady hunting russets. Sorin had to roll the sleeves up a few times. Willem had loaned Edin one of his more "spirited" horses, since she was, naturally, an expert rider.

Sorin had her metal knife displayed in her belt-sheath, but she'd tucked the dragonbone blade into the small of her back. In her saddlebags, she had her potions and poisons, her salt, and everything she'd had in the forest as an Eye. Some habits were hard to shake.

Sorin heaved herself up into the horse's saddle, and Jaculus fluttered down to perch on the pommel. Arcady looked dubious of their
steed.

"Good gods, Arc," Willem exclaimed once they'd finally mounted.
"One would think you'd never ridden a horse in your life, your seat's
so bad."

"I'll admit it's been a while," they said. "I was never much one for
the great outdoors, even out in the Northwilds."

Sorin resisted the urge to shake her head as Willem swallowed
the obvious lie.

The four of them took off down the steep slope from the lodge.
Willem was in the lead, followed by Edin, then Arcady, and Sorin.
She relaxed once they were under the winter canopy of the forest.
The air was sharp from the previous night's rain. Water dripped off
bare branches and dark pine needles. Some of the younger birch
trees still had their red, new bark, as if the trees were bleeding. The
older ones were white as bone, and the rocks were covered in a car-
pet of lichen and moss. The horses' hooves squelched through the
mud, and Jaculus took off with a flap of feathers and a joyful call at
being somewhere wilder than the city's spires. He, Livet, and Verdell
would keep an eye out for prey.

Willem took the lead and found a game trail. Arcady was restless,
shifting in the saddle. The deeper they went into the forest, the more
the knots in Sorin's shoulders loosened.

"Be quiet," she told them. "Listen to the forest and what it wants
to tell you." Arcady shot her a look but settled.

Willem grew frustrated as the day wore on and they had nothing
to show for it, not even a rabbit. Even Edin's usual good spirits were
fraying at the edges.

"Where are they?" Willem complained as they stopped to eat the
sandwiches packed in their saddle bags by a small cascade of water

that fell into a series of fairy pools down a rocky slope. "We'd usually have seen at least one doe or young buck by now, even if they're on the other side of the glen."

"I've heard of a few complaining of poor hunting on their estates, too," Edin said. "Maybe they just didn't rut as well this year?"

"I was never any good at hunting anyway," Arcady said, with a shrug. "But it's been nice spending the day out here, even if my arse hasn't enjoyed this saddle."

Sorin made a sound of agreement, tilting her head back to catch the winter sunlight. The forest had been too quiet, though, and it made her uneasy.

The hunting party mounted their horses and set out again. The afternoon lengthened and the air grew colder.

"We should head back," Edin said, pointing to the clouds gathering overhead. "The weather will turn."

"Let's try for another candlemark," Willem urged. "We're close to something. I can feel it."

Even Sorin was all too ready to be back in front of a fire, drinking warmed wine, but she dutifully nudged her horse forward.

As they followed the trail, the forest had grown even quieter. No birds, no rustling. The clouds overhead thickened, and a few snowflakes began to fall. Sorin huddled deeper into her cloak.

A warning cry from Jaculus caught her attention.

Willem paused his horse as they reached the outskirts of a meadow. "What . . . is that?" he asked. Edin's back stiffened. Sorin half-stood in her saddle, peering over Arcady's shoulder for a better view, dread unfurling within her.

There was a dark spot on the trunk of a birch tree, shaped like a star. It was stark against the white bark, small tendrils spreading from the points.

"Is it . . . dead?" Arcady asked.

"It is. That tree won't grow leaves come spring." Edin leaned closer, chewing her lip.

Willem's brow knit. "The groundskeeper didn't mention any blight to me."

"We lost a few copses of beech. Had to burn them." Edin's voice was hushed.

Sorin's mind spun, letting their voices wash away. She suspected a wraith had come through the Veil. Last night, she guessed, since this was the darker phase of the moon. They were close to the leyline — she could just catch the rush of the Red River from here.

Most wraiths were too weak to take form and do much more than kill a few plants, but some had the strength to linger long enough to cause trouble. Where was the Eye who was meant to guard this part of the forest?

Edin had dismounted. "Look," she said, pointing.

Sorin spied the gray spot in the dried winter grass of the meadow. The snow flurries remained light enough that it hadn't covered the track. A human bootmark. She shivered as she realized what the star shape on the tree was: a handprint.

Overhead, Jaculus, Verdell, and Livet circled like vultures.

Sorin took an arrow from her quiver and notched it into her bow, moving in front of Edin. Willem and Arcady readied their bows, still mounted on their horses. Arcady's hands were shaking, but they set their jaw.

Sorin followed the dark gray spots marring the meadow, Edin trailing behind her. Sorin's muscles tightened. Definitely human footprints.

"Oh, cursed saints," Edin exhaled.

Here was the Eye. They were curled on their side, one hand clutching their dragonbone blade.

Sorin gestured for Edin and the others to stay back. Edin looked like she wanted to protest, but she halted.

Sorin circled the body, her arrow at the ready. When she saw the Eye's face, she sucked in a breath. Her gaze memorized every detail, knowing Magnes might read this memory. The skin was hardened and cracked, like it could turn to ash at the slightest touch. She recognized one of the Eyes she'd seen in her brief stops at Nalore Monastery.

They also weren't yet dead.

Though something had torn open their torso, and their innards were scattered on the frozen ground, their eyes were open, the whites bloodshot. Their breaths were shallow. She could only hope that the Eye's body had put them in a shock so deep they no longer felt pain.

Sorin kept her face unmoving. From this angle, the others couldn't see the Eye still clung to life. If this could be called life.

The Eye met her gaze, eyes widening slightly in recognition. Their lips moved.

"Be careful," Edin warned.

"This soul needs last rites." Sorin bowed her head, as if in prayer.

"It's . . . still . . . here," the Eye rasped. She barely caught the words. "It . . . *jumped*."

Sorin's body spiked with fear. Her hand went to her stomach, feeling the scars from the wolf-monster's claws, always cooler than the surrounding skin.

"I'll find it," she promised the Eye. They gave the barest nod. Sorin reached for her magic, the seal's green flare hidden beneath her clothing. A few months ago, she wouldn't have been strong enough to do much more than twist her healing magic to cause pain instead of relief. But between the Elixir, the university, Magnes's secret training, and how close the Eye was to death, it took only the smallest spark.

Another inhale, an exhale . . . and nothing.

Sorin kept her head bowed a moment longer. A few moons ago, she'd thought she'd never have to kill again. This, like Widow

Girazin's death, had been a mercy. She raised her head, blinking away tears.

Sorin and Arcady had dismounted, coming to Edin's side. Willem cocked his arrow. Arcady drew their knife. Edin's hand was splayed across their chest in a gesture to the five gods.

When he caught sight of the corpse's face, Willem doubled over and vomited. Arcady pressed their hand to their mouth, and Edin was pale. Sorin swallowed hard, fighting her own rising gorge.

"Have you seen this person before?" Sorin asked Willem.

Willem shook his head, sneaking another glance and wincing away. "Maybe . . . maybe a poacher?"

"No," Arcady murmured. "I don't think so." Arcady's eyes flicked to the trees, searching for the wraith that they, too, knew might be lurking nearby. Did Arcady recognize these robes? There had been other Eyes in the forest on the night of the Feast of Flowers.

"It's as though they've been . . . gouged," Edin said. "A boar, maybe?" She looked equally dubious and horrified.

Silence grew between the four of them.

"We should make a pyre," Sorin said, finally.

"But . . . they might have been murdered," Willem said. "We have to report it to the authorities, don't we? They'll need to identify them, find the family . . ."

"I don't think it's safe to wait that long," Sorin said.

"You think this is a Struck or a Starveling?"

"Their corpse wouldn't be a risk if it was," Arcady said, the words sharp. "The Strike is long finished, and the Struck can't pass their marks on."

Edin backed away, putting her hand over her seal as if that would protect her magic from becoming infected. It was the first time Sorin had seen her even close to afraid.

Magnes had always stressed that wraiths must be dealt with quickly, and the blight treated, but he had never deigned to tell her exactly why. Could the Strike return if too much chaos slipped through the Veil?

Sorin met Willem's eyes as the wind whipped the snow in circles around them. "I say we burn the corpse," she said. "To be safe."

"Me too," Edin agreed, without hesitation. Arcady wrapped their arms around themselves.

Willem dithered. "I don't know. I don't know what's right."

"Then trust that I do," Sorin said. "We can't leave them like this. I suspect this person has no family to find." *None save the Order of the Dragons*, she added in her head. "Let their soul ascend. The gods will forgive us."

He gave a shaky exhale. "Right."

"We're agreed, then. Let's gather what firewood you can that isn't completely soaked," Edin ordered the others.

"I'll tie up the horses and take a quick loop around the meadow before the snow covers up any other tracks. Just in case," Sorin said.

"Don't go far," Arcady warned, looking at her too intently. "None of us should be on our own."

Sorin nodded.

She calmed the horses and took the bag of salt from her saddlebag, thanking her past self for her paranoia. She salted the dying tree, searching for any other hints of blight. She circled the clearing and found a set of black hoof prints leading off into the forest.

Her dread grew.

She'd have to return and hunt the wraith, but she first had to make sure the others were safe. The snow thickened, and the wind shrieked through the trees. She hurried back to Arcady, Willem, and Edin, slyly scattering salt on each of the stained footprints before the snow covered them from view.

"The weather's too poor for us to make it back before night-fall," Willem said, throwing another few sodden twigs on top of the corpse. The Eye was nearly covered, but Sorin noticed the corpse's hands were empty.

Sorin's gaze flicked to Arcady, suspecting a dragonbone blade was hidden in one of their pockets. She cursed herself. She should have taken it when she "prayed" over the Eye, but she hadn't been thinking clearly.

A soaked Jaculus landed on her shoulder, huddling close. She picked him up and placed him beneath her cloak, warming him with her body's heat.

"Definitely wouldn't be safe in the dark," Edin said. "You have shelters scattered through your estate, though, yes?"

"Aye," Willem said. "There's one not far from here. It'll be basic, but it should be fine for one night. Livet can make it back to the lodge with a message we'll return in the morning."

"I'm fairly sure your family's version of basic will be more than fine," Arcady said.

"I'll try to draw some of the water from the wood," Edin said, "but I think lighting the pyre will be left to you, Arcady. I saw your display in the first trial."

Arcady nodded.

Edin closed her eyes. "*A vojra, ðźaj léavam.*" Her seal flared. Water wept from the pyre, leaving the branches drier.

"Right." Arcady's lips thinned. The sodden corpse seemed so pitiful beneath the thicket of wood. "Let's send the lost soul on their way. Any last words, Sorin?"

Sorin swallowed. "May the dragon gods take their soul on swift, soft wings." She had been too nervous to get close enough to the corpse to read their seal. They'd died without their name on her lips.

A Jaskian would have found that abhorrent—a name to them was sacred. "By the gods' wing, and scale, and claw."

"By wing, scale, and claw," the others echoed.

Arcady's hands rose and they focused on the corpse.

"*Reukas*," Arcady said, hands twisting.

The fire over their palms lit up the clearing. With a push of power, they sent it toward the pyre. The wood caught immediately, burning so hot Sorin took a few steps back from the flames. Arcady closed their hands into fists.

The hairs on the back of Sorin's neck stood up. Magnes was right to be so interested in their magic. The feeling of their power was different, even if it was subtle enough someone might not know unless they were searching for it.

Who are you? Sorin wondered, not for the first time, as the four of them watched the pyre burn until it was nothing but ash.

By the time the hunting party reached the small log cabin, soaked through and cold, the wind howled through the forest. The rain stung Sorin's face, numbing her skin and making her eyes water, and the remaining two bedraggled wyverns were desperately unhappy. Sorin hoped Livet hadn't found it too difficult flying back to the lodge in the storm.

The hut was small—one main room and a covered stable. While it wasn't warded, the shelter was locked up tight against potential poachers or squatters. Inside smelled faintly of damp and mold, but it was weatherproofed and well-stocked with dry firewood. The four of them worked in silence. Arcady lit the fire in the hearth and Willem unloaded the saddlebags. While there were no heatstones, there was a brazier in the stable. Sorin and Edin went to see to the horses, who were skittish from the storm and whatever lurked in the forest.

"What do you think that person was doing out in the middle of the woods?" Sorin asked, soothing one of the horses after a gust of wind rattled the walls. Better to appear less certain after the way she'd behaved in the clearing.

"Must have been a poacher, like Willem said," Edin said. "The Red River is good for rafting, and they weren't that far from the water. Maybe they were simply passing through and had the bad luck to fight the wrong prey. Still. A shame to go like that, whoever they were." Edin's gaze was distant.

Sorin shuddered. "Agreed."

They went back to the main hut. The wind rattled the windows and the shutters, but the fire soon stole the worst of the chill. Sorin wrapped herself in a saddle blanket that smelled of horse and huddled near the flames. Jaculus and Verdell were curled in a tangle of scales and feathers on the hearth.

As the group had already eaten most of the food Arine had packed during their midday meal, dinner was a sad affair of dried fruit, some squashed sweetspheres, and jerky. Sorin thought longingly of the meal they would have eaten back at Willem's estate.

Willem, of course, had packed a flask of brandy. Sorin poured generous drams, slyly slipping a mild sleeping draft into the others' cups. It was wrong to dose people without their knowledge, of course, but she had to go back out into that storm to find the wraith, and she didn't want to risk anyone following.

Willem downed his drink in one go and topped it up. Edin sipped at hers, but Arcady toyed with their cup. The fire sputtered as the gale blew outside. Willem shivered.

"I can't stop thinking about that corpse," he said, voice low. "I've seen bodies wrapped for the pyre before but . . . but nothing like that. Have you?"

Arcady hesitated. "I've seen my share of death, yes. Wish I hadn't." They stared into the fire.

"I have seen it, too," Sorin whispered. *And brought it about*, she added silently.

"Not me, really." Edin said. "I was there when my taie died, but it was of old age. It was sad, but not, you know, like that. They gave her a lot of laudanum to send her on her way. It was peaceful. Holy, even."

"I've been so lucky, I know," Willem said. "I haven't lost as many as most. I sometimes feel guilty about that. Even in the Strikes, our family was largely spared because we could hide ourselves out here." He gulped more brandy. "And I guess I almost saw death in the second trial. When Lowe came for me, and there was nothing in their eyes . . . I thought that was the end. I know you're embarrassed I keep bringing it up, Edin, but if the professors had been a little slower . . . I dunno. I'm more aware than ever that if things had gone that bit differently, I wouldn't be here right now. And it feels like more luck I didn't earn."

Edin reached over and clasped the back of Willem's hand. "It was a tragedy, like what happened today. It wasn't anyone's fault. Only . . . rotten luck, like you say."

"Exactly," Arcady said. "And you're still here, Willem. Tonight, and tomorrow, and the night after that."

Willem gave them both a watery smile that fled as soon as it appeared.

"Tonight is the Night of Locked Tombs," Sorin said. "Let us honor those whose stories have ended."

"The Night of Locked Tombs," Arcady echoed. They gazed into the fire, pensive.

Sorin passed Willem a piece of kindling to light. "It's not a candle, but it'll do. Who do you honor on the Night of Locked Tombs, Sar

Willem Ansel?" she asked. She used the tone and cadence of a priest during a ritual.

He lit the thin piece of wood, lulled into the ceremony. "I light this flame for those I've lost. My uncle. My friends at the academy who didn't survive the Strikes." He closed his eyes. "I wish their spirits well, and I promise to remember them." He threw the kindling on the fire.

Arcady lit a stick of wood next. "I light this flame for those I've lost. I've lost my parents and all of my family line. I'm the last to carry on their name and legacy." They swallowed. "I also lost one of my closest friends a few years ago, and I miss them every day. I wish their spirits well, and I promise to remember them." They tossed the sliver of wood into the grate.

Edin went next. "I light this flame for those I've lost. My taie. My three cousins, a nephew, two uncles, and my little sibling during the Strike. I promise to remember them." The fire flared with the next bit of kindling. She bowed her head. Sorin had seen Edin visiting the cathedral more often than many of the students. She was far more devout than someone like Willem or Arcady.

"And you, Sorin?" Arcady nudged.

Sorin lit her makeshift candle, weighing her words. "I light a flame for those I've lost. I remember seven souls." A merchant's scion, choking on widow's sleep poison. A Jaskian captain and the slash of a shard of glass by their own hand before she could wield her knife. A drakine widow, screaming in a dungeon until the sound cut off with a gurgle. Ikari Dwell and the two guards felled by her crossbolts. The Eye in the forest that very afternoon. All strangers Magnes had told her to kill, save the last, and she had done it without question. She pictured their faces. "I wish their spirits well, and I promise to remember them." *Even if they will never forgive me,* Sorin finished internally. The kindling sputtered in the flame, then caught.

Arcady was watching her closely. They might have found it odd she'd given no specifics. Let them wonder.

Sorin raised her glass. "On the Night of Locked Tombs, we, the living, honor the dead. Those fallen and lost are now safe in the claws of the gods." She wished she could still believe that, but after all she'd seen, she had no idea where the dead went when they were gone. Maybe they were simply . . . gone.

"To the lost," Willem and Arcady echoed.

"In Saint Wyndyn's name," Edin said. "Our patron saint of the lost and wandering." Willem, already yawning, drained his glass, and Arcady, finally, drank their brandy and its sleeping draft.

Willem took the bed, and Sorin, Edin, and Arcady settled into their blankets on the floor. Willem was asleep as soon as his head hit the pillow, and it didn't take Arcady and Edin long to follow. Sorin watched Arcady's features, relaxed in sleep, completely defenseless.

She could, right here, foil Magnes's plan. She took out the dragonbone blade. The banked fire stained the white of the blade orange. She let herself consider it.

If she killed Arcady, though, she could very well lose the sole person who might help her find out what was in her mind, and how to break it.

Sorin sheathed her knife and put on her still-sodden boots and cloak. Jaculus protested when she tapped him on the head and woke him up, but he disentangled himself from Verdell, who cheeped sleepily.

With her wyvern perched on her shoulder, Sorin headed out into the night in search of a monster.

35.
EVEREN:

THE RETURN

The last time I had flown toward a rip in the Veil, I had stolen a prophecy and fled as fast as my wings could carry me. I had been too frantic to second-guess myself. Only my sister had followed me as I'd raced towards the horizon. She had pretended she had wanted to stop me, but in truth she and Miligrist had let me find that scroll, knowing how desperate I would be to take fate in my claws.

This time, even if I believed destiny, I knew what I faced, and had even packed a sack of things I might need in the human world and tied it to one of my spines. Cassia and half a dozen of our strongest dragon warriors flanked me as we flew over the Lady of Vere Celene, her carved snout pointing toward the horizon. Once more, I hoped she would show me the way. Even my mother came, in preterit on Mace's back and dressed in full armor. She sat tall, despite how much her wound obviously still pained her. Miligrist had stayed behind, but I had said my farewell to her.

—*The magic within holds the key*, she had told me. *Trust your heart and it will guide you.* I would have preferred more specific advice.

I hovered in mid-air, the dragons behind me in a V shape.

Last time, the rip had emerged at sunset, but this time it was full night before the Veil opened into a nearly invisible seam. I felt the power of it calling to me and smelled the sharpness of the storm within.

The first wraith slipped free, long and thin, like a snake with wings. Mace dove, her jaws snapping. A second emerged, and Thist and Hyacinth made quick work of them. The wraiths screamed as they disintegrated. A third, a fourth. Mace roared, letting loose a plume of fire and burning them to ash. The dragons had grown practiced at holding the monsters at bay. Soon enough, the wraiths' shrieks and clicking faded, and no more monsters streamed through the gap.

While I was grateful for their protection, unease also rippled through me. Was this a delegation, or an ambush? What if, once more, my mother was willing to risk everything for a chance to take the human world?

—*Go, Everen. We will not follow*, the Queen said, as if guessing my thoughts.

I stared at the dragon who no longer thought herself my mother. —*Is that your word as Queen?* I asked her, privately.

Her nostrils flared, but she drew herself tall, adjusting the furs around her. The jewel of her office glowed. —*It is.*

—*Thank you*, I sent, softly.

The storm plucked at my magic, and the golden bond curled through me like a spool of thread, ready to unwind and show me the way.

—*Find the tree*, Cassia said. *Heal the serpent and send it to slumber. Help us leave this broken world behind once and for all.*

It sounded so easy, but I knew too well fate was never that simple. I met my mother's eyes. This, right here, was the last moment we pretended to be on the same side.

I wanted dragons to come back to the Lumet, but I did not want Queen Naccara to lead them. If she came through, still thirsting for war, would I have to challenge her? And if I killed my mother, how would Cassia react? Would the dragons want her as Queen? Or if I were the victor, would they choose me?

The Queen blinked slowly.

—*I wish it could have been different between us, Everen,* she sent privately. *I do.*

—*Your title and what I was born never allowed for that. Fortune has made us what we are.*

—*Go,* the Queen ordered publicly.

—*Be safe,* Cassia said. *And help guide us home.*

The rip grew wider. I sensed, with deep certainty, that I would not return to this world. I took one last look at the dragon warriors surrounding me and the Lady of Vere Celene in the distance.

—*We cannot change the past,* I said, sending the thought wide, *but I hope for a brighter future. I have seen a future where dragons and humans live in harmony. I know it is possible. And I vow on starfire that, one way or another, I will bring it to pass.*

My mother's lips pulled back from her teeth in a hiss. I had issued an open challenge, even if I had not backed it with magic. Other dragons roared their displeasure, but my words would spread through Vere Celene by morning. Some might listen. Some might believe that fate had told me true.

For the third time, I entered the Veil, opening my wings and twisting as I dove into the storm.

I flew through the bruised clouds, my forked tongue tasting lightning on the air. My wings disturbed the frozen, suspended rain, each drop burning and freezing my scales. The bond was there, but it was such a thin, delicate thread.

—*Arcady*, I sent, following the path. I flew harder, working my wings.

The clouds shifted, allowing me the occasional glimpse of what looked like a river of wraithwright.

The serpent undulated far below me, impossibly large. I knew I could fly for hours, following its looping coils, and never reach its head. I held my breath, terrified of drawing any attention to myself or risking disturbing its slumber. Even asleep, its presence was tempting. It was a dream, and it was a nightmare. For all my magic and long life, I was nothing but a speck compared to this.

Humans thought dragons were gods, but there in the storm, I faced something truly divine. The Dreamer was the beginning and the end and everything in between. If I joined it, could I be more? Hypnotized, I made a mistake: I strayed from the golden path.

I was drawn to the wound. The gash glowed, red-orange as fire, the edges charred black. My every scale and feather sensed the wrongness of it.

Scattered details rose from the past. The serpent had been hurt, and the rot had been festering for more than eight centuries.

—*Whatever you do, remember this*, fate whispered. *You must not wake the Dreamer.*

I drifted just that bit lower, wishing I could soothe the serpent's pain. Smoke rose from the wound, twisting over its scales.

The smoke folded into shapes, spots of violet lights winking into being as the wraiths quickened and opened their eyes.

As one, the creatures turned their smoky heads toward me, their mouths opening to reveal the purple at the base of their throats. As one, they let loose that unearthly clicking, the discordant sounds echoing over each other. The serpent shifted.

The wraiths were the serpent's nightmares.

My surprise brought me back to myself. I shook my head, as if I could clear my eyes of sleep.

Heart pounding, I pulsed my wings, flying up, up. But I had lost the thread.

Where was the gold? Where were you?

—Arcady! I called across the storm. Below me, the wraiths hissed, the clicking rising to a shriek. *Arcady! You have to call me through. Please!*

I heard nothing, felt nothing. For a moment, I was drenched in fear. Surely, we had moved beyond the dance of secrets and betrayal by now? After everything, you would not leave me here, would you?

I had been within the storm too long. The storm's rain burned, and the wraiths screamed again, growing nearer. The edges of myself blurred. If I did not leave the storm soon, I might never be able to at all.

I focused, with everything I had, on our bond. There. A shimmer in the darkness.

There you were. You slept. You dreamed.

For a moment, I swore you appeared before me, as transparent as the beginning and the end of our nightly dreams. You hovered, surrounded by stars, outlined in gold. Your eyes were closed, but the edges of your lips rose in a knowing smile.

— Whatever you do, remember this: you must not wake the Dreamer.

As the shrieks of the wraiths grew closer, I had no choice. I was drawn to you like a flower to sunlight, like roots to water, like lungs to air.

Your dreaming self's lips moved, whispering the spell. You reached up, beckoning, and I answered your call as you pulled me out of one storm and into another.

36.

ARCADY:

THE STAG

One moment, I had closed my eyes in a warm hut. The next, I awoke ankle-deep in a snow-swept forest, magic so thick in the air I choked on it. I felt as though I was still dreaming as I watched a dragon fall to earth.

My dragon.

Awe spread through me as he stretched his great wings before landing too gently, too softly for something so large. His glowing scales stained the snow scarlet. He arched his neck, tucking his wings behind him.

I had no memory of speaking the spell or bringing him through. Had my sleeping self chosen this, or had fate forced my hand?

I should have been afraid of him, and on some level, I was. Dazed, I walked through the snow on numb feet, taking in every detail.

The dragon bent his head low, great eyes level with mine, as if he bowed to me. The scales on his face were small compared to the ones on his sides, stronger than any armor and the edges sharp as any knife. Flat, circular scales covered the ridges of his brow, leading to a great crest of feathers on the top of his head that matched the ones at the upper ridge of his bat-like wings. Spikes rose along the back of his neck and down his spine to the tip of his tail, where another cluster of feathers curled like a question mark. There was something tied to one of the spines on his back. His fangs were as long as my forearm. There were those great claws that had dragged me up to the sky the last time I had seen him like this. I shivered.

I reached out my hand and placed it on the tip of his nose, feeling the hardness of his scales and the heat that radiated from them. His eyes closed as a shiver of pain shuddered through his body. The bond between us deepened from the golden wisp between worlds to something more.

Everen's dragon body glowed brighter around the edges. I dropped my hand as he transformed, shrinking and shifting.

And there he was.

Everen, winged and fanged, but almost human. He wore nothing, his skin creamier than the bright white of the snow. His expression was full of relief and a tenderness that cut me.

Everen crouched down, opening the bag that had been tied to the spines on his back and fallen when he transformed. His wings were tucked tight along his back, but in a blink, they disappeared. He pulled on the robe I'd seen him wear in his dreams.

He looked at me and he held out his arms.

I should have been wary. I should have remembered that even if we worked together, even if we trusted each other, we'd inevitably find ourselves on opposite sides after this was all finished.

I went to him all the same. We didn't touch skin to skin. He lifted me. I tucked my head against his shoulder, my legs settling around his waist, my feet burning, reminding me how close I was to frostbitten. His body heat warmed me enough to shiver as I clung to him.

"For a moment, there, I thought I was lost," he whispered into my ear. "Thank you, thank you for bringing me back." He pulled away. He was clearly haunted by whatever he'd seen in the Veil. But he was here. He was *here*. My eyes stung and my throat closed.

Reluctantly, I pulled away. I stood on the tops of his feet so I wouldn't have to put my soles back in the snow. Ridiculous, to think of myself standing on a dragon's humanoid toes, like how I used to dance with my taie when I was a small child. I had to laugh. Though he sounded beyond tired, Everen echoed it. I had missed that sound rumbling in the depths of his ribcage more than I could say.

The burst of energy at being reunited faded. Exhaustion pulled at my limbs. My hunger grew, and Everen, sensing it, rummaged in his pack and gave me a strip of dried, salted fish. I chewed it, disliking the taste but marveling that I was technically eating something from another world.

My magic was muted again, as if my hearing had grown more muffled or my vision misted. The half-bond moved between us like breath. We had completed it, and we had broken it. What would we do with it this time?

An unearthly shriek echoed through the forest and my muscles clenched in fear. Everen's eyelids opened wide. I turned, stumbling back into the snow, and Everen sank into a crouch.

A stag arrived at the edge of the clearing, its antlers casting long shadows across the snow. And there was something very, very wrong with it.

The eyes glowed as purple as a wraith's. It pulled back its lips and instead of the flat teeth of an herbivore, it bared black fangs. Ropes of saliva dripped from its mouth. Its pelt was stained black as the blight we'd found in the forest, and smoke clung close to its fur.

One of the wraiths had somehow possessed the stag.

Next to me, Everen hissed, his wings emerging from the slits at the back of his robe.

The tainted deer pawed at the snow with a hoof, breathing out smoke rather than steam. It hissed, a deeply unnerving clicking coming from deep in its throat. There was nothing in those glowing eyes but hunger.

The stag lowered its antlers.

"Oh, fuck," I said.

The disemboweled corpse we'd found in the forest flashed in my mind's eye.

Everen's wings flapped, and he rose, hovering a few feet above the snow. If Everen had still been a full dragon, the wraith would have been no match for his teeth and claws. But he was smaller, and drained. How well could either of us fight the thing?

I reached for my magic, and it flared weakly. I sent what I could at the deer, but it was little better than a child trying to cast their first spell. Everen dove at the creature with a roar, landing on its back and grabbing its antlers with his hands, forcing it to swerve so it didn't hit me.

It bucked, throwing Everen off, and he crashed to the ground, skidding through the snow.

"Everen!" I cried.

The stag slowed at the edge of the clearing, turning around and snorting out smoke. It let out another screech that made the hair on my arms stand up.

Everen tried to rise once more, but fell onto his knees. His eyes rolled up in his head before he collapsed into the snow. I ran toward him.

—*I'm . . . I'm all right*, he sent, faintly. *Give me . . . a moment.*

The stag lowered its antlers as Everen pushed himself onto an elbow. We didn't have a moment.

Spots danced in my vision, but I forced myself to stay standing.

"Get up, Everen," I said. "Please, *get up.*"

The stag's muscles bunched. I gathered what was left of my magic. Everen believed in fate, even if I wasn't sure I did. I was ready for it to lend a helping hand.

I heard the *thwunk* of a bowstring. An arrow hit the stag in the side of the neck. Its mouth opened in a strangled scream, the smoke writhing along its patchy coat. The arrow should have be enough to take it down, if it was a normal animal, but it seemed to feel no pain.

A wyvern cried and dived toward the stag. In the dark, it took me a moment to recognize Sorin's wyvern, Jaculus. The stag tossed its antlers, narrowly avoiding hitting the creature with the sharp points. The monster prepared to charge us once more. Fear spiked through me; I didn't fancy its chances of missing a second time.

Something whipped over my shoulder, narrowly missing me. Instead of an arrow, a knife hit the creature right between the eyes. The stag tossed its head, letting out a mournful, echoing sound. It took three wavering steps before falling to its knees. The lights of its eyes sputtered and darkened. Smoke rose from its corpse before drifting, slowly, into nothing.

The snow blanketed everything in silence. I caught my breath, still hungry and shivering, but at least not in danger of immediately turning Starveling. I hoped.

Sorin came into the clearing, bow slung over one shoulder.

I staggered through the snow to the monster's side. It was undeniably dead, its tongue lolling from its mouth. The teeth remained sharp as obsidian. Everything in me screamed to run as far from it as fast as I could, but I forced myself to grab the handle of the knife and pry it from the stag's skull. The blade was bone-white except where it was stained dark with blood. It was the mirror of the knife still tucked into the small of my back: the one I'd stolen from the corpse in the woods.

Everen, even weakened, moved faster than most humans. He grabbed Sorin before she had time to blink, hands firmly pinning her arms behind her back.

"*You*," he said, voice low and dangerous, twisting around to peer at her features as I blinked, still struggling to put the pieces together. The white-bladed knife. Her expression when she'd seen the corpse that afternoon. How Sorin fought on the practice grounds like she'd been born with a blade in her hand, even if she tried to hide it. The way she'd just taken down that stag. I should have realized as soon as I'd laid eyes on Sorin's green Jaculus. I had seen that same wyvern before, circling over the head of the hooded assassin at the barrow hill who had been about to kill me before Everen rescued me in his claws. Sorin met my eyes, resigned.

"I remember you," I said.

37.
SORIN:

UNMASKED

Sorin had lost the tracks of the beast in the snow, but as soon as she'd seen the gap in the sky, she'd known it would be drawn to the magic sizzling in the air like lightning.

She'd arrived to see the monster readying to kill Arcady and the celestial she'd seen at the auction. She'd shot the arrow without thinking, and thrown the knife deliberately.

The celestial being gripped Sorin tightly, and Their sharp nails— almost talons—dug into her flesh. She felt the heat of Their presence against her back. They forced her to the ground, magic pinning her in place. Arcady crouched, holding Sorin's own dragonbone blade to her neck.

Above them, Jaculus screeched, circling anxiously. The dragon shaped like a human hissed up at her wyvern, and Jaculus gave a frightened cry and perched on a branch, his neck straining.

Peace, little protector, she thought at him. *Peace.*

Something tightened around her wrists as the celestial pushed her to her knees.

"Do not run," the celestial warned.

Her legs likely wouldn't carry her even if she tried. Her whole body was shaking—from cold, from fear, and from the very sight of the being before her. She'd felt that sense of awe at the tower. Even if this creature was not a god, as Magnes claimed, They had come down from the sky on reddened wings. She knew, without a doubt, that she was still staring at something far beyond her ken.

"I think you have much to explain, Sorin," Arcady said. Their face and voice were hard as stone.

The snowfall had lightened. The celestial's body was so warm the snow around Their feet had begun to melt, revealing a patch of dark grass around the three of them as if spring had arrived early.

The silence was strangling, but any word she spoke could ensnare her further. If Magnes ever found out how she had failed, he would definitely kill her. He had given her so many chances, and this would be the last. Unless she found a way to break free of whatever lurked in her mind, she was a corpse walking.

"Why were you at the barrow hill?" Arcady asked. "Who are you, really?" They emphasized each question with a press of the knife.

Sorin considered her words. As with Magnes, she would tell the truth but leave holes. "My name is truly Sorin of the Order of the Dragons. I was raised at the Citadel. You are the one who crafted an entire false life." She paused. "But I, too, have been living a hidden one."

Arcady said nothing, but the line between their eyes deepened.

The celestial leaned closer, peering at her so intensely Sorin faltered. Recognition spread over Their unearthly features. "You were not merely at the barrow hill. You were one of the guards in the tower at the auction." Their voice was deep, the accent light but unlike any she'd ever heard. "Arcady, do you remember?"

Arcady searched Sorin's face but looked unsure. "I wasn't exactly in my best state."

"I fought you," the celestial said to Sorin. "You were the one who threw the knife as I leaped from the window."

Arcady exhaled. "Gods. You tried to kill us twice?" they said. "And then as soon as I enrolled at the university, there you were, pretending to be a poor little priest student, even lower on the hierarchy than me." They shook their head. "You clearly hated me, but you were always hanging about. Gods. How did I miss this? It was right in front of my sarding nose."

Because I am his Eye and his Knife, Sorin thought. *You were only meant to see me as a priest student, so for a long time, you did.* She knew she hadn't played the perfect game, but while Arcady had had their suspicions, in the end, she had tricked the trickster. Sorin supposed she should be proud of that.

"You even managed to be both my alchemy partner *and* my partner in the second trial." Arcady's impatience bubbled over, their voice coiling with fury. "How'd you manage that? Why? You are going to tell me the truth, Sorin of the Order of the Dragons. One way or another."

They played with the dragonbone knife, and Sorin felt a ripple of unease. Would Arcady, whoever they really were, hurt her to find out the truth?

"I was working on behalf of someone," Sorin said.

"As an assassin."

Sorin's eyes cast downward.

"And what does this person you work for want?" Arcady demanded. "Who are they?"

Her ears rang, and her heartbeat hammered in her throat. She tested her bonds, but they were tight.

"Untie me," she said. "I won't run. Please." She hated being trussed up like a hunted animal.

Arcady and the celestial exchanged glances, conferring silently.

"I swear it on the one I work for and the five gods," she said. "I won't run, and I won't try to harm you."

"I've heard that before," Arcady muttered, and the celestial, Sorin swore, hid a smile.

"I can help you," Sorin said, but she wouldn't let herself beg. "There's a deal to be made. Let's strike it."

Sorin's blade left her skin, and, after an aching pause, Arcady cut the bonds.

She worked her fingers open and closed before folding her arms tight to her chest. She kept her word and made no move. Jaculus called out softly and fluttered closer.

Arcady's chest subconsciously turned toward the dragon. Sorin found herself strangely envious.

Sorin wanted to know the truth of this bond between them. Not for Magnes, but for her own curiosity.

Arcady raised their chin, staring Sorin down. Sorin just managed not to flinch. "Why should we ever trust you?"

The celestial cocked Their head. "Something has been troubling me since the night of the tower." Their green eyes narrowed, and Sorin once more struggled under the sheer power of that gaze. "You missed."

"Definitely didn't," Arcady said with a grimace. "I set that broken bone myself."

The celestial shook Their head. "You did not aim for my wing. It was meant to be a killing blow to my back." They leaned forward. "You missed on purpose."

Arcady sucked in a breath.

"Yes," Sorin whispered. "I didn't harm you at the barrow hill, either." Sorin paused, readying her metaphorical next arrow. "Or in the clearing in the forest when the gods tried to break back through." She turned her head toward Arcady. "Or within that cave."

Arcady's skin blanched.

"I have seen you more murderous than I've ever been, 'Arcady Dalca,'" Sorin said, pronouncing their false name with derision. "I have seen your eyes black and your skin stained with marks. I have seen you so very *hungry*. You don't even remember, do you?" Her lips pulled back from her teeth. "I do."

Sorin pulled up her sleeve and showed the scars on her forearm. "You *bit me*."

Both Arcady and the celestial stared at the red scars on her forearm with something like revulsion. Each tooth indent was permanently etched into her skin. Sorin kept the scars visible, even as she wanted nothing more than to shove the sleeve down.

Even now, Arcady looked hungry. Sorin's stomach roiled in unease. Had Arcady used too much magic?

"But you didn't lose yourself entirely," Sorin pressed. "Someone brought you back from the brink."

"The ambrosia," Arcady whispered. "That was you?"

"My master." The ringing in her ears grew louder. At the time, Sorin hadn't understood why Magnes hadn't simply killed Arcady and been done with it. Now, of course, she knew Magnes had some other need of them.

"If the one I worked for had wanted to kill you, you would already be dead. I have been your protector, if anything. But my master *will* kill you when you've outlived your usefulness. I'm certain of that."

"This person . . ." Arcady began. "They're the one who made you take that Vow of Silence, aren't they?"

Sorin nodded.

"Fuck. That means the spymaster is someone in the priesthood."

Sorin clenched her jaw, which was answer enough.

"Tell us the name," the celestial said, Their voice low and mesmerizing. "Tell us who you work for, and do not lie."

The ringing grew to a dull roar. She felt as though she were falling, gathering speed before she hit the ground.

"Say it, Sorin," Arcady commanded.

Sorin opened her mouth. One word. Two syllables. Once the name
was uttered, there'd be no taking it back.

"I work . . . I work for—"

Her tongue froze.

Magnes, she tried to say. Her lips pressed together for the "M."
Mag—

Her throat closed, and she sputtered. She fell forward on her
hands and knees, to her side, her limbs jerking. The knot in her mind
tightened. She was choking on her tongue. Her brain was boiling,
every nerve on her skin afire. Still, she tried to say the name, but managed only strangled noises, like a panicked animal caught in a trap.

—*Stop*, the celestial said in her mind. *Let it go. Let it go for now.*

As soon as Sorin stopped reaching for the name, her muscles
relaxed. She panted, her cheek on the cold, wet grass, sucking in air
that smelled like snow, the sharpness of the Veil, and the unnatural,
rotten-smoke scent of the stag. Its unholy corpse was not six paces
away, staring at her with blank eyes.

"What was *that*?" Arcady asked. "Did you seal sign not to say
their name?"

"No," she gasped. She would have remembered setting her seal
into the ink or wax, dragging it across the contract.

Unless he made you forget, a tiny corner of her mind reminded her.

"There's a block on her mind," the celestial said. Part of her was
annoyed the celestial dared to be so informal to refer to her as "she"
before they'd been properly introduced, but the rest was in far too
much pain to care.

"I've . . . I've put together that my mind has been meddled with,"
Sorin said through gritted teeth. "As we practiced for the second

trial and you warded me, I started to . . . remember. There's a . . . knot, but I don't know how to untangle it."

She sat up, wiping her face of spittle, snot, and tears. "I know, now, why my master was so confident I would remain loyal. Letting me take the Vow of Silence was for their own amusement more than anything." She laughed, bitterly. She had defaulted back to the neutral pronoun, afraid even gendering Magnes aloud might trigger the block.

"It was the illusion of choice," she said, bowing her head. "That's why I've come to you. Maybe a liar and a false god can help me." She raised her head and met their eyes.

Arcady and the celestial stared at each other, and then at her.

The dragon spoke slowly. "You think we can save each other."

"Yes," she breathed. "Help me break it, and I'll tell you everything I know. You need me, too. There's something about you my master can't yet defeat. Once they figure out how, you won't stand a chance. An alliance gives us a hope. Do we have a deal?"

Another silence. She realized, with a prickling of unease as she waited for their answer, that they were *speaking* to each other with forbidden magic.

Sorin had learned many things that night, but most of all, she knew she was no longer Magnes's unthinking, unflinching Eye.

She had blinked.

38.

ARCADY:

THE AFTERMATH

What do you think? I asked Everen as Sorin knelt before us. *Can we trust her?*

—*No*, he replied without hesitation. *We should kill her.*

—*If we kill her, we can't very well get any answers, can we?* I pointed out. Never mind that I wasn't a murderer, and despite being a dragon who had killed one of his own, he wasn't, either.

He paused, considering, as Sorin's eyes bounced between us.

I was *furious* with myself. I had spent so much of my energy making Arcady Dalca appear like a real drakine student, I'd forgotten the obvious: that I might not be the sole student pretending.

My stomach churned from both hunger and the sight of Sorin's scars. I wanted to call her a liar, but deep down, I knew she was telling the truth about what had happened in that cave.

—*Can you read her mind?* I asked. *Figure out who she works for that way?*

A subtle shake of the head. —*No. Dragons read emotions and speak to each other like this, but as in the human world, it is anathema to pry into another's mind. I have not learned the way of it, nor do I want to. But she has already discovered warding magic that might allow her to unblock herself.*

—So what do we do?

He heaved a sigh. *—I think you know.*

Indeed I did.

"All right, Sorin," I said aloud. "You have your deal. But I swear, I *swear*, if you pull anything, I will personally gut you like that corpse we found earlier. Do you understand?"

"I understand," she whispered.

I shivered. The snow had stopped, but even with Everen's heat, it was freezing. The dead stag was motionless.

—Can you head back to the city tonight? I asked Everen.

—Maybe. Just. But I would not be able to carry you that far in preterit, especially now.

I shuddered. I had not enjoyed either of my two flights so far with Everen, whether he was preterit or dragon.

"Right," I said aloud. "No one tries to kill each other tonight. We're all too tired for that. Sorin and I head back to the hut, and Everen will head back to Vatra."

"Everen," Sorin echoed, as if tasting the name.

"I suppose proper introductions are in order," I said, with the fake levity that was my token response when things grew too heavy. "Everen," I signed "he," "is a dragon prince from the land of Vere Celene beyond the Veil. Sorin," I signed "she," "is from the Order of the Dragons and is a warrior-priest assassin posing as a student." I waved my hand between them.

Sorin blinked. *Vere Celene*, she mouthed. Everen dragged himself up to his full human height. Sorin took in his dragon-green eyes, the too-smooth way he moved. She was awed by him, and I couldn't blame her.

"Everen," I said, nodding my head to the stag's corpse that raised gooseflesh on my arms whenever I caught sight of it. "Will you kindly get rid of that nightmare thing?"

With an elegant wave of his hand, the stag burst into flame. Sorin's eyes widened.

Though flames from the stag helped warm me, I pressed against Everen's side, and his arm came around me. Sorin wrapped her arms around herself as we watched the stag burn down to cinders, its noxious smoke rising to the sky.

When the fire guttered out, Sorin reached for her pocket.

"It's salt," she said at our suspicion, drawing out a small bag. She clicked to her wyvern, and Jaculus perched on her shoulder. Sorin scattered the white granules on the worst of the black tracks from the monster.

"The blight marks seem to fade, in time," she said. "But salt helps ensure it doesn't spread, though of course nothing else will grow in its place." She paused, as if waiting to see if the magic in her mind would punish her for revealing that. It didn't.

We walked back in silence, mistrust so thick in the air between us I could almost taste it.

We paused just out of sight of the hut.

"For better or worse," Sorin said. "We're in this together."

"For now, at least," I said.

"For now," Sorin agreed.

Everen hesitated. *—Are you sure I should not stay? I could sleep in the stables and be gone before you wake, but I would be close.*

—You'd smell like a predator to the horses, and we need them rested to get back to the lodge tomorrow.

—Are you sure it is safe? he asked, flicking his eyes to Sorin, lips pulling back from his teeth. *What if she hurts you?*

—I doubt she's allowed to kill me. I shifted my shoulders uncomfortably. Someone back at the Citadel knew far too much and had from the beginning. I would worry about that tomorrow.

I didn't want Everen to leave, either. We had so much to work through. I reached out and grabbed his arm, his sleeve protecting him from my touch, but I had to prove to myself he was really here and I wasn't dreaming. Whether or not I'd chosen it, he was back, a year to the day after he'd crashed into this world the first time.

I was still afraid, suspicious of his true motives, and I had no idea what would happen next. Our magic was compromised, and I didn't like being weaker. Yet he was familiar, and he was so beautiful, and for better or worse, he knew me better than any other living creature. No small part of me wished we were properly alone, and I knew he wished the same.

— Tomorrow, I promised. *As soon as I'm back in Vatra, I'll meet you at the lock shop.* I chanced leaning my head against his chest. His arms squeezed me tight. Reluctantly, he let go, backing away, not breaking my gaze.

His wings emerged, lighting up the forest, and Sorin couldn't suppress her gasp.

— Tomorrow, he agreed, and he rose from the ground. With a few flaps of his wings, he was gone, the clouds hiding his glow.

When Sorin and I could finally bear to lower our gazes, we stared at each other.

"I take it you won't return my knives?" she asked.

"No."

She gave a mirthless smile and pushed open the door.

Willem was tangled in his blanket on the bed, his head thrown back, snoring softly. Edin lay on her side, Verdell curled in her arms.

They had slept through it all.

We headed back to the lodge at first light, ate our weight in food, and tidied ourselves up. Willem wanted to stay longer, but Sorin and I convinced him we needed to make it back to Vatra, and Edin was happy to do whatever we thought best.

It was a long, awkward carriage ride back to the capital. Willem was well-rested and far too aware something between Sorin and me had changed.

"What is *up* with you two?" he said roughly once every quarter candlemark. "I could cut this tension with a knife. Did you two fight or kiss? I really can't tell. I'm hoping kiss, to be honest."

Edin smirked.

I don't think our glowers helped dissuade either of them that we weren't in some sort of lover's tiff. Better that than suspecting the truth, I supposed. I stared out the window, willing the spelled carriage to go faster.

When we finally arrived at the Citadel, the sky was stained orange. We'd missed the evening meal, sadly. Willem, bless him, asked Sorin some question about wyverns, and it distracted her long enough for me to slip away and make my way back down to the city.

I doubled back and took a few strange detours to cover my tracks. When I was sure no one was following me, I made my way back to the Loc & Key and the dragon that waited for me there.

39.
EVEREN:

REUNION

The first thing I did once I broke into the Loc & Key was attempt to scry my sister.

I first tried with the little mirror in the washroom on the upper level. When that failed, I gathered my strength and headed through the trapdoor to the back room that had once been your sanctuary.

My heart constricted at the sight of it coated in a layer of soot and ash. I wiped off the mirror, grateful that the heat had not cracked it.

As I attempted another scry, I tried not to imagine the worst: another wraith attack after I went through the rip in the Veil. The Reek erupting, raining fire and smoke. I even poured the flask of precious scrysilver I had brought through to the human world into the bowl and attempted to scry that way.

—*Please*, I sent out like a prayer. *Please be all right.*

Exhausted from the effort with my dampened magic, I eventually gave up and returned the scrysilver to its leather bladder and hid it at the bottom of my bag.

On this side of the Veil, I had to hope I would be able to find more about the dragonstone tree. Sorin, after all, was a member of the Order of the Dragons, but she was likely too young to know the priesthood's innermost secrets, I guessed, even if she had worked as one of its Eyes. Perhaps she had seen something she should not have, and that is why she had been spelled to forget?

No small part of me wondered if I should have ripped her throat out there in that forest and been done with it, no matter her secrets. It would have kept us both safer.

The day lengthened as I waited for your return. Even though I was drained from the flight through the storm and the fight with the tainted stag, I could not stay idle. When you finally unlocked the door in the evening, I was strangely nervous.

"Hello," I said, and despite everything, I could not keep the smile from my face.

"Hullo," you said, taking in my handiwork.

I had cleaned the worst of the dust from the upper level of the shop and shaken out the bedding in the back courtyard. I had lit the candles you had stolen from churches long ago, and the air was filled with the smell of food.

I had used what you taught me to pickpocket that afternoon before spending the coins at the market. I laid out the meat pies and roasted vegetables and poured the wine into ceramic cups.

You closed your eyes at the first bite, savoring the suet and salt. We ate in near-silence, both wanting to taste the odd near-normalcy a moment longer. I had missed those evenings in this very lock shop almost as much as I had missed human food. I let myself enjoy the meal.

When the last bite had been swallowed, you sighed and swirled the wine in your cup. "What are the next steps, then?" you asked, breaking the spell. "Beyond hoping Sorin doesn't kill us in our sleep."

"I attempted to scry, but without success. I believe we must discover what this Sorin knows. I do not trust her, but I do trust fate sent her to us."

"It must be comforting," you said, still staring into the depths of the cup. "To still believe that fate does have a grand plan for us."

"I have seen it," I said. "I have seen dragons flying over Vatra, with peace between our kind and yours. There is a way to bring it to pass. I have to believe it. I have to."

You glanced at me, then away.

"Even after a full day of rest and food, I'm back to barely being able to hold a shapeshift for a candlemark, much less waterweave for my Kalsh class or have a hope of making it through the third trial." You drained your cup. "Though I suppose it doesn't matter, in the end."

The sadness rose off you in waves, and I ached to reach for you.

"Let us see what Sorin knows," I said. "And if we complete the bond, we will have our full magic to face whatever comes next."

"If we complete the bond," you echoed, softly, not looking at me. "I don't know if it'd be easier or harder for us a second time."

"I expect that is largely up to you," I said, and your shoulders hunched. "I know that you gave me your trust only for me to ruin it by reacting with nothing but my fear, my anger, and my guilt. I swear I have learned from it. This time, I will hold nothing back, and nothing—nothing—will shake my loyalty to you. I swear it. But that does nothing if you do not trust me as well."

"I—" Your eyes were wet and shining.

"Think about it," I said. "We have a little time. Not much, but some. Get used to me being here. Let me prove myself to you."

You nodded in obvious relief, and I tried to hide my own stab of disappointment.

We finished cleaning up, and you hesitated. "I . . . I probably shouldn't go back to the Citadel until classes return," you said.

"Yes," I said. "Please stay."

You made your bed, and we settled down on our respective sides of the lock shop. You turned from me, but it was still something that you trusted me enough to show me your back. I watched your breath rise and fall, rise and fall, until you finally settled into sleep. Eventually, I followed.

Neither of us dreamed.

40.
ARCADY:

BETTER THAN ALONE

The days ticked down until term began again.

On the second morning after we'd returned from the lodge, I snuck out and put a note at the agreed drop point, telling Wren and Larkin while I hadn't yet found anything, I had a few solid leads. I could only hope it was enough to buy me time. I might not have discovered any specifics, but it had only driven home for me that whatever Hayden was working on — Larkin probably shouldn't get her mitts on it.

I came back to find Everen poring over the few sources I'd found that referenced the crystal tree, his feathered hair falling into his face. I tried not to think about Sorin and halfheartedly read my history textbook chapters. I was meant to practice spells for Kalsh, but each time I tried, my magic flickered and the water splashed back into the bowl. Part of it was that my magic was muted. Part of it was frustration that there was no point any longer.

Mostly, though, I was preoccupied.

With every candlemark, the distraction grew. For moons, my sleeping-self had been far too honest about how very much I wanted

Everen. Once we'd realized we were connected in those dreams, I'd been too mortified to act on it, and Everen had been respectful.

Now, he was back, close enough to physically touch in the real world. As another day lengthened to evening, the tension only swelled.

The way his eyes lingered told me he wanted me just as much. *Maybe I want you to hurt me*, he'd said once, when I feared my kiss would cause him pain. He'd dragged my lips to his first.

That night, sleep wouldn't find me. I stared at the back of Everen's head and the curve of his spine. I knew every line of his body, and my fingers itched to trace them. What if I was brave enough to cross the distance between us and press my cheek to the space between his shoulder blades? To drape my arm over his waist? I laid on my back.

He turned over, and my head turned toward him. His pupils were wide in the darkness. So close, yet so far.

"This is torture," he whispered.

"Yes," I said, even if part of me found the anticipation of it delicious.

We stared at each other. Which of us would break first? I'd once tangled my gloved hands in his scalp when I dyed his hair darker. There was that time we had practiced dancing on that abandoned rooftop and ended up practicing something entirely different, our clothes a barrier between us. After the auction but before the barrow hill, I'd shown him my marks and he hadn't flinched.

"I'm not ready to fully bond," I said. I knew we should, but the thought filled me with fear. "Not yet."

"Instruct, then, and I'll follow." His voice was low, warm with something that kindled a fire deep in my belly. It was heady knowing I could tell a dragon to do anything, and he might very well do it.

"Gloves," I said. "Behind the counter."

He was there in a blink, and he slipped them on.

We took each other in. We both wore long shirts, and mine didn't cover the Struck marks on my legs.

"Kneel." I didn't recognize my tone of voice. He fell to his knees. I walked toward him. Slow, deliberate.

His face tilted up, his head level with my hip. I reached out and pulled off his shirt. He leaned forward and pressed his cheek against my lower stomach, my shirt protecting us. My fingers toyed with his hair, not touching his scalp, and his head moved slightly with my breath.

This was playing with all sorts of fire.

"Tell me, if it becomes too much," I said, pulling away. He nodded and looked up at me with such trust it almost broke me.

I gripped his jaw in my hand, hard, and he gasped. His magic flowed to me, my palm glowing where our skin touched. I wanted more. Him giving up his control made me feel so powerful.

I leaned down, my lips barely brushing his. He arced toward me, but I pulled away. I took a step back, and then another, until I reached my tangle of blankets. Not breaking eye contact, I pulled my shirt over my head and stepped out of my small clothes. I kept my shoulders back as his eyes drank me in. The metal setting at my chest with my stolen seal. The Struck marks that snaked their way up my legs, tangled around my torso, my upper arms, ending above my collarbone.

Slowly, I lowered myself onto the bed.

"Crawl to me," I said.

The dragon's eyes darkened, and on all fours, he came.

"Make me forget," I said. "Make me forget my fear."

I felt his gloved hand on my ankle, skimming up my leg. I leaned back, letting him take control.

He kissed his way up my calf, the inside of my knee, and up my thigh. The brush of his lips was light, reverent, and each sent a shock of pleasure through me. Red and blue veins of power rose on my skin as each kiss fed me more magic, and he willingly gave it.

One hand came to the back of my thigh, below my arse, and the other rested on the crease of my hip. He came close enough to the place I desperately wanted him to be. I felt his breath as his hands came away, no longer touching.

He shifted so his hands were on the blankets at either side of my head. Resting his weight on them, his body hovered over mine just as he had in one of my dreams. Our dreams.

He blinked first, slow, content, and bent his head. The tip of his tongue traced the shell of my ear.

He moved lower again. My heart had been armored for so long by the cage of my ribs. I'd hidden myself with various false faces and personas. With Everen, I had no more defenses.

He made a sound deep in his throat as his mouth found my neck.

"Don't—don't break the skin," I said, the fear snaking its way back through me. I could feel the half-bond hovering between us, desperate to complete.

He paused, raising his head. I caught the flicker of sorrow at my holding back, but he nodded. I ran my hands down his back in apology, though I knew my touch hurt as much as it soothed.

He pulled away. I sensed he'd given me as much magic as he could, and I nodded.

He lay at my side and his gloved hand came between my legs, and my hips bucked at his grasp. My hand reached out toward his groin, gathering the bedsheet and gripping him through it. He gave a strangled groan. I threw my forearm over my eyes, the sight of him suddenly too much as he set the rhythm, and I matched it.

I felt his breath on my neck, but our skin didn't touch. We rode the pressure and the friction. My hips moved to meet his hand, focusing on a point deep within myself. At times, I worried I'd lost it, but then, the crest rose, and he urged me over as I cried out. My hand's movement faltered as I briefly lost myself.

As my climax finished, he freed himself, bringing his gloved hand beneath my bare one. I opened my eyes as, with one last burst of magic for me and pain for him, he moved our hands thrice more and followed me over the cliff. I watched his face—the way his mouth opened and his head fell back. I realized I wanted to see that expression on him again and again.

I'd given myself something like this, of course, but I'd always reached the crescendo on my own. We stayed like that as our breath quieted, coming back to ourselves.

Everen shifted onto his back, and he laughed in that way I loved so much, and I echoed it. It had been a dangerous relief to finally release the tension. We cleaned ourselved and slid into fresh bedding. His stolen power flowed through me—still not enough compared to my usual magic. Within a few days, it would drift back to fueling the bond and keeping us from the rest of our power. Even if we'd come together, we remained apart.

But even like this was so much better than being alone.

The next morning, though neither of us regretted what we'd done, we were awkward and silent as we ate our breakfast.

I'd put my sleep shirt back on, but his gaze kept catching on my thighs. Tempted as I was to push him back down to the bed, the Citadel called. I dressed, packed my things, and hesitated by the door.

"I feel useless here," Everen said.

"Keep looking through what I found—perhaps I missed something. I'll be back as soon as I can."

I paused, wanting to kiss him, but holding back. I'd taken too much magic from him last night. I suspected as soon as I left, he'd go back to bed and sleep most of the day.

"Be safe," was all he said, and I slung my bag over my shoulder and headed back up the hill to whatever waited for me there.

When I arrived, the Citadel had a strange air about it that reminded me of my first day at university when we'd all, as one, learned that Chancellor Yrsa of Swiftsea had died. People clustered close together, whispering. I paused in the courtyard long enough to eavesdrop. It seemed the public had heard what I'd already learned from Willem: the Jaskian shipwreck off the coast of the Edge Isles.

In my history lecture, Professor Fullin gave additional context to the recently unveiled diplomatic snarl. I knew I should care about the possible threat of war, and the part I'd helped play in it by trying to sell a relic to Jask myself. But I had far more on my mind. Sorin was missing, and I kept half-expecting guards to burst in any moment and drag me down to the dungeon.

Halfway through the lecture, she slunk in, looking rough as anything.

"Tardy, tardy," Professor Fullin admonished, mildly, before diving back into an over-detailed breakdown of another past tension between Loc and our neighbor to the south. I tried to ignore Sorin for the rest of the lecture.

When class finally finished, Professor Fullin passed back our essays. I glanced at the professor's increasingly exasperated questions in the margins. The professor thought I had focused too much on the consorts, particularly the final one, at the expense of analyzing the wider political tensions.

I'd passed, but not much more than that. It should have disappointed me, but I felt numb. I hadn't been allowed to research what I really wanted to know or gain access to the higher levels of the archives. Trying to do everything the official way, even with my false seal, had gotten me next to nowhere so far. I shoved the paper into my bag.

Sorin waited for me in the hallway. We stared at each other in silence until the other students left and we were alone.

I searched her face. "You haven't turned me in, it seems," I said, keeping my voice low.

"We made a deal," Sorin said. "I've already cast my die. Even before we spoke in the forest, I lied in my reports."

"About what?" I demanded.

"I put in nothing about the Night Market after I followed you there."

My mouth opened, but no sound came out.

Sorin stepped forward, crowding me. "I know you're looking into the professor's research, and I've said not a word about it for over a moon. No one's come to your lock shop either, have they?"

I stiffened.

One side of Sorin's mouth quirked. "Did you think I didn't follow you?" She leaned even closer until our noses nearly touched. All trace of mirth left her voice. "I gave you your moment to recover from the forest, but time grows short. I need—"

"Sorin. Arcady!"

We broke apart as Rahela trotted in our direction.

"Did I . . . interrupt?" she hesitated.

"No," I said, shortly. "What is it, Rahela?"

"Haven't you heard?" She took my sleeve. "Come on, the six of us have been called. The administration made a decision." She broke into a grin, unable to contain her excitement. "The Trials are going ahead."

41.

SORIN:

THERE AND BACK AGAIN

Instead of gathering on the amphitheater grounds, six students clustered in Professor Plink's classroom, though it was Professor Hayden who introduced the third trial. Professor Plink sat in the corner, marking more papers.

Beneath lowered lashes, Sorin took in the other remaining students. Everyone suspected Edin Vayne would likely come in first place and receive the full scholarship. Which two would receive second and third place, and the support and glory that would come with it, was anyone's guess. Rahela had proven herself well, especially for a second year. Cind and Jordin were strong contenders. Sorin knew she and Arcady were the underdogs, but she'd heard whispers that a few at the Citadel were rooting for them all the same.

While the third trial might be anyone's game, Sorin knew it was ultimately Magnes's. He'd pulled his strings to ensure Arcady remained in the Trials. She felt as though a clock was ticking down the time within her skull.

"Welcome," Professor Hayden said, but Their smile didn't reach Their eyes. It was strange to see the professor back in the context of the university, even though Sorin had been too shy to speak to Hayden beyond the bare minimum at the lodge. Their wife, Sar Ansel, remained with the rest of the delegation sorting out the Jaskian shipwreck. Sorin suspected talks were not going well. Selfishly, she hoped this meant Magnes would be away from the Citadel for longer.

"Today I'm honored to be the one to introduce you to the third trial. This is a task that cannot truly be studied or practiced, as it tests how you react in the moment. It'll all culminate in one sennight, which means soon enough the Trials will be finished and you'll have the rest of the term to fully focus on your coursework and final exams." Professor Hayden raised Their eyebrows. "I know some of you have been . . . slightly distracted."

A few of the students smirked or looked guilty. Sorin knew her progress in her classes had stalled, but she had also learned enough over her last few moons at the university that, if she could break free of Magnes, she might be able to scrape a living doing something other than hiring out her muscles, her sword, or the various other ways she knew how to kill.

"I can't help but give you a wee test, so forgive me in advance," Professor Hayden said. "If the first trial was magic versus self, and the second was magic versus others, does anyone have any guesses as to what the third might be?"

Edin Vayne raised her hand. The professor nodded.

"Magic against nature," she said. "We'll be tested by the land itself."

"Very good," Professor Hayden said, "Unlike the other trials, you won't have a captive audience around you. There'll be a grand display at the start—the Citadel does love a spectacle, after all, and the third trial falls on the Feast of Storms—and you'll all be paraded through the city. The whole of Vatra will see you off and wish you well. Once you're out of the city, though, you'll be transported in individual carriages to the starting points of the race."

Professor Hayden waved toward the large map of Loc on the wall. They reached into the pocket of Their robe and brought out a simple copper medal, not unlike the one Sorin had won at the wyvern race.

"You'll all start separately, but eventually the paths will converge. At each obstacle, you must claim one of these. First bronze, then silver, then gold. For these tasks, you'll have to cross, climb, or break through these natural barriers with the aid of magic. Each obstacle is set up in a way that you could use several branches to achieve the same effect. So, for example, if you came across fire in your path, you could either snuff it out using Aura magic, starve it of air with Zama's power, quench it with Kalsh's magic, or block it by moving boulders or soil with the aid of Piater. Only Jari might not be so useful. Does everyone follow so far?"

The students nodded.

"Excellent. You will each have parallel paths where you face your first and second obstacles separately. You'll all face the same third obstacle before returning to your carriages. The official finishing point is the Citadel amphitheater, and we will all be waiting to greet you and celebrate the winners."

Professor Hayden cleared Their throat. "Safety is something of which you must be mindful for this task. Take extra care. While professors will be in the general area, we won't be as physically near as we were in the first and second trials." They paused and swallowed, obviously pushing aside the memory of Their son's attack. Willem's face that night in the hut as he stared into the fire flashed in Sorin's mind's eye.

Professor Hayden passed them each a necklace with a sphere of thin metal.

"If you are in distress, all you have to do is break one of these using the same spell you did for the sword in the second trial—*tiś-té*—and help will come as quickly as possible."

They all practiced. Sorin triggered hers with ease, but she noticed that it took Arcady a couple of tries, like they were trying to light kindling in the wind.

"Well done," the professor said, bringing their attention back to the front of the room. "Remember that magic is in everything. The earth, the sky, the air, the water. It moves through the world along leylines, following its own rules. Listen to the power within yourself, too. Respect it, and it will respect you in turn. May you be lifted upon the dragon gods' wings."

Arcady frowned, staring absently at the map of Loc.

The professor released them, and Sorin streamed into the hallway with the rest. Cind invited the others to a tavern for drinks, but Arcady and Sorin made their excuses. Arcady remained pensive.

"I saw you struggle with that basic charm," Sorin said when they reached a secluded corridor. "What's wrong with your magic?"

Sorin's words failed to interrupt whatever was going on in Arcady's head.

"Arcady," Sorin said.

Arcady hesitated, their expression shifting.

"My life's tied up in yours now," Sorin pressed, her heart hammering. "I deserve to know."

Arcady searched Sorin's face. "Everen and I . . . we're only half-bonded, you see," they admitted. "It'll take time for us to finish the connection. Until then, our magic is dampened."

"Dampened?" Sorin's voice was too loud. Arcady winced.

"It's temporary."

"*How* temporary?"

Arcady didn't answer.

"How will you help me if you can't cast a simple spell?" Sorin demanded, her heartbeat rising.

"Between the both of us, Everen and I should be able to ward you." But even they looked doubtful.

"And if you can't? If you don't complete this bond by the third trial?"

Arcady's face rippled in unease.

Sorin ran her palm over the short stubble of her skull. They were running out of options and running out of time. "We've delayed long enough." She tapped her temple. "I need to know. You have to find a way."

Arcady rubbed their face with a shaking hand. They glanced up at the stone ceiling of the corridor, making a few internal calculations.

"Fuck," they sighed. "All right. Let's go."

"A moment. I need to fetch something."

"What?"

It was Sorin's turn for silence.

Arcady exhaled. "Be quick, then. I'll wait by the gates."

Back in her monk's cell, Sorin took one of the vials of Elixir from its hiding place. She knew, whatever happened next, she'd need all the help she could get. She took a small dose, letting its glow flow through her veins.

She debated taking it with her, but she didn't know how it would affect a dragon and a human's magic, and, deep down, she wasn't willing to share either the secret or the drug.

As Arcady led Sorin down through the city and to their hidden lock shop, they glanced at her out of the corner of their eye.

"I have a feeling once we lay out our secrets, the pieces will add up to a painting of what's coming." They swallowed. "I don't think we'll like what it shows us."

Sorin suspected they were right.

42.
SORIN:
AN UNRAVELING

Outside, it was a golden winter afternoon, but inside Arcady's lock shop, with the curtains drawn, it was dim as night.

Arcady rolled a large map of Loc onto the floor, weighing down the corners with locks. It was marked up with handwritten notes and dates in different colored ink.

"This shows the spread of the Strike in the early days of the plague," Sorin said, slowly, putting it together.

The celestial—Everen—looked as though he wanted to put himself between Sorin and Arcady. The mistrust rose off him like smoke. Sorin knew she must play this carefully: if she gave them enough that this Everen believed she was no longer useful, she had no doubt he'd try to kill her. She'd been trained well, but was she strong enough to face down a dragon?

"Do you know the children's story of *The Mage Tree*?" Arcady rose, taking a book from the bar at the back of the lock shop and passing it to her.

Sorin blinked at the cover. A book of fairy tales? "Vaguely. That's the one about the youth who wants to live forever and becomes trapped as fruit on the branch of the Tree of Life instead?"

"That's the one." Arcady crouched, hooking their elbows around their knees as Sorin opened it to the correct page. Arcady and Everen watched her every move. Sorin ran a fingertip along the illustration.

"We think the tree might be real," Arcady said.

Sorin glanced up sharply. Arcady leaned forward and tapped a passage and read the line aloud: "'The mage told the youth the tree could be found where the veins meet the sharpened teeth at the heart of truth.'"

Sorin's gaze returned to the map.

"Yes," they said, gaze intent. "Do you see it?"

"The veins . . ." Sorin walked her fingertips along the Crystal River. Everen touched the Red River, and Arcady the Vatran.

"Seven rivers that spread through Loc and Myria all begin in the glaciers of the Fangs," Arcady tapped the mountains.

"That is still a large area," Everen said. "Where exactly is this 'heart'?"

"It's not marked on that map," Sorin said, her voice flat. "It's the—" She tried to form the words, but she sputtered, struggling past the block.

Everen seemed like he would happily let her choke, but Arcady shook her by the shoulder. "Let it go," they said.

"I have to break this spell," Sorin gasped, pressing a finger to her temple once the worst of it had passed. "It's all in here."

Arcady exhaled. "Right. Let's try, then."

Everen went to the counter and took out a leather bladder and a large, shallow bowl. He set the bowl between them and poured a strange liquid into it. The silver surface shimmered like oil mixed in water.

"It looks . . . it looks like a ward made into quicksilver," Sorin said, mesmerized. "What is it?"

Everen hesitated.

"Just tell her, Everen," Arcady said.

Everen scowled but relented. "We call it scrysilver. It is a liquid drawn from the depths of the earth that my kind uses to scry the past and future. The hope is this may help us follow what you see when the spell is broken."

Sorin blinked. "The . . . future?"

Arcady spread their hands. "Welcome to the cluster of fate, Sorin. Looks like you're as tangled up in it as we are. I'm afraid it's largely terrible."

"Will this even work?" Sorin asked, her foreboding growing.

"I have a way to access more power, at least for a time." Arcady held out their hand toward Everen's cheek. "May I?"

A silent conferral, and Everen nodded.

When Arcady brushed Everen's skin, his eyes closed and he shuddered as if in pain, even though the touch was gentle. Sorin felt like she was intruding but couldn't glance away from the soft glow of red, blue, and gold where their skin met. Everen hissed and pulled away, and Arcady's palm and seal glowed before settling.

Everen fell back, breathing harder. Sorin had never seen magic pass *between* people like that, not even during the second trial and the ward.

"There," Arcady said, panting slightly. "This might be enough. Then again, it might not. Only one way to find out. Are you ready?"

"Yes," Sorin said.

"What do I do, Everen?"

"Try the Celenian words to create the ward," the dragon said. "But make the 'friends' part plural, so we might both try."

Arcady paused. "I may understand the Old Tongue better thanks to you, but my fundamental grasp of Celenian grammar is still . . . rather shit."

"*Kaṣutak* versus *kaṣutul.*"

Sorin blinked. The Old Tongue was the dragons' language?

"Ah. Right." They cleared their throat. "*Vanoté leu ek kaṣutak al-lei.*" Arcady's seal glowed as they used their power mixed with their dragon's. The ward fell over the three of them.

At first, Sorin felt the ward wobble. It was only once she reached out and joined the spell that the boundary rose around the three of them, steadied . . . and held.

"Find the knot, Sorin," Arcady instructed.

Sorin closed her eyes and focused within.

At first, all was silent.

—*There,* Everen said, and Sorin cringed at the sound of another's voice in her head. She could feel the dragon rooting around her mind like—like *him.*

Everen guided her, and the spell held. The ward chased away occluded shadows, revealing the nearly invisible tangle that blended into the rest of her thoughts.

"What do I do next?" Sorin asked aloud. Magic continued to flow between the three of them, feeding the ward.

—*Untie it,* he commanded.

Sorin tried not to second guess as she groped within herself until she found a tendril and gripped it tightly. The pain was like when she'd cracked a tooth as a child. Whenever her tongue had brushed it, her whole body had reverberated in agony. Her muscles locked. The longer she held it, the more likely she'd start to seize.

—*We cannot help you from here,* Everen said in her mind. *It has to be you, Sorin of the Order of Dragons.*

Sorin reached for a corner of the knot and *pulled.*

She doubled over, gasping as the memories streamed back through her consciousness, jumbled and out of order. Out of the corner of her eye, Sorin caught Everen and Arcady leaning forward toward the shimmering scrysilver as she lost herself to the past and all that came with it.

She arrives at Nalore Monastery, tired and dirt-stained. It is the end of her second moon of being an Eye. The monks who live here year-round, hidden in the depths of the mountains, have taken a Vow of Silence just as she once had. Perhaps, in the archives, they might whisper a spell to copy ink, but in front of her, they do not even communicate in Trade. They flit through the monastery like ghosts.

She knows, though, from the fluid way the monks move, that they all have been trained for combat. Sorin suspects if she tugged one of the dagger hilts at their waists, she'd find the white of dragonbone.

The priests here are scholars, but they are also guards.

What are they protecting?

Sorin sees herself from above, as if through her wyvern's eyes. She's racing through the dawn-dyed forest, urging her horse to go faster, faster, leaning low over the saddle. She glances over her shoulder.

Her horse is running too fast across a forest path that might have hidden roots. If her beast trips, it'd be a broken leg or worse. But if she can make it in time—if she can get just a little further—

The forest lightens. She's been riding all night.

She and the horse are almost out of the cover of the trees. Then it is only another short ride down to the coast to the small harbor at the mouth of the Crystal River. She knows she should head further down the coast to Cardia, but she needs to leave, she needs to go to where He can't follow.

Faster—faster—if she can make it to the sea by morning, if she can find a ship that will take her—if she can get far enough, fast enough before He realizes she's gone—

The branches of the trees reach for her, twigs breaking and falling to the dirt. The wyvern calls out, wings beating hard, keeping pace. Does he, too, dream of the horizon?

A shadow falls over them both. The wyvern gives a mournful sound. He knows what is coming. He drops lower, flying toward his human.

"Hush," she says. "We had to try, didn't we?" She always remembers, right at the end.

The wyvern lands on her shoulder.

The horse screams as a figure appears in front of them on the path. Sorin grabs the reins, Jaculus's talons digging into her flesh as the horse rears. She fights to keep her seat.

The horse lowers, snorting and stamping in fear.

The figure before her is half-hidden in fog, but she would recognize Magnes anywhere.

He has found her once again. He wears nothing, and His naked body is as muscled as a much younger man's.

"How many times will we play this game, Sorin?" He asks, voice amused, but there is sharp steel beneath each word.

His spell has broken. She knows who He is and why He does this. She's still afraid, but the fight has gone out of her. "Kill me or let me go." This is the third time. Perhaps the fourth.

"Where's the fun in that?" He says, His smile widening. His teeth grow more pointed, eyes glowing as orange as the coming dawn. He holds out His palm as the wings rise from His back like dark purple flames.

All goes strange and distant. He touches her hand with His bare skin. She watches herself stare blankly into the distance.

Magnes gives the horse enough magic to carry her through the forest and back up the mountain. Some part of her knows that she'll awaken in her bed, as she has before, with no memory of this night.

He toys with her, like a cat with a mouse, over and over, because it amuses Him to let her wake up enough to almost be free, only to make her His once more.

She is already forgetting the wings, the fangs, the glowing eyes.

Some part of her will still know, deep down: whether she is a knife or an Eye, He is always the hunter, and she is always the prey.

Sorin lay on the ground, feeling the smooth floorboards against her cheek. The ward had dropped, the rest of the lock shop coming into focus.

Sorin sobbed, once, before forcing herself to swallow the sound. Arcady and Everen wore matching expressions of horror and pity.

"Say his name now, Sorin," Arcady said. "Say his name."

Sorin forced herself upright. Her eyes were gritty, and she struggled to get enough air into her lungs.

"The one I worked for . . . " she said, dragging each word from somewhere deep, "is Ma—is Magnes, the Head Priest of the Order of the Dragons." She exhaled. A missing part of herself had returned. The piece was jagged, and broken, but she was finally complete.

Arcady closed their eyes. "Gods," they whispered. "He's right at the top. But he can't also be . . ."

"A dragon," Everen finished. "And I suspect I know exactly who he is." He laughed, the sound so bitter it further soured the fear in Sorin's stomach.

Everen swallowed, his voice shaking with fear. "His true name is Ammil, the former last male dragon. We have thought him dead for over three centuries." He blinked, long and slow. "But if he has been here the whole time, working his way into positions of power . . . then I fear we are doomed."

43.

ARCADY:

NAUŚTJE

I shivered as Everen's words echoed throughout the shop.

The glowing seal at Sorin's chest faded, and she swayed with exhaustion.

I passed Sorin a sweetsphere, and she ate it. I held one out for Everen, but he didn't even seem to see it, so I popped it in my mouth and chewed.

Even through our muted bond, I felt how thunderstruck he was. Sorin and Everen had both had a heap of revelations dumped on their head, but Everen had discovered something that completely upended the story he'd been told since he was a hatchling—that he was the last and sole male dragon. I was reeling too.

"Now that you remember, I want you to tell us everything like you promised," I said. "Seal sign for it for the next candlemark."

It was a small risk, to activate a private seal promise, but if I released it quickly like I had with Kelwyn just before Larkin stole my seal, it shouldn't draw the attention of the Citadel. Or so I hoped.

She hesitated before gesturing for a piece of paper, ink, and a pen. The nib scratched before she passed the sheet over to me.

I, Sorin of the Order of the Dragons, hereby promise Arcady Dalca that everything I say in the next candlemark is as true as I know it.

At my nod, she rolled her seal in the ink and pressed it to the paper. I signed it next.

"*Naustje,*" Sorin said. Her seal flared, and the spell held.

Sorin began, her words halting as the sharp teeth of truth bit into her.

"I was found as a babe, left on the steps of the Citadel. I was raised in the Order, and Magnes recruited me in secret. I trained for years, but I made my first kill last year."

"How many have you killed? Seven?" That was the number of souls she'd mentioned in the hut in the woods.

She inclined her head.

"What did Magnes tell you about us?" I pressed.

"He said that you were an agent of chaos from the Veil."

"No," Everen said, voice flat and distant. "We dragons live in a land beyond the Veil, and we were trapped there by humans who betrayed us eight centuries ago."

"Not gods?" Sorin already knew they weren't, I was sure, but she obviously couldn't help asking all the same.

"No," Everen said. "We are powerful, and there are plenty of reasons to fear us, but we have never been divine. Your kind's worship . . . it does not come to us."

It was strange to watch someone who had been raised a priest lose the last of their faith right in front of my eyes. The knot might have frayed, and Sorin hadn't broken her seal promise, but it was obvious that she still hurt in every way it was possible for someone to hurt.

"I think we have both been raised on lies," Everen offered, and some gentleness broke through the flatness.

Sorin ducked her head, blinking fast.

After she gathered herself, she continued, her words waterlogged. The scrysilver's surface stayed unmoving. After seeing echoes of someone's memories in scrysilver, I could understand the dragons' lure. Who wouldn't want to be able to see what had happened and what might come? Who wouldn't want to try and change fate if they didn't like what they saw?

Sorin told us of an evening last year when Magnes brought her to the forest to show her a wraith and the dangers they faced. Sorin raised the bottom of her shirt, showing the black scars of claw punctures on her stomach.

"You see," she said, voice shaking with effort. "You see what I risk by defying him?"

"We do," I whispered. "We do."

Sorin dipped her head, lowering her shirt.

When she told us of the auction and that Magnes had also wanted the claw, I gasped.

"Gods. He spoke to me, that night at the auction, didn't he?" I said, putting it together. "When Everen went to fetch me a drink. I thought he was some obscenely rich drakine. He told me he would be bidding on the claw, and he wished me 'happy hunting.' You've said that to me before, Everen."

"Yes." Everen drew the *s* into a near-hiss, pulling his lips back from his teeth. "It is a common dragon's saying. He was playing with you. And me. All of us."

I remembered that frantic bidding at the auction, the number growing higher and higher until I was afraid that the false jewels I'd brought with me wouldn't be enough to pay for it. The stranger had leaned back at a certain point, letting me win the lot. Magnes had known that no matter what, he'd find a way to get it in the end.

Sorin's mouth opened, closed. Opened again. "He said . . . he said he needed that relic to seal the Veil."

"Did you ever see him actually use it?" Everen asked, his tone intense.

Sorin paused, searching her memories, and shook her head in a sharp jerk.

"I am fairly certain it was his own claw," Everen said.

Sorin sucked in a breath.

Everen sat cross-legged, leaning forward to rest his elbows on his knees. "If a dragon loses a part of themselves, it can affect their magic," he said. "If he was missing some of his magic for that long, and now he has it back . . ." He trailed off. "Miligrist always said Ammil's magic had left dragons awe-struck. That it had been something to fear."

The silence lengthened.

"After all that happened on the Feast of Flowers," Sorin continued, "he sent me to the forest to guard the Veil as one of his Eyes. Like the one we saw in the clearing."

I stiffened.

"During the full moon when the Veil was strongest," Sorin said. "I rested up in the mountains."

She pointed to the map where the rivers converged. "Nalore Monastery. Right in the heart of the Fangs. This is where all the leylines meet."

I remembered falling golden flakes behind glass. "In alchemy class, Professor Hayden said something made with magic liked to make the shape of a tree. Do you remember?"

Sorin nodded.

"Have you seen it?" Everen asked Sorin. "A tree made of dragonstone?"

Another shrug. "If I have, I don't remember. There are still gaps. But I do know there are caves beneath the monastery, and the Eyes weren't allowed there. Only the monks." She paused.

"What else?" I pushed.

"Near the end of the summer, Magnes appeared in my room. He asked me to come back to the university, to study the interloper I'd seen at the auction. He said he needed to understand their magic. Your magic."

I stared at her, horror thrumming through me. "The Trials were a trap all along, weren't they?" My mouth was dry. The Head Priest must have known I didn't have much in the way of money and that I wouldn't be able to resist a scholarship dangled in front of my face.

Everen's eyes glowed with anger.

"Yes," Sorin admitted. "And I did what he asked, at first. I watched you and I reported what I saw. But the doubt, this time at least, kept growing." She closed her eyes. "Without that knot, I finally feel . . . whole. And you helped make that happen. We have had our differences, but . . . " Her light brown eyes pinned mine as her voice caught. "Thank you."

I didn't know what to say. Everen and I had done it for our own gain, yes, but I was glad that we'd helped liberate her all the same. Exposing the wound was painful, but taking out the poison was also the only way she'd be able to heal.

Everen had disappeared back into himself. I was having trouble wrapping my head around the fact that the Head Priest of the Order of the Dragons was an actual dragon. A dragon who had been here in the Lumet for three centuries. Magnes had been Head Priest for my entire life. How long had he been pulling the strings of the world before that?

"What does Magnes, or Ammil, *want*, Sorin?" I asked. "All this effort, all this planning . . . what is he working toward?"

Sorin shifted, resting back against the lock shop wall. "For so long, I wasn't meant to ask questions. At the start of term, he told me . . ." She took a moment. "He told me he needs to heal chaos. That something sleeping must never wake. And that you're both somehow at the center of it."

That got Everen's attention. He straightened, focusing on her. "He knows of the Dreamer?"

"The Dreamer?" Sorin echoed, blankly.

He hesitated.

Lay down the cards, Everen, I sent. *No point bluffing any longer.*

"There is a serpent, intertwined deep between the whorls of the world," Everen dipped a fingertip into the scrysilver and brought it to his lips. "It has slept since the dawn of time. The wraiths are its nightmares. It is wounded, perhaps since humans banished us to our world, and it sleeps too lightly. If it wakes, then both worlds will be destroyed in flame."

Sorin's eyes went wide.

"I told you," I said. "Fate is a headache."

Everen looked so thrown, so utterly lost, that I regretted being flippant.

"Is Magnes still away from the capital?" I asked.

"As far as I know, yes," Sorin said.

"We don't want to draw attention to ourselves. Magnes won't know the spell is broken unless he physically touches you. Is that right, Everen?"

He was staring into the scrysilver.

"Everen?"

He blinked at me, belatedly processing my words. "I believe so. But it is not magic I am as familiar with."

I leaned close, staring Sorin down. "This isn't a ruse, is it? This isn't all a ploy to get us to trust you?"

Sorin's eyes blazed, her nostrils flaring. "You saw what he did to me. I swear, I am no longer his creature. He taught me many ways to kill, over the years." Her voice quivered with emotion. "Dragon or not, he's still mortal. And I vow it, right here and now, under the seal promise I made you, that I will do whatever I can to end him."

Her voice rang with such finality that I believed her. So did the spell.

"He's laid his plans so carefully," Sorin said. "The third trial will send students towards the Monastery so he can capture you. I'm certain of it."

I nodded, my eyes catching on the map. "Even now that we know it's coming, I'm not sure how we can avoid it."

We lapsed into silence, but already something like a plan began to form in my mind.

"Well. We might have the element of surprise," I said. "That's something. Going into the third trial seems a decidedly foolish idea if it's what he wants."

"We've seal signed for it, though," Sorin pointed out. "Breaking the spell won't kill us, but it'll hurt, and it'll draw attention."

"I studied the words of that contract very carefully before I rolled my seal in the ink. We need to *start* the trial," I said. "It doesn't mean we have to *finish*. If we throw it at the first obstacle, then we'd be free to run."

"He might watch for that, too."

I considered. "What if, on the morning of the trial, we put as much distance between us and Vatra as we can? By the time the Citadel realizes we're not there and the spell activates, we'll be near the Myrian border, or we'll be on a ship to Jask." I'd heard of criminals trying to flee Loc to avoid being tracked down via their seal. Most of the time, it didn't work, but if the criminal had enough of a head start, they sometimes escaped.

"Distance and time," Everen said, as if he were dreaming. "Two things that undo all magic, in the end, no matter how powerful."

His words made me shiver.

Sorin considered. "Maybe that's why he stopped me from reaching the coast. If I was far enough from him, his control would lessen." She shuddered. "It will be painful, and difficult. But it might work." The corners of her mouth turned up in hope. "It might."

I nodded. "For now, head back to the Citadel, and Everen and I will stay here." I picked up the seal promise and let it catch in the flame, freeing Sorin from the spell. "Tomorrow. Tomorrow, we'll decide what to do."

"Yes." She paused by the door. "I saw how powerful you were when you were bonded on the Feast of Flowers. You opened a door between worlds. I think you know this as well as I do: if we want to have any hope of surviving what's to come next, you two need to find a way to become that strong again."

44.

CASSIA:

THE QUEEN

Cassia pulled back from the scrysilver. She'd searched for Everen every morning and evening since he had left Vere Celene. Finally, Cassia had her first vision of the present in weeks. She'd watched Everen and his human lean over a bowl of scrysilver, pushing another human to release a spell on her mind and spill out her secrets.

Cassia's shock had broken the vision, slamming her back to her body in the caves before she could even try to reach out to Everen.

No. *No.*

The previous last male dragon, the prophet who burned so many prophecies—he couldn't have survived. She tried to scry, but the images slithered away.

There was something familiar about the human with Everen and his bond partner. Months ago, after a vision, she'd been so sick that Miligrist had had to carry her back to her cavern. By the time she was well enough to record the details, she had forgotten almost everything, save that there had been a priest and their disciple in the forest, fighting a wraith that had taken the twisted shape of a wolf.

The priest had tortured the young acolyte, refusing to heal her until she made a promise.

"Yes, my child," the priest had said. "You are mine."

Cassia raced through the corridors of Vere Celene, trying to piece together her memories of the older priest's face. The tawny color of his eyes. The angle of his cheekbones. The . . . oily feel of his thoughts and emotions. Had she truly been that close to the truth and not even recognized it?

Cassia found Miligrist resting. She awoke, raising her head. —*Cassia? It's late.*

—*Ammil is alive*, Cassia said.

Miligrist's confusion radiated off her in waves, but she couldn't hide her undercurrent of fear.

—*Everen discovered that Ammil did not perish in the fire. He's been in the Lumet all this time.*

While it was fresh in Cassia's mind, she relayed everything she had seen, writing it down on a fresh scroll. Her handwriting was so rough she could barely read it, but she could not risk forgetting anything. Not again.

Miligrist's crest flattened to her skull. —*He can't have.* Her mental voice was so anguished that Cassia paused. Though none spoke of Ammil, there had been whispered rumors.

—*Who, exactly, was Ammil to you?* she asked.

Miligrist blinked her milky eyes in surprise. —*You truly do not know? None whispered the truth to you?*

—*I would hear it from you.*

Miligrist closed her eyes, her features anguished. —*Ammil was not mine by blood. His mother died not long after he hatched. I raised him even before he had his first vision when he came of age. I trained him to be an Archivist and a Seer. He was my son, in the end, in all the ways that mattered.*

Cassia felt a strange absence of surprise.

The Seer opened her milky eyes. — *I should have realized I taught him too much of his own future. Ammil learned to hide from them. From us.*

—*But Everen is still the last male dragon*, Cassia said. *That means he remains at the center of the prophecies. Isn't he?*

—*If the prophecies can be trusted*, Miligrist admitted.

Cassia's jaw slackened. —*Miligrist?*

—*I fear I have been a poor custodian of fate. All the faithful recording, all that time spent trying to unpick a vision of a prophecy. What have I truly changed, in the end?*

—*What are you saying?* Cassia said, her scales tingling.

Miligrist lowered her head. —*I do not know. I thought him surviving that fire an impossibility. I do, however, know what he might be capable of.* She stared sightlessly into the distance. *Perhaps Ammil was right, on some level. To know too many futures drives us to madness.*

Cassia swallowed past the ember in her throat. —*Do you think Everen can do what Ammil, or you, could not?*

Miligrist exhaled tendrils of smoke. — *We can but hope.*

The Reek rumbled, the stone vibrating beneath Cassia's claws. One of the storage caves had collapsed the other day from a particularly strong tremor. The pressure was building, and she feared it would soon break.

— *We must have faith all will unfurl in the way that hurts the least*, Miligrist said.

Cassia felt a shiver along her scales.

—*So do what must be done. Stop waiting for her to wake up, Cassia. Become the Queen you are meant to be.*

Cassia bowed her head, but she knew the old Seer was right.

—*Say nothing of Ammil to any dragon. This is our—and Everen's—burden to bear*, Miligrist said. *May starfire tell us true.*

Cassia took her leave of Miligrist and wound her way deeper into the labyrinth of the weyr, her mind spinning as she transformed back into her full self.

Mace stood guard in dragon form at the last curve of the corridor that led to the Queen's chambers. She let Cassia pass. The scab on Mace's eye from the first wraith attack had healed to a white scar, making her stare all the more accusatory.

The Queen, in preterit, lay on a bed of feathers and furs.

Cassia's nostrils flared at the sweetly rotten scent of infection and medicine. Queen Naccara's pebbled skin was bone pale, her eyes closed. She looked small. Vulnerable.

The dragons had destroyed the wraiths that came through after Everen returned to the human world, but there was a cost. Three more dragons had died, their bodies lost among the waves and their souls sung into starfire.

Mace had protected the Queen on her back and kept her from the worst of the fight, but it had been too much for her. As a smoky dawn broke over Vere Celene, the battered and bruised dragons had returned to the weyr. When Queen Naccara dismounted, she had fainted.

She still had not awakened.

The wound's rot had spread, and the healers said she hovered on the cusp of life and death. The last hope was that enough rest might give her the strength to recover.

Cassia sat back on her haunches. —*Any change?* she asked Mace.

Mace shook her great head.

Foreboding slid over Cassia's scales.

Whatever you do, remember this: you must not wake the Dreamer.

Cassia lowered her head toward her mother, gently touching the Queen's cheek with the back of one talon as Mace kept watch.

Though Cassia had known Mace since she was a hatchling, she was never entirely sure what the warrior thought of her. There had always been a brusque kindness, but Mace saved her loyalty and love for the Queen and Vere Celene. Cassia wasn't sure there was space for anything more.

— *The dragons must meet in the council chamber*, Cassia said. *They are restless and they need guidance. I will greet them.*

— *You would take on all the Queen's duties?* Mace asked. Her chin lifted, and she could not hide her heartache. The silence between them was heavy.

— *We cannot afford to wait any longer, Mace. The dragons need a ruler. There will be more wraiths, and the Reek* . . . She trailed off, unwilling to even state her fear, as if the very thought might make it erupt.

Mace's eyes gleamed with a mixture of pride and warning. — *I was wondering how long it would take you to see what must be done. Lead, then, Cassia, but remember that while there is breath in your mother's lungs, you are not truly Queen. And should she wake, you will bow your head and lower your crest to her. Do we have an understanding?*

Mace stared her down, blue eyes luminous in the semi-darkness of the cave.

— *Yes, Mace.*

Mace bowed low and allowed herself to shrink. She was muscled in preterit, as she was in dragon form, with short, feathered hair. The scar remained.

She went to a trunk in the corner of the room and took out the Queen's red jewel. It was larger than Mace's cupped preterit hands. Cassia ducked her head, and the warrior placed the jewel in the center of her forehead. With a flare of magic, the jewel attached to Cassia's scales.

— *I am at your service, Queen Regent Cassia Emberclaw.*

Cassia closed her eyes. The jewel was light as a feather and yet so very heavy.

— *I welcome your service, Mace*, Cassia sent. *Help guide me true.*

Cassia left her mother's chambers. On the way to the main common cave, Cassia told one of the gray dragons, Vania, to spread word that there would be a council that afternoon, where dragons could bring their concerns and look forward. Vania's silver-blue eyes widened at the sight of the jewel on Cassia's forehead. She, too, bowed, and Cassia hated how much part of her loved it.

It was only later at night, in her cave, that Cassia let herself ask the questions that frightened her. What if she was a worse queen than her mother?

But also: what if she was better?

45.

EVEREN:

A TASTE OF BLOOD

I barely heard the door shut after Sorin. I was not truly in the lock shop. My mind had flown.

I was not the last male dragon.

I never was.

Ammil had been a cudgel to keep me in line, a constant reminder of the monster I could become if I did not bow my head to the trifecta of Queen, Seer, and Heir. A reminder that male dragons were prone to violence and tempers that could not be controlled.

I leaned over the scrysilver again, probing the shallow depths for anything starfire might show me as my mind stormed with questions.

If Ammil knew of the Dreamer and sought to heal it . . . did that mean he, too, still had a hand in fate? Were we on opposite sides of the dragon scales?

Was only one of us a true Seer?

I gripped the edges of the bowl, reaching, searching for *anything* — for the world of dragons, for fate and any sign of what I should do next, or what it meant. Cassia. If I could reach my sister—

"Everen."

The sound of my name brought me crashing back to the lock shop. Your hand rested on my shoulder. Warm, present, real.

"Hey," you whispered. "Come back. Come here."

I shook off your hand. The scrysilver rippled from the movement, a drop spilling over the edge to stain the floorboards.

"If he is *here*, if he has always been here—" I broke off, my voice ragged. "We *saw him*. In our dreams, the dragon perched on the scales, or the branches of the tree. It was him all along—"

You turned me to face you, gripping my shoulders tight. "Everen. Look at me."

There were those sharp brows with three dark marks above them, like stars. Eyes the color of the sky after the sun had fled but before true night had fallen. I'd memorized your every feature—the shape of your nose, the angle of your jaw, the fullness of your lips. Your face was nearly as familiar to me as my own.

"Breathe," you said. "Just breathe."

Your right hand came to rest on my chest, over my heart. You must have felt it fluttering.

"Inhale, long and slow," you instructed, and my chest expanded.

"Now hold until it burns."

I did.

"Good. Now exhale, longer, slower. Until there's nothing left in your lungs. Then do it all again. In, and out. There's only breath. Nothing else." Your voice was soothing and low.

I followed your instructions. Only breath. We stayed like that until the tumble of my thoughts quieted and I felt I had landed back on the ground.

"Thank you," I whispered.

You inclined your head. I listened to your heartbeat. I breathed in the familiar scents of the lock shop, of you.

"I thought I knew what we were meant to do," I said, finally. "I don't know what this means. I cannot even reach Vere Celene. I am lost."

"You're not lost, Everen," you said, speaking to me like I was a spooked animal. I suppose I was.

You stepped closer, resting your cheek on my collarbone, the shirt fabric between us. My arms came around you, and you anchored me.

—*You're not lost because we found each other again.* You spoke the words in my mind, as if they were too much to admit aloud. *Everen. I think I'm ready.*

I pulled back, peering down at you. "What do you mean?" I hardly dared hope.

You brushed your hair back from your face. "Sorin's right. Whatever's coming next, we need to be united."

"Are you sure?" I searched your face for signs of doubt, but I found only determination. "If we complete the bond, I do not know if we will be able to break it again after this is all finished."

It was your turn to scrutinize me. "Are you saying you'd want to be rid of me?"

"*No.*" The force of the word startled us both. "No," I said, quieter. "I had the time to consider things when I was in my cell in Vere Celene." I gathered my courage. "We have reached each other across worlds, over and over, both before we knew of the other's existence and after. I have learned, over the last year, that even if we did not have to bond to face fate, that I would choose you, time and time eternal. In this world, or any other."

I could not meet your eyes.

"If you wish to be free," I forced myself to say, staring at the ground, "I would take any amount of pain to spare you more."

You made a small noise in the back of your throat.

"Then that's all I need to know," you said. You took one step, closing the distance between us. I raised my head.

"I don't think this will work if we don't go into this eyes open, heart forward," you whispered, breath playing along my skin, making me shiver.

"Eyes open," I echoed. "Heart forward."

"In some ways, we can't fully choose. You're right in that. But if I'm equally honest, I trust you, Everen. Saint Ini help me, but I do."

Your hand brushed my shoulder. Slowly, you traced my clavicle, pausing at the hollow of my throat. I focused on nothing but that point of faint pressure. Your fingertip reached my other shoulder.

"I'm going to say something I haven't said to anyone in . . . I don't know how long. Probably not since I was a child."

I waited, breathing.

"I love you."

The words were barely a whisper, and they were the sweetest sounds I had ever heard.

"You really have done the impossible," I said. "Making a dragon fall in love with a human. I echo all that love back to you, and more."

You savored the words, mouth curling up at the corners in quiet contentment. There was nothing between us any longer. Nothing holding us back. You met my gaze, and without breaking it, you tilted your head, exposing your neck.

Achingly slow, I placed my fangs against the pulse of your neck. It was strong, steady, sure.

I bit down.

You hissed in pain as I broke the skin just enough to taste warm iron. My hands ran down your arms over your shirt, your sides. I pulled back, and you reached up, grabbing the back of my neck, sending a shiver of pain through me. You bit my lip until you, too, drew blood.

Our previous embraces had often been fierce and hungry. Though we still felt our want, our need, and our pain, this kiss was unhurried. We let ourselves explore each other. Your mouth opened, and we deepened the caress as the magic swelled, the hum growing louder. Our shared power swirled, outlining us in blue, red, and gold, but I barely noticed. I was too focused on your taste, the way I gripped your waist and pulled you toward me, and how you went pliant enough to let me.

A high, pure note sounded in our minds. The glow of magic faded back into our skin. Your hand on the back of my neck no longer hurt.

For the second time, the bond had completed. We were in balance.

I drank it in, my heart lifting. Our magic was strong and sure. I would be able to become my full dragon self once more. I remembered that vision of a human and a dragon hatchling bonding, centuries ago, and launching themselves to their first shared flight.

"Come," I said, making for the door. "I wish to show you something."

"What?" you asked, but for once, without your usual trace of suspicion.

"The sky."

We reached a deserted stretch of stone wall. No guards were nearby, and the street was quiet. I took off my shirt and let my wings emerge.

It was a cloudy night, but I dimmed my feathers, and you cast a notice-not charm for good measure.

I held out my arms, and you came to me. I picked you up, your arms circling my neck, and we flew over the wall and out to the forest.

Under the cover of the trees, I set you down and stepped back. I spread my hands and tilted my head up to the sky, feeling your eyes on me as I left my preterit form behind and became my full self.

Magic rippled along my skin. You watched as my pallor turned to armored red.

When the change was complete, you gazed up at me. I bowed low and extended my neck.

You stared at the spines along my back with no small amount of trepidation. "What if I fall off?"

— *You will not fall*, I said. *If you did, I would catch you.*

Still, you hesitated.

— *Trust me, Arcady*, I said.

You straightened your shoulders and climbed along my arm, over my shoulder blade, and settled between two spikes, the perfect fit for a human. You clutched the spine as hard as you could. My scales would keep you warm once we took to the skies, and our bond would make sure you could breathe despite the altitude.

"Sometimes, I can't believe this," you said. "You, a dragon. Me, here."

I rumbled low in my throat, a draconic chuckle, but my head was already tilted toward the stars.

— *Hold on*, I said.

I coiled my muscles and with another burst of magic, I took to the air.

We were far from the city, but there was a risk someone might see a red streak as I made for the cover of the clouds.

Through the bond, I felt the wind whip the hair from your face and sting your eyes, but you let out a whoop that was closer to a scream.

My wings caught the wind. It felt so good to leave the ground behind. Below us was the black swathe of the forest, but in the distance shone the bright lights of Vatra. You laughed, this time with joy. No other human had seen the city from this vantage point for centuries.

The lights disappeared as we entered the cool wisps of cloud.

I rose higher, higher, until we burst beyond the cloud line. Above us, stars scattered across the sky. The moon was half-full, lighting the cloud banks below. From here, they looked almost solid enough to land on.

I moved my wings, flying smoothly, banking carefully. You let out another incredulous sound. I flew faster, until I was skimming the tops of the clouds. Your excitement spurred me on, and I swooped, though I did not roll or dive. Next time, or the next, or all the many flights we would have together.

The bond grew stronger between us as we flew up into the heavens, until it was only us, the clouds, the sky, and the moon.

Eventually, I dipped back below the clouds and returned to the quiet part of the forest. I sensed the magic of the leylines below, leading the way off toward the mountains and Nalore Monastery.

—*No, Everen*, you said, sensing the direction of my thoughts. *We can't go there unprepared. We don't even know what we'd do if we found the tree, do we?*

I knew you were right, even as I yearned follow the leyline to the heart of the Fangs.

—*Nothing else of fate, Everen*, you said. *The rest of the night is ours.*

I dipped my head and landed back on the forest floor. You dismounted, carefully, stretching your legs, your cheeks chapped from the wind, your grin wide in the darkness.

I returned to my preterit form, and again you watched until I stood before you wearing only my wings. Your expression changed, a small smile playing about your mouth. We both knew what would come next.

When you were close enough to touch, I pushed your coat from your shoulders, letting it pool on the mossy forest floor. One less layer of distance between us. Carefully, I finished undressing you, taking my time. I traced the marks on your skin, feeling you tremble.

I spread your clothes on the ground, and you lay down on them. We said nothing, for we didn't need to. Our lips met, the kiss growing deeper and more urgent. My wings covered us both, keeping us warm as we pressed skin to skin.

We were no longer confined by how long I could stand the pain or endure you siphoning my magic. We were not asleep, doomed to wake at a moment's notice. Fingertips, lips, tongue, and the gentle nip of teeth. It was you, and me, slowly catching fire.

I kissed my way down your body until I reached your hipbone. You arched when I took you in my mouth. Your hands tangled in my hair, and you let out a sound I wanted to hear, again and again. Through the bond, you guided me. We set a rhythm, my hands gripped your hipbones as they rocked, drawing you closer to me. My world sharpened to a pinpoint—to only you and what you needed.

"More," you said. "I want more."

I raised my head, and the sight of your eyes half-lidded in pleasure nearly undid me. You dragged me up, and I paused. This was the furthest we'd ever gone. This was the last way we could join. I lined myself up against you.

I bowed my head, my whole body shaking as I began to slide into you. You shook, too, and I gave you a moment to adjust.

"All right?" I whispered.

"Yes, yes, yes," you said, and we intertwined in mind, body, and magic.

Your hands scraped along the skin of my back, pulling me closer until our hips joined. I moved slower, but soon enough I quickened my pace, reveling in you. You arched up, catching your lips with mine, and we laughed as our teeth bumped together.

Your eyes closed, and I watched your face as you concentrated, focusing inward. A wave of possessiveness rushed over me.

"Harder," you said, and I obeyed.

Thought fled, and we threw ourselves into the bond and the way our bodies joined, retreating only to meet once more.

You gripped my upper arms, your fingernails digging into my skin. I focused, giving all I could. I would give you everything and hoard nothing.

I felt the moment the climax broke in you. It was a lightning strike, followed by thunder. I managed a few more movements, making sure you finished, before the storm found me, too.

There was the bond, completed. There we were, sated.

This was a pause before whatever fate brought us next. Trees, serpents, dragons, storms, monsters. It would all be in our future.

But that night, as you said, was ours. And how we cherished it.

46.

ARCADY:

THE LABORATORY

The next evening, I climbed up the drainpipe to Kelwyn's window. As ever, he startled when I rapped on the glass, but dutifully came over to let me in.

"You still have the keys to both the front and the back doors, you know," he said as I slid into the familiar room.

"I know. But this is more fun."

"Tea?"

"Please, though I won't be staying long."

He put on the kettle and set out a plate of biscuits. I chomped on a few quite happily and sighed in relief when I took a sip of milky tea. He passed me the silver coins from selling the bracelet, and I inclined my head and tucked them in my pocket.

"You're . . . chirpy," Kelwyn said, peering at me. "What's changed?"

I smiled into my cup.

"Well, I expect you're here for another favor, so out with it." He sipped his tea.

"Everen's back," I began.

Kelwyn set down his cup with a clatter. He narrowed his eyes. "Ah. *That's* why you're in a good mood. Took you long enough."

"Kel!"

"What?" He smirked. "You've wanted that pretty boy since the moment you laid eyes on him. We all saw it."

I coughed.

Kelwyn leaned back in his chair. "Where did he go, then, and why is he back?"

I stirred my tea. "It's . . . it's a long story, and you wouldn't believe half of it."

He crossed his arms. "Try me."

"I mean it. It's unbelievable."

"As unbelievable as dragons?"

I froze.

"I'd usually let you slither out of it, but we have danced around it all too long." Kelwyn licked his lips. "Consider it payment for your favor. I saw things that night at the barrow hill that I couldn't explain. A flash of red in the sky . . . " He trailed off. "I've been trying to put it from my mind. But I can't."

I swallowed. I supposed I should have known it'd come to this eventually. "There's no going back. You won't be able to unlearn . . . that dragons exist."

"Gods above and below," he exhaled. "I thought you'd tell me . . . I don't know. Something rational—that I'd been drugged, or it was some sort of craft from wherever Everen was from. You're telling me it was a god?"

"A dragon, but not a god."

He shook his head, struggling to believe me, but deep down, I knew he did. "And Everen? Did he call it down somehow?"

I fiddled with my teaspoon, then met his eyes. *Cards on the table*, like I'd told Everen. "Kel . . . come now, surely you guessed. Everen *is* the dragon."

Kel sucked in a breath, various emotions tumbling across his face. To my surprise, I didn't think he had quite put it together, at least not consciously. It was a jump to make.

"Look," I said. "It doesn't much matter how or why he's back. I've already told you more than I should. We need to leave Vatra on the morning of the third trial and get as far away from the city as we can. Can you arrange to smuggle three out of Loc?"

"Who's the third?" His voice was faint as he wrangled with what I'd just dropped on him.

"Another who needs to run from the person after us," I said. "She's uh, not a dragon," I added, belatedly.

Kelwyn made a choking sound. He closed his eyes, gathering himself, before continuing. "Who's after you?"

I shook my head. "I can't tell you. It would put you in danger."

He rubbed his mouth. "What of Larkin and her blackmail? Is it related to that?"

I shrugged. "Yes, and no. Larkin can't hold shit over me any longer. Arcady Dalca's life is already ashes."

Kelwyn reached out and put his hand on top of mine. "Oh, Arc."

I pulled my hand away. "It's fine. It was never going to last."

"Still. I'm sorry."

"Me too. My only hope is to get us out of here and away from the much larger threat."

"Is there anything else you can or are willing to tell me? Or anything else I should know, to protect myself in case whatever this is comes back to bite me in the arse?" His eyes were intense and unblinking.

I hesitated. "That's all I can share, and it's already too much. I swear it. The sooner I'm away, the safer you'll be, too. I'm sorry." My words felt inadequate.

He exhaled, staring into the distance. "If you leave . . . will you ever come back to Loc?"

"I don't know," I said, hoarsely.

He leaned back in his chair. "Fine. I'll ask around for a way to get you out of Loc discreetly. After that though, you're on your own."

I nodded, too overcome to speak.

He lifted the teapot, refilling my cup before I even had to ask.

We drank our tea in silence.

The night before the final trial, the common room was full to bursting. Those of us competing were guests of honor. Other students had made us crowns of holly, and the sharp leaves tickled my forehead. Externally, I was as delighted as all the other students. Edin Vayne had once more taken on the role of cupbearer, and I held up my empty mug to be re-filled, and acted like I had all the confidence in the world that I'd win the third trial—or at least do well enough to cover myself in glory.

Inside, I wanted to cry.

Students were sprawled across the sofas like a tangle of puppies. Rahela's cheeks were flushed pink. Willem and Damon were speaking intently in the corner. At one point their fingers intertwined. Not long after, they left together, and I smiled. Whatever had come between them, they seemed to have finally worked it out, and I was glad for them.

Everen felt all my emotions, the golden bond hovering between us though he was at the lock shop.

A few candlemarks later, Sorin sidled up to me, equally sober.

"Time to leave?" I asked, and she nodded.

We slipped from the common room, and I followed Sorin to her quarters. If anyone saw us together, we'd simply lean into what Willem and a few others already thought.

Sorin's bag was by the door. I'd already moved most of my possessions to the Loc & Key over the last couple of days, hoping no one noticed. In my pocket was the last thing: the glass dragon eye Wren had given me at the Night Market.

"Before we go . . ." Sorin began. "I'd ask a favor of you. You're a thief. Help me steal something."

"Steal what?"

"Hayden's research."

Whatever I'd been expecting her to say, it wasn't that.

"I know where it might be," she continued. "The wards on it are too tricky for me to break alone. Magnes is still away from the Citadel. If he comes after us, I suspect we'll need this if we want a hope of facing him."

"What . . . what exactly is Hayden's research?" I asked. "I know what my source told me, but I want to hear it from you."

"Hayden mentioned it the first day of class."

I whistled. "You can't mean it's *actually* the Elixir of Life?"

"No, not exactly. Magnes said that what Hayden developed doesn't grant immortality, but I've seen firsthand that it can focus and enhance magic while lessening the cost." She hesitated. My mind was spinning. "Magnes has been dosing me with it . . . for the trials."

My mouth fell open and I finally let the laugh escape. "Gods," I said. "That's how you got past the trials as a first year. We're a pair of cheats, aren't we?"

"For a rigged trial set by a dragon," Sorin said, her own mouth twisting. "Indeed. So. Will you help me or not?"

I spread my heads. "Aye, sure, Sorin. I'll help you steal my original blackmail now that it's too late to save my skin at the university. Why not?" Back in the lock shop, Everen sensed my amusement and apprehension.

Sorin pressed a stone in the corner of her room, and a hidden door opened. I stared at the secret passageway, my fingertips tingling.

—*Should I come to you?* he asked.

—*No,* I sent back. *Stay close, watch through me.* I didn't know how easy it would be for him to sneak onto the grounds of the university without a seal, and we didn't need additional complications. I felt his wave of reluctant assent.

"Are you ready?" Sorin asked.

I nodded and stepped into the dark.

It would have been dead handy to know there were hidden corridors threaded throughout the entire Citadel. I carefully unpicked wards and put them back up behind me as we made our way deeper into the depths of the university.

Finally, Sorin stopped us. "This is the hardest ward," she said. "Can you break it?"

"With some help," I said, reaching for the bond. Everen answered. He sent me a bit of power and we unpicked it like a lock. She was right. It wasn't easy. By the time the ward finally fell, I had sweat at my temples and my fingertips were shaking. I reached into my pocket and ate a few hazelnuts as Sorin nudged open the door.

The abandoned laboratory was larger than I thought it would be and reminded me of our alchemy classroom. Everything was dark stone. It took a moment for recognition to sink in. I'd been here before.

I'd thought they'd have destroyed it, but instead they'd bricked over the main door and left it as it'd been when I'd last been here as a child before the first Strike. This was my grandsire's laboratory.

How many times had I walked corridors right outside? It'd been hidden here all along.

One of the tables was full of equipment. A book of alchemical symbolism sat next to the beakers, opened to an illustration of the Tree of Life. I leaned over it. This one was an ornate woodcut engraving, finely detailed. Drawn over it were alchemical symbols in Hayden's hand.

"Professor Hayden really has been working with Magnes," I said. The disappointment hit me harder than expected. Did this mean she'd worked with him before? Had my grandsire? Part of me wish I'd never agreed to come here.

"There have to be more vials here," Sorin said, oblivious to my inner turmoil. She began searching. I, meanwhile, slowly walked the circumference of the laboratory, lost in fuzzed memories. Half-hidden behind one of the tables was a fireplace lined with green tile, the mantle black marble. I looked underneath it, and thought I caught something in the gloom. I pushed the heavy table out of the way with a grunt.

"What are you doing?" Sorin asked, barely glancing up from her increasingly desperate search.

I reached down into the dust and picked up a small, six-pointed metal object. It was one of a set of jackstones.

I rarely reached for the past, and my memory had never been keen, but I remembered throwing a ball and manipulating the jacks for candlemarks while my maire and taie worked on their various projects. I must have been six or so. There had been a third person there, sometimes, but I couldn't remember their face. A younger Professor Hayden?

I glanced up at Sorin. I still didn't know what we were. Allies by circumstance, maybe, but not friends. After this was all over, one way or another, where would we stand?

"There's no Elixir. We risked coming here for nothing," Sorin said, rubbing the stubble of her hair. "I thought for sure there'd be more." Her agitation caught my interest. Her . . . hunger.

I put the metal jack in my pocket, next to the glass dragon eye, and came back to the alchemy equipment. I ran my hands around the lower part of the table, drawn by another foggy, long-ago memory. I found the hidden catch, and the shelf popped open.

Sorin's breath caught behind me as we both stared down at five vials of a silvery mixture. She reached for them, gathering them with shaking hands.

"How . . . how did you know these were here?"

"Lucky guess?" I tried.

She shook her head. "I always assumed that Magnes was fascinated with you because of your involvement with a dragon," Sorin said. "But it's more than that, isn't it?"

I said nothing.

Sorin glanced at the room's stone walls. "I thought this was Professor Hayden's old lab. Is it?"

I took the jack out of my pocket again.

"Oh," she said, softly, putting it together. "Of course."

I chewed the inside of my cheek.

"You're too young to be the Plaguebringer's child. Grandchild, then?"

I finally raised my eyes, knowing they were wet. "Don't call him that."

"Ah." She paused. "Tell me your true name."

"My forename is actually Arcady. Dalca's the falsehood."

"Arcady Eremia," she said, and she spoke my name as hushed as if it were a spell. I half-expected the stone walls to shake.

"Let me see one of the vials," I said, holding out my hand.

She clutched them to her defensively. I wriggled my fingers, and she reluctantly passed me one. I moved the liquid this way and that before unstoppering it. A distinctive floral scent hit me.

"This has Pollen in it." I exhaled as another piece fell into place. "Let me guess. One of the side effects is perhaps puking your guts up on some ivy?"

She shot me a dirty look, but she didn't deny it. I gave a low whistle, glad, in the end, I hadn't found enough to risk Larkin getting her hands on it.

—*Ask her what else is in it*, Everen said, his thoughts insistent.

"Everen is asking about other ingredients," I said. I stretched my awareness, and I could catch the lingering scent of magic in the air. I paused, listening internally. "He guesses it has scrysilver in it, judging by the color and viscosity. But he thinks there's something else . . ."

Sorin's expression rippled.

"Sorin," I said.

She licked her lips. "When I first came into this laboratory, there were more than beakers and alchemical equipment," she whispered. "There was an entire dragon, carefully stripped down for parts. The one that had died in the forest."

"Glisten," I spoke Everen's anguished thoughts aloud. "Her name was Glisten."

Sorin bowed her head.

"The Elixir contains a few scales, I believe," Sorin said after a moment, and I almost staggered back with the wave of revulsion and fury from Everen.

—*It's not enough that humans stole our magic*, he said, *but an actual dragon would dare desecrate one of his own kind?*

I'm sorry, I said, unsure what else to say, but echoing his horror.

"Come on," I said to Sorin. "We shouldn't linger. You have what you came for."

Sorin gathered the Elixir reverently. At the door to the passage-way, I gave my taie's laboratory a last, lingering look. In some ways, I'd be leaving the university with more questions about him than answers. They might always haunt me.

We put the wards back up and wound through the passageways until we came out in the university courtyard. I tilted my head toward the darkened window of the dormitory where I would never sleep again. My seat in the lecture halls during my classes would remain empty for the rest of term. No more studying in the library with Rahela, Willem, Damon, and Edin. I never even had the chance to say good-bye.

—*Maybe this isn't good-bye,* my dragon said. *Perhaps one day you'll be able to return.*

—*Maybe,* I allowed.

Sorin didn't say anything, either. She didn't need to. Here were the familiar spires of the Cathedral she'd seen most mornings of her life. The monastery where she'd slept in that tiny priest's cell. The Great Hall where she'd taken so many meals. This had been her home far longer than mine. Was it harder for her to say good-bye?

"Come on," she said, hiking her bag higher on her shoulder. She led us to a secret door in the thick outer stone walls. The path down the hill was rockier and more treacherous in the dark, but Sorin knew the way.

Down in the city, it was my turn to lead. I knocked softly on the door of the Last Golden, and Kelwyn answered and gestured us inside, closing the door behind us.

"This is the third, then?" he said.

"This is Sorin," I said, but gave no more detail. Sorin signed "she."

"Kelwyn," he said, and I'd never seen someone sign their gender with such a wary expression.

Sorin stared at all the antiques lining the walls, drawn to one of the wolf figurines.

"Don't break that," Kelwyn snapped, and she put it back.

"Wren and Driscoll will be the ones to take you tomorrow," Kelwyn shared. "Said it was time for them to leave Loc anyway. They'll be going as far as the Glass Isles. You can either follow them there or slip away somewhere in Myria before they meet up with Larkin."

I wasn't sure if this was a better option than strangers or not. "Thank you." I buttoned my coat. "Give Sorin some of your best biscuits, would you please? We've had a day."

"I've made apricot cake," he said. "It turned out especially well, if I do say so myself. Fancy staying for a slice?"

I shook my head, even as I was tempted. "I'm heading back to the lock shop. But Everen and I will return before dawn."

"We'll be here," Kelwyn said. He took a moment to wrap up a couple of slices for us both. I took them gratefully.

Sorin met my eyes and nodded. "At dawn."

47.

EVEREN:

AS WHAT WAS

I've never left Loc before," you said, lying on your back at my side. "I always wanted to. Never expected it'd be quite like this."

"We will find somewhere safe," I said. I hoped I would be able to reach my sister and Miligrist across the Veil and gain more insight. I was still disturbed by what you had learned in that laboratory, and haunted by the realization that Ammil had been alive for centuries, pulling the strings here in the human world. I needed to ask them what to do next. How could I hope to heal the serpent if Magnes guarded the tree? We would have to find a way.

You turned, curling into my side, and my arm came around you. I bent down and kissed the top of your head. "Sleep," I said. "Dawn will be here soon enough."

It took another half a candlemark before your breath steadied into the shallows of sleep.

Eventually, I followed.

—To balance the scales, you must find the tree, *fate whispered.* Branches stretch high and roots run deep.

The dragonstone tree rose in my mind's eye, the hanging scales tipping one direction, and then the other. The snake coiled around its branches, the scarlet wound pulsing. Wraiths hovered around the Dreamer. The sleeping snake turned its head toward me, mouth opening as it exposed its fangs.

—Only the magic within holds the key.

The Dreamer's eyes opened.

The irises swirled with the colors of the storm, drawing me in. I was caught in the current of a gyre.

I fell.

You appeared next to me, drawn by the vision, our bond, and fate itself. You were as transparent as the beginning and end of our dreams.

"Everen," *you said aloud, your voice echoing, head craning toward the dragonstone tree. It looked like the one we had seen in Sorin's vision.* "What is this?"

—As above, so below, *I said in my mind, and I sounded as hazy as Miligrist after one of her visions.* As what was, so shall become.

I held out my hand, and you took it.

The white of the tree was echoed in the veins of dragonstone crawling across the cavern walls. The scrysilver pool at its roots reflected its light.

A group of mages stood in a circle around the trunk.

—This is the past, *I said.* I saw this the first night wraiths attacked Vere Celene. This is the night of the Great Betrayal.

The figures chanted their spells, the words distorted as if they spoke underwater. We caught the suggestion of hatred or fear on their blurred faces. Several had tears streaming down their cheeks. The dragonstone tree glowed brighter, until a rip in the fabric of the world appeared above the tree and drew us into it.

The snake undulated within the storm.

Magic made of starlight curled around the snake, directed by the humans'
spell. One coil of its great body wound unto itself, strangling tighter. Magic
shuddered over its scales and the snake rippled in pain, its great hide bursting
as it gave one last squeeze before it loosened.

—The first unlocking cut the world in twain, *said fate.* To leave
such a deep and festering cut.

A shimmer brought us out of one vision and into the next. We were once
more in that great cavern below the monastery. Your hand remained in mine
as the more recent past rose before us.

Six humans wearing the scale-embroidered robes of the Order of the Drag-
ons clustered around the dragonstone tree. No—five humans and one dragon.
From Sorin's visions, I recognized Ammil, disguised as Magnes, the Head
Priest of Loc. I hissed.

Your breath hitched, but you weren't looking at the dragon.

—That's . . . that's Professor Hayden, *you said, pointing to the young-*
est human.

—And that . . . *Your hand shook as you gestured to the older human next*
to the professor. That is my grandsire.

Barrow Eremia stood tall, graying hair trailing down his back. He had
your dark blue eyes, but his skin was paler. He exuded confidence and power.

—The others? *I asked.*

You studied their faces before gesturing to one with gray hair to their chin
and piercing hazel eyes. —That one is Yrsa of Swiftsea, I think. The
Chancellor that died. Those two . . . I'd guess Ketrel of Stormfell and
Carym of Redwing.

Ketrel had the appearance of a soldier long retired, with an old sword cut
scarring their cheek. Carym had the ruddy cheeks of too many nights of too much
drink. Even with magic lengthening their life, they must have been well over one
hundred years old. How much frailer would they be now, twelve years later?

—The entire Consul of Loc was here that night, *you breathed.*

Ammil gave a signal, and a procession of monks streamed into the cavern as though they walked down the aisle of the Cathedral at the Citadel. Each held an object reverently in outstretched hands.

Relics. Teeth. Claws. Scales. Carefully sawed-off pieces of bone. Pieces of long-dead dragons dug up from the earth. The hooded monks walked across the great roots. When they reached the trunk, they gave their offering. As soon as each piece touched the crystal, the tree absorbed it as though it was a tender morsel, and its light grew that much brighter.

With a shudder, I wondered if those humans long ago had also given entire dragons to the crystal. Whether they'd slaughtered their bond mate or banished them to the new world they had created—either option was horrific. I felt the same revulsion I had felt as I had watched you in the laboratory. Humans might have forgotten what their ancestors had done, but that did not stop them from using what remained of us for their own gain. And here was a dragon helping them do it.

"Leave us," Ammil commanded when the last bit of bone had been fed to the tree. The monks bowed low and quit the cavern. After a moment, the three Chancellors followed. Hayden left last, hesitating by the open door, her face creased with worry. She opened her mouth as if to speak.

"All will be well," Barrow Eremia reassured his assistant.

Hayden nodded, though she did not seem comforted. She closed the great door behind her, the sound echoing against stone.

"You're sure all is in order, Barrow?" Ammil asked. "This will give us what we need?"

Your grandsire nodded. "Should be more than enough to tap the tree and open the Veil." The first hint of doubt spread over his face. "It will be delicate work. We cannot take even one wrong step. Spend too long within the storm, and we might lose ourselves. Give the serpent too much, and it may heal the wound but drain the tree's power, leaving magic in our world too weakened. If we are successful, though . . ." His eyes gleamed. "All of magic's secrets will open to us. Both worlds will heal, and it'll bring about a new age. A new dawn."

Ammil and Barrow stepped forward, and, as one, they each drank a vial of Elixir.

Ammil's lips curled as the power took hold. His orange eyes grew brighter as he cast off his priest robes and his human form, spreading his violet wings wide. Barrow Eremia showed no surprise.

—He knew, *you said, eyes wide.* He knew a dragon walked among us.

Barrow mouthed the words of the spell you had spoken to draw me across the Veil. A rip appeared once more above the tree. Ammil transformed into a full dragon, and Barrow, without hesitation, climbed onto his back. The magic at Barrow's seal—the one that would become yours—glowed as bright as the starlit tree.

—Were they . . . bonded? *you asked.*

—I do not know, *I said.* I do not think so, but there is something between them.

With a great flap of his wings, Ammil leaped from the ground of the cave, the surface of the scrysilver pool around the roots rippling, and he and your grandsire disappeared into the Veil.

The vision shifted, showing a sleeping town deep in the mountains as dawn broke. A sleeping child woke, struggling to breathe, black marks crawling up their skin as their parents looked on in rising fear. I felt your horror.

—The second attempt to heal was in vain, *fate said, the echoing voice tinged with regret.* Illness struck and the future nearly shut.

Your dreaming self bent over, shaking your head, your mouth forming the word "no."

You had spent so long searching for the truth, determined to clear your grandsire's name. If fate had shown us true, then twelve years ago, Barrow Eremia may not have been the sole Plaguebringer . . . but he had been one of them. As had Ammil and the three Chancellors of Loc.

—Wake up. *The thoughts were desperate.* Wake up. *You twisted away from it all, disappearing from the echo, from the past that had deepened into a nightmare.*

I thought I would follow you to wakefulness, but the tree and the cavern remained.

I was not alone. Ammil, in preterit, took your place.

—Here we are, then, *he said.* We meet at last.

I stared at the other last male dragon. He was the one who had burned Vere Celene to ash, and I was the one meant to help our kind rise from the ashes.

—Why did you burn the Archives? *I asked him, unable to keep the curiosity at bay.* How did you survive?

The scrysilver around us rippled, and I saw flashes of orange flames, burning scrolls and books tumbling from collapsing shelves.

—I fully expected to die when I set that fire, you know, *he said.* I was fully done with prophecy, with fate, with life. I wanted no more part of it. I thought destroying the Archives would free our kind. After all, what would you have done with your life, Everen Emberclaw, without the prophecies weighing you down from the moment you hatched?

—I am no longer an Emberclaw, *I said.* That name was taken from me.

The fire in the scrysilver burned hotter, more scrolls shriveling to black.

—Would you take it back, if you could? *he asked.*

I had no answer. The edges of his lips curled in a smile. —As the flames surrounded me and I felt the heat of that fire, a rip in the Veil opened before me. I wanted to die, but I also feared the flames. So, like you, I jumped, and I left Vere Celene behind.

His gaze went distant as the scrysilver shifted to the purples and blues of the storm between worlds. —That was when I first saw the Dreamer. The sheer power of the serpent. Were you, too, tempted to join it?

A snake's coil the shade of wraithwright appeared in the scrysilver, so lifelike I half-expected it to breach the surface, like a whale coming up for air, before it slithered away.

—The Dreamer slept deeply and took no interest in me. Instead, the Veil spat me into the Lumet.

The scrysilver showed Ammil, in preterit form, sprawled in a desert made of black sand. He rose, naked and battered, and began to walk.

—Fate, or random chance, I no longer know, but I was stranded. I was alive whether I wished it or not. I've lived many lives since then, as the only dragon in the human world. Until now. We are not so different, you and I, *Ammil said.* We never were.

I backed away, skittish as prey.

Ammil smiled. —It was always leading to this. Surely you realize. Neither of us can do what comes next alone.

I said nothing, but my suspicion was palpable.

He waved a hand dismissively. —Ah, yes, I know. I've been watching your precious human. Have I harmed them? No. I even saved them from themselves. I have studied their magic because it is *you* I'm interested in, Everen. The last male dragon. A Seer who was never meant to exist. *He gestured to the tree, which glimmered as if in invitation.* Time grows short. The serpent sleeps so lightly. You feel it, don't you?

I hissed in a breath, but I didn't deny it.

—I know what needs to be done. I know how to open the tree and the Veil. I tried this once before, but I made the mistake of trusting a human. That is where I failed. I have worked hard to undo the damage caused, and I will not make the same mistake again. Not with you, fate's chosen, by my side.

I was desperate to believe him, but I made no move.

He held out his hand. —It has to be us: the new Seer and the old. As above, so below. As what was, so shall become. Whatever you do, remember this: you must not wake the Dreamer. *He spoke the prophecy so calmly. His palm was still outstretched toward mine.*

—Together, we could do what I could not before. So what will it be, Seer? Shall we put it all aside and, dragon and dragon, save our worlds?

What if my enemy was my ally, at least in this? Like my mother, I knew Ammil would not give up his power so easily, and if we triumphed here, we would turn back to foes. I did not know who would issue the challenge first, him or me, nor did I know who would win.

I, too, had learned from past mistakes, and knew I could not make the decision alone. I tried to wake up and return to you but, as if I sleepwalked, I watched my hand reach out and clasp his palm, and I was powerless to stop it.

48.

ARCADY:

NIGHTMARE

I gasped awake.

I had a near-memory of someone kissing the back of my eyelids, brushing a finger against my cheek, soothing me back to sleep. . . .

The details crystallized, and my stomach clenched with nausea. My grandsire's face as he spoke a spell and opened the Veil between worlds. The sight of him climbing onto the back of a dragon. They hadn't been bonded, not like me and Everen, but there had been something between them.

What had happened when they both went into the storm?

Had my taie unleashed the plague? Or was there, by some miracle, another explanation?

I reached out for Everen, but the space next to me was empty.

I forced myself upright, my head spinning. Cold air swirled into the room, and the open door of the lock shop swung on its hinges.

—*Everen?* I called, but the bond was so quiet I could barely feel it. He'd blocked me off like I'd tried to do to him after he'd burned my drawings.

I ran out into the street, barefoot and shivering in the pre-dawn cold. My heartbeat hammered in my throat. A few people were in the street, their faces craned toward the sky, body language slack with an awe I'd recognize anywhere.

They had seen something they couldn't explain.

The full brunt of my fear stabbed me. I almost fell to my knees. Some of the specifics of the dreams had already faded, but I knew. I knew.

Everen had gone to Magnes. Had he gone willingly?

In my mind, I heard something like laughter.

—*For him I used honey, but for you, I need only the stick*, came a far-off voice in my head. *If you want to save your dragon, then tomorrow, take your medicine, join the trial, and come to me. If you do not, he'll be dead by sunset, and the rest of the world along with it. Happy hunting, little Eremia.*

For all our attempts to twist out of it, his trap had so neatly snapped shut.

PART 4:
DECLENSION

By silver, by blood, by bone.
By the dragon scales, I am your storm.
By silver, by blood, and by bone:
you rage only for me.

49.

SORIN:

SCALDED

Mistrust rose off Kelwyn like steam in his aggressively cozy kitchen. Garlic, onions, and chilies hung from the ceiling, the stove was always warm, and mismatched chairs and a small table near the window showed a view of the Citadel lit up at night. Dinner was a simple affair of sausages, caramelized onion, and mashed potatoes, but it was well-made, the gravy thick and peppery. She ate every bite. After, he made her a cup of tea, and she devoured two slices of apricot cake. Throughout it all, they said as little as possible, and Sorin preferred it that way.

That night, she dozed in the cramped spare room, waiting for dawn.

A candlemark before the sun broke the sky, she dressed, packed her things, and went to set the kettle on the stove. She'd just poured herself a cup of tea when a frantic knocking at the window startled her. Scalding liquid spilled on her hand, and she hissed.

Kelwyn stumbled into the room, still half-asleep. Sorin grabbed a rag by the ewer, dunking it in water and pressing the cool cloth to her reddened skin.

Arcady was at the window of the lounge, face pinched with fear.

"That one never did learn how to use a door, I swear," Kelwyn muttered, crossing the room and letting them in.

"He took Everen." Arcady's words were breathless, their coat unbuttoned and shirt untucked, eyes wild.

Sorin's heart thudded.

"Wait. Who took Everen?" Kelwyn blinked the remnants of sleep from his eyes.

Arcady shook their head hard, once, their unbrushed curls whipping across their face. "Sorin, you should go with Wren and Driscoll. I'm sorry, I can't come with you."

Sorin's uninjured hand snaked out and grabbed Arcady's forearm.

"We need a moment," she said, dragging Arcady to the spare room and slamming the door behind her.

"What happened?" Sorin demanded, signing in Trade so Kelwyn couldn't eavesdrop.

"I don't—I don't know, exactly." Their signs were sharp and choppy. "I had a nightmare or a vision. Or a memory. Something. I think the Head Priest and my grandsire tried to heal the serpent twelve years ago, but something went wrong. Did you know that?"

Sorin searched her memories. "He's said he was righting an old wrong or that he had to fix what was broken. For every secret he told me, he kept three back."

"Whatever Magnes and my grandsire did, something went wrong, and it released—it might have started—" Arcady broke off with a strangled sob, pressing the heels of their palms against their eyes. Sorin's throat ached, but she forced the words aloud for them both.

"The Strike." All this time, Magnes had been so desperate to keep the wraiths from the Veil at bay because he knew what was truly at risk.

Arcady gave a muffled groan of frustration. "If what I saw was true . . . twelve years ago, the Consul tried to heal the serpent. I don't know what else Everen saw, or what lies Magnes fed him — I woke up and he was already gone. He probably thought he was protecting me, but instead, he's flown right into danger." Arcady briefly tangled their fingers in their hair before bringing their hands back up to sign. "He probably thinks he's being all noble and self-sacrificing. If he were here, I'd throttle him."

"Is he still alive?" Sorin asked.

"Yes," Arcady whispered aloud, too upset to sign clearly. "I would have felt if he'd died, I'm sure of it. It's like he's . . . deeply asleep, beyond where I can reach him."

Sorin's ears rang. She'd grown better at warding herself, and she'd checked, over and over, and found no sign of another knot in her mind. But what if he'd simply hidden it better?

"And then, before I came here, I heard a voice in my head — taunting me . . ." Arcady spread their hands.

"What did he say?" Sorin asked, stomach churning.

"'For him I used honey, but for you, I will need only the stick.'" Their voice caught. "And then he said if I wanted to save him, I'd have to enter the third trial and come to him. He's up at the monastery, waiting for me."

Sorin exhaled. She left Trade behind, too, but kept her voice low. "It didn't even matter that I broke free from his spell in the end, did it? He let me have that false sense of confidence." She wanted to be sick. "He let us feel like we were free before he snapped the cage shut. It's what he does. Over and over again."

"And that's why you should leave now while you have the chance," Arcady said. "Put as much distance between you and the spell as you can. It'll be hard, but you'll make it through. I have to do what Magnes demands. I have to go save my damned fool of a dragon."

Sorin stared down at her stockinged feet, her mind whirring. She was so *close*. So close to being free of it all, she could taste it. "You'd be confronting him alone."

"He'll *kill* Everen, Sorin. He'll kill him. He wasn't bluffing. I already thought I lost Everen once." Their voice shook. "I have to save him this time."

Sorin let herself imagine taking off, out of the city as soon as the gates opened, hidden down in the back of a cart. She would spend all day cramped and uncomfortable, the pain of the broken seal promise burning hotter and hotter until the distance between her and the Citadel finally helped it fade. She was supposed to cross the border at the coast and be in Myria by tomorrow's end.

"It would be the wiser choice to leave," Sorin said. "I do know that."

"Then go," Arcady said. "You've done enough—you told us who he is. This isn't your fight."

Even if Sorin found herself some out-of-the-way village and set up that life she'd dreamed of so many times, she would always be glancing over her shoulder. Every time she unlocked the door to her little cabin, she'd be half-expecting to see Magnes sitting right by the fireplace, ready to kill her with her own trident blade. Or he'd send one of his Eyes, not even doing the dirty work himself.

All it'd take is one sip of an unguarded cup at a tavern. One run-in somewhere quiet.

As long as Magnes breathed, she'd never be free.

"I'm not running," Sorin said. "Not anymore. It *is* my battle, and I'll fight at your side if you'll have me."

Arcady's gaze was intent. "You realize we might not survive."

Sorin inclined her head. "I know what I'm offering."

Arcady swallowed. Nodded. "Magnes . . . he said I had to 'take my medicine.'"

"If he wants you to take Elixir, then you shouldn't," Sorin said, immediately.

"If it makes your magic stronger, I need all the help I can get, don't I?"

Reluctantly, Sorin took out one of the vials, staring at the swirling liquid as she held it between her thumb and forefinger. "I don't know if it's safe, or how it might interfere with the connection between you and Everen." She passed it to Arcady.

Arcady tucked the vial into their coat pocket. "I've a few candle-marks to decide, I suppose."

The two of them left the spare room, but Kelwyn wasn't in the apartment. They heard voices downstairs in the main shop. Had Wren arrived early? Arcady took the stairs first and froze at the base.

Sorin hung back in the shadows of the stairwell. She had expected to see Wren, the Struck she'd seen at the Night Market.

Instead, it was Larkin Nash.

50.

ARCADY:

THE LARK SINGS

My hand went to the dagger hilt at my hip.

"Larkin," I said, warily.

"Arcady, dear," Larkin said, too sweetly. She'd spent some of Ikari Dwell's wraithwright coin on a large, stylish brown hat with an orange velvet ribbon and a gold buckle. Her floor-length coat matched, and her new boots were polished to a high shine.

Kelwyn's shoulder muscles were locked tight. He clearly hadn't expected Larkin, so it was either Wren or Driscoll who had sold me out. I wasn't surprised, but I thought I wouldn't have to deal with her until Myria.

"Oh don't blame Wren, dear," Larkin said with a wave of her hand as if reading my mind. "Go ahead and set off on your merry way with him and Driscoll when they arrive later. I don't care. But before you sard off, I do think I'm long overdue what I asked for, if you please." She held out her hand expectantly.

I exhaled, slowly. While the blackmail had been hanging over me for months, I was about to confront an actual dragon. Larkin didn't scare me one whit in comparison. I still had to be careful. This could get sticky.

"I don't have Hayden's research," I said, even as the Elixir burned a hole in my pocket.

"And we both know that's a mountain of pig's shit. Come now. The alchemist I've worked with has reached a dead end. We know Hayden's come close to cracking it. Her fool of a child got too loose-lipped one night in the pub, and it echoed what my other source already suspected."

Gods damn it, Willem.

"You're still not getting it, Larkin," I said. "I'm sorry you came all this way for nothing." I rubbed my forehead. "I don't care if you believe me or not, but I do know this Elixir has been kept secret for a reason. It's not ready. It's addictive, it's risky, and the ingredients are difficult to find and access. If I don't trust a master alchemist of the University of Vatra to make it safe, then I sure as shit don't trust you and whatever backwater quack you've found in Myria."

Larkin's nostrils flared. "You don't see how much the Struck in the communes struggle," she said. "Fatigue, pain, and being cut off from their magic. They're *suffering*, Arcady. This can help them. I know it."

"Who would you sell Elixir to in order to make sure you could afford to give it to the less fortunate? The Struck wouldn't be able to pay for ingredients, much less a profit." I gestured at Larkin's fine clothes. "Your head turns just as much as mine at a big pile of coin. Myrians would jump at the chance for enhanced magic. Jaskians might buy it for the same reason they want relics these days, what-ever that may be."

I put my finger to my lip. "What about Lochian drakines, despite how much you say you hate them? Would you still sell them this if it lined your pockets enough? Drakines getting addicted is good business, I suppose, but what about the Struck? Is it worth healing them of one issue by hurting them deeper?"

Something flickered in Larkin's face.

"You consistently underestimate me, Arcady. Of course I would ensure it was safe first. There will be a way to do that—my source is certain. This is about helping undo some of what Loc took from those whose sole crime was falling sicker than the rest. Everyone can pay the cost of magic, but the poor, and especially the Struck, pay the highest price. Don't you think Wren would choose to erase his marks, if he could, so someone could see *him* rather than only a Struck?"

I thought of Wren's face that night in the abandoned brewery, and how hopeful he'd been that Hayden's research might give him back his magic.

"I agree that the Struck deserve far better than what Loc has given them," I said. "But I'm not sure I trust you to be the one to save them. You may not understand how great the risk is, but I do."

Larkin's expression stormed over, and she took a step toward me. "You good for nothing—"

"Larkin," Kelwyn warned. "Stay civil under my roof."

She paused, quivering.

"I believe there's another matter to discuss," Sorin said from behind me. "You broke your promise to me, Larkin Nash. You shouldn't be here at all to threaten anyone."

Larkin jerked in shock and recognition. Sorin was good—someone like Larkin should have realized she was there. My suspicion flared. How did Larkin know Sorin? And what had Sorin done to Larkin for her to be so afraid?

Larkin recovered quicker than I expected, eyes flicking to Kelwyn. "You're bold," she said to Sorin. "Staying under the roof of someone you nearly killed."

"Ikari Dwell was my target that night," Sorin said, her voice mild as Kelwyn inhaled sharply. "Kelwyn was never on my list. My instructions were to get the claw back and kill you for taking it from the barrow hill."

A beat of silence.

Sorin tilted her head. "I banished you from Loc and yet here you are. Perhaps it was a mistake to let you live." With that quiet confidence, I suddenly saw the assassin in Sorin, and fear trickled through me. Kelwyn took a few steps backward.

Larkin's face was carefully unmoving, her eyes wary.

"Give Arcady back what's theirs," Sorin said, "and you may cross the border whenever you wish. The person I once worked for will never know, because with luck, he'll be dead by morning by my hand."

The tension between us was treacle-thick.

"What in the name of the five gods is going on?" Kelwyn asked.

"Arcady and their many, many secrets," Larkin taunted. She reached into her pocket and brought out a seal. My heart leaped at the sight of the dragonstone I'd worn the first nineteen years of my life.

Instead of passing it to me, she handed it to Kelwyn. My heart fell.

"Thought you might find this interesting, Kel," she said, eyes bright. "This, after all, was what I stole from Arcady. Now, why do you think they were so desperate to get it back they'd dance to the tune of my blackmail so easily?"

Kelwyn read the markings and the name, and his face rose, eyes meeting mine.

"You're . . . you're an Eremia?" he asked. The suspicion and hurt on his face cut me.

My silence answered him. His eyes roamed Larkin's face, then Sorin's.

"Even they knew?" he asked, unable to disguise his hurt. "But you didn't tell me?"

"I wanted to," I tried.

"Oh, but you could have," he said. "You could have even last night." His expression shuttered, and he set down the stone seal next to one of his figurines. "You chose not to."

"I was sure you would have hated me for it," I whispered.

He stared at me, dead-eyed. I'd been such a fool, for he hated me more now for keeping it from him.

"I don't care what you all decide between yourselves," he said, hollowly. "I want no part of any of this."

"Kelwyn—" I began.

"Once you leave, you are no longer welcome back at the Last Golden. None of you."

"Kel, please—"

"I'll keep your secret, Arcady, if that's what you're worried about." He shook his head. "My whole family died in the first Strike. My partner, my two children. You're not him, sure, but you're of him, and you couldn't even do me the courtesy of telling me. I'm sorry, Arcady. You're right. This is obviously dangerous. But I'm not risking my neck anymore, especially for the Plague-bringer's get."

I flinched.

He turned, and his footsteps were heavy on the stairs. Grief rose up to choke me.

Larkin's chin was raised, without a trace of regret. I picked up my original stone seal, my fingertips tracing the familiar carvings. My hand closed over it in a fist. I'd been desperate for it back, but I'd paid too dear a price. My magic was funneled through my taie's dragonstone, but I felt a spark from my old one, strong enough I almost dropped it.

"There," Larkin said. "Even if I went to the university with my suspicions, I have no proof. And yes, I should have known better than to blackmail you. I should have come back to Loc sooner, spoken to you one on one. Maybe we could have come to an agreement." Her eyes flicked to Sorin, still silent as a shadow behind me.

"So I ask you this again, without force, without leverage. Give me Hayden's research. I promise I will be careful. I'll even seal sign for it."

I sighed. "Larkin. The solution has always been simple: go to Professor Hayden yourself and ask Them for help directly. If I kill who I need to tonight, the professor might be able to help you, if They wish. You never needed me to steal Their research at all."

Her gaze slipped to Sorin. "And of my broken promise?" she asked, carefully.

"I release you from it," Sorin said. "You may stay in Loc. For I may not live to see the morning, either."

"May Saint Ini keep you both safe," Larkin said, her voice tight. We stared at each other. There was so much to say, but neither of us were willing to say it.

She tipped her hat at me, and the tinkle of the bell above the door was far too jolly.

My head twisted toward the stairs as the shop fell silent, but Kelwyn didn't come back down.

I put my old seal in my pocket and took out the vial of Elixir, my fingers fumbling as my breath came faster and faster, the panic rising like it had the night Wren had first blackmailed me.

"Arcady—it's not wise—"

"What choice do I have?" I snapped at Sorin. "I need whatever it takes to defeat him. How much?"

Sorin swallowed. "Half a vial. Especially for your first time."

"Bottoms up," I said, raising the vial.

My eyelids fluttered closed as I drank. "Saints and gods," I whispered as the drug took hold.

All that uncertainty, all that turmoil threatening to unravel me instantly fell away. Instead, my magic kindled like a flame roaring to life. While I couldn't reach Everen, I felt the bond better. He was alive.

There was still time to save him. And I felt, with Elixir in my arsenal, maybe there was a chance.

"Is this . . . is this what it's like to not fear anything?" I asked. "I feel like I could use all the magic in the world and never turn Starveling at all."

Sorin peered at me in concern. "Be careful. It'll give you focus and power, but it will also make it harder to know your limits or make you overly impulsive. It lessens the cost, but it doesn't eliminate it."

"Gods," I said. "No wonder the Consul was afraid of what my grandsire could do."

I held out the vial, and she snatched it from my hand and drained the rest. The tension left her body, bliss creeping across her face.

I straightened my shoulders. Everen had been taken, I'd confronted Larkin, and Kelwyn, my oldest true friend, had rejected me. A moment ago, I'd been wrecked, but with Elixir in my veins, I had no room for doubt or shame.

The morning bells tolled, echoing across the city. We'd tried so hard to leave, but the Citadel was calling us back all the same.

51.

SORIN:

THE FEAST OF STORMS

The seats of the Citadel amphitheater were full to bursting. Banners and ribbons fluttered in the breeze. The sky was a perfect, clear blue, and the winter chill had passed to the gentle coolness of a spring morning. Sorin wanted to be sick.

The two Chancellors sat straight on the dais on the other side of the grounds, wraithwright masks shining like coins. Next to them was someone dressed as the Head Priest, but it wasn't him. Sorin knew it instantly. She wondered who hid behind the horned mask. Did Magnes plan to make them forget they'd been a stand-in, or would he simply kill them afterward?

Arcady stared blankly, lost in the throes of the drug, and Sorin rode her own euphoria.

The six finalists stood on a grand float that would soon be pulled by Piater magic. Arcady and the others were all straight backs and raised chins. Edin Vayne beamed, and while Rahela seemed nervous, she still exuded quiet confidence. Jordin shifted from foot to foot, and Cind's mouth was a thin line. A fourth year, a second year, two third years, and, to the enduring confusion of many, two first years were the students left standing. Sorin could only hope none of the other students would be put at risk for Magnes's plan, whatever they were walking into.

"Welcome, welcome," the Herald said, magic-assisted voice floating out over the crowd and quieting some of the noise.

"On this Feast of Storms, we usher in the beginning of spring and also begin the third and final task of the University Trials. This will test our finalists to their limits. They will go forth into the land and face the elements with nothing but their grit, their will, and their magic. The first to return to the finish line with all three medals will be declared the winner, with the second and third still receiving partial scholarships. All six students should be beyond proud to have reached this stage. No matter the outcome, you all have bright futures ahead of you."

Arcady snorted.

"You represent the hope and the might of the University of Vatra and the Citadel of Loc. Once you are out of the city and on the path of the third trial, may you be lifted upon the dragon gods' wings and prove your might."

"Really wouldn't mind some bloody wings," Arcady said under their breath and Sorin fought the irrational urge to laugh. It was that or cry. She let the drug push it all away, wrapping her in warm sunlight. While the Elixir calmed Sorin down, Arcady was agitated, unable to stop fidgeting.

The float began to move, the wooden platform swaying beneath their feet. The Citadel crowd cheered louder, waving and wishing them all luck. By rote, Sorin lifted her arm with the others, an empty smile frozen on her face as the wyverns flew overhead, with Jaculus among them. She wondered if she'd ever see her little protector again. She wouldn't risk his safety. Where she was going, he couldn't follow. Below her were the students she'd studied with, the professors who'd taught her, the courtiers who had never seen her even as she'd grown up right in their midst.

The procession wound down the slope of the hill, and more people lined either side of the path.

"Come on, stop looking so dour," Edin Vayne said, nudging Sorin's shoulder. "It's meant to be a celebration."

Sorin brightened her false smile. Edin nodded and drifted to the other side of the float, leaning over the railings and taking a flower from a young, comely youth.

"I'd dreamed of doing this, once," Arcady murmured to Sorin. "I watched last year's Feast of Storms parade, vowing one day I'd be up here with them. Now here I am, and all I want to do is scream."

Sorin's eyes flicked to the other students. "Caution, Arcady."

Arcady straightened. "I know, I know. Let's give them a show, then. Might be the last time we can." Sorin watched Arcady's muscles loosen, their grin warming to seemingly sincere. The mask had slipped, but Arcady had tied it back on.

People half-hung from the open windows of the sandstone tenements, ribbon streamers fluttering in the breeze. It felt as if all of Vatra had come out to see them. It was too many eyes. Even with the drug, Sorin felt exposed and vulnerable. She was almost relieved when they passed the city gates.

Almost.

Several professors waited for them near the carriages that would take them to the official starting point of the third trial. Professor Hayden was among them. The carriages had been spelled so they'd reach the foothills of the mountains quicker. Her eyes watered at how much magic would be needed for six.

The students sobered once the crowd no longer distracted them from all that would come next. The professors gave the students their safety pendants, and they sized each other up—competitors once more.

"There is no shame in using this should you need it," Professor Plink said. "We'll come to your aid as quickly as we can. Your safety is more important than a token or a win. Understood?"

They all nodded, but Sorin suspected that whatever happened next, they were well and truly on their own.

"Good luck to all of you. May we all have the speed, strength, and favor of the gods," Professor Hayden said, and one by one, They gripped the students' forearms. Sorin tried not to flinch when it was her turn. Hayden paused, a line forming between Their brow, before pulling away.

"Take care," Professor Hayden said, but it sounded more like a warning. Sorin's heartbeat sped up. Did They know, or suspect? If so, why weren't They interfering?

The students shook each other's forearms next. *Don't do this*, Sorin wanted to yell at them. *Break the seal promise and sard the repercussions.* They were all powerful magic users. Did Magnes have a plan for them, too?

"See you on the other side," Arcady said.

Even with the drug in her veins, Sorin fought down her nerves as she climbed into the carriage. The door closed, locking her inside, before it took off down the Royal Road toward the mountains.

Toward two dragons: one to save, and one to kill.

52.

ARCADY:

MAGIC VERSUS NATURE

As the carriage barreled toward the mountains, I felt as though I'd swallowed a star. My magic lurked beneath my skin, and I was heady with the power of it. I felt strong enough to take on the world.

To take on a dragon.

Even with that extra power, I couldn't speak to Everen. When the carriage finally drew to a stop and the door snicked open, I wasted no time.

I knew we were in the forest somewhere near the foothills of the Fangs, but where exactly was a mystery. The carriage had come with a standard rucksack containing food and a few basic supplies. I slung it over my shoulder. We weren't meant to bring weapons—this being a test of magic and all—but Sorin and I had both taken our dragonbone blades, and I'd spirited away a few other blades for good measure. Professor Hayden hadn't searched us all that hard, and her expression had remained inscrutable after the cursory pat down before I'd climbed into the carriage. The professors were meant to be looking out for us, but Hayden was working for Magnes. Was she even now sending him word, somehow, that we were on our way? The carriage stopped, the door opening. Off in the distance, I spotted the other carriages, the students setting off on their individual paths without even a backward glance in my direction.

The way before me was lined with mage lights.

"Fate, you better help us out of this mess," I muttered.

I took the trail at a steady trot. The forest was thinner here, mostly birch and Lochian pine. Like Willem's estate, it was all too quiet, and I caught a few signs of the blight.

I heard the first obstacle before I saw it: a great river cut right across the path of mage lights. The Vatra or the Red River, was my guess. The white water tumbled over rocks. The first token glinted at me on the other side of the river, the bronze medal stuck into the top of a wooden stump.

I judged the distance across. At least ten yards.

"*Kjetim-lei ak-kalś.*" My Kalsh magic bubbled up like a fountain. It came with another burst of euphoria so intense I wanted to cry. I knew the fear was still there, deep down, but the Elixir wouldn't let me feel it.

I could get used to this.

"*Kiév vojra,*" I said. I imagined a straight path of smooth water and wading calmly through it. I held my palm up, urging the element to heed my will.

I grunted as my power flowed into the water. The river bubbled, but a line formed into a temporary dam to my right. The water sluiced over it, but it no longer raged. The aquatic wall rose higher. On the other side, the river quieted.

I stepped into the shallows, gasping with the cold. More of my magic flowed into the barrier to my right, and my seal glowed bright blue. Thanks to the dam, the water reached my waist instead of being deep enough to cover my head. Echoes of the current tugged at me, but they didn't knock me off my feet. The cold threatened to steal the air from my lungs, and I used a spark of Aura magic to warm me through. Using two types of magic at once should have drained me near-instantly, but between my dragon bond and the Elixir, I was barely winded.

I could become *so* used to this.

I reached the midpoint of the river. The dam to my right twisted as it struggled to free itself, the blue of my magic threaded through it like reflections of sunlight. The river was restless—the pressure growing. If I lost control, my body would be swept away before I could blink, and I doubted even Elixir would be able to save me.

I thought of Everen's green eyes and how they could be as hard as a predator's, yet grow so soft when they looked at me.

I poured more of my magic into the spell as I trudged forward. The other side of the bank was nearly within reach. Only a few more steps.

The water roiled, sluicing over the top of my spell. On the side of the bank where I'd first entered the river, the wall began to crumble. It was getting away from me. For all I'd taken my Kalsh class for a few moons, water-weaving was still new to me, and even with Elixir's help, I struggled.

Fighting panic, I dived beneath the surface and kicked as hard as I could, reaching for shore. My boots struggled for purchase on the slippery silt, and I scrabbled as the spell failed. I swallowed freezing water, my hands reaching out desperately, until I tangled my hands in roots, closing my eyes tight as the river flowed past, angry at being interrupted, my feet kicking in the current.

If I'd been in the middle of the river, I'd have had no chance, but in the shallows, I clung on with everything I had.

When the worst of the river's ire faded, I crawled out of the water on my hands and knees. I collapsed into the cold, sodden mud, coughing up water and gasping for breath.

I laid there as long as I dared, lungs burning, before I forced myself upright. The amount of magic I'd just used should have left me a starving, snarling Starveling. Instead, I felt . . . tired, sure, and hungry, but I was not in danger of losing myself.

Shaking my head in wonder, I opened my drenched bag and ate a damp and horrible sweetsphere as I made my way to the stump. With a tiny burst of magic, I freed the first token. It was a coin carved with the familiar wyvern heraldry of the University of Vatra. The other side was an open book with a five-pointed star above it. I shoved the token in my pocket, buttoning it closed.

The mage lights illuminated the way. I limped along the path, working warmth back into my limbs as my magic recovered.

Before long, I turned a corner and halted.

The way was blocked by the second obstacle: a giant wall of thorns. The dark brown branches were twice as tall as me. University green mages had been at work—there was no way the path could grow this dense without magical aid. Some of the thorns were longer than my hand and wickedly sharp. There was no way to walk around without adding hours to the journey at best.

Chewing my lip, I wondered how the other students would attack their respective thickets. Jari would be the easiest if someone was strong enough to peel back the thorns, but I had next no control of green magic. There was fire magic, of course, but the plants were dry and thirsty this high up the mountain, and it'd risk catching like kindling. Someone strong in Zama might be able to strike it with lightning, but with the same risks. Piater magic could help someone forge a path through by rolling stones through the thorns or using telekinesis. I wasn't anywhere near good enough with Piater magic for that, even with Elixir. Kalsh magic wasn't particularly useful here.

In the end, I decided on fire.

"*Reukas vé*," I said, and the magic leaped to my bidding. I felt the heat of the flames over my palms.

With a twist of my hands, I sent the fire forward. As I had with the river, I tried to imagine the path the fire could take through the thorns. Straight and true.

The thorns caught immediately, the flames rising high. Branches snapped and curled, the temperature of it playing against my face and reminding me of the pyre in the forest. My stomach clenched as the smoke rose to the sky.

Setting the fire had been the easy bit. Now I had to control it.

Like the river, the flame, too, wanted to escape. The fire wanted to burn every thorn and spread into the remains of the forest.

"*Sedžas*," I commanded, wrapping my magic tighter. *Extinguish.* I willed the air to starve the fire, but the flames fought me, licking their way closer. The heat of it was beginning to hurt, sweat trickling down my temples and the small of my back. There was a moment where I was afraid I'd lose control and the flames would use me for fuel as easily as the thorns.

I closed my eyes tight, letting my Elixir-enhanced power flare hotter than the blaze before me.

"*Sedžas!*"

With a last pulse of power, the flames snuffed out.

It was instant. Smoke rose, the blackened thorns hissing. More fell to ash.

I caught my breath, eating another sweetsphere and making sure the fire wouldn't return. The elation of the drug and seeing what I'd accomplished made my head spin. On the other side of the ruined thorns, I found the stone path.

My boots kicked up ash. It was so hot my skin felt scorched, but I didn't have so much as a blister.

The second token waited for me, this one stuck into a boulder. I tucked the silver next to the bronze in my pocket.

I glanced back at the still-smoking ruins of the thickets, then carried on as the ground sloped upward.

Even without the mage lights, I would have known the way. I felt it like a hook in the gut.

—*I'm coming*, I sent my dragon as the afternoon lengthened, even if he couldn't hear me. *I'll save you.*

I had no real plan, only a stubborn determination to make it out of this alive. It seemed as impossible as healing a serpent god who lurked between worlds.

I focused on the pain in my chest, the burning of my muscles. My ears rang. My breath came faster, and I forced myself to keep climbing. This high up, the forest looked as familiar as the ones where I'd spent my childhood.

My fingertips tingled when I passed a twisting pine tree at the next bend. There were the rocks on either side of the path that my paire had called the sentinels.

I knew exactly where I was.

When I reached the old market square of the mountain village of Atrel, my footsteps slowed. I'd lived in a little cabin on the outskirts of this town for three years, after my parents fled Vatra and everyone we'd ever known thought we'd died in the burning of our house near the Citadel. I'd come back this way not that long ago, searching for answers and finding my family grimoire in the ruins.

The plague had worked its way so quickly through the hamlet that no one had had time to even board or paint the windows to warn of the Strike. Instead, it had all burned, and only the skeletons of homes remained. Inside would be the black, cracked bones of people I'd once known.

I walked through the square, my feet kicking the loose cobbles. Their skittering echoed unnervingly.

Had Magnes made me pass through here on purpose? How many of my secrets did the dragon know?

My muffled hearing barely caught the sound of footsteps behind me. I turned, fear briefly breaking through the drug before relief spread through me at the sight of Sorin. She was just as damp and mud-splashed as me. She'd entered the town from the opposite side of the square—we must have all crossed the Vatra River at different points, but the paths converged here in Atrel.

"Take it you managed the first two obstacles?" I asked.

She pulled out her bronze and silver tokens. "Yes. Used Jari magic for both. Felled a tree for the river and cleared a path through the thorns." Sorin wouldn't have been able to do that without Elixir, either.

"Kalsh magic then Aura magic for me," I said.

"I'm not sure if anyone has triggered the safety spells. My guess is either Cind or Jordin tapped out already. Maybe both."

I thought of the jagged rocks, white water, and sharp thorns, and shivered.

"Have you spotted Rahela or Edin?" I asked. "I haven't seen a soul."

"Me neither." Sorin took in the burned buildings. "There are many villages like this up in the mountains. I passed through a few when I came to the monastery from the Red River. They all feel haunted."

"I lived in this one," I said.

Sorin stiffened in surprise.

"Aye. This was my home after we fled Vatra during the First Strike. In a cabin on the outskirts."

Sorin's frown deepened. "You lived this close to the monastery?"

"I'd always assumed we'd moved up here to hide . . ." I said, my words slow and halting. "Perhaps it was more than that. I knew my maire had been building on my taie's work as much as she could. She'd been waiting to tell me things when I was older . . ." I trailed off, shrugging. "She took her secrets to her grave save for the spell that gave me a new seal and a dragon. It all feels inevitable." I laughed bitterly. "It all feels like fucking fate."

The mage lights led off to another trail away from the village, and I hesitated.

"What?" Sorin asked.

"My parents always warned me to stay off this path. They said it was too dangerous and I never saw anyone come or go this way."

Sorin took a couple more steps. "Then I suspect we've found the way to the third obstacle."

I squared my shoulders and followed Sorin along the path, forcing the fear back down as we left Atrel behind.

53.
ARCADY:
THE THIRD TRIAL

The path grew higher, following the curve of Cragspeak Mountain. Sorin and I walked side by side, keeping a watchful eye on our surroundings. So far, the third trial hadn't been easy, exactly, but there hadn't been any surprises.

We reached the edge of a great cliff. A grand natural-looking bridge crossed over a sheer drop to the Vatra River below. I suspected magic had shaped it long ago. If all magic faded with time, did that mean it was still safe to cross?

The wind whistled across the gap. I knew if I fell, I'd have enough time to dread the landing.

We'd also found Rahela.

She was stuck halfway across the bridge, crouched low, clearly terrified to move in either direction. With each burst of wind that ruffled her short hair, she clung tighter.

"Rahela!" I called. She stiffened and twisted her head toward us.

"I can't do it," she sobbed. "I can't do it."

"It's not far," I said, pitching my voice to carry.

"I can't, I can't."

The wind was rising, whipping my hair across my face. Rahela muffled a scream as the wind rocked her. "Is there another way to the monastery?" Sorin asked, eyeing the bridge.

"You'd have to go back through Atrel and loop the other side of Cragspeak," I said. "It'd take time we don't have." I shifted from foot to foot.

"Rahela," Sorin called. "You're already over halfway, and this is the last obstacle. You've done the hardest part. Use your magic to quiet the wind and start moving. Going back is harder than going forward. You could be on the other side in a few minutes, and then it's over."

She ducked her head, rigid with fear.

"One of us has to help her," I said, putting one foot on the bridge as my impatience welled up.

Sorin grabbed my sleeve. "That bridge is delicate — I'm not sure it could handle more than one person at a time."

"What else can we do?" I said. "She's not moving."

Sorin peered at me. "The Elixir is making you reckless. Keep your wits about you. Give her a moment, and she won't need us at all."

If I could get her to the other side, then Sorin and I could be across in less than a quarter of a candlemark. The monastery was not far — we were nearly there. Everen *needed* me, and though I was sympathetic to Rahela's fear, she was currently another obstacle. The drug pulsed through me, my magic clamoring.

I stepped onto the bridge.

"Arcady!" Sorin hissed, but she couldn't risk following.

The bridge was barely wider than my hips. My determination hardened. If I was going to die, it would be facing down a dragon or a raging storm. Not here, not now. I had to help Rahela be on her way, and we could be on ours.

I tied my cloak tightly around myself, so I'd have no flapping fabric catching in the wind. I followed Rahela's approach and crawled across. The stone was rough beneath my hands, and the wind tugged stray hair from my hasty plait. Once I was away from the cliff's edge. I was acutely aware of how vulnerable I was to the wind and the elements. On the other side of the bridge, I just caught the light glinting off the gold tokens.

Don't look down, I told myself. *Whatever you do, don't look down.* I focused on a spot on the bridge ahead of me, pretending this was nothing more than a stone bridge over a creek in the woods. Nothing to fear. I forced myself to move slowly and steadily, keeping my breathing even.

My neck prickled as I realized that my back was exposed. My trust faltered. Sorin had an array of knives on her. We'd broken the spell in her mind, but what if she'd only agreed to come on the third trial because she still belonged to Magnes? If she'd threw a blade, as she had in Girazin's tower, she wouldn't miss. The space between my shoulder blades itched.

I turned my head. Sorin watched me, her hands empty.

Hardening my resolve, I faced forward and passed the thinnest part of the bridge.

"Rahela," I said.

"Arcady. I can't stand this. I don't even know how long I've been here. It feels like candlemarks. Days."

"Much longer than you needed to," I pitched my voice gently. "Come on. You're so close."

As I inched forward, I heard a sickening crack behind me. Rahela shrieked.

"Arcady, move!" Sorin's voice kicked me into action.

I staggered backward as I felt the stone shift beneath my feet. Part of the bridge ahead of me had cleaved away. Rahela screamed again, her legs nearly dangling, feet kicking. I clutched the stone beneath my hands, as if that'd make a lick of difference if the whole thing crumbled beneath us both.

The stone quieted.

There was a gap in front of me where it was narrow enough to cross, but the thought of hopping across made me want to puke.

"Push forward, Rahela," I said, breathing hard. "Get on the stronger part of the bridge."

She had her knees up on the stone, but her feet were over the gap.

Maybe the bridge was already fragile, and this would have happened anyway, but perhaps Sorin had been right and the bridge shouldn't have carried the weight of two people. "I'm sorry, I'm sorry. I should have given you more time."

The longer we stayed put, the greater the risk. Rahela was shivering badly. My heart was in my throat. I listened for cracks, but my weakened ears couldn't hear anything over the wind. My shoulders were hunched, and I was shaking as hard as Rahela.

I made a crucial mistake and glanced down. The green of the valley spread far below, the river nothing but a thin ribbon of blue.

"Come on," I urged Rahela past the lump of fear in my throat. "It'd help me out if you're not on the stone. You can kiss that final token and carry it down the mountain. You can be at the Citadel by sunset. You might even be in first place. Don't you want to win?"

Another sob. "Yes, yes, I want to win."

"And you deserve it. So act like it, Rahela. Save yourself, save me, and fight for it!"

She gave a cry that was closer to a scream. Behind me, I felt Sorin's magic flare as she shouted a Zama spell. A few seconds later, the wind around us quieted to a gentle breeze. Rahela's hands were stiff and probably half-frozen. I held my breath as, inch by painful inch, Rahela scuffled herself across. I clung to the rock and focused on Rahela; it helped me ignore my own fear of the long drop below.

Finally, finally, she reached the other side. She hugged herself, rocking back and forth.

"Don't tarry," Sorin called. "I can't keep back the wind much longer."

I stretched my awareness toward the stone. I had so little Piater magic. Would another fault reveal itself as soon as I started to move?

I took a few seconds, weighing my options, before I carefully took the water bladder hanging off the side of my pack.

"Yes," Sorin said behind me as she realized what I meant to do.

I spilled the water onto the stone in front of me. Using Kalsh, I whispered the spell, and the water moved, joining the cracks and filling in the missing gap of the bridge. I felt Rahela's magic reach across, helping me harden the water to ice. It simply had to hold for half a candlemark.

If it held.

Nothing for it. I crawled forward until I reached the part that was mainly ice. I tried not to imagine it shattering like glass. I used more magic to roughen the top of it for better grip, but it still meant putting a damn sight of faith in our combined spells, even with two of the three of us bolstered by Elixir.

Like I'd said to Rahela, I could only carry forward. I forced myself to go slowly. For the briefest moment, I had all four limbs on the section that was ice. My seal glowed bright blue.

I crawled until I was back on ice-cracked stone. It wasn't safe yet, but I took a beat to gather myself.

"Not far," Rahela called. "You're not far. If I did it, so can you."

I slithered along the thin stone bridge. Rahela gestured encouragingly.

When I reached the edge of the bridge, I jumped onto solid ground.

I let myself lie there for a moment, cheek to stone, as I had after the river.

Rahela rushed forward, rubbing my back. "Are you all right?" She was breathing shallowly. The air was thinner up here. Her cheeks were tear-stained and chapped red from the wind.

"Yeah. I . . . had a moment. You?"

She laughed and nodded. "Yeah. Just a moment."

My elation didn't last long. I stood and stared across the expanse of the canyon and the broken, spindly stone bridge that spanned it.

It was Sorin's turn.

54.

SORIN:

SILVER, BLOOD, BONE

Sorin took her first step onto the bridge. Her seal flared violet as she fought to keep control of the wind. Magnes had only given her a few lessons on Zama's magic for the first trial, but with the Elixir's help, she had taken to it well enough. Even so, the gusts tugged alarmingly at her. Instead of crawling like the other two, she crossed like an acrobat. Chin up, chest out, arms spread for balance. She walked heel to toe, her cloak wrapped securely around her waist.

Arcady's hands were clasped over the glowing blue seal at their chest, but Sorin couldn't quell her doubts as she approached the section of ice.

Sorin fell to hands and knees to help spread her weight and shuffled across. She didn't let herself think. She focused on putting one hand and one knee forward at a time. Once she was back on stone, she exhaled and brought herself to her feet.

An especially strong gust of wind made it through her spell, and she felt herself unbalance. Rahela gave a muffled shriek as Sorin windmilled her arms, desperately trying to right herself.

After an alarming tilt and a view of just how far she had to fall, Sorin steadied.

"You're almost there," Arcady urged. "Come on."

Sorin resisted the urge to run and made her careful way forward. Arcady reached out and Sorin grasped their wrist. They helped her down. Sorin bent over, resisting the urge to be sick.

"I'm sorry," Arcady was saying. "I'm sorry, you were right."

Sorin glanced back at the bridge. "We managed in the end."

"Don't fancy anyone else's chances if they come across it," Arcady said.

"One token is missing," Rahela plucked her gold one. "So someone's come this way." Four tokens remained.

"Edin," Sorin guessed.

"We all knew she'd win, didn't we?" Arcady said.

"Looks like second place is the best I can hope for, unless you two overtake me on the way back." Rahela shrugged, though her smile was wary.

Arcady grabbed her hand. "Head back to Vatra as fast as you can. We'll be right behind you, but you deserve to finish this ahead of us. You're brilliant, Rahela." Rahela had done well in both the first and the second trial, especially as a second year. She might have taken a bit of help from them on the third obstacle, but she had done this properly.

"Thank you," Rahela whispered. "Both of you."

Sorin inclined her head. "Fly fast and true."

Rahela nodded. "You, too."

Without a backward glance, she took off down the mountain.

As soon as she was out of sight, the mage lights of the path flickered, revealing another set of stairs carved into a gap between two boulders.

It headed further up the mountain, to Nalore Monastery and all the secrets within.

Nalore Monastery was so cleverly carved into the stone that it always surprised Sorin when it emerged from the rock. The monastery was brutish and unadorned; the windows were disguised as fissures along the natural lines of the stone, barely wide enough for a few arrows. The great wood and metal door was tucked beneath an outcropping that left it in permanent shadow.

Perhaps it was the Elixir in her system, but Sorin could feel the magic of this place in a way she hadn't when she'd last been here. It hummed in the air and the stone. The Elixir helped her sense the leylines converging at the heart of the Fangs.

Sorin passed the stables where she'd left her horse over the summer. Arcady wrapped their arms around themselves, breath misting in the air. Some deeper assassin's intuition made Sorin reach for her knife, lowering into a half-crouch.

A shadow broke from beneath the front door, and Edin Vayne stumbled closer to them. She cradled her arm close to her chest, head bowed. Sorin straightened. Had the mage lights led Edin up here instead of back down in the direction Rahela had gone?

"Edin? Are you hurt?" Arcady asked.

Edin coughed.

"Turn back, and head back down toward the city," Sorin said. "It's not safe up here."

Edin's head lifted when she was close enough, her nose red from the cold. Her expression was so blank, the hairs on the back of Sorin's neck rose.

"Edin?" Arcady's voice was hesitant, but Sorin understood in a blink.

Before she could warn Arcady, Edin reached for a knife at her belt. Even before Sorin saw the blade, she knew it would be white.

"Did you truly think that He would only have one Eye in the university, Sorin?" Edin smiled slyly, cocking her head. "That He wouldn't realize you were too weak for what would be needed when the time came?"

There had been three Eyes in the forest that day of the hunt.

"There is no point in fighting Him, Sorin. We both know it," Edin said, gripping the knife tighter. "We live solely to serve Him. To fulfill His glorious purpose as a dragon god living among us." Her eyes were wide and empty. "And He wants *them*." Her face turned toward Arcady, who was still frozen in shock.

Sorin knew surprise was her only advantage. She ducked, twisted, and kicked Edin's foot out from under her. Sorin had her blade at Edin's neck in less than ten seconds.

"Yes," Sorin hissed. "But if you're dead, what help can you be to your false god?"

Edin laughed, the sound echoing eerily against the stone. "Oh, Sorin, my little wyvern," she said, and the shift in her inflection froze Sorin to the core.

—*Over and over*, came his voice in her mind, *you try so very hard to flutter away. Haven't you realized by now that I will always keep what is mine?*

"No," Sorin whispered, her hand shaking enough the blade nicked Edin's skin.

—*By silver, by blood, and by bone*, Magnes said. *It's time to come home to roost.*

Edin's head tilted toward the sky, and she laughed exactly like Magnes as a shadow fell across the three of them.

Great wings, pointed as a bat's, blocked the fading light. The great dragon flapped his wings, circling the keep. Everything about him was sinuous: from his long neck, the undulation of his body, to the long tail. His scales were such a dark purple they were near-black, the shimmering feathers a glowing violet. He was all claws, talons, teeth, and those orange eyes, bright as fire. He looked divine and damned.

The wind from the dragon's wings made Sorin's eyes water as he hovered above them before landing on the stone in front of the monastery with surprising lightness. She wanted to run, but her feet were frozen to the rock. Arcady, too, seemed unable to move.

The white of a scar flashed at the base of one of his great fore-claws.

Magnes came closer, and one tip of that great talon carefully pressed into her shoulder, piercing her clothing and her skin. She felt the sheer force of it, how, with only a little more pressure, he could skewer her straight through.

He brought his talon to his great mouth and his forked tongue tasted her blood.

—*Tulaſ vraram, tulaſ pyu, tulaſ kajto*, the dragon intoned. *Tulaſ el-vanok vaugain, kjodžen-lei ar-džakain al-au. Tulaſ vraram, tulaſ pyu, ek tulaſ kajto. Fanau arlei el-vulo.*

"By silver, by blood, by bone," Arcady whispered the translation. "By the dragon scales, I am your storm. By silver, by blood, and by bone: you rage only for me."

A high note sang through Sorin's skull as the spell took hold. She tried to escape, but a dark gold wrapped around her mind, making the knot that had been there before look like nothing more than a ribboned bow. This one was made of thorned vines, sharp as the ones she'd faced during the second obstacle.

Sorin dropped the knife she held to Edin's throat.

Arcady scrabbled for their blade, but it was Sorin's hand that reached out and snatched their wrist. It was Sorin who pulled Arcady's arms behind them, pinning them in place.

"Sorin! Let me go." Arcady twisted desperately. Sorin willed her hands to open, but she couldn't even make herself blink. There was nothing but dark gold, sharp thorns puncturing her mind, and Magnes's magic sizzling through her like indigo lightning as the spell took deeper hold.

"*Tiś-té!*" With a burst of their magic, Arcady broke the pendant around their neck to call for help. The priest knew it would do nothing. Magnes had already set a boundary ward around the monastery. She felt its shimmer. Even if the professors were searching for them, they would never be able to find this place. No help was coming.

The priest watched, feeling nothing as the dragon came closer until His great head was level with them both. His head twisted to the side, His orange eye unblinking.

—*I have been waiting for this for such a long, long time,* the dragon said. *The players are all here. Let's see who wins this game.*

55.

CASSIA:

OMINOUS

The sky burned.

After threatening to erupt for so many years, lava finally spat fire and smoke into the sky. The sea churned. By morning, the entire island would be coated in a thick layer of ash.

As soon as the Reek had erupted, Cassia had felt a tug deep in her magic. Every dragon on the island felt it, and all knew what it meant.

Wraiths.

Cassia stood at the very tip of the Lady of Vere Celene. She wore her mother's armor—a chest plate to protect her heart, and chain-mail around her neck and stomach to protect the softer, thinner parts of her hide. Behind her, every dragon able to fight was at the ready. Three hundred strong, at best.

The dragons too infirm for physical confrontation sheltered in the caves below. They'd use their magic to feed the barrier around the island and protect themselves and the unhatched clutch of dragon eggs.

The last of the sunset was blotted out by black smoke and the orange-red of the volcano's anger.

Even through the smoke and fire, the rip across the fabric of the world was visible. Lightning flashed, and wisps of deeper darkness escaped from the storm.

—*This will be more wraiths than we've ever fought*, Cassia said, privately, to Mace. *Won't it?*

Mace nodded. —*We may not be able to hold them back. And if they make it to the barrier around the island . . .*

She didn't need to finish the thought.

The barrier would break. And dragonkind would fall.

—*We await your orders, Queen Regent*, Mace said, and Cassia's jaw gaped in a burst of grief. Cassia had done her best as their ruler, these last sennights. Some dragons had shifted their allegiance, and though no dragon had dared challenge her or her rule, many had made no secret that they wanted their true Queen to lead them through this.

Yet Queen Naccara remained underground, in a dream so deep none could reach her. Everen was in the human world, and Miligrist still had no visions of her own. Her mother would have known just what to do and how to act. Now there was only Cassia. Barely even a warrior. Young, untried, and untested.

—*Tonight, we fight with everything we have.* Cassia threw her thoughts wide. *With tooth, and claw, and scale. We must hold back the tide, and we must survive.*

—*What will become of us?* a dragon sent. Viola, perhaps. *Even if we survive, what future can there be for us?*

The other dragons growled, the uncertainty spreading. If they succumbed to fear, they stood no chance.

—*Take heart and heed*, Cassia cried. *If we defeat the wraiths, we will be rewarded with a bright and peaceful future. Fate has given us a winding path, I know, but we are so close. It tastes like plentiful prey. It tastes like clean water and clear air. If we are victorious, we will be rewarded and dragonkind will flourish. I know it.*

Mace narrowed her eyes, and Cassia nearly stumbled back from the sheer force and anger in the older dragon's gaze.

—*You would lie to your people?* Mace hissed, privately.

—*Everen told me he saw a peaceful future. The dragons need hope.*

—*How can you be so sure he saw true?*

—*Because I have faith in him.*

Cassia felt Miligrist's wordless approval, even as Mace seethed. Good. Let her channel that anger toward what was coming.

The air echoed with the distant shriek of wraiths.

—*For Vere Celene and the dragons,* Cassia sent to every dragon on the island, both above ground and below. *We fight for our future!* She opened her mouth in a roar, her whole body shaking with the force of it.

The dragons answered, the din loud enough to drown out the sounds of the wraiths.

As one, they rose to the sky, flying out to the horizon and the monsters that waited for them there.

Cassia caught sight of the first few wraiths, with their violet eyes and smoking wings. They opened their jaws unnaturally wide, their echoing clicks sending a shiver down her spine.

She hoped, when the sun rose, there would be dragons alive to greet it.

56.

EVEREN:

TWO DRAGONS

I blinked, my eyes struggling to focus as I caught the scent of stone, molten metal, and magic.

I . . . floated. I could not access my power. My head swam, my vision softening around the edges. My mouth tasted of scrysilver and something sickly sweet.

Elixir.

If I had been made to drink it, that meant I had ingested part of a dragon. I heaved, but nothing came up.

Gradually, the world around me stabilized. I was chained tight to something bright and shining as a star. I remembered nothing of waking or flying to this place.

I twisted my head. The dragonstone tree was exactly like Sorin's vision and my dream. The roots trailed off into a still pool of scrysilver that reflected the light. The branches stretched high above into darkness, and the heat and magic of it warmed the air. The cave was so deep I could not even see the ceiling. Everything tilted as I was lost in another rush of the drug.

When I could see again, the last male dragon stood on the far side of the scrysilver pool in preterit form. He was flanked by Sorin and another human I faintly recognized as another student through your memories. They were both stiff and blank as a pair of statues.

Ammil stepped onto a root, his footsteps leaving glowing tracks. He grew close enough for me to catch the amused smile playing across his lips. He paused opposite me and crouched until we faced each other, eye to eye.

His irises were the same brilliant orange I had seen in my dream, and his feathered hair was a dark black-purple. He was centuries older than me, but it barely showed on his face. Our height, our build, our features—although we were not direct kin, we were obviously kindred. Here was Ammil, the dragon I had always feared I would become. The one who had claimed we were meant to save the world together.

And here I was, the dragon foolish enough to have believed him.

He smiled at me, showing his pointed fangs, and reached out, letting the nail of his smallest finger sharpen to a talon. I flinched away, but there was nowhere to go. His claw was hot as a brand. His smile widened as he pricked my skin and brought the talon to his lips.

I felt the faint glimmer of the bond before I heard a groan. With effort, I turned my head. Your hair hung over your profile as you struggled to wakefulness.

No. *No.*

I struggled, but the bonds were tight, and I could not touch my magic. Even if I were to break free, I was not sure I would be able to stand. With a lurch of horror and an unintelligible moan, I realized that Ammil somehow had hold of our bond.

—*I do not need much more, my last male dragon.* His thoughts dripped sardonically. *Emotion is what powers the bond, after all. Let's see how long a dragon who is little more than a hatchling can keep his composure, hm?*

A dragon raised to believe he was the best, the chosen one. A dragon so furious and impetuous he'd run straight into a trap. Fight away. It only helps me.

I shook my head, groaning. He had drawn us here for a reason. He had tasted my blood.

"*Nyat,*" I said in Celenian, and my voice was faint. "No," I repeated in Lochian.

—*Once I found scrysilver in the human world, it was easy enough. All it took was sending a few crafted visions through the Veil to an old Seer already losing her touch.*

"This is a trick," I mumbled. "This is . . . another trick."

He smiled. —*For centuries, the dragons didn't even* try *to break through the Veil because they thought they had to wait for their chosen one—another male dragon. So they waited, and they waited, and this world remained mine.*

The glowing tree bathed both of us in soft, white light. I could feel the magic of the dragonstone behind me. Dread pulsed through me as my worldview cracked like an eggshell. I tried to push it down. If he wanted a rise out of me, then I could not give it to him.

—*The problem with dragons,* Ammil continued, as if we were two old acquaintances catching up rather than enemies, *is that our kind is, in many ways, remarkably incurious. I learned, long ago, that prophecies and religion are nothing more than tools. You use them to tell the story that gets you what you want. Humans learned that lesson, well enough, didn't they? They turned us from betrayed creatures to gods. To erase their guilty conscience, perhaps, or because they realized this was a more powerful story.*

My breathing came faster, the drug pumping through my veins.

Wake up, Arcady, I thought at you. *Wake up. Please.* Together, together we would have to be strong enough to face him. You whimpered.

Ammil cocked his head at me. —*Curious, though, isn't it? You, little dragon, were never actually meant to exist. And yet, here you are.* He grabbed my chin in his hands. I grunted, trying to wrench myself from his grasp, but he held me tighter. *Perhaps the belief of the dragons that a male dragon would come willed you into being. Fate still exists, after all, even if, often, it only whispers. If so, I suppose you have me to thank for existing almost as much as your mother. Unlike her, though, I do not fear you.*

"I claim nothing of you or from you," I spat.

His eyes lit up. *—There it is. Your little human has already opened themselves up to me by taking their medicine and using their magic. I've already tasted their blood, and yours. Soon, I'll be able to direct your power, almost as if I've bonded with you both.*

I tried to bat down my emotions, but the Elixir brought them all to the surface. I felt like an exposed nerve. I tried to remember what you had told me about breath, but I could not draw enough air into my lungs.

—Don't you see, Everen? Ammil gestured to the tree. *This is what the humans stole from us. Some of this is the natural magic of the world, but so much of it is ours. It's us. And even as humans continue to weaken it with their wasteful use of magic, it's dragons who make it stronger once more.*

I bit my tongue so hard it hurt.

—Over the centuries, humans have been draining the tree, Magnes continued. *They mine a cylinder of the dragonstone from the veins hidden in these very mountains. A priest carves it with symbols and uses a relic to tether it to a human child. One scale, a chip of bone, or even a hatchling's tooth is all it takes. The color of the original dragon relic affects what type of magic is easiest for the human to wield.*

I cringed in revulsion.

—It's barbaric, yes.

"And yet you fed me Elixir, despite what it contains," I bit out. "Maybe you, too, have been too changed by your time in the human world." Out of the corner of my eye, I caught your head moving.

Ammil gave an amused huff. *—If that is your attempt to get a rise out of me, you will have to work much harder than that. Perhaps I have perfected the art of lying from the humans. They are so very good at it, after all.*

He tilted his head toward the tree.

—For so long, humans have used magic without respecting the rules and the balance. So much was needed to help rebuild after the Strikes. Some spells leak back to the leylines and magic returns to the tree, but it's always a slow deficit. The lower it gets, the more the Veil weakens alongside it. I have lost count of the remnants of our kind the Order has fed the tree or the rips in the Veils over the years. Jask has begun stealing them from us for their own clandestine reasons, but, soon enough, it will no longer be a problem we need fear.

He leaned closer, those orange eyes burning. *—I need you to understand, Everen. Magic grows sicker. Sacrifices must be made. And I . . . I will not pretend I have not made my share of mistakes.* His expression flickered. *I'm getting ahead of myself.*

I tried to slow my breathing. I could not let him win.

—I didn't lie about it all, Everen Emberclaw. We aren't so far on opposite sides of this. If the serpent was healed, Vere Celene would no longer suffer. It is likely now too late for the dragons, but there is hope for us yet.

My heart froze. "What do you mean?"

His face creased into something like pity. *—You didn't know? Even as we speak, wraiths uncountable descend upon Vere Celene. They are not sent by me, but I am not above using their escape from the Veil for my own gain.*

The scrysilver rippled, showing shadowed wings and the flare of dragons' breath.

"The dragons will fight them off," I said. "My mother will lead them."

—Your mother has lain sleeping since the night you returned to this world. Your kind are led by your sister, who is as untried as you are. The dragons will fall by morning, I expect. It is a pity. But if I can heal the serpent, if I bring the worlds together and Vere Celene returns . . . He trailed off.

I swallowed down bile. If Vere Celene's island returned to the Lumet, then there would be a healthier Veil, with plenty of new dragon corpses to feed the tree and all the magic that came with them.

"You have been gone from Vere Celene a long time. You underestimate them," I said. "They are so much stronger than you can ever know." I hoped I was not bluffing. I hoped this was a trick and if I survived, I'd discover Vere Celene had never truly been in danger at all.

— *We shall see, soon enough,* he said, as if reading my thoughts.

"Let — let Arcady go." My words were thick and slurred. "Do what you will with me but leave them out of this. Please. Grant me this one mercy."

He smiled sadly. —*I am afraid for what happens next, I need both of you. Believe me, I would do it all myself if I could. You two are the key, for better or worse.*

He gave a jerk of our bond. I wanted to rip out his throat with my teeth. I wanted to disembowel him with such force my claws scraped his spine. He saw the murder in my eyes, and he did not even blink.

—*Hmm, closer,* he said, his smile widening. *Soon enough, we can begin.*

I willed myself to defeat my anger, but it was like telling myself not to breathe. Holding it back only made me gasp harder.

— *When I tried this twelve years ago, I made a crucial error. A human and a dragon had to do this together — a being from either side of the Veil. Barrow Eremia and I were not bonded, you see. But you. You and your human have done what I cannot.* His lip curled at the admission.

— *Through your connection, I can control the stream of magic. By draining you and others, I can leave my power intact.*

You moaned again, still coming to the surface.

Ammil glanced at Sorin and the shadowed figure, standing sentry on the other side of the scrysilver pool.

"Sorin!" I cried. "Help us!"

Sorin did not even blink.

—*She cannot heed you even though, deep down, she wants to*, he said. *I thought she would be more than she turned out to be. No matter. She'll serve her purpose well enough.* He flicked his hand dismissively. *I once believed the dragons when they said our kind could only bond once with one human. If the bond partner died and the dragon survived, or the opposite, then that was it. They would never find another. Yet when I discovered Elixir helped open humans' magic to me . . . it turns out it is so very easy to take them. If I had done it with your bond mate's grandsire. . . . how different might the Lumet be today?*

"Let Arcady go," I rasped. "And the other two. Whatever you wish to do with me, do it. Let this remain dragon against dragon."

—*You're in no position to negotiate, Everen Emberclaw.*

You groaned, and his eyes lit up as he focused his attention on you.

"*Jo néakya-iév sun, kéaltya-lei pau a kiéponkar,*" I swore at him, and nothing and no one could stop that wave of pure fury. Ammil came forward and pressed his hand to my forehead.

—*You were afraid of your anger undoing you as it did me. And it has. You were always going to become me, Everen. You have given me more than enough. Sleep*, he said.

—*Sleep. This will all be over soon.*

57.

ARCADY:

THE DRAGONSTONE TREE

My fear was dampened, and the world blurred around the edges. He must have dosed me with more Elixir.

White glowed behind me. I was tied to something, unable to move. To my left, Everen's head slumped forward. Mentally, I reached for him, but tugged at our bond, and I hissed in pain.

—Hello, little Eremia, he said, stepping forward to take my face in his hand.

I glared up at his dragonfire eyes with all the bravery I could dredge up. I'd caught some of his taunting of Everen as I'd come back to awareness, and what I'd heard had been more than enough.

—You hid from me well, you know, the dragon said. *I thought you had died with every other human who carried the Eremia name. I only realized who you truly were much, much later.*

I tried to twist from his grip, but he simply pinched me harder.

—I first met your grandsire when he was young and so very hungry to prove himself. Over the years, he did things with magic no other human could hope to accomplish. Your grandsire eventually saw through my disguises. He noticed

that my Laen seemed to live too long compared to the other humans, though we'd always claimed it was because she was a monarch blessed by the gods.

I sucked in a breath. "You were Consort Genat Lant?"

—Oh, I was Genat Lant, and I was Orden Isan, and I was Nortlyn Ildred. I lived at Monarch Laen's side as three lives, three consorts, for three centuries.

The scrysilver pool at the roots rippled. I wanted to look away, but I had been desperate for answers for so long that I'd take them from anywhere. Even from him. I saw my grandsire, first only a little older than me. Another ripple and his hair was greyer, but the blue eyes were the same shade as mine.

—I don't know when or how Barrow suspected Nortlyn Ildred might also have been the consorts who had 'died' before he was even born. When I finally returned to Loc after the Schism as a young priest twenty years ago, Barrow Eremia turned out to be my sole ally. He guessed some of the truth, but little by little, I fed him more of my secrets. He had already learned much of the Veil and how it behaved on his own. Eventually, I told him of the serpent.

He shifted, gazing up at the tree. *—It was Barrow who proposed that if we healed the Dreamer, magic would rebalance.*

A flare of hope. My grandsire had wanted to save the worlds.

Magnes chuckled, almost fondly. *—Your grandsire might have come from a poorer background and proved his worth to the Citadel with magic, but all the same, I would never call your grandsire idealistic. He cared about solving the problem. He fixated on it, really. Like you, like me, he hungered for answers. Knowledge and power. No matter the cost.*

The scrysilver shimmered to show Magnes and my grandsire, side by side, weaving together magic and ripping open the Veil above the tree I was now tied to.

Magnes shook his head, staring down at the rippled echoes of the past. *—I often wonder what would have happened if we'd simply left it all well enough alone. I may dislike most humans and think they don't deserve our magic, but I did not wish so many dead. I care not if you believe me in that.*

"I don't." I wanted to spit at him, but my mouth was too dry.

Magnes glanced at Edin Vayne and jerked his head. Edin left the cavern, moving stiff as a sleepwalker.

"You were all there twelve years ago," I said. "You were all involved. Yet you blamed him." My throat ached.

—*Someone had to take the fall,* Magnes's thoughts slithered in my mind. *Barrow was the most expendable, for all his brilliance. No family name, and he could no longer be trusted. And, after all, it was his faltering, his weakness, that broke the spell.*

"No," I whispered. "He didn't. He wouldn't."

Magnes had found the tenderest part of my fears, and he pushed hard on the bruise.

—*How many humans have turned Starveling since that night, and how many might still?* Magnes asked, not truly expecting an answer. *Strike or not, magic does not belong to your kind, Arcady Eremia. They'll destroy themselves with it. It belongs to dragons. It always has.*

"Yet you'd kill both your kind and mine. All for more power," I said.

—*Do you think I wanted the dragons to die? It was your grandsire who risked it all, including you and the rest of his family. And look at you, Arcady Eremia. A dragon used you for his own purposes, and you not only forgave him, you let him back into your magic and your heart. How did he repay you? He didn't trust you when it counted. He ran away to try and save you, and made it all the easier for you both to fall into my hands. Who protects you now?*

"I know what you're doing," I said. "You're trying to make me doubt him." Had he done this to Everen, too?

—*You already have,* Magnes said.

My gut twisted. Had Everen chosen to leave me behind? Sorin, my other ally, was bespelled. I couldn't access my magic, Elixir or no Elixir, because Magnes somehow had hold of it. Magnes had planned every eventuality.

I was well and truly alone.

—Do not judge young Everen too harshly, little Eremia, Magnes said. *It was always going to go this way. Humans and dragons cannot live together without hurting each other, no matter how hard they try. Love alone isn't enough to overcome.*

The emotion on his face was impossible to read, but it made me wonder what his relationship with Monarch Laen had truly been like.

Broken recognizes broken.

I didn't want to believe him, and I definitely didn't pity him, but his poison was slithering through the cracks. How had Sorin survived facing this, over and over again?

Edin returned, and two hooded figures trailed her. They moved unsteadily. Magnes turned from me, crossing the roots before lowering the figures' hoods.

It felt strangely inevitable to see the two Chancellors I'd seen in the scrysilver, now more than a decade older. Carym of Redwing stared ahead blankly, drool dribbling down his chin. Ketrel of Stormfell muttered nonsense, blinking like an owl.

Had the Chancellors even been at the Palace, or had Magnes spirited them away here before the trial ceremonies or Yrsa's funeral?

—I, too, know something of revenge, dear Eremia, he said, stroking a finger along Carym's cheek. *Here is the drakine who was most responsible for poisoning the Court against Laen.* He trailed his talon lightly across Ketrel's wrinkled neck. *And this is the general who gave the order for Laen's execution. They thought they won.* He smiled, showing his sharp teeth. *But I was a coup they never saw coming. Bit by bit, I made them mine. Now I only have one last use for these old fools. Shall I take that revenge for you and for me both?*

His hand balled into a fist, and Carym and Ketrel fell to their knees. Magnes took the dragonbone blade from his pocket, and before I could blink, he slit Ketrel's throat, and then Carym's.

Behind them, Edin and Sorin gave no reaction, but I couldn't stop my shocked cry. I might have dreamed of taking the Chancellors down, but it was something very different to see blood spurting from the gaping wounds in their necks and watching them gasp for air like fish.

I hadn't wanted revenge like this.

Streams of magic the color of starlight rose from their seals, twisting in the air. Magnes held out his hand and the magic came to him as if bidden, curling around his blood-splattered arms and wrists like a snake before settling into his skin. His expression was as blissful as if he'd taken a vial of Elixir.

He came back to the base of the tree, to me, and I wrenched my head to escape his touch, even if I knew it was futile. He leaned over me.

—*You see, I learned something very important from your grandsire, Arcady Eremia. All spells can be built upon or undone. All rules, of the worlds, of the Veil, of magic, or of fate itself, can be broken.*

His lips brushed my forehead. —*And I have been waiting so very long to shatter them all.*

I wanted to struggle, to do something —*anything*— but my eyelids grew heavy.

—*So we come to the next steps along the path I've forged.*

His hand caressed my cheek.

—*Sleep now, little Eremia. Sleep.*

58.

SORIN:

THE PRIEST'S VIGIL

The priest's eyes blinked. Her lungs rose and fell, and her heart beat steadily. The priest could not even turn her head to look at the other human tethered to a dragon. Her body was only a vessel.

Before her, the Chancellors' corpses were empty husks. The Head Priest glowed with magic as He stood on one of the thicker roots of the tree, raising His arms high.

"*Kjetim-lei ak ar-dźakain*," the dragon said, and through their twisted bond, the priest understood the words. *I call the storm.* "*Lei-turei, iév-turo.*" *Within you, within me.*

"*Ar-réal vanok vaugain, śajak val jain reno.*" *The dragon scales are upended. Two halves of a larger whole.*

The dragon and the human bodies tied to the tree glowed, threads emerging from their body to gild the tree.

"*Dźo eje loj el-dźakain,*" *And if we are the storm . . .*

"*Fanas arfan lo.*" *It must rage for us.*

The tree brightened, the air warming with magic until sweat broke out on the priest's skin.

There was a ripping in the fabric of the world, arcing over the tree's branches like a dark rainbow. Lightning flashed, throwing the cave into stark relief.

The Head Priest shucked His robes and transformed once more into a dragon. Power was in every line of His body. He spread his wings, glowing with triumph as He stretched His neck toward the rip in the Veil.

The Head Priest crouched, the muscles rippling in His haunches. In one smooth movement, He leaped toward the rip in the Veil. Power from the tree, white and gold, streamed after Him. With one push of His wings, the dragon and the stolen magic slipped into the storm between worlds.

The light from the tree drifted through the Veil, directed by the swirl of a golden bond between a human and a dragon.

Their heads were still bowed, their eyes closed in sleep. The priest knew that this was draining them as surely as the Chancellors had been burned down to the quick like wax candles.

The priest breathed and blinked in the eerie quiet of the cave, the storm raging above them. She waited, she watched, and she guarded the threshold between worlds.

59.
CASSIA:

THE BATTLE FOR VERE CELENE

Cassia crashed into another wraith, her claws tearing it to wisps. Her lungs burned with smoke from the Reek. Every dragon that fought alongside her was filled with the bloodlust of the hunt. Each knew what they risked and what they were willing to sacrifice. She let loose another plume of fire from her throat, charring two of the monsters to nothing.

She must have killed dozens, but for every one she destroyed, another three came through the Veil. On and on the monsters fought in an unending wave of screaming black. The rip in the Veil hovered over the mouth of the Reek. She could feel the heat against her scales. Though it was deepest night, the muted fire from the spitting volcano and the dragons' throats lit Vere Celene an eerie red.

Thist gripped a wraith by the neck in her jaws as another creature scraped the green scales of her back. Cassia dived to Thist's defense, snapping the wraith's neck. She roared, banking and searching for her next target, her tongue and throat coated with the too-familiar noxious taste.

Mace stopped another creature from escaping the pack and heading toward the barrier. Boreal dove, her purple scales the same color as the wraith's eyes. Cassia caught the shimmering of the boundary around the island of Vere Celene. While it still held, its magic was already weakening.

Cassia's keen eyes searched for dragons in trouble, and she dove to another's aid. Mace patrolled the outside of the horde, picking off stragglers. A few dragons, like pale red Coral and green Garder, worked in tandem, taking a part of the same wraith in their jaws and ripping it in two.

Cassia swallowed a roar of pain as she saw Ivy, a green dragon, overwhelmed by four monsters. Adile and Hyacinth tried to help, but Ivy gave a last roar, twisting and drawing the monsters to her as she fell, and fell, and splashed into the sea.

Cassia hoped she'd see Ivy emerge, but the sea had claimed her. At least she had taken some of the creatures with her, but Cassia's heart ached with the loss.

Opening her jaws, Cassia roared and breathed out more fire. She sent instructions to her warriors, urging some towards new targets, warning others about monsters at their backs. The dragons fought with all they had. Cassia's scales were scratched and bruised, and she bled from half a dozen cuts. Other dragons had rips in the leather of their wings, struggling to stay aloft. Blue Adile tried to send forth a burst of flame, but it sputtered out. Cassia sent her and another two dragons back to the weyr to lend their remaining strength to the barrier.

The air was full of the sound of frantically flapping wings, roars, the hideous clicking shrieks of the wraiths, and the deep rumbling of a dying world.

Cassia stopped thinking, relying entirely on her hunter's instinct. She fought, she fought, and she fought. With tooth, claw, and scale, she held nothing back.

Yet more came, and, with a lurch, Cassia watched the ward around the island flicker.

And fall.

60.

AMMIL:

THE EYE OF THE STORM

Ammil flew through the storm, every wing beat sure, leaving the vestiges of his humanity behind. Gold and white magic streamed behind him like a comet's tail.

It had been a tangled web to weave, but he was so close to fixing all that had broken. Between the return of his claw and the steady stream of power he'd accessed from the humans, their bond, and the tree, Ammil was stronger than he had been in centuries and robust enough to heal the serpent and bring the worlds together.

He would become powerful enough that nothing and no one could ever hurt him again.

Through Edin's eyes, part of Ammil's awareness saw Everen and Arcady's prone forms tied to the tree. The Lumet waited patiently for his return.

It had been twelve years since Ammil had last entered the Veil. He had missed the storm's dangerous beauty: its deep black sky, the suspended rain drops, and the distant pinpricks of stars. Ammil had wondered if each star was another world, and if the serpent guarded those, too.

A flash of dark purple lightning outlined the wisps of storm clouds. The eerie wind howled, but it could not blow him off course. Ammil banked, drawn to the Dreamer.

The tree's magic he had brought with him was like a surgeon's knife. Wielded well, it could heal, but he and Barrow had also learned too well how deeply it could cut. The longer he lingered, the more dangerous the storm would become for him and the worlds on either side of the Veil.

Before long, the Dreamer appeared far below him, twisting through the storm like a river, more powerful than any leyline.

Ammil lowered, lured to the serpent's power, drawing his stolen magic with him. He knew more about this creature than anyone. More than Miligrist or any past Archivist or Seer. The Dreamer, here in the gyre of the storm, was the closest thing Ammil had ever experienced to a god.

Wraithwright scales glimmered like scrysilver. Ammil flew alongside the beast until the storm clouds thickened to dark smoke. There was a suggestion of a wing or claws. A jaw opened in a yawn, showing obsidian teeth, but no purple glowed at the base of its throat, and the wraith's eyes remained closed. Ammil was surrounded by the Dreamer's unquickened nightmares.

The purple-blue storm gradually reddened as Ammil reached the wound. He shivered with the pain radiating from the Dreamer, his nostrils flaring as he scented the rot.

The angle of the serpent's coil was bent, forced by humans to create an unnatural world and seal the dragons within. The gash glowed like lava, crusted with black and the sickly green of infection. Crimson outlined the edges of the surrounding damaged scales. The red light dimmed and brightened with the slow, sluggish pulse of a great heart that kept time in a timeless place.

Ammil drew himself as close to the wound as he dared. This next part would be the most delicate.

Back in the cave, Arcady and Everen's bodies twitched as Ammil drew on their connection. For all his machinations, he had not been entirely sure he would be able to take control of their bond, yet here he was, the puppeteer of a magic no one, not even Barrow for all his brilliance, ever fully understood.

Ammil wove the white and gold between his claws. Even with his full power and the magic he had drained from the Chancellors and the dragonstone tree, he struggled. Ammil tapped more magic from the Nalore monks he'd claimed over the last few days. Deep within that fortress of stone, one of the monks fell, their heart giving out. Then a second. A third. No matter. He had more, and he would use as many as he needed.

Even after all that had happened, some part of him still wished Barrow Eremia was at his side.

Ammil knew that Everen and Arcady's awareness were in the storm with him. He sensed them, these dreamers without form trapped in his wake. All they could do was reach for each other, their souls tangling. It was almost sweet.

The human and the dragon were already blurring at the edges. The magic would take them soon enough, as surely as the dragonstone tree took a dragon relic. On the other side of the Veil, Ammil sensed more wraiths streaming toward the weyr that had once been his home. The dragons breathed fire and bared their teeth, trying in vain to slow the monsters. Their feathers were blood-soaked, their talons stained black with smoke. Ammil knew they would fight until the last warrior fell, and then what relics remained of the dragons would soon be his.

Despite everything, he felt a pang of regret that, centuries from now when time finally claimed him, he would be the last of his kind. Death came for all of them, in the end.

Back in the cave, the dragonstone tree beneath the monastery dimmed as more of its magic flowed into the storm. Arcady and Everen's golden bond wove around the starlight like a net, allowing Ammil to direct it.

—You will heal the wound and both worlds, Ammil sent to what remained of Everen Emberclaw and Arcady Eremia and the dragons of Vere Celene. *Take heart that your sacrifice was worth it.*

He inhaled the magic into himself, the power of it expanding his lungs, his heart, his veins, and he exhaled, breathing the tree's magic onto the wound.

Slowly, carefully, the rot rose from the cut, infecting some of the wraiths. He nudged them into a cluster. Their smoke was tinged with the same sickly green as the rot. They were even more dangerous than the lesser nightmares that had escaped through the Veil.

Standard wraiths were dangerous enough, but it was one of these rotting monsters that had escaped the Veil and slithered into a human's stone seal before it could disintegrate. That rot had jumped from seal to seal, sweeping through the Lumet and nearly destroying magic entirely. He could not risk it happening again.

Carefully, Ammil caged the rotten creatures with threads of gold and white. The Dreamer twitched, its scales rippling. The sleeping wraiths bobbed as if on an unseen current. One peeked open an eye, a single green star in the dark smoke. The storm whispered soft susurrations of a language too ancient to understand.

He must be quick.

Ammil breathed in more starlight and flamed it out once more. The power changed his body. His bones thickened, his scales hardened, and his claws burned. He was heady, as if his very blood was made of Elixir.

The edges of the serpent's wound began to shrink. The Dreamer shivered, rumbling low in its far-off throat, drifting even closer to awakening. Ammil could not falter.

The storm whispered, making him wordless promises.

—*Sleep*, he sent the Dreamer. *Sleep.*

As the Dreamer settled back into its slumber, Ammil hesitated. The storm's whispers grew more insistent. There was that same pull he'd felt the first time he'd seen this serpent in the storm three centuries ago. That temptation to fall, to join, to let go.

Yes, the storm whispered without words. *Yes.*

Ammil wrapped the magic tighter around his burning claws. The serpent's wound, though smaller and less rancid, still pulsed red. The rotten wraiths struggled against their cage.

He had been tempted by the serpent last time he had been here. It was Barrow who had tried to draw together the remnants of the spell. It was Barrow who had cried that they must leave the storm, even if their work was unfinished, or the risk was too great. Ammil was the one who had lingered, who had been too drawn by the serpent and the sheer scope of its power.

Barrow had drawn him back from temptation, but Ammil had learned more of magic and the way of things in the last twelve years, even in the last few moons. He could bond with humans whether they willed it or not. Even a bonded human and dragon had bowed to his will.

Magical as it might be, the Dreamer, too, was made of blood and bone.

The danger was great. But so, too, was the potential reward.

If he were to somehow bond with the Dreamer, here and now, then he could siphon as much of its magic as he wished. Far more than he could gain from bonding and draining humans. More than he could gain from every dragon corpse in Vere Celene fed to a dragonstone tree. More than he could ever imagine.

Take it, whispered the storm, or the rot within it. *You need only dare to take it.*

The Dreamer had settled, readying itself for a slumber. Once it did, it would be too deep for him to wake or reach.

It would have to be now.

If he dared.

In the storm and the Dreamer's wake, Ammil saw a future where he was more powerful than any dragon past or present. His scales were the color of wraithwright, and his claws glowed as ember-orange as his eyes. He spread his wings over a city that cowered beneath him. No one could stop him. No one could harm him. He could live as long as the serpent and break the rules of time and mortality itself.

Magnes gathered the remnants of power in his claws: from the tree, from the human and the dragon, and the monks of the monastery. The storm's whispers grew into the shrieks of wraiths.

He believed he dared.

61.

SORIN:

BROKEN CHAINS

A dragon between worlds dug its thorns deeper into the priest, stealing off more of her magic.

She existed for His bidding. She was the knife to His hand. She was the Eye through which He saw.

Magic still streamed from the tree up into the heart of the storm, but it had slowed to a trickle.

(Sorin had broken free once before, hadn't she? Elixir burned in her veins. If she tugged, if she cut, if she *fought*—)

The priest's finger twitched.

She blinked, eyes stinging with tears. Her eyes flicked toward Edin Vayne, who had not moved.

The priest's lips parted.

(Yes, *yes*, Sorin cried in the cage of her mind.)

The priest clenched her hand. Unclenched it. Like an unoiled gear, she moved her hand slowly to the hilt of the knife at her waist, every muscle protesting.

Edin Vayne blinked.

The priest took one small step toward the tree. Another. Magnes's magic plucked at her like a discordant string.

Her muscles shook, the threat of another fit rising the longer she rebelled. She grunted, barely able to take in breaths through her locked throat. Her tongue was thick and heavy in her mouth. In the space between worlds, she heard a distant roar.

She took another step, knowing she had to get to the human and the dragon.

(Sorin couldn't let Magnes win.)

She reached the edge of the pool. Pain tore through her, and her throat wanted nothing more than to scream.

Her seal glowed purple, the light catching on scrysilver that rippled with falling rain from the storm above. Each cold drop on her skin helped wake her.

(Sorin imagined Elixir and its power coating every sharp vine of dark gold rooted within her. She imagined it was caustic enough to burn away even the smallest taproot. To singe any seed that might be tempted to regrow. If he was a blight, she would make her mind barren to him.)

One thorn still drained her magic whether she willed it or not.

The storm raged.

She had just lifted her foot to step on one of the tree's roots when a hand closed over her wrist.

She twisted, her muscles unlocking further. Edin Vayne's face was blank.

"No," Edin said, voice wooden, eyes flat.

"Yes," Sorin snarled, bringing up her blade.

Edin ducked out of the way. At the edge of the scrysilver pool, they circled each other. It was an echo of so many mornings on the practice grounds, but this was a duel more deadly than the second trial.

"How did he get to you, Edin?" Sorin asked, her words thick. Her tongue was numb, and her skin tingled with pins and needles. "You're no priest."

Edin didn't answer, searching for any opening in Sorin's defense.

"He found me while I was in the academy. Even though I was older than He usually recruited, He said He saw the promise in me. I took the vows of the Order in secret." Her voice was vague, as though she spoke in her sleep. "Why wouldn't I follow a god?"

Edin darted forward, blade flashing, and Sorin danced back. She adjusted her grip, poised on the balls of her feet, willing her body to wake further.

"The moment you're no longer useful to him, he'll discard you without a thought," Sorin warned. "Maybe he could care for others, once, but now he doesn't know how to see anyone—dragon or human—as anything other than a tool." Sorin wriggled her toes. With each step, she felt more in control of her body, Magnes's influence retreating that little bit further. "Magnes is no god."

Edin's face grew sly. "Not yet, perhaps. But He may yet become one."

Sorin's face tingled. For a moment, she thought Edin Vayne was simply repeating whatever lie Magnes had told her, but there was a tug along the tether, and more of Sorin's power went along with it. Part of her awareness went into the storm . . .

"He couldn't," Sorin whispered.

"He might." Edin's eyes were bright with slavish devotion.

"I don't want this," Sorin said, sickened. "I don't want him. I don't want any of it."

"And that's where we differ. I want it all," Edin said.

"Did you? Or did he simply make you think you did? I know your parents are cruel, but Magnes is crueler still."

Edin attacked.

Sorin's breath left in a rush as she jumped backward. Only the fact that Edin's reactions were still slower saved Sorin. Edin slashed Sorin's sleeve, and she felt the sting of the shallow cut. For all Edin's training on the amphitheater grounds, Sorin realized something vital.

"He hasn't taught you to kill," Sorin said.

Edin breathed hard, eyeing her warily.

"He hasn't made you ingest the tiniest drop of poison, enough to make you sick but not enough to kill you, so that you could recognize its taste and effects," Sorin said. "He hasn't shown you exactly where to press someone, hard, to make them pass out. He never gave you a garrote or a three-bladed knife. You have never taken someone's past, present, and future from them. You have never taken a life."

Edin rushed forward, knocking Sorin back. She unbalanced, falling to the ground hard enough to push the air from her lungs. Pain burst along her ribs and shoulder. Edin pinned her in place, hips around her stomach, and punched Sorin, hard, in the face. Her cheekbone exploded with pain.

If this had been the practice grounds, Sorin would have banged her fist three times on the stone, and Edin would have immediately stood, offered her arm, and helped her opponent to her feet. There in the cavern below the monastery, Sorin knew Edin would give her no succor.

Edin held the dragonbone blade to Sorin's neck. Blood trickled down her skin and Edin's breath was hot on Sorin's face. Using her forearm, Sorin braced against Edin's chest, pushing away with everything she had.

"You don't . . . have to do this," Sorin gasped.

"I know," Edin said. "I don't even wish to. But I will, because I'd do anything—anything—for Him."

Sorin was sickened by that unquestioning devotion on Edin's face, knowing that she had once worn it, too.

Edin dropped the knife and before Sorin could push her away, Edin bared her teeth, her hands coming around Sorin's throat. "No, I haven't killed. But you can have the honor of being my first."

62.

EVEREN:

EYES OPEN, HEART FORWARD

I had no claws, no body, no scales. I had no teeth to bite. I had no mouth or throat to scream.

I was nothing but formless emotion. Foremost was regret. The storm saw me, and it, too, found me wanting.

Ever since I had discovered I was not the last male dragon, I had lost my destiny. I questioned starfire, fate, and my religion, and my beliefs. I doubted my very sanity.

Still. After those visions, even if I had doubted my own judgment, I should have found a way to wake from Ammil's dream. You, my clever thief, would have seen straight through Ammil. He had clouded me somehow, but I had been too weak to fight him off.

—*I am sorry,* I sent the thoughts into the stream. I had no idea if you could hear me as we were dragged deeper into the storm. *I am so very sorry.*

It had taken you so much to let down your last walls and lay down your weapons. To let yourself trust me enough to re-bond. How could you love someone who did not even know who they were any longer? With every second in the tempest, more of me drifted away, and I was glad to be rid of each bit of it. Being myself, even like this, was intolerable.

—*You should have left me*, I sent into the ether. *You could have saved yourself.* White and gold surrounded what remained of us. With every passing moment, our bodies back in the cave grew weaker, our link to them thinner. How long until they snapped?

—*No*, I heard back, your voice like a chime. *I made my choice, Everen. I don't regret it.*

I was aware enough to sense Ammil taking in the dragonstone tree's magic and breathing it back out like fire. With each breath, the angry red of the serpent's wound grew less tainted, and more wraiths joined the tangle. He was using our bond to direct the tree's magic so the creatures didn't dissipate like after being torn by a dragon's claws.

—*You will heal the wound and both worlds*, Magnes said to us. *Take heart that your sacrifice was worth it.*

Another piece of myself disappeared into the current of magic.

There were worse places to die, I supposed. The storm and the magic swirled around us. Perhaps it would not be so terrible to be lost in here forever. Would some part of us remain? Or would we simply join with everything else? Never dying, never living, like the youth in the fable who became a fruit on the branch of the tree of life.

Back in the cave in the human world, my body twitched. It was a lump of flesh, bone, meat, and gristle. The dragonstone tree flickered like a guttering candle. I found I no longer cared for it. How limiting, to have something like a body. How confining, to care what happened in other worlds. In here, we could be infinite.

Ammil used our bond to guide the magic. The wound closed a little more. The rot had been so deep, festering for centuries, and the serpent had hurt for so long. Its pain was everywhere—in the bruised clouds, the wind, its poisoned nightmares. I floundered my way toward you, but it was still so difficult to keep myself from drifting.

Though we were lost, I reached for you, though I had no body, and your soul reached back to mine.

On the other side of the Veil, dragons fought for their lives. I sensed Mace kill one of the monsters, and Cassia attack another. The sky was poisoned with wraiths and the Reek.

Even if, by some miracle, the Reek calmed and the dragons defeated the wraiths, the land of Vere Celene was as near-dead as my own body. I should care. I knew this. Here were the dragons who had raised me. My sister, my guardians, my protectors, and all that remained of my kind. But it was like it was all happening in a dream.

—*Everen, my love, your ability to pity yourself this intensely is nothing short of impressive, but I need you to focus. We've quite a bit more to do here.*

Your thoughts were so clear, so sardonic, that for a moment, it was like I was back in the lock shop, and you were teasing me for being too slow to pick up a skill. Your voice pierced the insidious whispers of the storm.

But Ammil's spell was nearly complete. I, too, was ready to rest, to let go, to become nothing but energy and light.

—*Don't you dare, Everen. You said you'd do anything I asked and more. So I'm commanding you, here and now: come back to me.*

Whereas I was blurring, you were stubbornly pulling all the threads of yourself together.

—*Don't you sarding leave me, Everen. Everyone in my life has abandoned me or died. Not you, too.*

Your anguish punctured the storm, reverberating through me. There were flashes of all your past pain. The loss of your grand-sire. The night you almost died of the Strike Barrow might have helped unleash, and the blood and pain that waited for you when you returned to the human world. The betrayal you had faced at my hand and others. Despite it all, the storm's whispers didn't tempt you. Even here, you were so fully yourself because you had chosen who you wanted to be all your life. You were always stronger than me, though, my Arcady. I was sorry to let you down at the last.

—*This is so much bigger than you or me. Look.*

I forced my scattering self to focus. Ammil's spell was shifting. The serpent's wound had partially healed. Rotten wraiths hovered above the bright red wound, barely caged by our bond.

—*By silver, by blood, by bone.* Ammil's thoughts were strong as he tangled more of the Lumet's starlit magic and *twisted.*

The serpent shuddered, and an unfathomable distance away, I sensed its tail lash in frustration. Ammil drank in more of his stolen power, his determination hardening. I knew, then, exactly what he planned to do: he was hoping to bond with the Dreamer.

—*We can't let him*, you said. *We can't let him win. There's a way out of this. There has to be.*

As Ammil, he had nearly destroyed Vere Celene. As Magnes, he had nearly ended the Lumet.

—*By the dragon scales, I am your storm,* Ammil intoned. The wind rose to a shriek. More violet eyes opened, bright spots in the darkness. Instead of attacking, they watched with something like curiosity, their clicks unnervingly soft.

How could we even hope to foil him? We were wrapped in his grasp as thoroughly as the humans in the Lumet and the magic of the tree itself.

—*Fight, Everen*, you said. *Please. You have to fight. For the dragons, for the humans. For you. For me.*

As the storm's whispers rose, we were on the verge of the scales unbalancing. It would be so much easier to surrender.

Ammil's neck arched. —*By silver, by blood, and by bone: you rage only for me.*

The serpent shuddered at Ammil's spell, but tendrils of burnished gold snaked into the wound, around the edges of the scales. Ammil renewed his efforts. Back in the monastery, more humans fell dead. Was Sorin among them?

—I'm still fighting, Everen. Don't you dare leave me here to face this alone, you said. *I need you here, with me. Eyes open, heart forward, remember?* Your fear was a burst of sickly orange against the white and gold. *We've come too far to give up here.*

You were a chime, a klaxon, a clarion call. Not even the storm could dim you.

You alone could call me home.

The pieces of myself floating through the storm wove back together. If I'd had a throat, I would have gasped.

—Eyes open, heart forward, I echoed. *You are not alone*, I said. My will to live, my devotion to you, all of it came rushing back, and I was grateful for it.

Back in the Lumet, my heartbeat flickered weakly. To do what we did next, I would have to leave my body even further behind.

We wove our souls together, tighter and tighter, until I did not know where you ended and I began. Even now, I am not sure how we knew what to do, but we were guided by gut feeling, by instinct, and a fierce and desperate hope. Later, I would wonder if fate directed us, but equally it could have simply been our will, our determination, and our love.

The bond between us brightened to white-gold. In the eye of the storm, we were closer than any dragon and rider had ever been.

—To banish the rot, trust not what you see, whispered the voice of fate. *Branches stretch high and roots run deep. Dig deeper: beyond golden must you be.*

We amalgamated. We transmuted. We became something *more*.

We spread our ghostly wings, opened our jaws, and roared. We were a dragon in the storm, as transparent as a dream.

Magnes, or Ammil, watched us rise, his great jaw slackening in surprise.

We opened our mouth and roared, the magic from the tree flowing through us instead of him.

—*By starfire as our witness, we challenge you, Ammil Aldwing. Here and now, we will see this through.*

He screeched as the challenge's magic took hold. He scrabbled for control of our bond, desperately trying to thicken those tendrils of gold and braid the serpent's will to his own. The boundary around the wraiths grew thinner as we battled for dominance, tendrils of green threatening to escape. The rotten monsters opened their jaws.

We gathered the white-gold around us, strengthening the cage as best we could.

—*Tis-té*, the part of us that was Arcady sent, the spell helping direct our power to the cage. *Breathe life.*

Magnes roared. He might be weakened, but he was still so strong. He reared, his wings spreading, before he dove towards us, but he flew straight through us. We were ephemeral. We were a dream.

Ammil banked, pouring more magic into the wisps of his nascent bond with the serpent. If he somehow tapped the serpent's power, neither our bond nor the magic of the human world could hope to stop him. Our challenge would fray, and what would become of us?

—*Tis-té*, we tried again, desperate. Yet more wisps threaded through the gaps like sand through a keyhole. We had so little left.

We felt more than heard a deep, echoing laugh, like a series of bells tumbling over each other.

—*I am afraid you will need far more magic than this.*

The words reverberated above, below, and within us. It was not the voice of the storm.

It was the Dreamer.

The serpent was on the very verge of waking, its thoughts thick with sleep. To the part of us that was Everen, it was the voice of fate he had heard so many times. The part of us that was Arcady heard the voice of their grandsire.

With a deep wave of awe, we realized: every soul that passed from this world to next went through the serpent. It consumed memories. Despite his death, while Barrow Eremia may not have bonded with the serpent, something of him remained.

One wraith escaped its cage. We braced when it dove, but it flew right through us.

—*No*, said fate, said the echoes of the one who had been Plaguebringer. *Not this time.*

The creature changed its flight and instead clipped Magnes on his wing. He swerved, and it broke his concentration. As he lost control of the magic, we tightened our control.

The wraith opened its mouth, its hissing and clicking joining the others until the sound was louder than the rising storm.

Instead of fleeing to the gaps in the Veil, it hovered, shifting its attention to Ammil, not us.

We might be ephemeral as dreams, but Ammil was physically within the Veil. He could be hurt, and the wraith wanted to hunt.

Magnes roared at the nightmare, scrabbling for control of our bond and the dregs of our magic. As his spell frayed to nothing, he lost his final tether to the dragonstone tree.

We glowed with victory, but not for long.

The tree's magic was diffusing, and the wraiths' cage began to unravel.

— *Tiś-té*, we tried again, but we were nearly spent.

—*Help us*, we cried to the storm, to the Dreamer, to all the souls housed within.

The serpent gave us the gentlest nudge. — *You know what to do. The magic within holds the key.*

And, somehow, we did. As on the night of the Feast of Flowers, we tapped into a deeper understanding. We gathered our bond and the fading remnants of the starlight magic to us.

Our magic flared, bright as a star. But instead of strengthening the cage, we unleashed the rotten wraiths to let them feast.

The monsters hit Ammil in the chest, the rot spreading across his scales and feathers. He bellowed in pain. Teeth flashed and jaws snapped as he was hidden from view by their writhing. He roared once more, the sound closer to a preterit scream.

The Dreamer, almost lazily, let loose a pulse of power that dwarfed anything that we had ever felt.

Ammil and the wraiths condensed and hardened until they transmuted into something like black stone. The shrieks cut to abrupt silence. The inert sphere hovered for a moment, rotating slowly. The Dreamer pushed it away, languidly, like a great whale breaching the surface to bat away a seabird.

What remained of the previous last male dragon and corrupted nightmares fell through the storm before the stone was lost and gone.

We reeled, flapping our ghostly wings. The serpent's wound remained, but it was smaller, with no trace of the rot left. It must still hurt, but with time, it might complete its healing.

We floated on the storm's currents for what could have been a moment, a season, a year, a century. Below us, the snake shuddered once more. There was regret, yes, but also peace.

The serpent was not yet fully asleep. Its hazy awareness surrounded us.

Across the Veil, we sensed Vere Celene. The wraiths that had been bearing down on the weyr faded to nothing in mid-air. The broken and exhausted dragons pulled up short, claws clasping at nothing. When they realized the last of the creatures were gone, they lifted their heads to let out triumphant calls. The fire of their breath rose towards the sky. The Reek sputtered but began to settle. It, too, was returning to its slumber.

The warriors landed on the Lady of Vere Celene as those who had hidden below came to the surface. Dozens of dragons had been lost. Those that remained began to sing their lament to stars hidden beneath a still-poisoned sky.

They had survived the night, but the sea had boiled and their prey was dead. How long could they hope to live?

—*Let the dragons survive,* we begged the serpent. *Please.*

—*Wait and see,* said the serpent in Barrow Eremia's voice. *Wait and see.*

The rip in the Veil to the human world was open, yet it was beginning to close. The magic from the tree was nearly spent. We could no longer feel our bodies.

Perhaps we were already dead.

—*Taie?* There were so many questions the part of us that was Arcady wanted to ask. Why he'd aligned with a dragon. Why his seal was different and he'd left it for me to find. Why he had risked both worlds. *Is that really you?*

Another eternity of a pause. —*Yes, and no. I am thousands, I am millions. I am the beginning and the end. I am the head and the tail. But the speck of me that is and was once Barrow Eremia tells you this, my little Arcady: the past cannot be changed. Do not let it poison what is yet to pass any longer. It had to happen.*

Gratitude, grief, and sorrow welled up in us. We were too overcome to say more, but it didn't matter. The Dreamer already knew all.

The serpent gave something like a sigh. —*Still you linger where you do not yet belong.*

— We don't know the way back. There was no golden thread to follow.

— Is that all? Listen.

At first, we sensed only the sounds of the storm until we caught a different, familiar voice. With a flick of its tail, the serpent sent us towards the friend guiding us home. It left us with a last few words as it sank into dreaming.

— Until we meet again.

63.

SORIN:

THE WARDER

Sorin gazed up at the flickering dragonstone tree and the storm beyond. She wanted to shout up at it that this shouldn't be her end, but Edin's hands were squeezing, squeezing, until her vision danced and her throat burned.

The storm screamed instead, echoing against the stone.

Wind from the space between worlds whipped through the cavern, stinging her eyes with the force of the breaking. The thinnest branches of the stone tree made a sound like chimes.

Sorin's back bowed as Magnes's bond was ripped from her with force. It made any pain she'd ever felt seem like nothing more than a prick to the finger. It drove out everything, *everything*.

Yet she welcomed it. Because with every rip of the thorn, that much more of him was gone.

When the wind died down and her vision finally returned, her ears rang. She heaved in air through her aching throat, her every nerve was on fire.

With a huff of effort, she pushed Edin's weight off her. Even before she saw the unblinking eyes, she knew: Edin Vayne was dead.

Sorin, for some reason, had lived.

She staggered to her feet. Everen and Arcady were tied to the base of the tree, their heads bowed. Were they still breathing? The tree behind them was too dim, its magic nearly spent.

She took one tottering step, and then another. She had no idea how deep the scrysilver pool was, or what would happen if she tumbled into it. Carefully, she made her way across the root toward the trunk.

She pressed her fingertips to Arcady's neck, sighing in relief when she caught first their flickering heartbeat, then Everen's. Above them, the storm seethed.

She untied them, and their heads lolled. She pulled up one of Arcady's eyelids to see only the whites.

"Wake up!" she said, shaking Arcady gently. "Wake up!" She was barely able to speak through the pain of her throat.

Sorin gazed up at the storm. She didn't know what to do. Her magic was shredded, and the Elixir was nearly gone from her system. As if it heard her silent plea, the storm answered. Awareness struck like lightning.

Sorin reached into her pocket and took out another precious vial of Elixir. She drank it down, and it stung in all the places Magnes's magic had ripped her apart. She shuddered as the potion filled in some gaps, but how much of her was permanently missing?

The potion kindled the dregs of her magic. She clung to Everen and Arcady's prone forms, grabbing one of their hands in each of hers.

The rip in the Veil above her was growing smaller. She knew what she must do.

"*Vanoté leu ek kasutak al-lei,*" she croaked, and the magic in her seal leaped to do her bidding. The ward rose around the three of them, shaky and unsure.

At first, she wasn't sure if it had worked. The rip in the Veil began to sew shut. She poured more of her magic into it.

"Come back," she called, then coughed. "Come home." She spoke the spell one last time.

Protect myself and my friends.

She waited, achingly, as the sounds of the storm quieted.

With twin gasps, Everen and Arcady awoke.

64.

ARCADY:

NALORE MONASTERY

After the night of the Feast of Flowers, I'd come back in pieces. In the cave beneath the Monastery, I thought I would be cold as I ebbed back to my body, but instead, I was too warm.

It would be easy to think of my body as a cage as I wriggled my toes and fingers and remembered what it was like to have lungs and to draw breath. My body was bruised and exhausted. My body was marked and scarred. It had been brought right to the edge of death more than once, but each time it had also welcomed me back. There, in the dark of the cave, I was so grateful for this vessel that I'd formed to fit the soul inside it.

And yet everything was all too *real*. Too small. Too separate. In the storm, I had been limitless. We had been one soul, and now we were split back into two bodies. It was a different sort of severing.

Before my eyes, Everen slowly shifted back into a dragon. When the transformation was completed, he curled around the base of the dragonstone tree, his snout touching his tail. The tips of his wings trailed in the scrysilver.

I had known what it was like to be a *dragon*. Part of me still did. There was a duality in my mind. I sensed the heaviness of his wings, the scales on his hide, the weight of his horns, and the heat of the fire at his throat. He lifted his head, and his green eyes met mine, the vertical pupils wide in the low light of the dragonstone tree. Whatever had happened to us within that storm, I knew, was uncharted territory.

Sorin was slumped against Everen's back leg. She groaned, dragging herself upright. A bruise bloomed on her cheekbone, and she had a shallow cut on her equally bruised neck that had bled alarmingly. She looked, frankly, like absolute shite, but I doubted I was much better.

Everen's hackles rose and I felt his surge of suspicion as if it were my own. I grabbed Sorin's shoulders and searched her face for any hint of *him*.

She met my gaze, her chin lifted. She pushed up her sleeve, baring her scars from my bite marks. I clasped her forearm, and the touch strengthened my awareness. Everen and I searched but we knew . . . there was no trace of Ammil left.

She was finally free.

"You could have left us in there," I said, my throat tight. "Instead, you saved us."

Sorin, the once-assassin, met my eyes and she shoved her sleeve down. "Now we're even."

Everen caught my tangled emotions. While our bodies were drained, the white-gold bond sang between us, somehow deeper and more harmonious than before.

I rose and made my unsteady way across the roots of the dragonstone tree. How much magic had Ammil taken from it? Would it recover and brighten as the leylines sent power back to its heart? Were there even enough relics left to feed it?

I decided that was not my—our—problem.

I stopped a few paces from the corpses. Edin Vayne's eyes were wide and staring. For all her strength in the Trials, she hadn't been able to untie his influence. Sorin turned her face away.

What remained of the last two Chancellors of Loc lay in a crumpled heap. I'd dreamed of killing them so many times over the years. Often, it'd been a macabre version of counting sheep or horses to soothe myself before falling asleep. I'd been so convinced it'd been their fault that my entire family was dead. I'd told myself if I could only make them pay, I'd finally be able to set down that stone of grief that had been weighing me down since the night we fled Vatra. The Dreamer's words came to me.

Let his legacy rest, and do not let it poison what is yet to pass. I took in the features of those who had been a core part of the Consul for close to thirty years, ruling Loc behind wraithwright masks. Or seeming to. They looked so . . . weak. In the end, it turned out I couldn't even muster up hatred for them.

They were dead. Ammil was gone, lost to the storm. The serpent was right: this didn't change the past. The Strike had still struck, and it had been partly my grandsire's fault. But together, at least Everen and I had stopped it from happening again.

Sorin paused at my side. Despite it all, I felt something bright and proud in my chest. Everen rose, spread those impossible wings, and flew over the scrysilver pool to settle behind me.

I threw my head back and laughed, the tension in me breaking like the dam I'd made in the river on the way here. Sorin stared at me strangely, but then her glee joined mine, though her laugh quickly turned into a hacking cough. Everen gave a draconic rumble from deep in his throat.

There, where the leylines converged in the cavern at the heart of the Fangs, we let ourselves revel in what we'd done. We'd achieved what not even my grandsire or Ammil had been able to. We'd healed the serpent. We'd stopped the rot escaping.

We'd done the impossible.

And we'd survived.

Two humans and a dragon walked the empty halls of Nalore Monastery.

Everen was far too tired to transform back to preterit, but the corridors were large enough for him. After all, this fortress was more than eight hundred years old. Dragons had walked these halls before.

Sorin's hand stayed on the hilt of her dagger, as did mine. Behind us, we had an armored dragon with claws and teeth.

We needed none of it.

When we came across the first corpse, we stuttered to a halt. The monk had collapsed, Their hands reaching forward. They'd been crawling, desperately trying to escape Ammil taking everything from Them.

I swallowed down my horror, Everen echoing it.

I tried to drag myself from his thoughts and feelings. It was like we were . . . porous. Without concentrating, it was still all too easy for *me* to become *us*.

I focused on putting my human feet one in front of the other and staying within my own mind and body as much as I could. Everen pulled away, too, and the small distance was welcome even as it felt equally jarring.

A second corpse. Then another. A cluster of three. They all wore identical dragon-scale embroidered robes. I'd once worn robes like that when I'd snuck into the caves beneath the Citadel to break into my grandsire's tomb. How many monks were in this monastery? Upstairs, were dozens more slumped over Their desks in the library, drained dry by Ammil as he'd fought so hard to bond with the serpent?

Sorin crouched by one of the bodies, her face rippling in pain.

"Gemiean," she whispered. I recognized one of the other acolytes who had left the university partway through the term. His face was frozen and twisted—we couldn't pretend he'd simply fallen asleep without pain when Ammil drained him. It had hurt.

"I should have been one of them," Sorin said.

"You can't change what happened," I said. "But you can make you being spared worth it."

She closed Gemiean's eyes and bent over him in silent prayer. Eventually, she rose. We continued through the mountain, saying nothing. I paused at the entrance to the library and archives.

"We should leave," Sorin said.

"When else would we get the chance to see what they have on us?" I said. "I have to know."

Everen stayed below, keeping guard, as Sorin and I entered the archives. Where the library at the Citadel was full of warm woods and honeyed light, this echo of it in Nalore Monastery was cold and gray.

As we'd feared, monks had died at Their desks, slumped over illuminated manuscripts. One inkwell had spilled, the black liquid dripping onto the stone floor. I shivered.

"Yes," I said. "Let's be quick."

Someone might be able to glean what we'd accessed through the catalog spells, I knew, but I couldn't let the opportunity slip from my grasp. Part of me was tempted to search up my grandsire's court trial transcript, but I didn't think I would find anything new.

Instead, we climbed the staircases to the highest levels. There had likely been wards meant to stop us, but they must have fallen along

with the monks. We reached the copy of the Citadel Records. Neat
rows of stacks spread into the distance. Sorin and I split up. I hunted
out both Arcady Dalca's and Arcady Eremia's files, but I was too afraid
to look at them right away, so I peeked at other folders at random.

The seal records were both more extensive and less explicit than
I thought they'd be. There were records of the individual carvings
and family trees linking files together, but only few seal signs showed
up in great detail. I saw one record of the Citadel casting a tracking
spell to find someone for debt. From the lowest peasant to the highest drakine, the Citadel could indeed locate them, but they weren't
constantly tracking everyone, even if they pretended to. It'd take far
too much magic for that. It still meant that only the Struck or the
few in very rural areas who were never visited by a wandering priest
moved through the country entirely unseen. In return, they had not
even the tiniest spark of magic.

"We should go." Sorin had given the monks Their last rites, I
was sure. I wondered if she'd done it for the Chancellors and Edin
Vayne, too, but I didn't ask.

I gestured to the two records that I'd kept out on one of the tables.

"Those are mine. Haven't looked yet. I'm tempted to burn them,"
I said.

"It'd possibly trigger them to pull your echoing records in Vatra.
You came this far. You may as well open it."

She was right. With trepidation, I opened them and began to
read. I'd signed for credit to buy a seal setting as Arcady Dalca in
a shop in Vatra, but I'd paid my debt, so the record had faded. The
only active one was joining the University Trials. I set it aside.

The Arcady Eremia file had my old seal carving marks, sure
enough, but I exhaled at the point where it said I'd died in the Strike
when the real Arcady Dalca had. Either the spell on the Night of
Locked Tombs had somehow switched it, or my maire had found

a way to doctor the records when we'd lived in Atrel even before I spoke my grandsire's words in the cave beneath the Citadel.

My fingertips tingled when I realized what this meant.

I had my original seal back from Larkin in the depths of my pocket. Arcady Dalca's file was thin, but that wasn't surprising for a poor drakine raised far from the capital. There was no real way for anyone to prove who I used to be.

This life was still open to me . . . if I wanted it.

"Come on," I said. "Let's go." There were so many other secrets in these stacks, I knew, but I didn't want to spend another second in this place.

The three of us left the monastery. Dawn was breaking, and the mountain was shrouded in light and purple-pink mist.

Rahela must have been back to the Citadel by now—did Vatra and Loc think that three students were missing? Did they know yet that the entire Consul was dead?

"It's a long way back to Vatra," Sorin said. Her skin was gray, but her eyes were bright and clear. Had she taken another dose of Elixir?

"I think . . . I think I want to see this through," I said, slowly. "I want to finish the trial. For myself." Everen might have helped guide me when I'd nearly lost control of the spell in the first trial, but I'd used the magic I could access through my seal. The second trial I'd done with no help from Everen at all. It'd been Sorin and I working together. For the third, Everen had been unreachable, though I could argue Elixir and having access to a dragon's magic was cheating, of course. I wasn't sure I deserved to win that partial scholarship, but if I walked right to the Citadel, I could steal it all the same.

Sorin stared at Everen as he craned his long neck and re-tucked his wings along his back before looking back at me. "Do you *want* to go back to the university?"

"Yes, I think so," I said. Despite everything—the unfairness, the danger . . . I'd barely scratched the surface in the last few months.

Everen gave me a warm pulse of understanding. Sorin seemed thoughtful.

—I'm too exhausted to fly all the way back to the capital, Everen said, and I felt his bone-deep fatigue as much as my own. I wasn't loving the idea of hiking back down that mountain.

I pressed my lips together. "Could you . . . could you fly us somewhere closer? There's one last thing I need to do in these cursed mountains."

He knew what I wanted, and he stretched out his neck. I climbed up without hesitation, but Sorin looked distinctly terrified. I leaned over and held my hand out toward her.

"Come on, Sorin," I said. "Haven't you ever wondered what it's like to fly?"

65.

SORIN:

THE GREEN WYVERN

With every flap of the dragon's wings, Sorin feared falling. Her hips ached as she clung onto Arcady's waist for dear life. Yet, though every dip made her heart leap to her throat, the changing landscape below them gave her an elation to rival Elixir's.

A candlemark later, the dragon set down in a valley outside the village of Atrel, near the ruins of a cottage. It must have once been a lovely if humble home, nestled in a dip that would protect it from the worst of the mountain winds and surrounded by the forest. When Sorin had had her daydreams of running away from Magnes, it had been to someplace not unlike this.

"I lived here with my parents for three years between the first and the second Strikes," Arcady said, taking in the cottage's collapsed thatch roof. They went around the side, Everen following quietly for such a large creature. She still couldn't stare at him for too long without being awed at the sight of a dragon's scales glinting in the sun and the wind ruffling his fire-bright feathers.

Arcady came to a pause near twin stone cairns, each at the base of a pine tree. They reached into their pocket and took out their old dragonstone seal. They held it in their fingertips, rolling it back and forth, their gaze distant. Eventually, they dug a small hole between the graves, planted the seal, and covered it with dirt and stone.

"I think some part of me thought that one day, I'd clear my family's name. That I'd once again take up the name Eremia and discard Arcady Dalca." They rested their hands against the metal seal setting at their chest. "But here, now, I hereby lay Arcady Eremia to rest, once and for all."

With a shiver of magic, they changed, briefly becoming the echo of their paire, Sorin guessed, and then their maire. Sorin thought they had kind faces. Arcady had their maire's eyes and their paire's chin. With a last burst of magic, Arcady became themselves again.

"Good-bye," they whispered. "And thank you."

The wind rustled through the trees, as if in answer.

"Everen," Arcady said. "I was too weak to build them a pyre when I first put them there. I was too afraid of the fire. Would you . . . ?"

They didn't have to finish the thought. The dragon's throat glowed as he breathed flame onto the stones. The gray rose to red, the heat warming Sorin's skin even from half a dozen paces away. Somewhere below those stone embers, bones blackened and cracked.

Before Arcady could ask it of her, Sorin bent her head and gave last rites. Arcady nodded in gratitude, their cheeks wet.

Everen drifted closer, bringing one wing around his human. Sorin caught Arcady pressing themselves against his scales before the leather membrane hid them from Sorin's sight. Sorin drifted away, giving them privacy.

Sorin lingered by the ruined cottage. There were worse places for Arcady to hide their past than way up here, near a forgotten stretch of mountain and what remained of their parents.

Sorin stared out at the trees. The air was so clear up here. There would be good hunting in the forest, and plenty of fish in the streams. There was life up here, even though the village was a graveyard and this peaceful part of the mountain had its share of bones and ghosts.

Sorin had seen so much death. The monks in the monastery. Edin and the Chancellors.

The closest thing she'd ever had to a parent had been the one who had hurt her the most, and he was now dead. There was relief, but grief, she knew, would come later. She'd hated him, but part of her had loved him, too. Or wanted so badly for him to love her. Was that the same thing?

Sorin's head rose as a shadow of wings crossed overhead. Her heart tightened in fear before she realized that, of course, the shadow was far too small for a dragon.

Jaculus screeched, circling once before coming to land on her outstretched arm. A silly grin spread across Sorin's face, hurting her cheeks. The call summoned Arcady and Everen.

"You were supposed to stay in the rookery, little protector," Sorin said, stroking Jaculus's head.

Her wyvern chittered in response, climbing over Sorin and sniffing her in concern to make sure she was unhurt. He glared at Everen, brave enough to hiss at the much larger dragon. Everen snorted.

"How did he find you?" Arcady asked.

Sorin shook her head. "I don't know."

—*Because he chose you*, Everen said.

She remembered how in those flashes of repressed memory, she'd seen herself as if from a wyvern's point of view. How Jaculus always seemed to know how she was feeling and she the same. It wasn't anything like Arcady and Everen, but perhaps it was a bond, all the same.

Everen nodded his great head, watching her put it together.

—*I believe he kept some of your memories, your doubt, and your desire to fly.*

Sorin's throat closed as she pressed her lips to the top of Jaculus's head.

"Come on," Arcady said. "We've a long way to go."

Sorin said nothing as she cradled the wyvern in her arms.

A line appeared between Arcady's eyes. "You're not coming back to Vatra, are you?"

Sorin shook her head. "You seem so very certain you want to take up your life again. I try to picture going back and sleeping in my quarters, but I know I would always be too afraid of waking up to a red flame at my bedside. Every corner of the Citadel will always remind me of him."

Arcady's face softened in understanding. "What do you plan to do?"

Sorin chewed her lip. "I would like to stay here for a time, with your permission. I could repair the cottage and set it to rights."

"The cottage has a sad history," Arcady said.

"It had happy memories in it, too, didn't it?"

"It did."

"I could make some new peaceful ones, at least." She glanced at Arcady out of the corner of her eye.

Arcady exhaled. "It's not truly mine to give, but you may have it. Would you really stay here for good, so far from anyone?"

"I'll stay until the silence grows too loud."

"What will you do next?" Arcady asked, softly.

Sorin finally voiced the plan she'd been turning over in her mind. "When I looked at my seal record . . . it said something of my parents. My sire is unknown, though I've long guessed they were Jaskian." Sorin gestured to the freckles on her cheeks and the blonde tint to her short, coiled hair. "But the one who bore me . . . I learned a name. When I have the means, I mean to go search for Them. I don't know if They're still living, what They're like, or if They want anything to do with a child They abandoned on the steps of a Citadel. But I mean to find out." She shrugged. "And then . . . who knows? Perhaps I'll come back to Loc. Or back here. Maybe eventually, other people will return to these mountains, too."

"Have you any money?" Arcady asked.

Sorin shook her head. "Next to none. But I know enough to live off the land."

"When you're ready to travel, you should call on Willem. I'm sure he'd give you help with passage. Or Rahela has family in Myria if you're going that way."

"I don't need their charity," Sorin bristled.

—Helping isn't always charity, Everen's thoughts were almost gentle. *Sometimes people simply wish to assist. Well do I know how hard it can be to let them.*

"Mmm." Sorin stared at the gentle current of the Vatra River, so much calmer than where they'd crossed it at the start of the trial. "Maybe."

"I feel like I've only just begun to know you," Arcady said.

Sorin laughed, softly, at how much everything had changed since Sorin first set eyes on Arcady at Widow Girazin's manor, or even since she'd sat next to them in alchemy a few moons ago.

"I think I'm only now getting to know myself," she said.

Arcady's expression went vague, and Sorin shivered as she watched them silently converse with Everen. They might have chosen to bond, but Sorin couldn't forget what it was like to have that forced upon her. Jaculus curled around her neck, offering wordless comfort.

"I hope you find your answers." Arcady held out their arm to Sorin, who took it. Everen inclined his head.

—Farewell, Sorin formerly of the Order of the Dragons.

Arcady's hand pressed against the scars they'd left, but they no longer hurt Sorin. "Farewell, Arcady Dalca. And Everen . . ." She trailed off.

—*Emberclaw*, he finished, his green eyes glowing.

Sorin nodded and pulled away.

Arcady climbed onto Everen's back. Sorin moved further away and let that wonder suffuse her as Everen crouched, spreading his wings. Not a god after all. Not a bit of chaos made flesh, either. Simply a dragon and his bonded human rider. Everen gathered his strength and launched triumphantly into the sky.

When they were gone, Sorin held Jaculus close, walking through the bright forest, listening to the sounds of the birds, the wind, and the hush of the river. Up here, at least, she saw no threat of the blight. No twisted creatures from the Veil. Blessed peace.

When she found a sun-kissed meadow, she laid out the thin blanket in her bag on the grass and took stock of all her worldly possessions. A few meals. Sweetspheres. Her normal knives and the three-pointed trident knife she hadn't used in nearly a year. A knife made of dragon bone. It would be enough. For now, she needed nothing from no one.

She lay down and listened to the sounds of nature and the quiet of her mind. Withdrawal was already setting in, and her hands were shaking. She had one vial of Elixir left to help her taper off the drug, so she forced herself to take the smallest sip. It would be a rough night, and another rough few days but eventually, it would pass. She'd fix that cottage roof and keep her promise to Arcady of clearing out the bad memories, and make new ones. Maybe they would even come visit her before she left. They could fly, after all.

Jaculus watched over her and, despite all that had happened, she eventually fell asleep with a smile playing at the corners of her mouth.

66.

ARCADY:

SEE IT THROUGH

E veren left me at the base of the mountain.
      He'd been prepared to fly me back to Vatra if I asked, but I
wanted to do this last part alone.

I reached up toward him, resting my hand on his nose, strengthening our connection before, reluctantly, pulling away.

—*Rest*, I said. *The worst of it is over.*

—*Is it?* he asked, and his grief crashed through me. As soon as
he could, I knew he'd try to find a mountain pool to try and scry his
sister. We knew the dragons had survived their battle against the
wraiths, but what would become of them in a still-broken world?

I limped through the forest along the path. I paused only to briefly
catch my breath, or to eat the last bit of food in my pack. The birds
sang, the sun shone, and all the horrors I'd seen seemed a nightmare.
Almost.

Finally, I reached the horseless carriages, clustered along the path
and waiting for students to return this way. I made a quick count.
One was missing. Rahela, I guessed. Cind and Jordin might not have

made it past the first obstacle. Sorin wouldn't claim her carriage, and neither, of course, would Edin.

It took me a moment to realize that one of the windows was open, and a face stared at me from the depths of the carriage.

"Professor Hayden," I said, keeping my voice neutral.

"The other professors are out searching for the missing students," she said. "I was asked to wait behind. I'm not exactly in a condition to be stomping through the woods." Her gaze was level. "Sorin and Edin . . . will they be coming?"

I debated playing dumb.

"No," I said, the word heavy.

Professor Hayden closed her eyes for a moment. "Get in," she said.

I hesitated.

"Tell me this: is the Dreamer asleep?"

For all my practice at pretending to be other people, for all the card games I'd played, I knew my reaction must have immediately given me away.

A few minutes' flight away, a dragon raised his head ready to come to my aid.

"Is the Dreamer asleep?" she repeated, more insistent.

"Yes," I whispered.

The corner of her lips quirked in triumph. "Get in." She paused. "Please."

Yet again curiosity got the better of me. Wordlessly, I told Everen to stand down as I climbed inside the carriage.

Professor Hayden's hands settled on her stomach. Her babe would be born before the moon was full. The door shut and I heard the *snick* of a lock. After an aching pause, Hayden spoke a spell, and the carriage began to move, taking us on the long road back to Vatra.

Hayden's face was half-shadowed by the small mage light in the corner.

"Magnes is dead, isn't he?" Professor Hayden's voice was free of inflection. She tapped her temple. "I felt it. Then I was able to urge the professors up towards the Monastery, though I feared it would be too late."

I blinked. Of course. Ammil had put a magical block on Hayden as he had Sorin. It was the best way to ensure secrets stayed kept.

She considered me, resting a finger on her lips. "I should have seen it sooner. Especially when we spoke that night at the lodge. You look like him, you know. The eyes are just the same."

Fear leaped up in me. My hand went to the carriage handle, even though I knew it was locked. Everen felt my fear, spreading his wings wide.

Professor Hayden leaned forward. "I've no desire to tell anyone. You're not under arrest. This is not a trick. I don't know how you enrolled under a false name, and I don't much care. But I do need to know what happened."

I stared her down. "Why should I trust you? You've been working with Magnes to make Elixir." I used his human name, unsure how much she truly knew.

"Not by choice." Her eyes blazed.

"You worked with him willingly enough twelve years ago," I said.

Her brows rose in surprise. "How did you learn of that?"

"You talk. Then maybe I will."

Hayden licked her lips. "Magnes came to me a year ago. I thought all of our research had been truly destroyed, but he had kept it. Later, when I realized how he meant to twist Barrow's work, it was too late. He wrapped that spell around me, and I couldn't say a word to anyone."

I remembered how Sorin had shuddered in a fit when the knot tightened its hold on her, and pity rose in me. Still. This could all be a ploy.

"If even the Chancellors, who are some of the most powerful magic users in Loc, fell under his spell, how in the gods' names did you manage to kill him *and* send the serpent back to sleep?" Her eyes were bright.

The carriage hit a stone in the path, jostling me. How much longer until we reached the city? I sensed Everen had flown closer. Even now, he was weaving his way through the trees on all fours, waiting for my signal. He wouldn't kill Hayden, not with her unborn babe, but he wouldn't hesitate to rescue me if I asked it of him. I wasn't afraid of Hayden. Elixir was in my veins and magic still roiled beneath my skin.

"It doesn't matter how I did it," I said. "But it's what happened. Magnes was lost to the storm." I decided I would give her something. "The Chancellors are dead. The entire Consul is gone."

She sucked in a breath. "Well," she said. "The Chancellors have done little these last few years. Magnes was the one making the decisions."

"What will happen next?"

"The court will find a way to play it. They'll appoint an emergency Consul until an election is called, and then I expect it'll be made permanent unless Myria uses this as an excuse to push for reunification under a monarchy."

"Would that happen?" I asked.

Professor Hayden shrugged. "I haven't a clue. I expect we'll find out."

The silence grew between us. A few minutes passed before she lobbed her next question at me.

"What happened to Edin and Sorin?"

"Edin is dead," I said, shortly. "Along with every monk in Nalore Monastery. Edin was one of Magnes's Eyes."

Her face rippled with sadness. "I had suspected that. Sorin as well. Is she also dead?"

"Yes," I said. Even if Hayden later realized I'd lied, it would give Sorin time. I could only hope the Council wouldn't bother tracking her seal.

Professor Hayden leaned back. "I sensed she was on Elixir during the Trials, but I couldn't warn anyone. I'd hoped she'd been able to escape him."

She closed her eyes, and we lapsed into silence long enough that, despite my suspicion, exhaustion took over and I nearly drifted off, Everen curled protectively around my mind.

"Arcady," she said, jolting my awareness back to the carriage some time later. "We're not far from the city gates. If you want to get out, now is the time."

"If you're not going to turn me in, then I want to finish the trial." I set my jaw. "I want the life that I'm owed. The life you helped steal from me, when you made sure Barrow Eremia took the fall."

The sheer force of my anger made her lean back in her seat.

"Ah. Then you haven't quite put it all together," she said.

I said nothing.

"Do you know why I testified against your grandsire?" Her voice was impossible to read.

"To save your own skin." Anger burned beneath every word.

She inclined her head. "That, yes, and to protect my family's. Despite the risks, though, I was willing to tell the full truth. The night before the trial, I visited Barrow in the dungeons."

Her face tightened, and I was glad none of my visions had ever shown me what a pitiful physical state he must have been in by then.

"He *asked* me to," she said.

My mouth opened, but no sound emerged.

"Yes," she said. "He wanted to be convicted. He said he wished to die, but that he didn't fear death because he knew something greater was coming. He swore to me that if he did this, it would begin a series of events that would one day bring back the gods. I thought, perhaps, the torture had driven him mad. He kept speaking of dragons and a serpent called the Dreamer who must not wake. He told me everything that he said had happened that night, but I didn't know how much of it to believe."

I bit back a curse. "You didn't know the Dreamer was even real for certain, did you?"

She smiled without mirth. "Not until you went and confirmed it for me before climbing into this carriage, no."

Magnes had never shown Hayden his true form, I guessed: only Barrow. She probably had had no idea that dragons were real, much less that I, too, was bonded to one. What else might she now suspect was true?

"That night in the dungeons, he made me promise," Hayden continued. "He made me swear I'd do what he asked of me." She grimaced in pain. "And so, gods help me, I did. Every day since, I've wondered if that was the right choice. I probably couldn't have taken the whole Consul down. Perhaps I would have ended up sealing myself up in a coffin next to him down in the Cave of Locked Tombs. At least I wouldn't have been so cowardly."

The self-hatred rolled off her in waves.

"Will others start to remember what Magnes made them forget?" I asked.

She shrugged. "I'm not sure. Most of his suggestions were very subtle. Even if he'd done a similar knot on someone else, they'd have to know to search for it. I suspect most of his spells will hold, at least for years yet."

"Would you testify against Magnes and the Chancellors now that you could tell the truth, then?"

"I would." The words rang with finality. "But at this stage, I am not sure what it would do." I hated that she might be right.

"What do you plan to do with your research now, then?" I asked after a moment.

She collected herself before touching her stomach. "After the babe is born, I will likely keep working on it in secret. If I can make Elixir safer, then there is a way to free anyone from turning Starveling. That, I think, is worth finishing what Barrow Eremia started. That might be a more fitting legacy, even if no one ever knows it was his work that made it possible."

"Legacy" was a word as poisoned to me as "fate." Flashes played behind my eyes. The Starveling I'd seen in the city with Everen after our night at Cinders. My mother, her face twisted into something unrecognizable. The fractured memories of when I'd turned Starveling myself. It'd been a near thing that I hadn't killed Sorin that night in the cave last spring. Without her by my side, what had happened in the mountain and the storm might have gone very differently.

I nodded, tentatively. "Yes. It's worth it." I swallowed, and my next words rushed out before I could second-guess them. "I know someone who is working with a Myrian alchemist. They have money and work closely with the Struck. This person blackmailed me into trying to find more of your research."

She pressed her lips together. "Not terribly trustworthy, then, I take it?"

I couldn't stop the scoff. "Trustworthy? No. Highly motivated to help the Struck? Yes. Her name is Larkin Nash."

Her mouth twisted. "Maybe I'll call on this Larkin, then. Eventually."

The carriage came to a halt outside the gates, and Hayden raised a finger to her lips.

"Name and seal," came the voice of a guard outside the carriage. The window cracked open, letting in a sliver of afternoon light.

Distantly, I heard the surge of the crowd waiting for the delayed return of the last of the students.

"Arcady Dalca," I said, passing my seal over.

A lengthy pause.

Finally, the guard handed it back. I clutched my seal in my sweaty palm as they closed the window and gave three raps on the outside of the carriage with the palm of their hand. The carriage veered to the right, bringing us through the gates and into the city. The sound of the people outside grew louder. A few others thumped on the carriage, I snapped my seal back into its setting before drawing my legs up onto the seat, hugging my knees to my chest.

Some out there were celebrating my return, but there'd also be plenty who hated me and all I represented. They'd hate me so much more if they ever discovered the surname I'd just left behind. My stomach churned, remembering Kelwyn's expression of revulsion at the Last Golden. Had that only been last night?

The carriage angle shifted—we'd made our way through the city and were climbing up the hill towards the Citadel.

"We're running out of time," she said. "Tell me: is there any proof that could be tied back to your true name?"

I shook my head. "No. Not anymore."

"Good." The carriage picked up speed, and before long we heard the crowd in the amphitheater.

"Go," Professor Hayden said. "Take the win and the scholarship and all that comes with it, but I'd like to give you a word of advice if you'll have it from me."

After a moment, I nodded.

"Keep your head down. Don't draw undue attention to yourself. There are plenty who would destroy you if they knew who you were, without blinking. Once the rest of the court learns the Consul is dead, everyone will be vying for power. They'd all sell their own souls for that bit more of it."

"Even you?" I asked.

"I learned from Magnes that yes, even I have the right price. Guard your trust." She licked her lips. "They might still call him Plaguebringer, but I know your grandsire had a good heart. He was always working to make magic and the world a fairer and kinder place. He didn't mean to release the Strike."

I didn't even know if I believed that any longer. "And yet," I said.

Her shoulders slumped. "And yet."

Professor Hayden leaned back into the shadows of the carriage as it came to a halt. "Go."

The door opened, bringing in the cool air and the growing roar of the crowd. I stumbled down the carriage steps, blinking fast. Even the sunset was too bright after so long in near-darkness. The court-yard was crammed with cheering people. Mage lights lit the top of the Citadel like candles on a cake. The path spread before me. With a few more steps, I'd enter the grand amphitheater, cross the official end point of the race, and that would be it.

—*Only a little further*, my dragon said. *I am with you.*

I took one step. And another. There were so many eyes on me. I resisted the urge to glance over my shoulder at the carriage where Hayden hid inside.

I forced my tired body through the gap in the crowd. The roar grew even louder when I reached the amphitheater. Rahela stood on the dais next to the Herald. The chairs for the Chancellors and the Head Priest were empty even of false actors.

Somewhere, I found the strength to pull on a smile and pre-tend to be a student who, over the last day, had faced merely a raging current, a thicket of thorns, and a perilous journey across a stone bridge before heading back to the capital like a good little competitor.

As soon as I staggered across the finish line, I collapsed to my knees. The din blended with the ringing in my skull. One of the Heralds hauled me to my feet and raised my arm above my head, declaring me second place. What they didn't yet know was that, technically, I'd also come in last.

I'd been running on sheer nerve and the dregs of Elixir, but both of those were running out fast. Everen had needed to rest, and now so did I. The world spun and I fell, boneless, to the ground.

67.

ARCADY:

A FADING LIGHT

Sorin hadn't lied about the comedown from Elixir. The nausea woke me, and I gagged as my stomach roiled. Someone shoved a bowl into my hands, and I bent over it just in time. Ambrosia came up, the sickly sweetness only making me queasier. I heaved harder. A hand rubbed my back.

"Steady on," came a familiar voice. When there was nothing left in my stomach, Willem pushed me back down into the soft pillows of the bed.

I was in my dormitory. Willem lounged right on top of the bed covers on his side, head propped up on one arm. There was Rahela by the window. Damon perched at the foot of the bed. Bouquets crowded every flat surface of the room.

I forced myself up on my elbows. Damon passed me a glass of water and a sweetsphere. I downed my cup, barely able to hold it steady, and forced myself to wash down the sweetsphere with a second glass of water. My hands gradually stopped shaking.

Sunlight streamed through the windows. It must be near noon, so I had slept for over half a day. I still wanted nothing more than to fall back asleep.

I reached out for Everen in my mind, and a rush of warmth and reassurance flowed through me. He'd come back to Vatra last night. He was out there, waiting for me.

Willem shifted on the bed. "The healers checked you over and thought you'd be more comfortable here. They asked someone to keep an eye on you, and so here we are, your loyal watchdogs."

Fear spiked through me. I was wearing a different shirt, and my skin was clean. Someone had changed me and sponged me down, but I hadn't been arrested or thrown out on my arse for being a Struck.

"I need . . . I need a moment," I said, my voice rough. "Please."

"I told you," Damon said, tugging at Willem. "Come on, give them their space. Time enough to fill them in on it all later."

My stomach clenched. "Fill me in on what?"

Damon grimaced.

Willem sat up, grabbing his coat off the back of the chair. "Oh, everything's a mess, Loc's in an uproar, and—"

Damon put their hand on Willem's shoulder, cutting him off.

"Right," Willem said, sheepish. "Later."

Rahela lingered after the others.

"Congratulations on winning," I said with a faltering smile, trying to dampen my panic. "You deserve it."

"Thanks," she whispered, but she wasn't triumphant. "Edin and Sorin never came back, you know."

I had a flash of Edin Vayne's unstaring eyes and the memory of Sorin's hand gripping my forearm as we parted ways.

"I'm hoping they're just lost," she said, a line appearing between her eyes. "But . . . I don't know. Something about the Trials . . . it doesn't sit well."

I licked my lips. "Sorin decided to leave the university and the priesthood behind. Please tell no one."

"Oh, I'm glad," Rahela said, shoulders slumping in relief. "I won't say anything. They say Edin is dead. Were . . . were you there?"

"No." My voice was sharp. "I saw nothing." I'd lied to Hayden about Sorin and told the truth of Edin, and I told Rahela the reverse. Maybe that was what I'd always be: half truthful, and half a liar.

Rahela stared at one of my bouquets. "I can't quite believe they're gone. All year, I'd been so excited to do well in the Trials. I'd worked so bloody hard. I thought I'd come second, and so to come in first . . . when the dust settles, I know they'll make a big song and dance about it. But Edin should have won, not me."

"You more than proved yourself, Rahela. Feel your feelings, and your grief, but also take the win. You deserve it."

"Sorry," Rahela said, shaking her head. "You're right. I'm being silly. Feel better, and I look forward to standing at your side when they do give us our medals and flowers." Her mouth quirked. "More flowers."

As soon as the door closed behind her, I sprang to my feet. I gripped the bedpost, steadying myself until the world stopped spinning. I ripped off my shirt and froze at my reflection in the mirror on my wardrobe.

My hearing was the same, but my Struck marks were almost entirely gone.

I'd no idea if this was from the Elixir, or the storm, or Everen's and my amalgamated bond, but it was a secret I no longer had to hide. And if it was from the Elixir . . . Larkin had been right. If the side effects could be fixed, it might help the survivors of the Strike.

I sat down, hard, on the bed. My eyes caught on a covered plate on my bedside table, and I lifted the top. The smell of lavender made my delicate stomach churn, but I stifled a sob. I spied the corner of a note and freed the slip of paper.

Give me some time, little imp. Give me some time.

My eyes stung. I'd hurt Kelwyn, but here was his peace offering. Both Hayden and Larkin knew I was an Eremia, but neither of them could prove it, and perhaps they could work together to solve the problem of Elixir. Maybe, judging by my fading marks, it wasn't far off. For one, blissful moment, though, I let myself bask in the knowledge that this life was mine once more.

—*Arcady* . . . came a dragon's aching plea. My world might have calmed, but his certainly hadn't.

— *Yes*, I said, pulling my shirt back on. *I'm coming.*

It took me nearly a candlemark to make my way from Sorin's secret exit from the Citadel to the city gates. On my back was a pack with supplies for Everen, but I was so weak it felt like it was full of cannon balls.

Once I was out of the city and on the outskirts of the Royal Forest, I was drawn to Everen like a moth to a flame. I finally came across my dragon, his red scales a bright contrast to the green of the forest. He cocked that great head at me, the feathers of his crest shifting, and my face broke out in a grin. I knew I'd never not be awed by the sight of him.

And he was *mine*.

With effort, Everen transformed down to preterit, wings and all, and I didn't waste another second. Our lips crashed together, and he cradled my jaw in his hands as he pressed our bodies together. His hands went to my waist, and he lifted me. My legs settled around him as I deepened the embrace. He kissed me as if he were Starveling and I alone could bring him back from the brink.

With us both in similar forms, it was even easier to meld mentally. Every touch was shared. With a flap of his wings, he brought us off the ground, spinning us, and I laughed into his mouth.

Our amusement quieted, our intensity growing as he set us back on solid ground. I ran my hand along the top of one of his wings, reveling in the softness of the feathers and the powerful muscles that, along with magic, helped him cheat gravity itself. Soon enough, they got in the way, and he banished them with a burst of magic. I spread out the blanket I'd brought before pressing him to the ground and straddling him. I took a moment to take him in—that feathered hair spread across the blanket, the green eyes catching the sun like gems, his pale skin gleaming in the light.

Mine.

I bent down to kiss him, but soon broke it as he helped me out of my shirt. He already knew my marks were faded, but it was his turn to study me. His fingertips skimmed over my torso and traced the outline of my seal setting. I'd always considered them hideous, but the lack of them made me feel more naked.

"They were not," he murmured, shaking his head as he drew me down. "Never."

We chased our pleasure, and we were unabashed about it. I let him think about nothing but me, and him, and our bodies and the various ways they could fit together. There was nowhere to hide. We took what we wanted and gave what we needed with tongue, lips, teeth, and fingers. I'd brought oil, and he massaged my aching muscles and chased away the aches and pain. I kissed my way down his body, following the lines of his muscles. I ran my tongue along the sensitive skin by his hip, and I eventually took him in my mouth, his head falling back with a groan.

Later, when he finally glided into me, I arched my back, his hand tangled in my hair, and I let him take control, guiding our movements. We were rough but also playful. He'd bring me to the brink but not let me cross it until I groaned and begged. Finally, he relented and let me go, and it was all the sweeter for the delay.

After, we lay there, spent, as the stars came out one by one. Everen turned back into a dragon to give us that bit more physic distance. He settled and I curled up against his side, his scales warming me through. He adjusted his wings so one of them covered me. It reminded me of the night we'd spent on the beach after the heist went wrong, except this time I wasn't afraid.

There was nowhere to hide from each other. Part of that scared me and made me want to run, but there was also nowhere I'd rather be.

Everen's grief for dragonkind returned. I'd only distracted him for a time. He'd been torturing himself ever since we returned from the storm, wondering what he could have done differently, what he should be doing now. He'd kept trying to scry, but he'd had nothing from Cassia, or Miligrist, or fate.

"Maybe the dragon world is healing, like ours is," I said.

But we'd both seen how damaged that world had been and how frail his kind had become even before the wraith attacks. There were so few dragons left. Even if by some miracle they had survived, how long could they last? No new eggs had hatched in years, he'd told me.

Through Everen, I knew that even though dragons lived a long time, they weren't immortal. He'd been called the last male dragon all his life, but what if I was bonded to the last *actual* dragon? The thought of something as magical as him being gone for good was overwhelming. I grieved with him.

I'd had some victories, but he had lost so much. What would Everen even do here in the human world? Hide as a human, lurking in the shadows and working a job that didn't require a seal? I couldn't imagine that.

I shuffled away from his scales, pulling my thoughts away, knowing they weren't helping.

—*Me, too*, he said. *Me, too.*

I lay beneath my dragon's wing, wishing I could offer him something more. It was a long time before we fell into a dreamless sleep.

68.

EVEREN:

THE COMING DAWN

A tremor both above and below woke us before dawn. The clouds above us glimmered purple, blue, and green. You craned your head to the sky, mouth opening with growing awe.

"I've seen colors like this up in the mountains," you said. "But this . . . this is different, isn't it?"

The Veil above us was not ripping but instead it . . . *rippled*. I tensed, waiting for wraiths to emerge or Ammil to have somehow survived and returned, but the sky stayed empty save for the shifting colors.

"Please," you pleaded. *"Please* don't let this be something terrible. Haven't we been through enough?"

You climbed onto my shoulder and settled in your rightful place, your knees gripping me tight. The night around us lightened. I took to the sky, rising above the cloud line. The rips in the Veil still played overhead, and I sensed the leylines of the world spreading below us like roots.

Previously, every breach in the Veil had felt like an act of violence. This time, the play of light was hypnotic as a dream.

I flew, careless of who might see. We crossed the Bay of Vatra, landing gently on one of the cliff faces of the Edge Isles. I took care not to jostle you.

You climbed down carefully, keeping one hand on my scales. Beneath the rippling of the Veil, we could make out the lights of the distant city of the capital, a scattering of gold glimmers among the black. How many people had already woken and realized what was happening above? The sky shifted. Pink, orange, and glimmers of yellow compared to the blue, green, and purple of the Veil. The stars were out, but instead of dimming with the coming dawn, their starfire brightened.

— *While a coil unkinks and worlds collide,* I echoed the voice of fate.

There was an easing of tension, another ebb of ancient, unknowable power. Between the worlds, a Dreamer shifted in its sleep and resettled. Magic fell from the sky like snow flurries, drifting on the wind. You stepped closer to me, your breath catching in your throat.

"There," you exhaled, pointing out to the sea.

It emerged like a mirage. A vague suggestion of a shape that gradually darkened and took form. An island, one side of it carved into the head of a dragon, mouth open in a roar.

The Lady of Vere Celene.

She had emerged at the same place the island had been before the severing. Long ago, dragons had nested there, in full view of Vatra and the human world. After more than eight centuries, it was back. Of the Reek, I saw no sign.

"It's beautiful," you whispered.

Your head turned toward the city. Humans would be scrambling to higher ground, wondering what it all meant, with no idea how thoroughly their understanding of everything was about to tilt.

My heart lifted when I spotted small, colored dots slowly growing larger. Dragons, their wings spread wide, their necks lifted proudly.

There was a red dragon at the front, followed by a contingent of dragon warriors. After so many years of waiting and broken prophecies and near misses . . . dragons had returned. They were *here*.

Fear rose in me—were they coming in peace, or to start a war? It took a few moments before I realized that red dot at the front was not Queen Naccara.

It was my sister.

Relief mixed with foreboding. If Cassia was leading the dragons . . . did my mother still sleep?

Fate showed us what would happen next, visions coming to us without even the need of scrysilver. Cassia would land at the heart of the Citadel. Loc was in turmoil, its leaders dead and gone, drakines already scrabbling for power. Guards would raise their arrows. Humans and dragons alike would hold their breath, wondering what would happen next.

The human known as Sar Ansel would be the one to step forward and greet Cassia. You knew her as Professor Hayden's wife. She would end up being one of the members of the emergency Consul.

What followed would not be easy. It would take time for the dragonstone tree to heal, for the blight to flee the woods and the red tide banished for good. Some would believe the gods had returned, with all the religious fervor that came with that assumption. Others would be afraid, and with that fear would come hatred. Myria would covet dragons and perhaps push for reunion, not least to have access to our kind. Jask would call us demons and might spark a war.

But you and I knew if we worked for it—if we played our cards right, to use one of your phrases—then that future of peace was a much stronger possibility than ever before.

You shivered, following our shared thoughts. Cassia, as Queen, had a decision to make as to how she would approach the humans, but we had a choice to make that dawn, too. Would we hide our bond, or would we step out of the shadows and into the light, to prove to an uncertain world that humans and dragons could live in harmony, respect, and love?

We stared at each other, weighing the options. You nodded, squared your shoulders, and climbed onto my back once more. With a last burst of magic, we took to the sky on the morning the Lumet learned that dragons were real. Nothing would ever be the same, and one way or another, you and I would be at the center of it all once again. Together.

Change was on the wind.

EPILOGUE:

THE ARCHIVIST

On that fateful sunrise, the dragon scales found their equilibrium. The Dreamer had returned once more to its slumber, and the Lumet, after eight centuries, was reunited. Dragons and humans were once more in the same world, even if much hung in the balance.

These two volumes contained the story of a woman who gave up being a priest and an assassin and found a measure of peace. This was the tale of the dragon Queen-in-Waiting and heir to the Emberclaw throne. With their permission, I scried into their pasts and asked them to edit or elaborate on what I found in the scrysilver.

This was the story of the last male dragon who was no longer the last. Two years after the dragons arrived, down in the depths of Vere Celene's caves, that clutch of dragon eggs warmed. One twitched, and then another. A small snout quested through the hole, forked tongue tasting the air for the first time. Three dozen dragons, male and female both, fought their way from their shells to emerge sticky and blinking, stretching their delicate wings to dry like a butterfly that has only emerged from a cocoon. Dragons waited to greet them, to love them, to cherish them.

As I wrote right at the very start, this is our story, Arcady. You told me you'd never write your part of this, but a few months later I heard your pen scratching on the paper late at night when you thought I slept.

There are plenty of dry, historical tomes written about this period. This account is far too personal, but it is, I feel, more honest.

You did not understand why I was so determined to collect this volume together, and swore you would never read it. If you ever do sneak down here and reach this point: you officially lost this wager and you owe me one kiss.

So here we are at the close, for now. I had cast off fate, but that does not mean that fate swore off us. We had our share of nightmares that later came true. But that is a story for another time, perhaps.

It is late, and I have been here for hours. I have stitched the binding closed. I shall go find you, now, and like these volumes, we will lie side by side.

With love,

—THE TWELFTH ARCHIVIST OF VERE CELENE

ACKNOWLEDGMENTS

The writing of this volume collided with a period of both extraordinarily good and extraordinarily bad luck in my life. Many thanks are in order.

Thank you firstly to myself. For over a year, every time it felt I got my feet underneath me, something else swept me under. I didn't swim very gracefully most of the time, and I lost pretty much all confidence at one point, but I did keep coming back up for air. I did not drown, even if at times I felt pretty soggy, and I made it back to shore.

Many people were life rafts and floatation devices. Thank you, as ever, to my agent, Juliet Mushens, and everyone at Mushens Entertainment: Kiya Evans, Emma Dawson, and Alba Arnau Prado, Liza DeBlock, and Rachel Neely. A million thank yous to my UK editor, Molly Powell at Hodderscape, for going above and beyond by looking at synopses (so many synopses) and partial drafts as I tried to fit the pieces of this book into something that made sense. Thank you to Leah Spann at DAW for eagle-eyed copyedits and line edits and I'm delighted to be working with you again. Thank you to publicists extraordinaires Kate Keehan (Hodderscape) and Laura Fitzgerald (DAW). Endless gratitude to Betsy Wollheim of DAW, the legend herself, and Ben Schrank at Astra. A special shoutout to Jack Perry at Astra Sales and Patrick Guaschino at Penguin Random House Sales. A blanket thank you to everyone at my publishers on both sides of the pond and in translation for their support, championship, and flexibility.

Thanks as usual to my partner, Craig, and my mother, Sally. A giant hug to my family, especially Gemma and Izzy. To save this being ten pages, a big hug to the friends I listed in the acknowledgments of *Dragonfall*—you remain wonderful and sorry for all the whining. An additional shout out to Katie Cummins, Beck O'Leary, Sam Eastop, Ally Kersel, Cal Howell, Alyssa Blair, for really going above and beyond for this book in particular. Thank you to Pete Freestone for being both an honest critique partner and a brilliant adventure buddy. Thank you to Vicky for continually reminding me to think of the middle ground and to hold it all lightly.

Thank you to my 'colleagues' at the 'office' (the baristas and the regulars at the café where I write). Thank you my more official colleagues at The Novelry and the writers I've worked with there. You're a lovely bunch. Another thank you to all at Argonaut Books and the various Edinburgh bookstores: Transreal, Portobello Books, Lighthouse, Rare Birds, Golden Hare, Waterstones, Blackwells, Edinburgh Bookshop, Typewronger, and Toppings. Thank you to the ESFF group for welcoming me with open arms and everyone in my local Edinburgh community.

I will forever be grateful to Barnes and Noble for selecting *Dragonfall* as the speculative fiction pick of the month last July. I never expected that type of visibility for a book like this, and the trip to New York was truly a career highlight. I also have to shoutout the US indies who got behind Dragonfall early on, like Fable Hollow Bookstore, Mysterious Galaxy, and many more.

Thank you to every bookseller, librarian, and reader who has championed this book as well as my rather eclectic backlist. I am very grateful. I hope to bring you many more stories.

Happy hunting.

GLOSSARY

Aldburn, Damon—a second-year student at the University of Vatra

Aldwing, Ammil—the last male dragon

Ansel, Willem—a second-year student at the University of Vatra. Offspring of Professor Hayden and Sar Ansel

Ansel, Sar—full name: Maude Ansel; a diplomat specializing in Jaskian relations, from a very powerful old family

Atrel—a mountain town in Loc

Aura—the red dragon god of fire and alchemy

Balcil, Lowe—a fourth-year student at the University of Vatra

Biela, Olwyn—a third-year student at the University of Vatra

Blackstone—a chancellery in Myria

Bryni—Saint of Righteous Anger, Patron Saint of Aura

candlemark—a measure of time equivalent to an hour

cantrip—a minor spell, not associated with a specific god

Carym of Redwing—one of the three Chancellors of the Consul of Loc

Celenian—the language of the dragons; see: Old Tongue

charm—a minor spell, not associated with a specific god

Cinders—an underground card den

Citadel, the—the seat of the Lochian government and former seat of the Locmyrian monarchy

Clearsight, Miligrist—the Seer of Vere Celene

Consul—the leadership of Loc, consisting of three Chancellors and the Head Priest of the Order of Dragons

Cote, the—the Marrick hideout outside of Vatra

Dolard—Saint of the Lost or Wandering, Patron Saint of Piater dragonstone—the stone seals are made from; their origins are only known to the Order of the Dragons

drakine—a person of noble birth

Dreamer, the—an enormous serpent within the Veil

Driscoll—one of the younger members of the Marricks

Easel, Rahela—a second-year student at the University of Vatra, who has family members in Myria

Elixir of Life, the—the mythical alchemical substance meant to impart ever-lasting life and heal any wound, but also a potion developed by Barrow Eremia and Professor Hayden which can enhance magic and cure the Struck

Etter—Saint of Clarity, Patron Saint of Zama

Eremia, Barrow—the Plaguebringer; the Traitor of the Lumet; Arcady's grandsire

Erisyn, the First—the founding monarch of Locmyria

Feast of Flowers, the—mid-spring celebration in Loc and Myria, celebrating Jari

Feast of Storms, the—early-spring celebration in Loc and Myria, celebrating Zama

Fangs, the—the smaller mountain range in the center of Loc

Fullin, Professor—a history professor at the University of Vatra

Glass Isles, the—traders tend to winter on some of the islands off the coast of Myria, whereas pirates or banished criminals live on others

Glimmerhail—a dragon holiday celebrated on the autumn equinox

Great Betrayal, the—the sealing of dragons and the isle of Vere Celene beyond the Veil

Greenscale—a chancellery in Myria

Haldvam—a Jaskian tradition of resting after dinner to "keep the warmth"

Hayden, Professor—full name: Kiera Hayden. A master alchemist at the University of Vatra.

Hulm, Armsmaster—the Citadel Armsmaster

Ini—Saint of Luck, Patron Saint of Kalsh

Jaculus—Sorin's green wyvern

Jari—the green dragon god of earth and healing

Jask—the land to the south who believe dragons are demons, not gods, and who were historically often at war with Locmyria

Jonrir, Kala—a fourth-year student at the University of Vatra

Kalsh—the blue dragon god of water and shapeshifting

Ketrel of Stormfell—one of the three Chancellors of the Consul of Loc

Kelwyn—the owner of the Last Golden and Arcady's fence for stolen goods; an excellent cook and baker

Lady of Vere Celene, the—the part of the island of Vere Celene that was carved with magic to look like a dragon's head

Laen the Ignited—the last monarch of Locmyria before the Schism

Last Golden, the—Kelwyn's antique shop

leyline—the lines of magic that occur in the natural world, which usually follow rivers

Lightfinger—Arcady's childhood friend and member of the Marricks; deceased

Loc—the main setting of *Dragonfall*; this country was previously joined with Myria before the Schism.

Locmyrian—the language spoken in both Loc and Myria

Loc & Key—the abandoned lockshop that Arcady made their home

Lumet, the—the overall name for the human world, consisting of Loc, Myria, Jask, and the Glass Isles

Lyn, Iona—a third-year student of the University of Vatra

Mace—Queen Naccara's closest advisor (a gray dragon)

Magnes—a dragon in disguise and the Head Priest of the Order of the Dragons and member of the Consul; see: Ammil Aldwing

maire—analogous to "mother" and/or the one who bears the child

Marricks, the—the band of thieves Arcady used to work with, who steal to help the Struck; members: Larkin Nash, Wren, Driscoll, Brev, Joana, Aby, and previously Lightfinger (deceased)

Melody, Cind—a third-year student of the University of Vatra

Miligrist—the Eleventh Archivist and current Seer of Vere Celene; one of the oldest (blue) dragons still living

Miti, Jordin—a third-year student of the University of Vatra

Miti, Teasel—a fourth-year student of the University of Vatra

monarchs—Myrian octagonal coins

Myria—the neighboring country to Loc, previously the other half of Locmyria before the Schism

Nalore Monastery—a monastery in the Fangs

Nash, Larkin—the leader of the Marricks

Night of Locked Tombs, the—the longest night of the year, where it's believed the barrier between the living and the dead grows thinner

Ocul—a peninsula to the west of Vatra

Old Tongue—what the humans call Celenian, the draconic language; they use a version of it for spells

Order of the Dragons, the—the priesthood, based in the Citadel

Pan—a blue dragon in Vere Celene; mate of Sidar

paire—analogous to "father" and/or the one who sires the child

Piater—the grey dragon god of stone, metal, and telekinesis

Plaguebringer, the—see: Eremia, Barrow

Plink, Professor—a Kalsh professor at the University of Vatra, specializing in water-weaving

Pollen—a high-inducing substance made from a flower grown in Myria

preterit—a term for a dragon in their humanoid form, from the term meaning "bygone, former"

pryde—a group of dragons

Redwing—a chancellery in Loc

Reek, the—the volcano in Vere Celene

Royal Forest, the—the forest outside of Vatra

saltsphere—a snack kept on hand for magic users, made of seeds, nuts, salt, and herbs

Sanron, Denlin—a fourth-year student at the University of Vatra

Sar—the title of a drakine (equivalent to "sir")

Schism, the—the coup that resulted in the death of Laen the Ignited and Locmyria breaking into two countries, 27 years before the start of *Dragonfall*

scrysilver—the magical substance, partially made of quicksilver, that dragons use to scry into the past, present, and future

seal—a stone cylinder all citizens of Loc wear to denote their identity and help funnel their magic

sennight—a week

Sidar—a (deceased) green dragon in Vere Celene; mate of Pan

smokemint—an herb humans smoke for euphoria

snap—a card game

Spine, the—the largest mountain range in the Lumet that bisects Loc and Myria

Spirit Moon, the—the darkest and coldest month of the year in the human realm

starfire—dragons worship the stars and their ever-burning fire, believing it helps steer fate

Starveling—someone who has used too much magic without adequately fueling it with food, meaning they briefly lose sense of themselves and seek only to eat and consume—even if that means attacking or killing a fellow human

Strike, the—the magical plague that killed many and increased the risk of humans turning Starveling, whether someone was Struck or not Struck—those who survived the Strike, who often have black markings following their veins; because they are believed to be more susceptible to turning Starveling, the Struck have their seals confiscated and replaced with marble

Struck—those who survived the Strike and bear dark markings along their veins as a result

suls—Lochian coins

sweetsphere—a snack kept on hand for magic users, made of seeds, nuts, honey, and sometimes dried fruits and spices

Swiftsea—a chancellery in Loc

taie—a more informal, gender-neutral term for grandparent

They/Them/Their—the capitalized honorific pronoun used for those in high station or esteem

Trade—the sign language and a lingua franca for many in the Lumet

Traitor of the Lumet—see: Eremia, Barrow

Trials, the—a contest held at the University of Vatra to test the magical prowess of its students

Ultred, Professor—a professor at the University of Vatra, specializing in wards and charms.

University of Vatra, the—an institution of higher learning for magic in Loc's capital

Vatra—the capital city of Loc

Vayne, Edin—a fourth year at the University of Vatra

Veil, the—the barrier between the Lumet and Vere Celene that opens into the storm between worlds

Vere Celene—the island home of the dragons

ward—a protective spell cast over a person or object, not associated with a specific god

waterweaving—a magical ability associated with Kalsh and Their chosen

weyr—the dwelling place of dragons

widow's sleep—a poison

Wren—a former member of the Marricks; an art forger and smuggler

wraith—a monster made of smoke that lives within the storm between worlds

wraithwright—a coin made of meteorite metal and worth fifty gold coins

wynd—a small street

Wyndyn—Saint of Faith, Patron Saint of Jari

Yrsa of Swiftsea—one of the three Chancellors of the Consul of Loc

Zama—the indigo or violet dragon god of weather and mind magic; mind magic is forbidden in Loc and punishable by death

ABOUT THE AUTHOR

Originally from sunny California, L.R. Lam now lives in cloudy Scotland. Lam is a Sunday Times Bestselling author whose work includes epic fantasy romance Dragonfall, the near-future space thrillers, Goldilocks, feminist space opera Seven Devils (co-written with Elizabeth May), BBC Radio 2 Book Club section False Hearts, the companion novel Shattered Minds, and the award-winning Micah Grey series: Pantomime, Shadowplay, and Masquerade. Their short fiction and essays have appeared in various anthologies such as Nasty Women, Cranky Ladies of History, Scotland in Space, and more.

IF YOU ENJOYED THE DRAGON SCALES SERIES, DON'T MISS L. R. LAM'S *PANTOMIME*:

A gaslamp fantasy trilogy about a circus aerialist's quest to escape his past and decipher the magical prophecy that will shape his future. Micah has much to learn, and he must do it quickly-before his past and future collide, with catastrophic consequences.

In the land of lost wonders, the past is stirring once more . . .

'Exotic and detailed'
Robin Hobb

'Fantastical, richly drawn'
Leigh Bardugo

WANT MORE?

If you enjoyed this
and would like to
find out about similar
books we publish,
we'd love you to
join our online Sci-Fi,
Fantasy and Horror
community, Hodderscape.

Visit hodderscape.co.uk for
exclusive content from our authors, news, competitions
and general musings, and feel free to comment, contribute
or just keep an eye on what we are up to.

See you there!